Swords and Sorcerers

Stories from the World of Fantasy and Adventure

Swords and Sorcerers

Stories from the World of Fantasy and Adventure

edited by Clint Willis

Thunder's Mouth Press
New York

SWORDS AND SORCERERS: *Stories from the World of Fantasy and Adventure*

Compilation copyright © 2003 by Clint Willis
Introduction copyright © 2003 by Clint Willis

Published by
Thunder's Mouth Press
An Imprint of Avalon Publishing Group Incorporated
161 William Street, 16th floor
New York, NY 10038

Book design: Michael Walters

Library of Congress Cataloging-in-Publication Data is available.

ISBN: 1-56025-415-7

9 8 7 6 5 4 3 2 1

Printed the United States of America

Distributed by Publishers Group West

For
Peyton McFarlain
and
Paige McFarlain
and
Nate Willis

Table of Contents

Introduction

Why are some stories so much fun to read? One reason is that when you read them, they become stories about you.

The best stories are a gift from the writer or storyteller to you. They are meant for your pleasure. When you read them, you bring them to life. That is your gift to the writer—and to yourself.

The best stories become just as real as breakfast or school or soccer practice—but there is one difference. When you read a story, you are in charge: You make many of the most important decisions. The writer offers clues about what to see or hear or feel or believe. But much of the time, you get to decide what the magician looks like, or how much it hurts to get stuck by a sword or how fast the horse is moving when the knight rides off. In those ways, you make up your own version of the story.

This book is full of good stories. Read it, and you will meet kings and musketeers. You will get to know magicians and heroes. You will become well acquainted with a very powerful monkey. You will fight duels to the death with villains and monsters and thieves and warriors. You will do battle with holy men.

You will make friends and some enemies. When you finish reading the stories, some of those people will stay with you—warning you, teaching you, liking or not liking you. It might be interesting to remember that all of these new friends and enemies are part of your magic: You helped to invent them by paying attention to the stories where they live.

I have known King Arthur since I was 7 years old—and Ali Baba since I was 10. I met the Three Musketeers when I was 11—and Robin Hood a year or so later. I met Monkey when I was already an adult. I know all of the characters in this book, and I'll tell you one of my secrets: People like King Arthur and Robin Hood and the rest are in some ways much more real to me then the people I read about in the newspaper—the President of the United States, say.

I also know that my storybook friends aren't the same characters you will meet in the book, even if they have the same names. You will reinvent each of them—and then they will reinvent you.

—CLINT WILLIS

from

The Princess Bride

by William Goldman

William Goldman's (born 1931) *The Princess Bride* is a kind of fairy tale. When three men kidnap a princess, a mysterious character—"the man in black"—gives chase. One of the kidnappers—a famous swordsman named Inigo—waits to confront the man in black at the top of a cliff.

Forty-seven feet to go now.

Now forty-six.

"Hello there," Inigo hollered when he could wait no more.

The man in black glanced up and grunted.

"I've been watching you."

The man in black nodded.

"Slow going," Inigo said.

"Look, I don't mean to be rude," the man in black said finally, "but I'm rather busy just now, so try not to distract me."

"I'm sorry," Inigo said.

The man in black grunted again.

"I don't suppose you could speed things up," Inigo said.

"If you want to speed things up so much," the man in black said, clearly quite angry now, "you could lower a rope or a tree branch or find some other helpful thing to do."

"I could do that," Inigo agreed. "But I don't think you would accept my help, since I'm only waiting up here so that I can kill you."

"That does put a damper on our relationship," the man in black said then. "I'm afraid you'll just have to wait."

Forty-three feet left.

Forty-one.

"I could give you my word as a Spaniard," Inigo said.

"No good," the man in black replied. "I've known too many Spaniards."

"I'm going crazy up here," Inigo said.

"Anytime you want to change places, I'd be too happy to accept."

Thirty-nine feet.

And resting.

The man in black just hung in space, feet dangling, the entire weight of his body supported by the strength of his hand jammed into the crevice.

"Come along now," Inigo pleaded.

"It's been a bit of a climb," the man in black explained, "and I'm weary. I'll be fine in a quarter-hour or so."

Another quarter-hour! Inconceivable. "Look, we've got a piece of extra rope up here we didn't need when we made our original climb, I'll just drop it down to you and you grab hold and I'll pull and—"

"No good," the man in black repeated. "You *might* pull, but then again, you also just *might* let go, which, since you're in a hurry to kill me, would certainly do the job quickly."

"But you wouldn't have ever known I was going to kill you if I hadn't been the one to tell you. Doesn't that let you know I can be trusted?"

"Frankly, and I hope you won't be insulted, no."

"There's no way you'll trust me?"

"Nothing comes to mind."

Suddenly Inigo raised his right hand high—"I swear on the soul of Domingo Montoya you will reach the top alive!"

The man in black was silent for a long time. Then he looked up. "I do not know this Domingo of yours, but something in your tone says I must believe you. Throw me the rope."

Inigo quickly tied it around a rock, dropped it over. The man in black grabbed hold, hung suspended alone in space. Inigo pulled. In a moment, the man in black was beside him.

"Thank you," the man in black said, and he sank down on the rock.

Inigo sat alongside him. "We'll wait until you're ready," he said.

The man in black breathed deeply. "Again, thank you."

"Why have you followed us?"

"You carry baggage of much value."

"We have no intention of selling," Inigo said.

"That is your business."

"And yours?"

The man in black made no reply.

Inigo stood and walked away, surveying the terrain over which they would battle. It was a splendid plateau, really, filled with trees for dodging around and roots for tripping over and small rocks for losing your balance on and boulders for leaping off if you could climb on them fast enough, and bathing everything, the entire spot, moonlight. One could not ask for a more suitable testing ground for a duel, Inigo decided. It had everything, including the marvelous Cliffs at one end, beyond which was the wonderful thousand-foot drop, always something to bear in mind when one was planning tactics. It was perfect. The place was perfect.

Provided the man in black could fence.

Really fence.

Inigo did then what he always did before a duel: he took the great sword from its scabbard and touched the side of the blade to his face two times, once along one scar, once along the other.

Then he examined the man in black. A fine sailor, yes; a mighty climber, no question; courageous, without a doubt. But could he fence? *Really* fence?

Please, Inigo thought. It has been so long since I have been tested, let this man test me. Let him be a glorious swordsman. Let him be both quick and fast, smart and strong. Give him a matchless mind for tactics, a background the equal of mine. Please, please, it's been so long: let—him—be—a—*master!*

"I have my breath back now," the man in black said from the rock. "Thank you for allowing me my rest."

"We'd best get on with it then," Inigo replied.

The man in black stood.

"You seem a decent fellow," Inigo said. "I hate to kill you."

"You seem a decent fellow," answered the man in black. "I hate to die."

"But one of us must," Inigo said. *"Begin."*

And so saying he took the six-fingered sword.

And put it into his left hand.

He had begun all his duels left-handed lately. It was good practice for him, and although he was the only living wizard in the world with his regular hand, the right, still, he was more than worthy with his left. Perhaps thirty men alive were his equal when he used his left. Perhaps as many as fifty; perhaps as few as ten.

The man in black was also left-handed and that warmed Inigo; it made things fairer. His weakness against the other man's strength. All to the good.

They touched swords, and the man in black immediately began the Agrippa defense, which Inigo felt was sound, considering the rocky terrain, for the Agrippa kept the feet stationary at first, and made the chances of slipping minimal. Naturally, he countered with Capo Ferro which surprised the man in black, but he defended well, quickly shifting out of Agrippa and taking the attack himself, using the principles of Thibault.

Inigo had to smile. No one had taken the attack against him in so long and it was thrilling! He let the man in black advance, let him build up courage, retreating gracefully between some trees, letting his Bonetti defense keep him safe from harm.

Then his legs flicked and he was behind the nearest tree, and the man in black had not expected it and was slow reacting. Inigo flashed immediately out from the tree, attacking himself now, and the man in black retreated, stumbled, got his balance, continued moving away.

Inigo was impressed with the quickness of the balance return. Most men the size of the man in black would have gone down or, at the least, fallen to one hand. The man in black did neither; he simply quickstepped, wrenched his body erect, continued fighting.

They were moving parallel to the Cliffs now, and the trees were behind them, mostly. The man in black was slowly being forced toward a group of large boulders, for Inigo was anxious to see how well he moved when quarters were close, when you could not thrust or parry with total freedom. He continued to force, and then the boulders were surrounding them. Inigo suddenly threw his body against a nearby rock, rebounded off it with stunning force, lunging with incredible speed.

First blood was his.

He had pinked the man in black, grazed him only, along the left wrist. A scratch was all. But it was bleeding.

Immediately the man in black hurried his retreat, getting his position away from the boulders, getting out into the open of the plateau. Inigo followed, not bothering to try to check the other man's flight; there would always be time for that later.

Then the man in black launched his greatest assault. It came with no warning and the speed and strength of it were terrifying. His blade flashed in the light again and again, and at first, Inigo was only too delighted to retreat. He was not entirely familiar with the style of the attack; it was mostly McBone, but there were snatches of Capo Ferro thrown in, and he continued moving backward while he concentrated on the enemy, figuring the best way to stop the assault.

The man in black kept advancing, and Inigo was aware that behind him now he was coming closer and closer to the edge of the Cliffs, but that could not have concerned him less. The important thing was to outthink the enemy, find his weakness, let him have his moment of exultation.

Suddenly, as the Cliffs came ever nearer, Inigo realized the fault in the attack that was flashing at him; a simple Thibault maneuver would destroy it entirely, but he didn't want to give it away so soon. Let the other man have the triumph a moment longer; life allowed so few.

The Cliffs were very close behind him now.

Inigo continued to retreat; the man in black continued advancing.

Then Inigo countered with the Thibault.

And the man in black blocked it.

He blocked it!

Inigo repeated the Thibault move and again it didn't work. He switched to Capo Ferro, he tried Bonetti, he went to Fabris; in desperation he began a move used only twice, by Sainct.

Nothing worked!

The man in black kept attacking.

And the Cliffs were almost there.

Inigo never panicked—never came close. But he decided some things very quickly, because there was no time for long consultations, and what he decided was that although the man in black was slow in reacting to moves behind trees, and not much good at all amidst boulders, when movement was restricted, yet out in the open, where there was space, he was a terror. A left-handed black-masked terror. "You are most excellent," he said. His rear foot was at the cliff edge. He could retreat no more.

"Thank you," the man in black replied. "I have worked very hard to become so."

"You are better than I am," Inigo admitted.

"So it seems. But if that is true, then why are you smiling?"

"Because," Inigo answered, "I know something you don't know."

"And what is that?" asked the man in black.

"I'm not left-handed," Inigo replied, and with those words, he all but threw the six-fingered sword into his right hand, and the tide of battle turned.

The man in black retreated before the slashing of the great sword. He tried to side-step, tried to parry, tried to somehow escape the doom that was now inevitable. But there was no way. He could block fifty thrusts; the fifty-first flicked through, and now his left arm was bleeding. He could thwart thirty ripostes, but not the thirty-first, and now his shoulder bled.

The wounds were not yet grave, but they kept on coming as they dodged across the stones, and then the man in black found himself amidst the trees and that was bad for him, so he all but fled before Inigo's onslaught, and then he was in the open again, but Inigo kept coming, nothing could stop him, and then the man in black was back among the boulders, and that was even worse for him than the trees and he shouted out in frustration and practically ran to where there was open space again.

But there was no dealing with the wizard, and slowly, again, the deadly Cliffs became a factor in the fight, only now it was the man in black who was being forced to doom. He was brave, and he was strong, and the cuts did not make him beg for mercy, and he showed no fear behind his black mask. "You are amazing," he cried, as Inigo increased the already blinding speed of the blade.

"Thank you. It has not come without effort."

The death moment was at hand now. Again and again Inigo thrust forward, and again and again the man in black managed to ward off the attacks, but each time it was harder, and the strength in Inigo's wrists was endless and he only thrust the more fiercely and soon the man in black grew weak. "You cannot tell it," he said then, "because I wear a cape and mask. But I am smiling now."

"Why?"

"Because I'm not left-handed either," said the man in black.

And he too switched hands, and now the battle was finally joined.

And Inigo began to retreat.

"Who are you?" he screamed.

"No one of import. Another lover of the blade."

"I must know!"

"Get used to disappointment."

They flashed along the open plateau now, and the blades were both invisible, but oh, the Earth trembled, and ohhhh, the skies shook, and Inigo was losing. He tried to make for the trees, but the man in black would have none of it. He tried retreating to the boulders, but that was denied him too.

And in the open, unthinkable as it was, the man in black was superior. Not much. But in a multitude of tiny ways, he was of a slightly higher quality. A hair quicker, a fraction stronger, a speck faster. Not really much at all.

But it was enough.

They met in center plateau for the final assault. Neither man conceded anything. The sound of metal clashing metal rose. A final burst of energy flew through Inigo's veins and he made every attempt, tried every trick, used every hour of every day of his years of experience. But he was blocked. By the man in black. He was shackled. By the man in black. He was baffled, thwarted, muzzled.

Beaten.

By the man in black.

A final flick and the great six-fingered sword went flying from his hand. Inigo stood there, helpless. Then he dropped to his knees, bowed his head, closed his eyes. "Do it quickly," he said.

"May my hands fall from my wrists before I kill an artist like yourself," said the man in black. "I would as soon destroy da Vinci. However"—and here he clubbed Inigo's head with the butt of his sword—"since I can't have you following me either, please understand that I hold you in the highest respect." He struck one more time and the Spaniard fell unconscious. The man in black quickly tied Inigo's hands around a tree and left him there, for the moment, sleeping and helpless.

Then he sheathed his sword, picked up the Sicilian's trail, and raced into the night. . . .

from

The Merry Adventures of Robin Hood

by Howard Pyle

Howard Pyle (1853–1911) was a distinguished American artist as well as a popular storyteller. His Robin Hood loves a practical joke and a good fight.

The dawning of a summer's day was fresh and bright, and the birds sang sweetly in a great tumult of sound. So loud was their singing that it awakened Robin Hood where he lay sleeping, so that he stirred, and turned, and arose. Up rose Little John also, and all the merry men; then, after they had broken their fast, they set forth hither and thither upon the doings of the day.

Robin Hood and Little John walked down a forest path where all around the leaves danced and twinkled as the breeze trembled through them and the sunlight came flickering down. Quoth Robin Hood, "I make my vow, Little John, my blood tickles my veins as it flows through them this gay morn. What sayst thou to our seeking adventures, each one upon his own account?"

"With all my heart," said Little John. "We have had more than one pleasant doing in that way, good master. Here are two paths; take thou the one to the right hand, and I will take the one to the left, and then let us each walk straight ahead till he tumble into some merry doing or other."

"I like thy plan," quoth Robin, "therefore we will part here. But look thee, Little John, keep thyself out of mischief, for I would not have ill befall thee for all the world."

"Marry, come up," quoth Little John, "how thou talkest! Methinks thou art wont to get thyself into tighter coils than I am like to do."

At this Robin Hood laughed. "Why, in sooth, Little John," said he, "thou hast a blundering hard-headed way that seemeth to bring thee right side uppermost in all thy troubles; but let us see who cometh out best this day." So saying, he clapped his palm to Little John's and each departed upon his way, the trees quickly shutting the one from the other's sight.

Robin Hood strolled onward till he came to where a broad woodland road stretched before him. Overhead the branches of the trees laced together in flickering foliage, all golden where it grew thin to the sunlight; beneath his feet the ground was soft and moist from the sheltering shade. Here in this pleasant spot the sharpest adventure that ever befell Robin Hood came upon him; for, as he walked down the woodland path thinking of nought but the songs of the birds, he came of a sudden to where a man was seated upon the mossy roots beneath the shade of a broad-spreading oak tree. Robin Hood saw that the stranger had not caught sight of him, so he stopped and stood quite still, looking at the other a long time before he came forward. And the stranger, I wot, was well worth looking at, for never had Robin seen a figure like that sitting beneath the tree. From his head to his feet he was clad in a horse's hide, dressed with the hair upon it. Upon his head was a cowl that hid his face from sight, and which was made of the horse's skin, the ears whereof stuck up like those of a rabbit. His body was clad in a jacket made of the hide, and his legs were covered with the hairy skin likewise. By his side was a heavy broadsword and a sharp, double-edged dagger. A quiver of smooth round arrows hung across his shoulders, and his stout bow of yew leaned against the tree beside him.

"Halloa, friend," cried Robin, coming forward at last, "who art thou that sittest there? And what is that that thou hast upon thy body? I make my vow I ha' never seen such a sight in all my life before. Had I done an evil thing, or did my conscience trouble me, I would be afraid of thee, thinking that thou wast some one from down below bringing a message bidding me come straightway to King Nicholas."

To this speech the other answered not a word, but he pushed the cowl back from his head and showed a knit brow, a hooked nose, and a pair of fierce, restless, black eyes, which altogether made Robin think of a hawk as he looked on his face. But beside this there was something about the lines on the stranger's face, and his thin cruel mouth, and the hard glare of his eyes, that made one's flesh creep to look upon.

"Who art thou, rascal?" said he at last, in a loud, harsh voice.

"Tut, tut," quoth merry Robin, "speak not so sourly, brother. Hast thou fed upon vinegar and nettles this morning that thy speech is so stinging?"

"An thou likest not my words," said the other, fiercely, "thou hadst best be jogging, for I tell thee plainly, my deeds match them."

"Nay, but I do like thy words, thou sweet, pretty thing," quoth Robin, squatting down upon the grass in front of the other: "moreover, I tell thee thy speech is witty and gamesome as any I ever heard in all my life."

The other said not a word, but he glared upon Robin with a wicked and baleful look, such as a fierce dog bestows upon a man ere it springs at his throat. Robin returned the gaze with one of wide-eyed innocence, not a shadow of a smile twinkling in his eyes or twitching at the corners of his mouth. So they sat staring at one another for a long time, until the stranger broke the silence suddenly. "What is thy name, fellow?" said he.

"Now," quoth Robin, "I am right glad to hear thee speak, for I began to fear the sight of me had stricken thee dumb. As for my name, it may be this or it may be that; but methinks it is more meet for thee to tell me thine, seeing that thou art the greater stranger in these parts. Prythee, tell me, sweet chuck, why wearest thou that dainty garb upon thy pretty body?"

At these words the other broke into a short, harsh roar of laughter. "By the bones of the Daemon Odin," said he, "thou art the boldest spoken man that ever I have seen in all my life. I know not why I do not smite thee down where thou sittest, for only two days ago I skewered a man over back of Nottingham Town for saying not half so much to me as thou hast done. I wear this garb, thou fool, to keep my body warm; likewise it is near as good as a coat of steel against a common sword-thrust. As for my name, I care not who knoweth it. It is Guy of Gisbourne, and thou mayst have heard it before. I come from the woodlands over in Herefordshire, upon the lands of the Bishop of that ilk. I am an outlaw, and get my living by hook and by crook in a manner it boots not now to tell of. Not long since the Bishop sent for me, and said that if I would do a certain thing that the Sheriff of Nottingham would ask of me, he would get me a free pardon, and give me tenscore pounds to boot. So straightway I came to Nottingham Town and found my sweet Sheriff; and what thinkest thou he wanted of me? Why, forsooth, to come here to Sherwood to hunt up one Robin Hood, also an outlaw, and to take him alive or dead. It seemeth that they have no one here to face that bold fellow, and so sent all the way to Herefordshire, and to me, for thou knowest the old saying, 'Set a thief to catch a thief.' As for the slaying of this fellow, it galleth me not a whit, for I would shed the blood of my own brother for the half of two hundred pounds."

To all this Robin listened, and as he listened his gorge rose. Well he knew of this Guy of Gisbourne, and of all the bloody and murderous deeds that he had done in Herefordshire, for his doings were famous throughout all the land. Yet, although he loathed the very presence of the man, he held his peace, for he had an end to serve. "Truly," quoth he, "I have heard of thy gentle doings. Methinks there is no one in all the world that Robin Hood would rather meet than thee."

At this Guy of Gisbourne gave another harsh laugh. "Why," quoth he, "it is a merry thing to think of one stout outlaw like Robin Hood meeting another stout outlaw like Guy of Gisbourne. Only in this case it will be an ill happening for Robin Hood, for the day he meets Guy of Gisbourne he shall die."

"But thou gentle, merry spirit," quoth Robin, "dost thou not think that mayhap this same Robin Hood may be the better man of the two? I know him right well, and many think that he is one of the stoutest men hereabouts."

"He may be the stoutest of men hereabouts," quoth Guy of Gisbourne, "yet, I tell thee, fellow, this sty of yours is not the wide world. I lay my life upon it I am the better man of the two. He an outlaw, forsooth! why, I hear that he hath never let blood in all his life, saving when he first came to the forest. Some call him a great archer; marry, I would not be afraid to stand against him all the days of the year with a bow in my hand."

"Why, truly, some folk do call him a great archer," said Robin Hood, "but we of Nottinghamshire are famous hands with the longbow. Even I, though but a simple hand at the craft, would not fear to try a bout with thee."

At these words Guy of Gisbourne looked upon Robin with wondering eyes, and then gave another roar of laughter till the woods rang. "Now," quoth he, "thou art a bold fellow to talk to me in this way. I like thy spirit in so speaking up to me, for few men have dared to do so. Put up a garland, lad, and I will try a bout with thee."

"Tut, tut," quoth Robin, "only babes shoot at garlands hereabouts. I will put up a good Nottingham mark for thee." So saying he arose, and going to a hazel thicket not far off, he cut a wand about twice the thickness of a man's thumb. From this he peeled the bark, and, sharpening the point, stuck it up in the ground in front of a great oak tree. Thence he measured off fourscore paces, which brought him beside the tree where the other sat. "There," quoth he, "is the kind of mark that Nottingham yeomen shoot at. Now let me see thee split that wand if thou art an archer."

Then Guy of Gisbourne arose. "Now out upon it!" cried he. "The Devil himself could not hit such a mark as that."

"Mayhap he could and mayhap he could not," quoth merry Robin, "but that we shall never know till thou hast shot thereat."

At these words Guy of Gisbourne looked upon Robin with knit brows, but, as the yeoman still looked innocent of any ill meaning, he bottled his words and strung his bow in silence. Twice he shot, but neither time did he hit the wand, missing it the first time by a span and the second time by a good palm's breadth. Robin laughed and laughed. "I see now," quoth he, "that the Devil himself could not hit that mark. Good fellow, if thou art no better with the broadsword than thou art with the bow and arrow, thou wilt never overcome Robin Hood."

At these words Guy of Gisbourne glared savagely upon Robin. Quoth he, "Thou hast a merry tongue, thou villain; but take care that thou makest not too free with it, or I may cut it out from thy throat for thee."

Robin Hood strung his bow and took his place with never a word, albeit his heartstrings quivered with anger and loathing. Twice he shot, the first time hitting within an inch of the wand, the second time splitting it fairly in the middle. Then, without giving the other a chance for speech, he flung his bow upon the ground. "There, thou bloody villain!" cried he fiercely, "let that show thee how little thou knowest of manly sports. And now look thy last upon the daylight, for the good earth hath been befouled long enough by thee, thou vile beast! This day, Our Lady willing, thou diest—I am Robin Hood." So saying, he flashed forth his bright sword in the sunlight.

For a time Guy of Gisbourne stared upon Robin as though bereft of wits; but his wonder quickly passed to a wild rage. "Art thou indeed Robin Hood?" cried he. "Now I am glad to meet thee, thou poor wretch! Shrive thyself, for thou wilt have no time for shriving when I am done with thee." So saying, he also drew his sword.

And now came the fiercest fight that ever Sherwood saw; for each man knew that either he or the other must die, and that no mercy was to be had in this battle. Up and down they fought, till all the sweet green grass was crushed and ground beneath the trampling of their heels. More than once the point of Robin Hood's sword felt the softness of flesh, and presently the ground began to be sprinkled with bright red drops, albeit not one of them came from Robin's veins. At last Guy of Gisbourne made a fierce and deadly thrust at Robin Hood, from which he leaped back lightly, but in so leaping he caught his heel in a root, and fell heavily upon his back. "Now, Holy Mary aid me!" muttered he, as the other leaped at him, with a grin of rage upon his face. Fiercely Guy of Gisbourne stabbed at the other with his great sword; but Robin caught the blade in his naked hand, and, though it cut his palm, he turned the point away so that it plunged deep into the ground close beside him; then, ere a blow could be struck again, he leaped to his feet, with his good sword in his hand. And now despair fell upon Guy of Gisbourne's heart in a black cloud, and he looked around him wildly, like a wounded hawk. Seeing that his strength was going from him, Robin leaped forward, and, quick as a flash, struck a back-handed blow beneath the sword arm. Down fell the sword from Guy of Gisbourne's grasp, and back he staggered at the stroke, and, ere he could regain himself, Robin's sword passed through and through his body. Round he spun upon his heel, and, flinging his hands aloft with a shrill, wild cry, fell prone upon his face upon the green sod.

Then Robin Hood wiped his sword and thrust it back into the scabbard, and, coming to where Guy of Gisbourne lay, he stood over him with folded arms, talking to himself the while. "This is the first man I have slain since I shot the King's forester in the hot days of my youth. I ofttimes think bitterly, even yet, of that first life I took, but of this I am as glad as though I had slain a wild boar that laid waste a fair country. Since the Sheriff of Nottingham hath sent such a one as this against me, I will put on the fellow's garb and go forth to see whether I may not find his worship, and perchance pay him back some of the debt I owe him upon this score."

So saying, Robin Hood stripped the hairy garments from off the dead man, and put them on himself, all bloody as they were. Then, strapping the other's sword and dagger around his body and carrying his own in his hand, together with the two bows of yew, he drew the cowl of horse's hide over his face, so that none could tell who he was, and set forth from the forest, turning his steps toward the eastward and Nottingham Town. As he strode along the country roads, men, women, and children hid away from him, for the terror of Guy of Gisbourne's name and of his doings had spread far and near.

And now let us see what befell Little John while these things were happening.

Little John walked on his way through the forest paths until he had come to the outskirts of the woodlands, where, here and there, fields of barley, corn, or green meadow lands lay smiling in the sun. So he came to the highroad and to where a little thatched cottage stood back of a cluster of twisted crab-trees, with flowers in front of it. Here he stopped of a sudden, for he thought that he heard the sound of someone in sorrow. He listened, and found that it came from the cottage; so, turning his footsteps thither, he pushed open the wicket and entered the place. There he saw a gray-haired dame sitting beside a cold hearthstone, rocking herself to and fro and weeping bitterly.

Now Little John had a tender heart for the sorrows of other folk, so, coming to the old woman and patting her kindly upon the shoulder, he spoke comforting words to her, bidding her cheer up and tell him her troubles, for that mayhap he might do something to ease them. At all this the good dame shook her head; but all the same his kind words did soothe her somewhat, so after a while she told him all that bore upon her mind. That that morning she had three as fair, tall sons beside her as one could find in all Nottinghamshire, but that they were now taken from her, and were like to be hanged straightway; that, want having come upon them, her eldest boy had gone out, the night before, into the forest, and had slain a hind in the moonlight; that the King's rangers had followed the blood upon the grass until they had come to her cottage, and had there found the deer's meat in the cupboard; that, as neither of the younger sons would betray their brother, the foresters had taken all three away, in spite of the oldest saying that he alone had slain the deer; that, as they went, she had heard the rangers talking among themselves, saying that the Sheriff had sworn that he would put a check upon the great slaughter of deer that had been going on of late by hanging the very first rogue caught thereat upon the nearest tree, and that they would take the three youths to the King's Head Inn, near Nottingham Town, where the Sheriff was abiding that day, there to await the return of a certain fellow he had sent into Sherwood to seek for Robin Hood.

To all this Little John listened, shaking his head sadly now and then. "Alas," quoth he, when the good dame had finished her speech, "this is indeed an ill case. But who is this that goeth into Sherwood after Robin Hood, and why doth he go to seek him? But no matter for that now; only that I would that Robin Hood were here to advise us. Nevertheless, no time may be lost in sending for him at this hour, if we would save the lives of thy three sons. Tell me, hast thou any clothes hereabouts that I may put on in place of these of Lincoln green? Marry, if our stout Sheriff catcheth me without disguise, I am like to be run up more quickly than thy sons, let me tell thee, dame."

Then the old woman told him that she had in the house some of the clothes of her good husband, who had died only two years before. These she brought to Little John, who, doffing his garb of Lincoln green, put them on in its stead. Then, making a wig and false beard of uncarded wool, he covered his own brown hair and beard, and, putting on a great, tall hat that had belonged to the old peasant, he took his staff in one hand and his bow in the other, and set forth with all speed to where the Sheriff had taken up his inn.

A mile or more from Nottingham Town, and not far from the southern borders of Sherwood Forest, stood the cosy inn bearing the sign of the King's Head. Here was a great bustle and stir on this bright morning, for the Sheriff and a score of his men had come to stop there and await Guy of Gisbourne's return from the forest. Great hiss and fuss of cooking was going on in the kitchen, and great rapping and tapping of wine kegs and beer barrels was going on in the cellar. The Sheriff sat within, feasting merrily of the best the place afforded, and the Sheriff's men sat upon the bench before the door, quaffing ale, or lay beneath the shade of the broad-spreading oak trees, talking and jesting and laughing. All around stood the horses of the band, with a great noise of stamping feet and a great switching of tails. To this inn came the King's rangers, driving the widow's three sons before them. The hands of the three youths were tied tightly behind their backs, and a cord from neck to neck fastened them all together. So they were marched to the room where the Sheriff sat at meat, and stood trembling before him as he scowled sternly upon them.

"So," quoth he, in a great, loud, angry voice, "ye have been poaching upon the King's deer, have you? Now I will make short work of you this day, for I will hang up all three of you as a farmer would hang up three crows to scare others of the kind from the field. Our fair county of Nottingham hath been too long a breeding-place for such naughty knaves as ye are. I have put up with these things for many years, but now I will stamp them out once for all, and with you I will begin."

Then one of the poor fellows opened his mouth to speak, but the Sheriff roared at him in a loud voice to be silent, and bade the rangers to take them away till he had done his eating and could attend to the matters concerning them. So the three poor youths were marched outside, where they stood with bowed heads and despairing hearts, till after a while the Sheriff came forth. Then he called his men about him, and quoth he, "These three villains shall be hanged straightway, but not here, lest they breed ill-luck to this goodly inn. We will take them over yonder to that belt of woodlands, for I would fain hang them upon the very trees of Sherwood itself, to show those vile outlaws therein what they may expect of me if I ever have the good luck to lay hands upon them." So saying he mounted his horse, as did his men-at-arms likewise, and all together they set forth for the belt of woodlands he had spoken of, the poor youths walking in their midst guarded by the rangers. So they came at last to the spot, and here nooses were fastened around the necks of the three, and the ends of the cords flung over the branch of a great oak tree that stood there. Then the three youths fell upon their knees and loudly besought mercy of the Sheriff; but the Sheriff of Nottingham laughed scornfully. "Now," quoth he, "I would that I had a priest here to shrive you; but, as none is nigh, you must e'en travel your road with all your sins packed upon your backs, and trust to Saint Peter to let you in through the gates of Paradise like three peddlers into the town."

In the mean time, whilst all this had been going forward, an old man had drawn near and stood leaning on his staff, looking on. His hair and beard were all curly and white, and across his back was a bow of yew that looked much too strong for him to draw. As the Sheriff looked around ere he ordered his men to string the three youths up to the oak tree, his eyes fell upon this strange old man. Then his worship beckoned to him, saying, "Come hither, father, I have a few words to say to thee." So Little John, for it was none other than he, came forward, and the Sheriff looked upon him thinking that there was something strangely familiar in the face before him. "How, now," said he, "methinks I have seen thee before. What may thy name be, father?"

"Please your worship," said Little John, in a cracked voice like that of an old man, "my name is Giles Hobble, at your worship's service."

"Giles Hobble, Giles Hobble," muttered the Sheriff to himself, turning over the names that he had in his mind to try to find one to fit to this. "I remember not thy name," said he at last, "but it matters not. Hast thou a mind to earn sixpence this bright morn?"

"Ay, marry," quoth Little John, "for money is not so plenty with me that I should cast sixpence away an I could earn it by an honest turn. What is it your worship would have me do?"

"Why, this," said the Sheriff. "Here are three men that need hanging as badly as any e'er I saw. If thou wilt string them up I will pay thee twopence apiece for them. I like not that my men-at-arms should turn hangmen. Wilt thou try thy hand?"

"In sooth," said Little John, still in the old man's voice, "I ha' never done such a thing before; but an a sixpence is to be earned so easily I might as well ha' it as anybody. But, your worship, are these naughty fellows shrived?"

"Nay," said the Sheriff, laughing, "never a whit; but thou mayst turn thy hand to that also if thou art so minded. But hasten, I prythee, for I would get back to mine inn betimes."

So Little John came to where the three youths stood trembling, and, putting his face to the first fellow's cheek as though he were listening to him, he whispered softly into his ear, "Stand still, brother, when thou feelest thy bonds cut, but when thou seest me throw my woolen wig and beard from my head and face, cast the noose from thy neck and run for the woodlands." Then he slyly cut the cord that bound the youth's hands; who, upon his part, stood still as though he were yet bound. Then he went to the second fellow, and spoke to him in the same way, and also cut his bonds. This he did to the third likewise, but all so slyly that the Sheriff, who sat upon his horse laughing, wotted not what was being done, nor his men either.

Then Little John turned to the Sheriff. "Please your worship," said he, "will you give me leave to string my bow? for I would fain help these fellows along the way, when they are swinging, with an arrow beneath the ribs."

"With all my heart," said the Sheriff, "only, as I said before, make thou haste in thy doings."

Little John put the tip of his bow to his instep, and strung the weapon so deftly that all wondered to see an old man so strong. Next he drew a good smooth arrow from his quiver and fitted it to the string; then, looking all around to see that the way was clear behind him, he suddenly cast away the wool from his head and face, shouting in a mighty voice, "Run!" Quick as a flash the three youths flung the nooses from their necks and sped across the open to the woodlands as the arrow speeds from the bow. Little John also flew toward the covert like a greyhound, while the Sheriff and his men gazed after him all bewildered with the sudden doing. But ere the yeoman had gone far the Sheriff roused himself. "After him!" he roared in a mighty voice; for he knew now who it was with whom he had been talking, and wondered that he had not known him before.

Little John heard the Sheriff's words, and seeing that he could not hope to reach the woodlands before they would be upon him, he stopped and turned suddenly, holding his bow as though he were about to shoot. "Stand back!" cried he, fiercely. "The first man that cometh a foot forward, or toucheth finger to bowstring, dieth!"

At these words the Sheriff's men stood as still as stocks, for they knew right well that Little John would be as good as his word, and that to disobey him meant death. In vain the Sheriff roared at them, calling them cowards, and urging them forward in a body; they would not budge an inch, but stood and watched Little John as he moved slowly away toward the forest, keeping his gaze fixed upon them. But when the Sheriff saw his enemy thus slipping betwixt his fingers he grew mad with his rage, so that his head swam and he knew not what he did. Then of a sudden he turned his horse's head, and plunging his spurs into its sides he gave a great shout, and, rising in his stirrups, came down upon Little John like the wind. Then Little John raised his deadly bow and drew the gray-goose feather to his cheek. But alas for him! for, ere he could loose the shaft, the good bow that had served him so long, split in his hands, and the arrow fell harmless at his feet. Seeing what had happened, the Sheriff's men raised a shout, and, following their master, came rushing down upon Little John. But the Sheriff was ahead of the others, and so caught up with the yeoman before he reached the shelter of the woodlands, then leaning forward he struck a mighty blow. Little John ducked and the Sheriff's sword turned in his hand, but the flat of the blade struck the other upon the head and smote him down, stunned and senseless.

"Now, I am right glad," said the Sheriff, when the men came up and found that Little John was not dead, "that I have not slain this man in my haste! I would rather lose five hundred pounds than have him die thus instead of hanging, as such a vile thief should do. Go, get some water from yonder fountain, William, and pour it over his head."

The man did as he was bidden, and presently Little John opened his eyes and looked around him, all dazed and bewildered with the stun of the blow. Then they tied his hands behind him, and lifting him up set him upon the back of one of the horses, with his face to its tail and his feet strapped beneath its belly. So they took him back to the King's Head Inn, laughing and rejoicing as they went along. But in the mean time the widow's three sons had gotten safely away, and were hidden in the woodlands.

Once more the Sheriff of Nottingham sat within the King's Head Inn. His heart rejoiced within him, for he had at last done that which he had sought to do for years, taken Little John prisoner. Quoth he to himself, "This time to-morrow the rogue shall hang upon the gallows tree in front of the great gate of Nottingham Town, and thus shall I make my long score with him even." So saying, he took a deep draught of Canary. But it seemed as if the Sheriff had swallowed a thought with his wine, for he shook his head and put the cup down hastily. "Now," he muttered to himself, "I would not for a thousand pounds have this fellow slip through my fingers; yet, should his master escape that foul Guy of Gisbourne, there is no knowing what he may do, for he is the cunningest knave in all the world,—this same Robin Hood. Belike I had better not wait until to-morrow to hang the fellow." So saying, he pushed his chair back hastily, and going forth from the inn called his men together. Quoth he, "I will wait no longer for the hanging of this rogue, but it shall be done forthwith, and that from the very tree whence he saved those three young villains by stepping so boldly betwixt them and the law. So get ye ready straightway."

Then once more they sat Little John upon the horse, with his face to the tail, and so, one leading the horse whereon he sat and the others riding around him, they went forward to that tree from the branches of which they had thought to hang the poachers. On they went, rattling and jingling along the road till they came to the tree. Here one of the men spake to the Sheriff of a sudden. "Your worship," cried he, "is not yon fellow coming along toward us that same Guy of Gisbourne whom thou didst send into the forest to seek the outlaw, Robin Hood?"

At these words the Sheriff shaded his eyes and looked eagerly. "Why, certes," quoth he, "yon fellow is the same. Now, Heaven send that he hath slain the master thief, as we will presently slay the man!"

When Little John heard this speech he looked up, and straightway his heart crumbled away within him, for not only were the man's garments all covered with blood, but he wore Robin Hood's bugle horn and carried his bow and broadsword in his hand.

"How now!" cried the Sheriff, when Robin Hood, in Guy of Gisbourne's clothes, had come nigh to them. "What luck hath befallen thee in the forest? Why, man, thy clothes are all over blood!"

"An thou likest not my clothes," said Robin, in a harsh voice like that of Guy of Gisbourne, "thou mayst shut thine eyes. Marry, the blood upon me is that of the vilest outlaw that ever trod the woodlands, and one whom I have slain this day, albeit not without wound to myself."

Then out spake Little John, for the first time since he had fallen into the Sheriff's hands. "O thou vile, bloody wretch! I know thee, Guy of Gisbourne, for who is there that hath not heard of thee and cursed thee for thy vile deeds of blood and rapine? Is it by such a hand as thine that the gentlest heart that ever beat is stilled in death? Truly, thou art a fit tool for this coward Sheriff of Nottingham. Now I die joyfully, nor do I care how I die, for life is nought to me!" So spake Little John, the salt tears rolling down his brown cheeks.

But the Sheriff of Nottingham clapped his hands for joy. "Now, Guy of Gisbourne," cried he, "if what thou tellest me is true, it will be the best day's doings for thee that ever thou hast done in all thy life."

"What I have told thee is sooth, and I lie not," said Robin, still in Guy of Gisbourne's voice. "Look, is not this Robin Hood's sword, and is not this his good bow of yew, and is not this his bugle horn? Thinkest thou he would have given them to Guy of Gisbourne of his own free will?"

Then the Sheriff laughed aloud for joy. "This is a good day!" cried he. "The great outlaw dead and his right-hand man in my hands! Ask what thou wilt of me, Guy of Gisbourne, and it is thine!"

"Then this I ask of thee," said Robin. "As I have slain the master I would now kill the man. Give this fellow's life into my hands, Sir Sheriff."

"Now thou art a fool!" cried the Sheriff. "Thou mightst have had money enough for a knight's ransom if thou hadst asked for it. I like ill to let this fellow pass from my hands, but as I have promised, thou shalt have him."

"I thank thee right heartily for thy gift," cried Robin. "Take the rogue down from the horse, men, and lean him against yonder tree, whilst I show you how we stick a porker whence I come!"

At these words some of the Sheriff's men shook their heads; for, though they cared not a whit whether Little John were hanged or not, they hated to see him butchered in cold blood. But the Sheriff called to them in a loud voice, ordering them to take the yeoman down from the horse and lean him against the tree, as the other bade.

Whilst they were doing this Robin Hood strung both his bow and that of Guy of Gisbourne, albeit none of them took notice of his doing so. Then, when Little John stood against the tree, he drew Guy of Gisbourne's sharp, double-edged dagger. "Fall back! fall back!" cried he. "Would ye crowd so on my pleasure, ye unmannerly knaves? Back, I say! Farther yet!" So they crowded back, as he ordered, many of them turning their faces away, that they might not see what was about to happen.

"Come!" cried Little John. "Here is my breast. It is meet that the same hand that slew my dear master should butcher me also! I know thee, Guy of Gisbourne!"

"Peace, Little John!" said Robin in a low voice. "Twice thou hast said thou knowest me, and yet thou knowest me not at all. Couldst thou not tell me beneath this wild beast's hide? Yonder, just in front of thee, lie my bow and arrows, likewise my broadsword. Take them when I cut thy bonds. Now! Get them quickly!" So saying, he cut the bonds, and Little John, quick as a wink, leaped forward and caught up the bow and arrows and the broadsword. At the same time Robin Hood threw back the cowl of horse's hide from his face and bent Guy of Gisbourne's bow, with a keen, barbed arrow fitted to the string. "Stand back!" cried he, sternly. "The first man that toucheth finger to bowstring dieth! I have slain thy man, Sheriff; take heed that it is not thy turn next." Then, seeing that Little John had armed himself, he clapped his bugle horn to his lips and blew three blasts both loud and shrill.

Now when the Sheriff of Nottingham saw whose face it was beneath Guy of Gisbourne's hood, and when he heard those bugle notes ring in his ear, he felt as if his hour had come. "Robin Hood!" roared he, and without another word he wheeled his horse in the road and went off in a cloud of dust. The Sheriff's men, seeing their master thus fleeing for his life, thought that it was not their business to tarry longer, so, clapping spurs to their horses, they also dashed away after him. But though the Sheriff of Nottingham went fast, he could not outstrip a clothyard arrow. Little John twanged his bowstring with a shout, and when the Sheriff dashed in through the gates of Nottingham Town at full speed, a gray-goose shaft stuck out behind him like a moulting sparrow with one feather in its tail. For a month afterwards the poor Sheriff could sit upon nought but the softest cushions that could be gotten for him.

Thus the Sheriff and a score of men ran away from Robin Hood and Little John; so that when Will Stutely and a dozen or more of stout yeomen burst from out the covert, they saw nought of their master's enemies, for the Sheriff and his men were scurrying away in the distance, hidden within a cloud of dust like a little thunder-storm.

Then they all went back into the forest once more, where they found the widow's three sons, who ran to Little John and kissed his hands. But it would not do for them to roam the forest at large any more; so they promised that, after they had gone and told their mother of their escape, they would come that night to the greenwood tree, and thenceforth become men of the band.

Thus end the bravest adventures that ever befell Robin Hood and Little John.

from

Monkey

by Wu Chêng-ên,
translated by Arthur Waley

Arthur Waley's (1889–1966) translation of Monkey is based upon a work by 16th-century Chinese magistrate Wu Chêng-ên (c. 1505–1580). The story begins with a monkey born from stone, who strives to become immortal. He finds a cave of immortals and asks for instruction from the patriarch, who gives him his new school-name, "Aware-of-Vacuity."

Monkey was so pleased with his new name that he skipped up and down in front of the Patriarch, bowing to express his gratitude. Subodhi then ordered his pupils to take Monkey to the outer rooms and teach him how to sprinkle and dust, answer properly when spoken to, how to come in, go out, and go round. Then he bowed to his fellow-pupils and went out into the corridor, where he made himself a sleeping place. Early next morning he and the others practised the correct mode of speech and bearing, studied the Scriptures, discussed doctrine, practised writing, burnt incense. And in this same way he passed day after day, spending his leisure in sweeping the floor, hoeing the garden, growing flowers and tending trees, getting firewood and lighting the fire, drawing water and carrying it in buckets. Everything he needed was provided for him. And so he lived in the cave, while time slipped by, for six or seven years. One day the Patriarch, seated in state, summoned all his pupils and began a lecture on the Great Way. Monkey was so delighted by what he heard that he tweaked his ears and rubbed his cheeks; his brow flowered and his eyes laughed. He could not stop his hands from dancing, his feet from stamping. Suddenly the Patriarch caught sight of him and shouted, 'What is the use of your being here if, instead of listening to my lecture, you jump and dance like a maniac?'

'I am listening with all my might,' said Monkey. 'But you were saying such wonderful things that I could not contain myself for joy. That is why I may, for all I know, have been hopping and jumping. Don't be angry with me.'

'So you recognize the profundity of what I am saying?' said the Patriarch. 'How long, pray, have you been in the cave?'

'It may seem rather silly,' said Monkey, 'but really I don't know how long. All I can remember is that when I was sent to get firewood, I went up the mountain behind the cave, and there I found a whole slope covered with peach-trees. I have eaten my fill of those peaches seven times.'

'It is called the Hill of Bright Peach Blossom,' said the Patriarch. 'If you have eaten there seven times, I suppose you have been here seven years. What sort of wisdom are you now hoping to learn from me?'

'I leave that to you,' said Monkey. 'Any sort of wisdom—it's all one to me.'

'There are three hundred and sixty schools of wisdom,' said the Patriarch, 'and all of them lead to Self-attainment. Which school do you want to study?'

'Just as you think best,' said Monkey. 'I am all attention.'

'Well, how about Art?' said the Patriarch. 'Would you like me to teach you that?'

'What sort of wisdom is that?' asked Monkey.

'You would be able to summon fairies and ride the Phoenix,' said the Patriarch, 'divine by shuffling the yarrow-stalks and know how to avoid disaster and pursue good fortune.'

'But should I live forever?' asked Monkey.

'Certainly not,' said the Patriarch.

'Then that's no good to me,' said Monkey.

'How about natural philosophy?' said the Patriarch.

'What is that about?' asked Monkey.

'It means the teaching of Confucius,' said the Patriarch, 'and of Buddha and Lao Tzu, of the Dualists and Mo Tzu and the Doctors of Medicine; reading scriptures, saying prayers, learning how to have adepts and sages at your beck and call.'

'But should I live forever?' asked Monkey.

'If that's what you are thinking about,' said the Patriarch, 'I am afraid philosophy is no better than a prop in the wall.'

'Master,' said Monkey, 'I am a plain, simple man, and I don't understand that sort of patter. What do you mean by a prop in the wall?'

'When men are building a room,' said the Patriarch, 'and want it to stand firm, they put a pillar to prop up the walls. But one day the roof falls in and the pillar rots.'

'That doesn't sound much like long life,' said Monkey. 'I'm not going to learn philosophy!'

'How about Quietism?' asked the Patriarch.

'What does that consist of?' asked Monkey.

'Low diet,' said the Patriarch, 'inactivity, meditation, restraint of word and deed, yoga practised prostrate or standing.'

'But should I live forever?' asked Monkey.

'The results of Quietism,' said the Patriarch, 'are no better than unbaked clay in the kiln.'

'You've got a very poor memory,' said Monkey. 'Didn't I tell you just now that I don't understand that sort of patter? What do you mean by unbaked clay in the kiln?'

'The bricks and tiles,' said the Patriarch, 'may be waiting, all shaped and ready, in the kiln; but if they have not yet been fired, there will come a day when heavy rain falls and they are washed away.'

'That does not promise well for the future,' said Monkey. 'I don't think I'll bother about Quietism.'

'You might try exercises,' said the Patriarch.

'What do you mean by that?' asked Monkey.

'Various forms of activity,' said the Patriarch, 'such as the exercises called "Gathering the Yin and patching the Yang", "Drawing the Bow and Treading the Catapult", "Rubbing the Navel to pass breath". Then there are alchemical practices such as the Magical Explosion, Burning the Reeds and Striking the Tripod, Promoting Red Lead, Melting the Autumn Stone, and Drinking Bride's Milk.'

'Would these make me live forever?' asked Monkey.

'To hope for that,' said the Patriarch, 'would be like trying to fish the moon out of the water.'

'There you go again!' said Monkey. 'What pray do you mean by fishing the moon out of the water?'

'When the moon is in the sky,' said the Patriarch, 'it is reflected in the water. It looks just like a real thing, but if you try to catch hold of it, you find it is only an illusion.'

'That does not sound much good,' said Monkey; 'I shan't learn exercises.'

'Tut!' cried the Patriarch, and coming down from the platform, he caught hold of the knuckle-rapper and pointed it at Monkey, saying, 'You wretched simian! You won't learn this and you won't learn that! I should like to know what it is you do want.' And so saying he struck Monkey over the head three times. Then he folded his hands behind his back and strode off into the inner room, dismissing his audience and locking the door behind him. The pupils all turned indignantly upon Monkey.

'You villainous ape,' they shouted at him, 'do you think that is the way to behave? The Master offers to teach you, and instead of accepting thankfully you begin arguing with him. Now he's thoroughly offended and goodness knows when he'll come back.' They were all very angry and poured abuse on him; but Monkey was not in the least upset, and merely replied by a broad grin. The truth of the matter was, he understood the language of secret signs. That was why he did not take up the quarrel or attempt to argue. He knew that the Master, by striking him three times, was giving him an appointment at the third watch; and by going off with his hands folded behind his back, meant that Monkey was to look for him in the inner apartments. The locking of the door meant that he was to come round by the back door and would then receive instruction.

The rest of the day he frolicked with the other pupils in front of the cave, impatiently awaiting the night. As soon as dusk came, like the others, he went to his sleeping place. He closed his eyes and pretended to be asleep, breathing softly and regularly. In the mountains there is no watchman to beat the watches or call the hours. The best Monkey could do was to count his incoming and outgoing breaths. When he reckoned that it must be about the hour of the Rat (11 p.m.–1 a.m.) he got up very quietly and slipped on his clothes, softly opened the front door, left his companions, and went round to the back door. Sure enough, it was only half shut. 'The Master certainly means to give me instruction,' said Monkey to himself. 'That is why he left the door open.' So he crept in and went straight to the Master's bed. Finding him curled up and lying with his face to the wall, Monkey dared not wake him, and knelt down beside the bed. Presently the Patriarch woke, stretched out his legs and murmured to himself.

> *Hard, very hard!*
> *The Way is most secret.*
> *Never handle the Golden Elixir as though it were a mere toy!*
> *He who to unworthy ears entrusts the dark truths*
> *To no purpose works his jaws and talks his tongue dry.*

'Master, I've been kneeling here for some time,' said Monkey, when he saw the Patriarch was awake.

'You wretched Monkey,' said Subodhi, who on recognizing his voice pulled off the bed-clothes and sat up. 'Why aren't you asleep in your own quarters, instead of coming round behind to mine?'

'At the lecture today,' said Monkey, 'you ordered me to come for instruction at the third watch, by way of the back gate. That is why I ventured to come straight to your bed.'

The Patriarch was delighted. He thought to himself 'This fellow must really be, as he says, a natural product of Heaven and Earth. Otherwise he would never have understood my secret signs.'

'We are alone together,' said Monkey, 'there is no one to overhear us.

Take pity upon me and teach me the way of Long Life. I shall never forget your kindness.'

'You show a disposition,' said the Patriarch. 'You understood my secret signs. Come close and listen carefully. I am going to reveal to you the Secret of Long Life.'

Monkey beat his head on the floor to show his gratitude, washed his ears and attended closely, kneeling beside the bed. The Patriarch then recited:

> To spare and tend the vital powers, this and nothing else
> Is sum and total of all magic, secret and profane.
> All is comprised in these three, Spirit, Breath, and Soul;
> Guard them closely, screen them well; let there be no leak.
> Store them within the frame;
> That is all that can be learnt, and all that can be taught.
> I would have you mark the tortoise and snake, locked in tight
>   embrace.
> Locked in tight embrace, the vital powers are strong;
> Even in the midst of fierce flames the Golden Lotus may be
>   planted,
> The Five Elements compounded and transposed, and put to
>   new use.
> When that is done, be which you please, Buddha or
>   Immortal.

By these words Monkey's whole nature was shaken to the foundations. He carefully committed them to memory; then humbly thanked the Patriarch, and went out again by the back door.

A pale light was just coming into the eastern sky. He retraced his steps, softly opened the front door and returned to his sleeping place, purposely making a rustling noise with his bed-clothes. 'Get up!' he cried. 'There is light in the sky.' His fellow pupils were fast asleep, and had no idea that Monkey had received Illumination.

Time passed swiftly, and three years later the Patriarch again mounted his jewelled seat and preached to his assembled followers. His subject was the parables and scholastic problems of the Zen Sect, and his theme, the tegument of outer appearances. Suddenly he broke off and asked, 'Where is the disciple Aware-of-Vacuity?'

Monkey knelt down before him and answered 'Here!'

'What have you been studying all this time?' asked the Patriarch.

'Recently,' said Monkey, 'my spiritual nature has been very much in the ascendant, and my fundamental sources of power are gradually strengthening.'

'In that case,' said the Patriarch, 'all you need learn is how to ward off the Three Calamities.'

'There must be some mistake,' said Monkey in dismay. 'I understood that the secrets I have learnt would make me live forever and protect me from fire, water and every kind of disease. What is this about three calamities?'

'What you have learnt,' said the Patriarch, 'will preserve your youthful appearance and increase the length of your life; but after five hundred years Heaven will send down lightning which will finish you off, unless you have the sagacity to avoid it. After another five hundred years Heaven will send down a fire that will devour you. This fire is of a peculiar kind. It is neither common fire, nor celestial fire, but springs up from within and consumes the vitals, reducing the whole frame to ashes, and making a vanity of all your thousand years of self-perfection. But even should you escape this, in another five hundred years, a wind will come and blow upon you. Not the east wind, the south wind, the west wind or the north wind; not flower wind or willow wind, pine wind or bamboo wind. It blows from below, enters the bowels, passes the midriff and issues at the Nine Apertures. It melts bone and flesh, so that the whole body dissolves. These three calamities you must be able to avoid.'

When Monkey heard this, his hair stood on end, and prostrating himself he said, 'I beseech you, have pity upon me, and teach me how to avoid these calamities. I shall never forget your kindness.'

'There would be no difficulty about that,' said the Patriarch, 'if it were not for your peculiarities.'

'I have a round head sticking up to Heaven and square feet treading Earth,' said Monkey. 'I have nine apertures, four limbs, five upper and six lower internal organs, just like other people.'

'You are like other men in most respects,' said the Patriarch, 'but you have much less jowl.' For monkeys have hollow cheeks and pointed nozzles.

Monkey felt his face with his hand and laughed saying, 'Master, I have my debits, but don't forget my assets. I have my pouch, and that must be credited to my account, as something that ordinary humans haven't got.'

'True enough,' said the Patriarch. 'There are two methods of escape. Which would you like to learn? There is the trick of the Heavenly Ladle, which involves thirty-six kinds of transformation, and the trick of the Earthly Conclusion, which involves seventy-two kinds of transformation.'

'Seventy-two sounds better value,' said Monkey.

'Come here then,' said the Patriarch, 'and I will teach you the formula.' He then whispered a magic formula into Monkey's ear. That Monkey King was uncommonly quick at taking things in. He at once began practising the formula, and after a little self-discipline he mastered all the seventy-two transformations, whole and complete. One day when master and disciples were in front of the cave, admiring the evening view, the Patriarch said, 'Monkey, how is that business going?'

'Thanks to your kindness,' said Monkey, 'I have been extremely successful. In addition to the transformations I can already fly.'

'Let's see you do it,' said the Patriarch. Monkey put his feet together, leapt about sixty feet into the air, and riding the clouds for a few minutes dropped in front of the Patriarch. He did not get more than three leagues in the whole of his flight.

'Master,' he said, 'that surely is cloud-soaring?'

'I should be more inclined to call it cloud-crawling,' said the Patriarch laughing. 'The old saying runs, "An Immortal wanders in the morning to the Northern Sea and the same evening he is in Ts'ang-wu." To take as long as you did to go a mere league or two hardly counts even as cloud-crawling.'

'What is meant by that saying about the Northern Sea and Ts'ang-wu?' asked Monkey.

'A real cloud-soarer,' said the Patriarch, 'can start early in the morning from the Northern Sea, cross the Eastern Sea, the Western Sea, and the Southern Sea, and land again at Ts'ang-wu. Ts'ang-wu means Ling-ling, in the Northern Sea. To do the round of all four seas in one day is true cloud-soaring.'

'It sounds very difficult,' said Monkey.

'Nothing in the world is difficult,' said the Patriarch, 'it is only our own thoughts that make things seem so.'

'Master,' said Monkey, prostrating himself, 'you may as well make a good job of me. While you're about it, do me a real kindness and teach me the art of cloud-soaring. I shall never forget how much I owe to you.'

'When the Immortals go cloud-soaring,' said the Patriarch, 'they sit cross-legged and rise straight from that position. You do nothing of the kind. I saw you just now put your feet together and jump. I must really take this opportunity of teaching you how to do it properly. You shall learn the Cloud Trapeze.' He then taught him the magic formula, saying, 'Make the pass, recite the spell, clench your fists, and one leap will carry you head over heels a hundred and eight thousand leagues.'

When the other pupils heard this, they all tittered, saying, 'Monkey is in luck. If he learns this trick, he will be able to carry dispatches, deliver letters, take round circulars—one way or another he will always be able to pick up a living!'

It was now late. Master and pupils all went to their quarters; but Monkey spent all night practising the Cloud Trapeze, and by the time day came he had completely mastered it, and could wander through space where he would.

One summer day when the disciples had for some time been studying their tasks under a pine-tree, one of them said, 'Monkey, what can you have done in a former incarnation to merit that the Master should the other day have whispered in your ear the secret formula for avoiding the three calamities? Have you mastered all those transformations?'

'To tell you the truth,' said Monkey, 'although of course I am much indebted to the Master for his instruction, I have also been working very hard day and night on my own, and I can now do them all.'

'Wouldn't this be a good opportunity,' said one of the pupils, 'to give us a little demonstration?'

When Monkey heard this, he was all on his mettle to display his powers. 'Give me my subject,' he said. 'What am I to change into?'

'How about a pine-tree?' they said.

He made a magic pass, recited a spell, shook himself, and changed into a pine-tree.

The disciples clapped and burst into loud applause. 'Bravo, Monkey, bravo,' they cried. There was such a din that the Patriarch came running out with his staff trailing after him.

'Who's making all this noise?' he asked.

The disciples at once controlled themselves, smoothed down their dresses, and came meekly forward. Monkey changed himself back into his true form and slipped in among the crowd, saying, 'Reverend Master, we are doing our lessons out here. I assure you there was no noise in particular.'

'You were all bawling,' said the Patriarch angrily. 'It didn't sound in the least like people studying. I want to know what you were doing here, shouting and laughing.'

'To tell the truth,' said someone, 'Monkey was showing us a transformation just for fun. We told him to change into a pine-tree, and he did it so well that we were all applauding him. That was the noise you heard. I hope you will forgive us.'

'Go away, all of you!' the Patriarch shouted. 'And you, Monkey, come here! What were you doing, playing with your spiritual powers, turning into—what was it? A pine-tree? Did you think I taught you in order that you might show off in front of other people? If you saw someone else turn into a tree, wouldn't you at once ask how it was done? If others see you doing it, aren't they certain to ask you? If you are frightened to refuse, you will give the secret away; and if you refuse, you're very likely to be roughly handled. You're putting yourself in grave danger.'

'I'm terribly sorry,' said Monkey.

'I won't punish you,' said the Patriarch, 'but you can't stay here.'

Monkey burst into tears. 'Where am I to go to?' he asked.

'Back to where you came from, I should suppose,' said the Patriarch.

'You don't mean back to the Cave of the Water Curtain in Ao-lai!' said Monkey.

'Yes,' said the Patriarch, 'go back as quickly as you can, if you value your life. One thing is certain in any case; you can't stay here.'

'May I point out,' said Monkey, 'that I have been away from home for twenty years and should be very glad to see my monkey-subjects once more. But I can't consent to go till I have repaid you for all your kindness.'

'I have no desire to be repaid,' said the Patriarch. 'All I ask is that if you get into trouble, you should keep my name out of it.'

Monkey saw that it was no use arguing. He bowed to the Patriarch, and took leave of his companions.

'Wherever you go,' said the Patriarch, 'I'm convinced you'll come to no good. So remember, when you get into trouble, I absolutely forbid you to say that you are my disciple. If you give a hint of any such thing I shall flay you alive, break all your bones, and banish your soul to the Place of Ninefold Darkness, where it will remain for ten thousand aeons.'

'I certainly won't venture to say a word about you,' promised Monkey. 'I'll say I found it all out for myself.'

So saying he bade farewell, turned away, and making the magic pass rode off on his cloud trapeze, straight to the Eastern Sea. In a very little while he reached the Mountain of Flowers and Fruit, where he lowered his cloud, and was picking his way, when he heard a sound of cranes calling and monkeys crying.

'Little ones,' he shouted, 'I have come back.'

At once from every cranny in the cliff, from bushes and trees, great monkeys and small leapt out with cries of 'Long live our king!' Then they all pressed round Monkey, kowtowing and saying, 'Great King, you're very absent-minded! Why did you go away for so long, leaving us all in the lurch, panting for your return, as a starving man for food and drink? For some time past a demon has been ill-using us. He has seized our cave, though we fought desperately, and now he has robbed us of all our possessions and carried off many of our children, so that we have to be on the watch all the time and get no sleep day or night. It's lucky you've come now, for if you had waited another year or two, you'd have found us and everything hereabouts in another's hands.'

'What demon can dare commit such crimes?' cried Monkey. 'Tell me all about it and I will avenge you.'

'Your Majesty,' they said, 'he is called the Demon of Havoc, and he lives due north from here.'

'How far off?' asked Monkey.

'He comes like a cloud,' they said, 'and goes like a mist, like wind or rain, thunder or lightning. We do not know how far away he lives.'

'Well, don't worry,' said Monkey; 'just go on playing around, while I go and look for him.'

Dear Monkey King! He sprang into the sky straight northwards and soon saw in front of him a high and very rugged mountain. He was admiring the scenery, when he suddenly heard voices. Going a little way down the hill, he found a cave in front of which several small imps were jumping and dancing. When they saw Monkey, they ran away. 'Stop!' he called, 'I've got a message for you to take. Say that the master of the Water Curtain Cave is here. The Demon of Havoc, or whatever he is called, who lives here, has been ill-treating my little ones and I have come on purpose to settle matters with him.'

They rushed into the cave and cried out, 'Great King, a terrible thing has happened!'

'What's the matter?' said the demon.

'Outside the cave,' they said, 'there is a monkey-headed creature who says he is the owner of the Water Curtain Cave. He says you have been ill-using his people and he has come on purpose to settle matters with you.'

'Ha, ha,' laughed the demon. 'I have often heard those monkeys say that their king had gone away to learn religion. This means that he's come back again. What does he look like and how is he armed?'

'He carries no weapon at all,' they said. 'He goes bareheaded, wears a red dress, with a yellow sash, and black shoes—neither priest nor layman nor quite like a Taoist. He's waiting naked-handed outside the gate.'

'Bring me my whole accoutrement,' cried the demon.

The small imps at once fetched his arms. The demon put on his helmet and breastplate, grasped his sword, and going to the gate with the little imps, cried in a loud voice, 'Where's the owner of the Water Curtain Cave?'

'What's the use of having such large eyes,' shouted Monkey, 'if you can't see old Monkey?'

Catching sight of him the demon burst out laughing. 'You're not a foot high or as much as thirty years old. You have no weapon in your hand! How dare you strut about talking of settling accounts with me?'

'Cursed demon,' said Monkey. 'After all, you have no eyes in your head! You say I am small, not seeing that I can make myself as tall as I please. You say I am unarmed, not knowing that these two hands of mine could drag the moon from the ends of Heaven. Stand your ground, and eat old Monkey's fist!'

So saying he leapt into the air and aimed a blow at the demon's face. The demon parried the blow with his hand.

'You such a pigmy and I so tall!' said the demon. 'You using your fists and I my sword—No! If I were to slay you with my sword I should make myself ridiculous. I am going to throw away my sword and use my naked fists.'

'Very good,' said Monkey. 'Now, my fine fellow, come on!'

The demon relaxed his guard and struck. Monkey closed with him, and the two of them pommelled and kicked, blow for blow. A long reach is not so firm and sure as a short one. Monkey jabbed the demon in the lower ribs, pounded him in the chest, and gave him such a heavy drubbing that at last the demon stood back, and picking up his great flat sword, slashed at Monkey's head. But Monkey stepped swiftly aside, and the blow missed its mark. Seeing that the demon was becoming savage, Monkey now used the method called Body Outside the Body. He plucked out a handful of hairs, bit them into small pieces, and then spat them out into the air, crying 'Change!' The fragments of hair changed into several hundred small monkeys, all pressing round in a throng. For you must know that when anyone becomes an Immortal, he can project his soul, change his shape, and perform all kinds of miracles. Monkey, since his Illumination, could change every one of the eighty-four thousand hairs of his body into whatever he chose. The little monkeys he had now created were so nimble that no sword could touch them or spear wound them. See how they leap forward and jump back, crowd round the demon, some hugging, some pulling, some jabbing at his chest, some swarming up his legs. They kicked him, beat him, pommelled his eyes, pinched his nose, and while they were all at it, Monkey slipped up and snatched away the demon's sword. Then pushing through the throng of small monkeys, he raised the sword and brought it down with such tremendous force upon the demon's skull, that he clove it in twain. He and the little monkeys then rushed into the cave and made a quick end of the imps, great and small. He then said a spell, which caused the small monkeys to change back into hairs. These he put back where they had come from; but there were still some small monkeys left—those that the demon had carried off from the Cave of the Water Curtain.

'How did you get here?' he asked.

There were about thirty or forty of them, and they all said with tears in their eyes, 'After your Majesty went away to become an Immortal, we were pestered by this creature for two years. In the end he carried us all off, and he stole all the fittings from our cave. He took all the stone dishes and the stone cups.'

'Collect everything that belongs to us and bring it with you,' said Monkey. They then set fire to the cave and burnt everything in it.

'Now follow me!' said Monkey.

'When we were brought here,' they said, 'we only felt a great wind rushing past, which whirled us to this place. We didn't know which way we were coming. So how are we to find the way home?'

'He brought you here by magic,' said Monkey. 'But what matter? I am now up to all that sort of thing, and if he could do it, I can. Shut your eyes, all of you, and don't be frightened.'

He then recited a spell which produced a fierce wind. Suddenly it dropped, and Monkey shouted, 'You may look now!' The monkeys found that they were standing on firm ground quite close to their home. In high delight they all followed a familiar path back to the door of their cave. They and those who had been left behind all pressed into the cave, and lined up according to their rank and age, and did homage to their king, and prepared a great banquet of welcome. When they asked how the demon had been subdued and the monkeys rescued, he told them the whole story; upon which they burst into shouts of applause.

'We little thought,' they said, 'that when your Majesty left us, you would learn such arts as this!'

'After I parted from you,' said Monkey, 'I went across many oceans to the land of Jambudvipa, where I learnt human ways, and how to wear clothes and shoes. I wandered restless as a cloud for eight or nine years, but nowhere could I find Enlightenment. At last after crossing yet another ocean, I was lucky enough to meet an old Patriarch who taught me the secret of eternal life.'

'What an incredible piece of luck!' the monkeys said, all congratulating him.

'Little ones,' said Monkey, 'I have another bit of good news for you. Your king has got a name-in-religion. I am called Aware-of-Vacuity.'

They all clapped loudly, and presently went to get date-wine and grape-wine and fairy flowers and fruit, which they offered to Monkey. Everyone was in the highest spirits.

Monkey, having returned in triumph, after slaying the Demon of Havoc and snatching the demon's huge cutlass, practised sword-play every day and taught the small monkeys how to sharpen bamboos with spears, make wooden swords and banners to carry; how to go on patrol, advance and retreat, pitch camp, build stockades, and so on. They had great fun doing this; but suddenly, sitting in a quiet place, Monkey thought to himself, 'All this is only a game; but the consequences of it may be serious. Suppose some human king or king of birds or beasts should hear what we are at, he may very well think that we are hatching a conspiracy against him and bring his armies to attack us. Bamboo spears and wooden swords wouldn't help you much then. You ought to have real swords and lances and halberds. How are we to get hold of them?'

'That's an excellent idea,' they said, 'but there's nowhere we can possibly get them from.'

At this point four old monkeys came forward, two red-bottomed horse-apes and two tailless apes with plain behinds. 'Great King,' they said, 'if you want to get weapons made, nothing could be easier.'

'Why do you think it so easy?' asked Monkey.

'East of our mountains,' they said, 'there are two hundred leagues of water. That is the frontier of Ao-lai, and at that frontier there is a king whose city is full of soldiers. He must certainly have metal-works of all sorts. If you go there, you can certainly buy weapons or get them made for you. Then you can teach us to use them, and we shall be able to defend ourselves. That is the way to protect us against extinction.'

Monkey was delighted with this idea. 'You stay here and amuse yourselves,' he said, 'while I go off and see what can be done.'

Dear Monkey! He set out on his cloud trapeze, and in a twinkling he had crossed those two hundred leagues of water, and on the other side there was indeed a city with walls and moat, with wards and markets, and myriad streets where men walked up and down in the happy sunshine. He thought to himself, 'In such a place there are sure to be ready-made weapons. I'll go down and buy some. Or better still, I'll get some by magic.' He made a magic pass, recited a spell and drew a magic diagram on the ground. He then stood in the middle of it, drew a long breath and expelled it with such force that sand and stones hurtled through the air. This tempest so much alarmed the king of the country and all his subjects that they locked themselves indoors.

Monkey lowered his cloud, made straight for the government build-
ings, and soon finding the arsenal he forced open the door, and saw a
vast supply of swords, lances, scimitars, halberds, axes, scythes, whips,
rakes, cudgels, bows, and crossbows—every conceivable weapon.
'That's rather more than I can carry,' he said to himself. So, as before,
he changed his hairs into thousands of small monkeys, who began
snatching at the weapons. Some managed to carry six or seven, others
three or four, till soon the arsenal was bare. Then a great gale of magic
wind carried them back to the cave. The monkeys at home were
playing in front of the cave door, when suddenly they saw a great
swarm of monkeys in the sky above, which scared them so much that
they all rushed into hiding. Soon Monkey lowered his cloud and
turned the thousands of little monkeys into hairs. He stacked the
weapons on the hillside and cried, 'Little ones, all come and get your
arms!' To their astonishment they found Monkey standing all alone on
the ground. They rushed forward to pay homage, and Monkey
explained to them what had happened. When they had congratulated
him on his performance, they all began to grab at swords and cut-
lasses, pick up axes, scramble for spears, drag off bows and crossbows.
This sport, which was a very noisy one, lasted all day.

Next day they came on parade as usual, and the roll-call disclosed
that they numbered forty-seven thousand in all. All the wild beasts of
the mountain and demon kings of every kind, denizens of no less than
seventy-two caves, came to pay homage to Monkey, and henceforward
brought tribute every year and signed on once in every season. Some
supplied labour and some provisions. The Mountain of Flowers and
Fruit became as strong as an iron bucket or wall of bronze. The demon
kings of various districts also presented bronze drums, coloured banners, helmets, and coats of mail. Day after day there was a tremendous
bustle of drilling and marching. Everything was going well, when suddenly one day Monkey said to his subjects, 'You seem to be getting on
well with your drill, but I find my sword very cumbersome, in fact not
at all to my liking. What is to be done?'

The four old monkeys came forward and said, 'Great King, it is quite natural that you, being an Immortal, should not care to use this earthly weapon. Do you think it would be possible for you to get one from the denizens of the sea?'

'Why not, pray?' said Monkey. 'Since my Illumination I have mastery of seventy-two transformations; greatest wonder of all, I can ride upon the clouds. I can become invisible, I can penetrate bronze and stone. Water cannot drown me, any more than fire can burn me. What's to prevent me getting a weapon from the Powers of the Sea?'

'Well, if you can manage it,' they said. 'The water that flows under this iron bridge comes up from the palace of the dragon of the Eastern Sea. How about going down and paying a call upon the Dragon King? If you asked him for a weapon he would no doubt be able to find you something suitable.'

'I'll certainly go,' said Monkey. He went to the bridgehead, recited a spell to protect himself from the effects of water, and jumped in, making his way along the water-course till he came to the bottom of the Eastern Sea. Presently he was stopped by a Yaksha who was patrolling the waters.

'What deity is that,' he asked, 'pushing along through the water? Give me an account of yourself and I will announce your arrival.'

'I am the monkey-king of the Mountain of Flowers and Fruit,' said Monkey. 'I am a near neighbour of the Dragon King, and consider that I ought to make his acquaintance.'

The Yaksha brought in the message, and the Dragon King rose hastily and came to the door of his palace, bringing with him his dragon children and grandchildren, his shrimp soldiers and crab generals.

'Come in, High Immortal, come in,' he said.

They went into the palace and sat face to face on the upper seat. When they had taken tea, the dragon asked, 'How long, pray, have you been Illumined, and what magic arts have you learned?'

'I have led a religious life since my infancy,' said Monkey, 'and am now beyond birth and destruction. Recently I have been training my subjects how to defend their home; but I myself have no suitable weapon. I am told that my honoured neighbour within the shell-portals of his green jade palace certainly has many magic weapons to spare.'

The Dragon King did not like to refuse, and ordered a trout-captain to bring out a huge sword.

'I'm no good with a sword,' said Monkey. 'Can't you find something else?'

The Dragon King then told a whitebait-guardsman with the help of an eel-porter to bring out a nine-pronged fork. Monkey took hold of it and tried a few thrusts.

'It's much too light,' he said. 'And it does not suit my hand. Can't you find me something else?'

'I really don't know what you mean,' said the Dragon King. 'The fork weighs three thousand six hundred pounds.'

'It doesn't suit my hand,' said Monkey, 'it doesn't suit my hand.'

The Dragon King was much upset, and ordered a bream-general and a carp-brigadier to bring out a huge halberd, weighing seven thousand two hundred pounds. Monkey seized it and after making a few thrusts and parries tossed it away saying, 'Still too light!'

'It's the heaviest weapon we've got in the palace,' said the Dragon King. 'I have nothing else I can show you.'

'The proverb says "It's no use the Dragon King pretending he's got no treasures," ' said Monkey. 'Just look again, and if you succeed in finding something suitable, I'll give you a good price.'

'I warn you I haven't got anything else,' said the Dragon King.

At this point the Dragon Mother and her daughter slipped out from the back rooms of the palace and said, 'Great King, we can see that this Monkey Sage is of no common capacities. In our treasury is the magic iron with which the bed of the Milky Way was pounded flat. For several days past it has been glowing with a strange light. Was this not perhaps an omen that it should be given to the Sage who has just arrived?'

'This,' said the Dragon King, 'is the thing that was used by the Great Yü, when he subdued the Flood, to fix the depth of the rivers and seas. It's only a piece of holy iron. What use could it be to him?'

'Don't worry about whether he uses it or not,' said the Dragon

Mother. 'Just give it to him, and if he can cope with it, let him take it away with him.'

The Dragon King agreed, and told Monkey.

'Bring it to me and I'll have a look at it,' said Monkey.

'Out of the question!' said the Dragon King. 'It's too heavy to move. You'll have to go and look at it.'

'Where is it?' asked Monkey. 'Show me the way.'

The Dragon King accordingly brought him to the Sea Treasury, where he at once saw something shining with innumerable beams of golden light. 'There it is,' said the Dragon King. Monkey respectfully tidied himself and approached the object. It turned out to be a thick iron pillar, about twenty feet long. Monkey took one end in both hands and raised it a little. 'A trifle too long and too thick!' he said. The pillar at once became several feet shorter and one layer thinner. Monkey felt it. 'A little smaller still wouldn't do any harm,' he said. The pillar at once shrunk again. Monkey was delighted. Taking it out into the daylight he found that at each end was a golden clasp, while in between all was black iron. On the near end was the inscription 'Golden Clasped Wishing Staff. Weight, thirteen thousand five hundred pounds'. 'Splendid!' thought Monkey. 'One couldn't wish for a better treasure than this.' But as he went along, he thought to himself, fingering the staff, 'If only it were a little smaller, it would be marvellous.' And sure enough, by the time he got outside it was not much more than two feet long. Look at him, how he displays its magic, making sudden thrusts and passes on his way back to the palace. The Dragon King trembled at the sight, and the Dragon Princes were all in a flutter. Tortoises and turtles drew in their heads; fishes, crabs, and shrimps all hid themselves away. Monkey, with the treasure in his hand, sat down by the Dragon King.

'I am deeply grateful for my honoured neighbour's kindness,' he said.

'Pray don't mention it,' said the Dragon King.

'Yes, it's a useful bit of iron,' said Monkey, 'but there is just one more thing I should like to say.'

'Great Immortal,' said the Dragon King, 'what else have you to say?'

'Before I had this iron,' said Monkey, 'it was another matter, but with a thing like this in my hand, I begin to feel the lack of anything suitable to wear with it. If you have got anything in that line, please let me have it. I should really be grateful.'

'I have nothing at all,' said the Dragon King.

'You know the old saying,' said Monkey, ' "One guest should not trouble two hosts". You won't get rid of me by pretending you haven't got any.'

'You might try another sea,' said the Dragon King, 'it's just possible they would be able to help you.'

' "Better sit in one house than run to three," ' said Monkey. 'I insist on your finding me something.'

'I assure you I don't possess anything of that sort,' said the Dragon King. 'If I did you should have it.'

'All right,' said Monkey. 'I'll try my iron on you, and we shall soon see whether you can give me one.'

'Steady, steady, Great Immortal,' said the Dragon King. 'Don't strike! Just let me find out whether my brothers haven't got anything that you could have.'

'Where do they live?' asked Monkey. 'They are the dragons of the southern, northern, and western seas,' said the Dragon King.

'I am not going as far as that,' said Monkey. ' "Two in hand is better than three in bond." You must find me something here and now. I don't mind where you get it from.'

'I never suggested that you should go,' said the Dragon King. 'We've got an iron drum and a bronze gong here. If anything important happens, I have them sounded, and my brothers come immediately.'

'Very well,' said Monkey. 'Look sharp and sound the drum and gong.'

A crocodile accordingly beat the drum and a turtle sounded the gong, and in a twinkling the three dragons arrived.

'Brother,' said the Dragon of the South, 'what urgent business has made you beat the drum and sound the gong?'

'You may well ask,' said the Dragon King. 'A neighbour of mine, the

Sage of the Mountain of Flowers and Fruit, came to me today asking for a magic weapon. I gave him the iron with which the Milky Way was pounded. Now he says he must have clothes. We have nothing of that sort here. Couldn't one of you find me something, so that we can get rid of him?'

The Dragon of the South was furious. 'Brothers,' he cried, 'let us summon men-at-arms and arrest the rascal.'

'Out of the question!' said the Dragon King. 'The slightest touch of that iron is deadly.'

'It would be better not to tamper with him,' said the Dragon of the West. 'We'll give him some clothes, just to get rid of him, and then we'll complain to Heaven, and Heaven will punish him.'

'That's a good idea,' said the Dragon of the North. 'I've got a pair of cloud-stepping shoes made of lotus-fibre.'

'I've got a cap of phoenix-plume and red gold,' said the Dragon of the South.

'I've got a jerkin of chain-mail, made of yellow gold,' said the Dragon of the West.

The Dragon King was delighted and brought them in to see Monkey and offer their gifts. Monkey put the things on and, with his wishing-staff in his hand, strode out. 'Dirty old sneaks,' he called out to the dragons as he passed. In great indignation they consulted together about reporting him to the powers above.

The four old monkeys and all the rest were waiting for their king beside the bridge. Suddenly they saw him spring out of the waves, without a drop of water on him, all shining and golden, and run up the bridge. They all knelt down, crying 'Great King, what splendours!' With the spring wind full in his face, Monkey mounted the throne and set up the iron staff in front of him. The monkeys all rushed at the treasure and tried to lift it. As well might a dragon-fly try to shake an ironwood-tree; they could not move it an inch.

'Father,' they cried, 'you're the only person that could lift a thing as heavy as that.'

'There's nothing but has its master,' said Monkey, lifting it with one hand. 'This iron lay in the Sea Treasury for I don't know how many hundred thousand years, and only recently began to shine. The Dragon King thought it was nothing but black iron and said it was used to flatten out the Milky Way. None of them could lift it, and they asked me to go and take it myself. When I first saw it, it was twenty feet long. I thought that was a bit too big, so I gradually made it smaller and smaller. Now just you watch while I change it again.' He cried 'Smaller, smaller, smaller!' and immediately it became exactly like an embroidery needle, and could comfortably be worn behind the ear.

'Take it out and do another trick with it,' the monkeys begged. He took it from behind his ear and set it upright on the palm of his hand, crying 'Larger, larger!' It at once became twenty feet long, whereupon he carried it up on to the bridge, employed a cosmic magic, and bent at the waist, crying 'Tall!' At which he at once became a hundred thousand feet high, his head was on a level with the highest mountains, his waist with the ridges, his eye blazed like lightning, his mouth was like a blood-bowl, his teeth like sword-blades. The iron staff in his hand reached up to the thirty-third Heaven, and down to the eighteenth pit of Hell. Tigers, panthers, wolves, all the evil spirits of the hill and the demons of the seventy-two caves did homage to him in awe and trembling. Presently he withdrew his cosmic manifestation, and the staff again became an embroidery needle. He put it behind his ear and came back to the cave.

One day when Monkey had been giving a great banquet to the beast-monarchs of the neighbourhood, after seeing them off and giving presents to the leaders great and small, he lay down under a pine-tree at the side of the iron bridge, and fell asleep. In his sleep he saw two men coming towards him, bearing a document on which was his name. Without giving him time to say a word, they brought out a rope and binding Monkey's dream-body, they marched him away, presently bringing him to the outskirts of a walled city. Coming to himself and looking up, he saw that on the wall of this city was an iron placard saying 'Land of Darkness'.

'Why,' said Monkey to himself, suddenly realizing with an

unpleasant shock where he had got to, 'that's where Yama, the King of Death, lives. How did I get here?'

'Your time in the World of Life is up,' said the two men, 'and we were sent to arrest you.'

'But I have got beyond all that,' said Monkey. 'I am no longer compounded of the Five Elements, and do not come under Death's jurisdiction. What's all this nonsense about arresting me?'

The two men took no notice, and continued to drag him along. Monkey now became very angry, snatched the needle from behind his ear, changed it to a formidable size, and pounded the two messengers into mincemeat. Then he freed himself from his bonds, and swinging his staff strode into the city. Bull-headed demons and horse-faced demons fled before him in terror. A mass of ghosts rushed to the palace, announcing that a furry-faced thunder-god was advancing to the attack. In great consternation the Ten Judges of the Dead tidied themselves and came to see what was afoot. Seeing Monkey's ferocious appearance, they lined up and accosted him in a loud voice: 'Your name, please!'

'If you don't know who I am, why did you send two men to arrest me?' asked Monkey.

'How can you accuse us of such a thing?' they said. 'No doubt the messengers made a mistake.'

'I am the Sage from the Water Curtain Cave,' said Monkey. 'Who are you?'

'We are the Ten Judges of the Emperor of Death,' they said.

'In that case,' said Monkey, 'you are concerned with retribution and rewards, and ought not to let such mistakes occur. I would have you know that by my exertions I have become an Immortal and am no longer subject to your jurisdiction. Why did you order my arrest?'

'There's no need to lose your temper,' they said. 'It's a case of mistaken identity. The world is a big place, and there are bound to be cases of several people having the same name. No doubt our officers have made a mistake.'

'Nonsense,' said Monkey. 'The proverb says "Magistrates err, clerks

err, the man with the warrant never errs." Be quick and bring out the
registers of the quick and the dead, and we'll soon see!'

'Come this way, please,' they said, and took him to the great hall,
where they ordered the official in charge of the record to bring out his
files. The official dived into a side room and came out with five or six
ledgers, divided into ten files, and began going through them one by
one—Bald Insects, Furry Insects, Winged Insects, Scaly Insects . . . He
gave up in despair and tried Monkeys. But the Monkey King, having
human characteristics, was not there. Not however being subject to the
unicorn, he did not come into any animal category, and as he was not
subject to the phoenix, he could not be classed as a bird. But there was
a separate file which Monkey insisted on examining himself, and there,
under the heading 'Soul 3150', he found his own name, followed by
the words 'Parentage: natural product. Description: Stone Monkey.
Life-span: 342 years. A peaceful end.' 'I haven't got a life-span at all,'
said Monkey. 'I'm eternal. I shall cross my name out. Give me a brush!'
The official hastened to provide a brush, soaked in heavy ink, and
Monkey put a stroke not only through his own name, but through
those of all the monkeys named in the Monkey File. Then throwing
down the ledger, 'There's an end of the matter,' he exclaimed. 'Now at
any rate you've got no hold over us!'

So saying he picked up his staff and forced his way out of the
Palace of Darkness. The Ten Judges dared not protest; but all went off
at once to the Kshitigarbha, Guide of the Dead, and discussed with
him the advisability of laying a complaint about the matter before
the Jade Emperor in Heaven. As Monkey rushed naked out of the city,
his foot caught in a coil of creeper and he stumbled. He woke with a
start, and found that it had all been a dream. Sitting up, he heard the
four old monkeys and the others who were mounting guard over him
saying, 'Great King, isn't it time you woke up? You drank so heavily that
you've been sleeping here all night.' 'I must have dozed off for a time,'
said Monkey, 'for I dreamt that two men came to arrest me.' And he told
them his dream. 'I crossed off all our names,' he said, 'so the fellows
won't be able to interfere with us any more.' The monkeys kow-towed

and thanked him. From that time onward it has been noticed that many mountain monkeys never grow old. It is because their names were crossed out from the registers of the King of Death.

One morning when the Jade Emperor was sitting in his Golden-doored Cloud Palace, with all his ministers civil and military, an officer announced, 'Your majesty, the Dragon of the Eastern Sea is outside, with a plea to lay before you.' The dragon was shown in and when he had paid his respects, a fairy boy presented a document, which the Jade Emperor began to read. 'This small dragon of the Eastern Sea informs your Majesty that a certain counterfeit immortal from the Water Curtain Cave has maltreated your servant, forcing a way into his watery home. He demanded a weapon, using gross intimidation, and forced us to give him garments, by violence and outrage. My watery kinsmen were dismayed, tortoises and turtles fled in panic. The Dragon of the South trembled, the Dragon of the West was appalled, the Dragon of the North collapsed. Your servant was obliged to part with a holy iron staff, a phoenix-plume hat, a coat of mail and a pair of cloud-stepping shoes, before we could get rid of him. But even then he threatened us with arms and magic, and called us dirty old sneaks. We are ourselves quite unable to deal with him, and must leave the matter in your hands. We earnestly beg that you will send soldiers to control this pest and restore peace to the World Below the Waves.'

Having read the document, the Jade Emperor gave judgement. 'The dragon,' he said, 'is to return to his sea, and I will send officers to arrest the criminal.' The Dragon King bowed and retired. Whereupon another officer immediately appeared, announcing that the First Judge of the Dead, supported by Kshitigarbha, the Advocate of the Dead, had arrived with a petition. With them was a fairy girl, who presented a document which read as follows: 'We respectfully submit that Heaven Above is for spirits, and the Underworld is for ghosts. Darkness and Light must have their succession. Such is the way of Nature, and cannot be changed. But a counterfeit Sage from the Water Curtain Cave has violently resisted our summons, beating to death our emissaries and menacing the Ten Judges. He made an uproar in the Palace of Death, and erased names from our books, so that in future monkeys and apes will enjoy improper longevity. We therefore appeal to your Majesty to show your authority by sending spirit soldiers to deal with this monster, restore the balance of Dark and Light and bring back peace to the Underworld.'

The Jade Emperor gave judgement: 'The Lords of Darkness are to return to the Underworld, and officers shall be sent to arrest this pest.' The First Judge of the Dead bowed and retired.

'How long has this pernicious monkey been in existence?' the Jade Emperor asked of his ministers, 'and how comes it that he acquired Illumination?'

At once the Officer of the Thousand League Eye and the Officer of the Down the Wind Ear stepped forward. 'This monkey,' they said, 'was emitted three hundred years ago by a stone. At first he displayed none of his present powers; but since then he has managed somehow to perfect himself and achieve Immortality. He now subdues dragons, tames tigers, and has tampered with the Registers of Death.'

'Which of you deities will go down and deal with him?' asked the Jade Emperor.

The Spirit of the Planet Venus came forward. 'Highest and Holiest,' he said, 'all creatures that have nine apertures are capable of achieving Immortality. Small wonder then that this monkey, produced by the natural forces of Heaven and Earth, nurtured by the light of the sun and the moon, fed by the frost and dew, should have achieved Immortality and subdued dragons and tigers. I suggest that an indulgent course should be followed. Let us send a rescript, commanding him to appear in Heaven. We will then give him official work of some kind, so that his name will appear on our rolls, and we shall be able to keep an eye on him here. If he behaves well, he can be promoted, and if he misbehaves, he must be put under arrest. This course will save us from military operations and will add to our numbers an undoubted Immortal.'

This suggestion pleased the Jade Emperor. He ordered the Spirit of the Book Star to draw up a summons and bade the Planet Venus deliver it. He went out at the southern gate of Heaven, lowered his magic cloud and soon reached the Water Curtain Cave, where he said to the crowd of monkeys, 'I am a messenger from Heaven, bearing a command that your king is to proceed at once to the Upper Realms. Tell him of this immediately.' The little monkeys outside the cave sent word to the interior that an old man had come with some writing in his hand. 'He says he is a messenger from Heaven, sent to ask you to go with him.' 'That's very convenient,' said Monkey. 'I have been thinking lately of making a little trip to Heaven!'

Monkey hurriedly tidied himself and went to the door. 'I am the Spirit of the Planet Venus,' the messenger said, 'and I bring an order from the Jade Emperor that you are to come up to Heaven and receive an Immortal appointment.'

'Old Star,' said Monkey, 'I am much obliged to you for your trouble,' and he told the monkeys to prepare a banquet.

'With the sacred command about me, I dare not linger,' said the Star. 'After your glorious ascension we shall have ample opportunity for conversation.'

'I will not insist,' said Monkey. 'It is a great honour for us that you should have paid this visit.' Then he called the four old monkeys to him. 'Don't forget to put the young monkeys through their paces,' he said. 'I'll have a look round when I get to Heaven, and if it seems all right there, I'll send for the rest of you to come and live with me.' The old monkeys signified their agreement, and the Monkey King, following the Star Spirit, mounted the cloud and soared up.

from

A Connecticut Yankee at King Arthur's Court

by Mark Twain

Mark Twain was the pen name of Samuel Clemens (1835–1910). His 1889 novel is about an American transported to King Arthur's Camelot.

I am an American. I was born and reared in Hartford, in the State of Connecticut—anyway, just over the river, in the country. So I am a Yankee of the Yankees—and practical; yes, and nearly barren of sentiment, I suppose—or poetry, in other words. My father was a blacksmith, my uncle was a horse doctor, and I was both, along at first. Then I went over to the great arms factory and learned my real trade; learned all there was to it; learned to make everything—guns, revolvers, cannon, boilers, engines, all sorts of labour-saving machinery. Why, I could make anything a body wanted—anything in the world, it didn't make any difference what; and if there wasn't any quick new-fangled way to make a thing, I could invent one—and do it as easy as rolling off a log. I became head superintendent; had a couple of thousand men under me.

Well, a man like that is a man that is full of fight—that goes without saying. With a couple of thousand rough men under one, one has plenty of that sort of amusement. I had, anyway. At last I met my match, and I got my dose. It was during a misunderstanding conducted with crowbars with a fellow we used to call Hercules. He laid me out with a crusher alongside the head that made everything crack, and seemed to spring every joint in my skull and made it overlap its neighbour. Then the world went out in darkness, and I didn't feel anything more, and didn't know anything at all—at least for a while.

When I came to again, I was sitting under an oak tree, on the grass, with a whole beautiful and broad country landscape all to myself—nearly. Not entirely; for there was a fellow on a horse, looking down at me—a fellow fresh out of a picture-book. He was in old-time iron armour from head to heel, with a helmet on his head the shape of a nail-keg with slits in it; and he had a shield, and a sword, and a prodigious spear; and his horse had armour on, too, and a steel horn projecting from his forehead, and gorgeous red and green silk trappings that hung down all around him like a bed-quilt, nearly to the ground.

'Fair sir, will ye just?' said this fellow.

'Will I which?'

'Will ye try a passage of arms for land or lady or for—'

'What are you giving me?' I said. 'Get along back to your circus, or I'll report you.'

Now what does this man do but fall back a couple of hundred yards and then come rushing at me as hard as he could tear, with his nail-keg bent down nearly to his horse's neck and his long spear pointed straight ahead. I saw he meant business, so I was up the tree when he arrived.

He allowed that I was his property, the captive of his spear. There was argument on his side—and the bulk of the advantage—so I judged it best to humour him. We fixed up an agreement whereby I was to go with him and he was not to hurt me. I came down, and we started away, I walking by the side of his horse. We marched comfortably along, through glades and over brooks which I could not remember to have seen before—which puzzled me and made me wonder—and yet we did not come to any circus or sign of a circus. So I gave up the idea of a circus, and concluded he was from an asylum. But we never came to an asylum—so I was up a stump, as you may say. I asked him how far we were from Hartford. He said he had never heard of the place; which I took to be a lie, but allowed it to go at that. At the end of an hour we saw a far-away town sleeping in a valley by a winding river; and beyond it on a hill, a vast grey fortress, with towers and turrets, the first I had ever seen out of a picture.

'Bridgeport?' said I, pointing.

'Camelot,' said he.

'Camelot—Camelot,' said I to myself. 'I don't seem to remember hearing of it before. Name of the asylum, likely.'

It was a soft, reposeful summer landscape, as lovely as a dream, and as lonesome as Sunday. The air was full of the smell of flowers, and the buzzing of insects, and the twittering of birds, and there were no people, no waggons, there was no stir of life, nothing going on. The road was mainly a winding path with hoof-prints in it, and now and then a faint trace of wheels on either side in the grass—wheels that apparently had a tire as broad as one's hand.

Presently a fair slip of a girl, about ten years old, with a cataract of golden hair streaming down over her shoulders, came along. Around her head she wore a hoop of flame-red poppies. It was as sweet an outfit as ever I saw, what there was of it. She walked indolently along, with a mind at rest, its peace reflected in her innocent face. The circus man paid no attention to her; didn't even seem to see her. And she— she was no more startled at his fantastic make-up than if she was used to his like every day of her life. She was going by as indifferently as she might have gone by a couple of cows; but when she happened to notice me, *then* there was a change! Up went her hands, and she was turned to stone; her mouth dropped open, her eyes stared wide and timo- rously, she was the picture of astonished curiosity touched with fear. And there she stood gazing, in a sort of stupefied fascination, till we turned a corner of the wood and were lost to her view. That she should be startled at me instead of at the other man, was too many for me; I couldn't make head or tail of it. And that she should seem to consider me a spectacle, and totally overlook her own merits in that respect, was another puzzling thing, and a display of magnanimity, too, that was surprising in one so young. There was food for thought here. I moved along as one in a dream.

As we approached the town, signs of life began to appear. At intervals we passed a wretched cabin, with a thatched roof, and about it small fields and garden patches in an indifferent state of cultivation. There were people, too; brawny men, with long, coarse, uncombed hair that hung down over their faces and made them look like animals. They and the women, as a rule, wore a coarse tow-linen robe that came well below the knee, and a rude sort of sandals, and many wore an iron collar. The small boys and girls were always naked; but nobody seemed to know it. All of these people stared at me, talked about me, ran into the huts and fetched out their families to gape at me; but nobody ever noticed that other fellow, except to make him humble salutation and get no response for their pains.

In the town were some substantial windowless houses of stone scattered among a wilderness of thatched cabins; the streets were mere crooked alleys, and unpaved; troops of dogs and nude children played in the sun and made life and noise; hogs roamed and rooted contentedly about, and one of them lay in a reeking wallow in the middle of the main thoroughfare and suckled her family. Presently there was a distant blare of military music; it came nearer, still nearer, and soon a noble cavalcade wound into view, glorious with plumed helmets and flashing mail and flaunting banners and rich doublets and horse-cloths and gilded spear-heads; and through the muck and swine, and naked brats, and joyous dogs, and shabby huts it took its gallant way, and in its wake we followed. Followed, through one winding alley and then another,—and climbing, always climbing—till at last we gained the breezy height where the huge castle stood. There was an exchange of bugle blasts; then a parley from the walls, where men-at-arms, in hauberk and morion, marched back and forth with halberd at shoulder under flapping banners with the rude figure of a dragon displayed upon them; and then the great gates were flung open, the drawbridge was lowered, and the head of the cavalcade swept forward under the frowning arches; and we, following, soon found ourselves in a great paved court, with towers and turrets stretching up into the blue air on all the four sides: and all about us the dismount was going on, and much greeting and ceremony, and running to and fro, and a gay display of moving and intermingling colours, and an altogether pleasant stir and noise and confusion.

The moment I got a chance I slipped aside privately and touched an ancient common-looking man on the shoulder, and said, in an insinuating, confidential way—'Friend, do me a kindness. Do you belong to the asylum, or are you just here on a visit or something like that?'

He looked me over stupidly, and said—

'Marry, fair sir, me seemeth—'

'That will do,' I said; 'I reckon you are a patient.'

I moved away, cogitating, and at the same time keeping an eye out for any chance passenger in his right mind that might come along and give me some light. I judged I had found one, presently; so I drew him aside and said in his ear—

'If I could see the head keeper a minute—only just a minute—'

'Prithee do not let me.'

'Let you *what?*'

'*Hinder* me, then, if the word please thee better.' Then he went on to say he was an under-cook and could not stop to gossip, though he would like it another time; for it would comfort his very liver to know where I got my clothes. As he started away he pointed and said yonder was one who was idle enough for my purpose, and was seeking me besides, no doubt. This was an airy slim boy in shrimp-coloured tights that made him look like a forked carrot; the rest of his gear was blue silk and dainty laces and ruffles; and he had long yellow curls, and wore a plumed pink satin cap tilted complacently over his ear. By his look, he was good-natured; by his gait, he was satisfied with himself.

He was pretty enough to frame. He arrived, looked me over with a smiling and impudent curiosity; said he had come for me, and informed me that he was a page.

'Go 'long,' I said; 'you ain't more than a paragraph.'

It was pretty severe, but I was nettled. However, it never phazed him; he didn't appear to know he was hurt. He began to talk and laugh, in happy, thoughtless, boyish fashion, as we walked along, and made himself old friends with me at once; asked me all sorts of questions about myself and about my clothes, but never waited for an answer— always chattered straight ahead, as if he didn't know he had asked a question and wasn't expecting any reply, until at last he happened to mention that he was born in the beginning of the year 513.

It made the cold chills creep over me! I stopped, and said, a little faintly:

'Maybe I didn't hear you just right. Say it again—and say it slow. What year was it?'

'513.'

'513! You don't look it! Come, my boy, I am a stranger and friendless: be honest and honourable with me. Are you in your right mind?'

He said he was.

'Are these other people in their right minds?'

He said they were.

'And this isn't an asylum? I mean, it isn't a place where they cure crazy people?'

He said it wasn't.

'Well, then,' I said, 'either I am a lunatic, or something just as awful has happened. Now tell me, honest and true, where am I?'

'IN KING ARTHUR'S COURT.'

I waited a minute, to let that idea shudder its way home, and then said:

'And according to your notions, what year is it now?'

'528—nineteenth of June.'

I felt a mournful sinking at the heart, and muttered: 'I shall never see my friends again—never, never again. They will not be born for more than thirteen hundred years yet.'

I seemed to believe the boy, I didn't know why. *Something* in me seemed to believe him—my consciousness, as you may say; but my reason didn't. My reason straightway began to clamour; that was natural. I didn't know how to go about satisfying it, because I knew that the testimony of men wouldn't serve—my reason would say they were lunatics, and throw out their evidence. But all of a sudden I stumbled on the very thing, just by luck. I knew that the only total eclipse of the sun in the first half of the sixth century occurred on the 21st of June, A.D. 528, O.S., and began at 3 minutes after 12 noon. I also knew that no total eclipse of the sun was due in what to *me* was the present year—*i.e.*, 1879. So, if I could keep my anxiety and curiosity from eating the heart out of me for forty-eight hours, I should then find out for certain whether this boy was telling me the truth or not.

Wherefore, being a practical Connecticut man, I now shoved this whole problem clear out of my mind till its appointed day and hour should come, in order that I might turn all my attention to the circumstances of the present moment, and be alert and ready to make the most out of them that could be made. One thing at a time, is my motto—and just play that thing for all it is worth, even if it's only two pair and a jack. I made up my mind to two things; if it was still the nineteenth century and I was among lunatics and couldn't get away, I would presently boss that asylum or know the reason why; and if on the other hand it was really the sixth century, all right, I didn't want any softer thing: I would boss the whole country inside of three months; for I judged I would have the start of the best-educated man in the kingdom by a matter of thirteen hundred years and upwards. I'm not a man to waste time after my mind's made up and there's work on hand; so I said to the page—

'Now, Clarence, my boy—if that might happen to be your name— I'll get you to post me up a little if you don't mind. What is the name of that man that brought me here?'

'My master and thine? That is the good knight and great lord Sir Kay the Seneschal, foster brother to our liege the King.'

'Very good; go on, tell me everything.'

He made a long story of it; but the part that had immediate interest for me was this. He said I was Sir Kay's prisoner, and that in the due course of custom I would be flung into a dungeon and left there on scant commons until my friends ransomed me—unless I chanced to rot, first. I saw that the last chance had the best show, but I didn't waste any bother about that; time was too precious. The page said, further, that dinner was about ended in the great hall by this time, and that as soon as the sociability and the heavy drinking should begin, Sir Kay would have me in and exhibit me before King Arthur and his illustrious knights seated at the Table Round, and would brag about his exploit in capturing me, and would probably exaggerate the facts a little, but it wouldn't be good form for me to correct him, and not over safe, either; and when I was done being exhibited, then ho for the dungeon; but he, Clarence, would find a way to come and see me every now and then, and cheer me up, and help me get word to my friends.

Get word to my friends! I thanked him; I couldn't do less; and about this time a lackey came to say I was wanted; so Clarence led me in and took me off to one side and sat down by me.

Well, it was a curious kind of spectacle, and interesting. It was an immense place, and rather naked—yes, and full of loud contrasts. It was very, very lofty; so lofty that the banners depending from the arched beams and girders away up there floated in a sort of twilight; there was a stone-railed gallery at each end, high up, with musicians in the one, and women, clothed in stunning colours, in the other. The floor was of big stone flags laid in black and white squares, rather battered by age and use, and needing repair. As to ornament, there wasn't any, strictly speaking; though on the walls hung some huge tapestries which were probably taxed as works of art; battle-pieces, they were, with horses shaped like those which children cut out of paper or create in gingerbread; with men on them in scale armor whose scales are represented by round holes—so that the man's coat looks as if it had been done with a biscuit-punch. There was a fireplace big enough to camp in; and its projecting sides and hood, of carved and pillared stone-work, had the look of a cathedral door. Along the walls stood men-at-arms, in breastplate and morion, with halberds for their only weapon—rigid as statues; and that is what they looked like.

In the middle of this groined and vaulted public square was an oaken table which they called the Table Round. It was as large as a circus ring; and around it sat a great company of men dressed in such various and splendid colours that it hurt one's eyes to look at them. They wore their plumed hats, right along, except that whenever one addressed himself directly to the King, he lifted his hat a trifle just as he was beginning his remark.

Mainly they were drinking—from entire ox-horns; but a few were still munching bread or gnawing beef bones. There was about an average of two dogs to one man; and these sat in expectant attitudes till a spent bone was flung to them, and then they went for it by brigades and divisions, with a rush, and there ensued a fight which filled the prospect with a tumultuous chaos of plunging heads and bodies and flashing tails, and the storm of howlings and barkings deafened all speech for the time; but that was no matter, for the dog-fight was always a bigger interest anyway; the men rose, sometimes, to observe it the better and bet on it, and the ladies and the musicians stretched themselves out over their balusters with the same object; and all broke into delighted ejaculations from time to time. In the end, the winning dog stretched himself out comfortably with his bone between his paws, and proceeded to growl over it, and gnaw it, and grease the floor with it, just as fifty others were already doing; and the rest of the court resumed their previous industries and entertainments.

As a rule the speech and behaviour of these people were gracious and courtly; and I noticed that they were good and serious listeners when anybody was telling anything—I mean in a dog-fightless interval. And plainly, too, they were a childlike and innocent lot; telling lies of the stateliest pattern with a most gentle and winning naïveté, and ready and willing to listen to anybody else's lie, and believe it, too. It was hard to associate them with anything cruel or dreadful; and yet they dealt in tales of blood and suffering with a guileless relish that made me almost forget to shudder.

I was not the only prisoner present. There were twenty or more. Poor devils, many of them were maimed, hacked, carved, in a frightful way; and their hair, their faces, their clothing, were caked with black and stiffened drenchings of blood. They were suffering sharp physical pain, of course; and weariness, and hunger and thirst, no doubt; and at least none had given them the comfort of a wash, or even the poor charity of a lotion for their wounds; yet you never heard them utter a moan or a groan, or saw them show any sign of restlessness, or any disposition to complain. The thought was forced upon me: 'The rascals— *they* have served other people so in their day; it being their own turn now, they were not expecting any better treatment than this; so their philosophical bearing is not an outcome of mental training, intellectual fortitude, reasoning; it is mere animal training; they are white Indians.'

Mainly the Round Table talk was monologues—narrative accounts of the adventures in which these prisoners were captured and their friends and backers killed and stripped of their steeds and armour. As a general thing—as far as I could make out—these murderous adventures were not forays undertaken to avenge injuries, nor to settle old disputes or sudden fallings out; no, as a rule they were simply duels between strangers—duels between people who had never even been introduced to each other, and between whom existed no cause of offence whatever. Many a time I had seen a couple of boys, strangers, meet by chance, and say simultaneously, 'I can lick you,' and go at it on the spot; but I had always imagined until now, that that sort of thing belonged to children only, and was a sign and mark of childhood; but here were these big boobies sticking to it and taking pride in it clear up into full age and beyond. Yet there was something very engaging about these great simple-hearted creatures, something attractive and lovable. There did not seem to be brains enough in the entire nursery, so to speak, to bait a fish-hook with; but you didn't seem to mind that, after a little, because you soon saw that brains were not needed in a society like that, and indeed, would have marred it, hindered it, spoiled its symmetry—perhaps rendered its existence impossible.

There was a fine manliness observable in almost every face; and in some a certain loftiness and sweetness that rebuked your belittling criticisms and stilled them. A most noble benignity and purity reposed in the countenance of him they called Sir Galahad, and likewise in the King's also; and there was majesty and greatness in the giant frame and high bearing of Sir Launcelot of the Lake.

There was presently an incident which centered the general interest upon this Sir Launcelot. At a sign from a sort of master of ceremonies, six or eight of the prisoners rose and came forward in a body and knelt on the floor and lifted up their hands toward the ladies' gallery and begged the grace of a word with the Queen. The most conspicuously situated lady in that massed flower-bed of feminine show and finery inclined her head by way of assent, and then the spokesman of the prisoners delivered himself and his fellows into her hands for free pardon, ransom, captivity, or death, as she in her good pleasure might elect; and this, as he said, he was doing by command of Sir Kay the Seneschal, whose prisoners they were, he having vanquished them by his single might and prowess in sturdy conflict in the field.

Surprise and astonishment flashed from face to face all over the house; the Queen's gratified smile faded out at the name of Sir Kay, and she looked disappointed; and the page whispered in my ear with an accent and manner expressive of extravagant derision—

'Sir *Kay*, forsooth! Oh, call me pet names, dearest, call me a marine! In twice a thousand years shall the unholy invention of man labour at odds to beget the fellow to this majestic lie!'

Every eye was fastened with severe inquiry upon Sir Kay. But he was equal to the occasion. He got up and played his hand like a major—and took every trick. He said he would state the case, exactly according to the facts; he would tell the simple straightforward tale, without comment of his own; 'and then,' said he, 'if ye find glory and honour due, ye will give it unto him who is the mightiest man of his hands that ever bare shield or strake with sword in the ranks of Christian battle—even him that sitteth there!' and he pointed to Sir Launcelot. Ah, he fetched them; it was a rattling good stroke. Then he went on and told how Sir Launcelot, seeking adventures, some brief time gone by, killed seven giants at one sweep of his sword, and set a hundred and forty-two captive maidens free; and then went further, still seeking adventures, and found him (Sir Kay) fighting a desperate fight against nine foreign knights, and straightway took the battle solely into his own hands, and conquered the nine; and that night Sir Launcelot rose quietly, and dressed him in Sir Kay's armour and took Sir Kay's horse and gat him away into distant lands, and vanquished sixteen knights in one pitched battle and thirty-four in another; and all these and the former nine he made to swear that about Whitsuntide they would ride to Arthur's court and yield them to Queen Guenever's hands as captives of Sir Kay the Seneschal, spoil of his knightly prowess; and now here were these half dozen, and the rest would be along as soon as they might be healed of their desperate wounds.

Well, it was touching to see the Queen blush and smile, and look embarrassed and happy, and fling furtive glances at Sir Launcelot that would have got him shot in Arkansas, to a dead certainty.

Everybody praised the valour and magnanimity of Sir Launcelot; and as for me, I was perfectly amazed, that one man, all by himself, should have been able to beat down and capture such battalions of practised fighters. I said as much to Clarence; but this mocking featherhead only said—

"An Sir Kay had had time to get another skin of sour wine into him, ye had seen the accompt doubled."

I looked at the boy in sorrow; and as I looked I saw the cloud of a deep despondency settle upon his countenance. I followed the direction of his eye, and saw that a very old and white-bearded man, clothed in a flowing black gown, had risen and was standing at the table upon unsteady legs, and feebly swaying his ancient head and surveying the company with his watery and wandering eye. The same suffering look that was in the page's face was observable in all the faces around—the look of dumb creatures who know that they must endure and make no moan.

'Marry, we shall have it again,' sighed the boy; 'that same old weary tale that he hath told a thousand times in the same words, and that he *will* tell till he dieth, every time he hath gotten his barrel full and feeleth his exaggeration-mill a-working. Would God I had died or I saw this day!'

'Who is it?'

'Merlin, the mighty liar and magician, perdition singe him for the weariness he worketh with his one tale! But that men fear him for that he hath the storms and the lightnings and all the devils that be in hell at his beck and call, they would have dug his entrails out these many years ago to get at that tale and squelch it. He telleth it always in the third person, making believe he is too modest to glorify himself— maledictions light upon him, misfortune be his dole! Good friend, prithee call me for evensong.'

The boy nestled himself upon my shoulder and pretended to go to sleep. The old man began his tale; and presently the lad was asleep in reality; so also were the dogs, and the court, the lackeys, and the files of men-at-arms. The droning voice droned on; a soft snoring arose on all sides and supported it like a deep and subdued accompaniment of wind instruments. Some heads were bowed upon folded arms, some lay back with open mouths that issued unconscious music; the flies buzzed and bit, unmolested, the rats swarmed softly out from a hundred holes, and pattered about, and made themselves at home everywhere; and one of them sat up like a squirrel on the King's head and held a bit of cheese in its hands and nibbled it, and dribbled the crumbs in the King's face with naïve and impudent irreverence. It was a tranquil scene, and restful to the weary eye and the jaded spirit.

This was the old man's tale. He said:

'Right so the King and Merlin departed, and went until an hermit that was a good man and a great leech. So the hermit searched all his wounds and gave him good salves; so the King was there three days, and then were his wounds well amended that he might ride and go, and so departed. And as they rode, Arthur said, I have no sword. No force,[*] said Merlin, hereby is a sword that shall be yours and I may. So they rode till they came to a lake, the which was a fair water and broad, and in the midst of the lake Arthur was ware of an arm clothed in white samite, that held a fair sword in that hand. Lo, said Merlin, yonder is that sword that I spake of. With that they saw a damsel going upon the lake. What damsel is that? said Arthur. That is the Lady of the lake, said Merlin; and within that lake is a rock, and therein is as fair a place as any on earth, and richly beseen, and this damsel will come to you anon, and then speak ye fair to her that she will give you that sword. Anon withal came the damsel unto Arthur and saluted him, and he her again. Damsel, said Arthur, what sword is that, that yonder the arm holdeth above the water? I would it were mine, for I have no sword. Sir Arthur King, said the damsel, that sword is mine, and if ye will give me a gift when I ask it you, ye shall have it. By my faith, said Arthur, I will give you what gift ye will ask. Well, said the damsel, go ye into yonder barge and row yourself to the sword, and take it and the scabbard with you, and I will ask my gift when I see my time. So Sir Arthur and Merlin alight, and tied their horses to two trees, and so they went into the ship, and when they came to the sword that the hand held, Sir Arthur took it up by the handles and took it with him. And the arm and the hand went under the water; and so they came unto the land and rode forth. And then Sir Arthur saw a rich pavilion: What signifieth yonder pavilion? It is the knight's pavilion, said Merlin, that ye fought with last, Sir Pellinore, but he is out, he is not there; he hath ado with a knight of yours, that hight Egglame, and they have fought together, but at the last Egglame fled, and else he had been dead, and he hath chased him even to Carlion, and we shall meet with him anon in the highway. That is well said, said Arthur, now have I a sword, now will I wage battle with him, and be avenged on him. Sir, ye shall not so, said Merlin, for the knight is weary of fighting and chasing, so that ye shall have no worship to have ado with him; also, he will not lightly be

[*] No matter.

matched of one knight living; and therefore it is my counsel, let him pass, for he shall do you good service in short time, and his sons after his days. Also ye shall see that day in short space ye shall be right glad to give him your sister to wed. When I see him, I will do as ye advise me, said Arthur. Then Sir Arthur looked on the sword, and liked it passing well. Whether liketh you better, said Merlin, the sword or the scabbard? Me liketh better the sword, said Arthur. Ye are more unwise, said Merlin, for the scabbard is worth ten of the sword, for while ye have the scabbard upon you ye shall never lose no blood, be ye never so sore wounded; therefore, keep well the scabbard always with you. So they rode into Carlion, and by the way they met with Sir Pellinore; but Merlin had done such a craft that Pellinore saw not Arthur, and he passed by without any words. I marvel, said Arthur, that the knight would not speak. Sir, said Merlin, he saw you not; for an he had seen you ye had not lightly departed. So they came unto Carlion, whereof his knights were passing glad. And when they heard of his adventures they marvelled that he would jeopard his person so alone. But all men of worship said it was merry to be under such a chieftain that would put his person in adventure as other poor knights did.'

It seemed to me that this quaint lie was most simply and beautifully told; but then I had heard it only once, and that makes a difference; it was pleasant to the others when it was fresh, no doubt.

Sir Dinadan the Humourist was the first to awake, and he soon roused the rest with a practical joke of a sufficiently poor quality. He tied some metal mugs to a dog's tail and turned him loose, and he tore around and around the place in a frenzy of fright, with all the other dogs bellowing after him and battering and crashing against everything that came in their way and making altogether a chaos of confusion and a most deafening din and turmoil; at which every man and woman of the multitude laughed till the tears flowed, and some fell out of their chairs and wallowed on the floor in ecstasy. It was just like so many children. Sir Dinadan was so proud of his exploit that he could not keep from telling over and over again, to weariness, how the immortal idea happened to occur to him; and as is the way with humourists of his breed, he was still laughing at it after everybody else had got through. He was so set up that he concluded to make a speech—of course a humorous speech. I think I never heard so many old played-out jokes strung together in my life. He was worse than the minstrels, worse than the clown in the circus. It seemed peculiarly sad to sit here, thirteen hundred years before I was born, and listen again to poor, flat, worm-eaten jokes that had given me the dry gripes when I was a boy thirteen hundred years afterwards. It about convinced me that there isn't any such thing as a new joke possible. Everybody laughed at these antiquities— but then they always do; I had noticed that, centuries later. However, of course, the scoffer didn't laugh—I mean the boy. No, he scoffed; there wasn't anything he wouldn't scoff at. He said the most of Sir Dinadan's jokes were rotten and the rest were petrified. I said 'petrified' was good; as I believed, myself, that the only right way to classify the majestic ages of some of those jokes was by geologic periods. But that neat idea hit the boy in a blank place, for geology hadn't been invented yet. However, I made a note of the remark, and calculated to educate the commonwealth up to it if I pulled through. It is no use to throw a good thing away merely because the market isn't ripe yet.

Now Sir Kay arose and began to fire up on his history-mill, with me for fuel. It was time for me to feel serious, and I did. Sir Kay told how he had encountered me in a far land of barbarians, who all wore the same ridiculous garb that I did—a garb that was a work of enchantment, and intended to make the wearer secure from hurt by human hands. However he had nullified the force of the enchantment by prayer, and had killed my thirteen knights in a three-hours' battle and taken me prisoner, sparing my life in order that so strange a curiosity as I was might be exhibited to the wonder and admiration of the King and the court. He spoke of me all the time, in the blandest way, as 'this prodigious giant,' and 'this horrible sky-towering monster,' and 'this tusked and taloned man-devouring ogre;' and everybody took in all this bosh in the naïvest way, and never smiled or seemed to notice that there was any discrepancy between these watered statistics and me. He said that in trying to escape from him I sprang into the top of a tree two hundred cubits high at a single bound, but he dislodged me with a stone the size of a cow, which 'allto brast' the most of my bones, and then swore me to appear at Arthur's court for sentence. He ended by condemning me to die at noon on the 21st; and was so little concerned about it that he stopped to yawn before he named the date.

I was in a dismal state by this time; indeed, I was hardly enough in my right mind to keep the run of a dispute that sprung up as to how I had better be killed, the possibility of the killing being doubted by some, because of the enchantment in my clothes. And yet it was nothing but an ordinary suit of fifteen-dollar slop-shops. Still, I was sane enough to notice this detail, to wit: many of the terms used in the most matter-of-fact way by this great assemblage of the first ladies and gentlemen in the land would have made a Comanche blush. Indelicacy is too mild a term to convey the idea. However, I had read 'Tom Jones' and 'Roderick Random,' and other books of that kind, and knew that the highest and first ladies and gentlemen in England had remained little or no cleaner in their talk, and in the morals and conduct which such talk implies, clear up to a hundred years ago; in fact clear into our own nineteenth century—in which century, broadly speaking, the earliest samples of the real lady and real gentleman discoverable in English history—or in European history, for that matter—may be said to have made their appearance. Suppose Sir Walter, instead of putting the conversations into the mouths of his characters, had allowed the characters to speak for themselves?

We should have had talk from Rachel and Ivanhoe and the soft Lady Rowena which would embarrass a tramp in our day. However, to the unconsciously indelicate all things are delicate. King Arthur's people were not aware that they were indecent, and I had presence of mind enough not to mention it.

They were so troubled about my enchanted clothes that they were mightily relieved, at last, when old Merlin swept the difficulty away for them with a common-sense hint. He asked them why they were so dull—why didn't it occur to them to strip me. In half a minute I was as naked as a pair of tongs! And dear, dear, to think of it: I was the only embarrassed person there. Everybody discussed me; and did it as unconcernedly as if I had been a cabbage. Queen Guenever was as naïvely interested as the rest, and said she had never seen anybody with legs just like mine before. It was the only compliment I got—if it was a compliment.

Finally I was carried off in one direction, and my perilous clothes in another. I was shoved into a dark and narrow cell in a dungeon, with some scant remnants for dinner, some moldy straw for a bed, and no end of rats for company.

I was so tired that even my fears were not able to keep me awake long.

When I next came to myself, I seemed to have been asleep a very long time. My first thought was, 'Well, what an astonishing dream I've had! I reckon I've waked only just in time to keep from being hanged or drowned or burned, or something. . . . I'll nap again till the whistle blows, and then I'll go down to the arms factory and have it out with Hercules.'

But just then I heard the harsh music of rusty chains and bolts, a light flashed in my eyes, and that butterfly, Clarence, stood before me! I gasped with surprise; my breath almost got away from me.

'What!' I said, 'you here yet? Go along with the rest of the dream! scatter!'

But he only laughed, in his light-hearted way, and fell to making fun of my sorry plight.

'All right,' I said resignedly, 'let the dream go on; I'm in no hurry.'

'Prithee, what dream?'

'What dream? Why, the dream that I am in Arthur's court—a person who never existed; and that I am talking to you, who are nothing but a work of the imagination.'

'Oh, la, indeed! and is it a dream that you're to be burned to-morrow? Ho-ho—answer me that!'

The shock that went through me was distressing. I now began to reason that my situation was in the last degree serious, dream or no dream; for I knew by past experience of the life-like intensity of dreams, that to be burned to death, even in a dream, would be very far from being a jest, and was a thing to be avoided, by any means, fair or foul, that I could contrive. So I said beseechingly:

'Ah, Clarence, good boy, only friend I've got,—for you *are* my friend, aren't you?—don't fail me; help me to devise some way of escaping from this place!'

'Now do but hear thyself! Escape? Why, man, the corridors are in guard and keep of men-at-arms.'

'No doubt, no doubt. But how many, Clarence? Not many, I hope?'

'Full a score. One may not hope to escape.' After a pause— hesitatingly: 'and there be other reasons—and weightier.'

'Other ones? What are they?'

'Well, they say—oh, but I daren't, indeed daren't!'

'Why, poor lad, what is the matter? Why do you blench? Why do you tremble so?'

'Oh, in sooth, there is need! I do want to tell you, but—'

'Come, come, be brave, be a man—speak out, there's a good lad!'

He hesitated, pulled one way by desire, the other way by fear; then he stole to the door and peeped out, listening; and finally crept close to me and put his mouth to my ear and told me his fearful news in a whisper, and with all the cowering apprehension of one who was venturing upon awful ground and speaking of things whose very mention might be freighted with death.

'Merlin, in his malice, has woven a spell about this dungeon and there bides not the man in these kingdoms that would be desperate enough to essay to cross its lines with you! Now God pity me, I have told it! Ah, be kind to me, be merciful to a poor boy who means thee well; for an thou betray me I am lost!'

I laughed the only really refreshing laugh I had had for some time; and shouted—

'Merlin has wrought a spell! *Merlin*, forsooth! That cheap old humbug, that maundering old ass? Bosh, pure bosh, the silliest bosh in the world! Why, it does seem to me that of all the childish, idiotic, chuckle-headed, chicken-livered superstitions that ev—oh, damn Merlin!'

But Clarence had slumped to his knees before I had half finished, and he was like to go out of his mind with fright.

'Oh, beware! These are awful words! Any moment these walls may crumble upon us if you say such things. Oh, call them back before it is too late!'

Now this strange exhibition gave me a good idea and set me to thinking. If everybody about here was so honestly and sincerely afraid of Merlin's pretended magic as Clarence was, certainly a superior man like me ought to be shrewd enough to contrive some way to take advantage of such a state of things. I went on thinking, and worked out a plan. Then I said:

'Get up. Pull yourself together; look me in the eye. Do you know why I laughed?'

'No—but for our blessed Lady's sake, do it no more.'

'Well, I'll tell you why I laughed. Because I'm a magician myself.'

'Thou!' The boy recoiled a step, and caught his breath, for the thing hit him rather sudden; but the aspect which he took on was very, very respectful. I took quick note of that; it indicated that a humbug didn't need to have a reputation in this asylum; people stood ready to take him at his word, without that. I resumed.

'I've know Merlin seven hundred years, and he—'

'Seven hun—'

'Don't interrupt me. He has died and come alive again thirteen times, and traveled under a new name every time: Smith, Jones, Robinson, Jackson, Peters, Haskins, Merlin—a new alias every time he turns up. I knew him in Egypt three hundred years ago; I knew him in India five hundred years ago—he is always blethering around in my way, everywhere I go; he makes me tired. He don't amount to shucks, as a magician; knows some of the old common tricks, but has never got beyond the rudiments, and never will. He is well enough for the provinces—one-night stands and that sort of thing, you know—but dear me, *he* oughtn't to set up for an expert—anyway not where there's a real artist. Now look here, Clarence, I am going to stand your friend, right along, and in return you must be mine. I want you to do me a favour. I want you to get word to the King that I am a magician myself—and the Supreme Grand High-yu-Muckamuck, and head of the tribe, at that; and I want him to be made to understand that I am just quietly arranging a little calamity here that will make the fur fly in these realms if Sir Kay's project is carried out and any harm comes to me. Will you get that to the King for me?'

The poor boy was in such a state that he could hardly answer me. It was pitiful to see a creature so terrified, so unnerved, so demoralised. But he promised everything; and on my side he made me promise over and over again that I would remain his friend, and never turn against him or cast any enchantments upon him. Then he worked his way out, staying himself with his hand along the wall, like a sick person.

Presently this thought occurred to me: how heedless I have been! When the boy gets calm, he will wonder why a great magician like me should have begged a boy like him to help me get out of this place; he will put this and that together, and will see that I am a humbug.

I worried over that heedless blunder for an hour, and called myself a great many hard names, meantime. But finally it occurred to me all of a sudden that these animals didn't reason; that *they* never put this and that together; that all their talk showed that they didn't know a discrepancy when they saw it. I was at rest, then.

But as soon as one is at rest, in this world, off he goes on something else to worry about. It occurred to me that I had made another blunder: I had sent the boy off to alarm his betters with a threat—I intending to invent a calamity at my leisure; now the people who are the readiest and eagerest and willingest to swallow miracles are the very ones who are the hungriest to see you perform them; suppose I should be called on for a sample? Suppose I should be asked to name my calamity? Yes, I had made a blunder; I ought to have invented my calamity first. 'What shall I do? What can I say, to gain a little time?' I was in trouble again; in the deepest kind of trouble: . . . 'There's a footstep!—they're coming. If I had only just a moment to think. . . . Good! I've got it. I'm all right.'

You see, it was the eclipse. It came into my mind, in the nick of time, how Columbus, or Cortez, or one of those people, played an eclipse as a saving trump once, on some savages, and I saw my chance. I could play it myself, now: and it wouldn't be any plagiarism, either, because I should get it in nearly a thousand years ahead of those parties.

Clarence came in, subdued, distressed, and said:

'I hasted the message to our liege the King, and straightway he had me to his presence. He was frighted even to the marrow, and was minded to give order for your instant enlargement, and that you be clothed in fine raiment and lodged as befitted one so great; but then came Merlin and spoiled all; for he persuaded the King that you are mad, and know not whereof you speak; and said your threat is but foolishness and idle vapouring. They disputed long, but in the end, Merlin, scoffing, said, "Wherefore hath he not *named* his brave calamity? Verily it is because he cannot." This thrust did in a most sudden sort close the King's mouth, and he could offer naught to turn the argument; and so, reluctant, and full loth to do you the discourtesy, he yet prayeth you to consider his perplexed case, as noting how the matter stands, and name the calamity—if so be you have determined the nature of it and the time of its coming. Oh, prithee, delay not; to delay at such a time were to double and treble the perils that already compass thee about. Oh, be thou wise—name the calamity!'

I allowed silence to accumulate while I got my impressiveness together, and then said:

'How long have I been shut up in this hole?'

'Ye were shut up when yesterday was well spent. It is nine of the morning now.'

'No! Then I have slept well, sure enough. Nine in the morning now! And yet it is the very complexion of midnight, to a shade. This is the 20th, then?'

'The 20th—yes.'

'And I am to be burned alive to-morrow.' The boy shuddered.

'At what hour?'

'At high noon.'

'Now then, I will tell you what to say.' I paused, and stood over that cowering lad a whole minute in awful silence; then in a voice deep, measured, charged with doom, I began, and rose by dramatically graded stages to my colossal climax, which I delivered in as sublime and noble a way as ever I did such a thing in my life: 'Go back and tell the King that at that hour I will smother the whole world in the dead blackness of midnight; I will blot out the sun, and he shall never shine again; the fruits of the earth shall rot for lack of light and warmth, and the peoples of the earth shall famish and die, to the last man!'

I had to carry the boy out myself, he sunk into such a collapse. I handed him over to the soldiers, and went back.

In the stillness and the darkness, realisation soon began to supplement knowledge. The mere knowledge of a fact is pale; but when you come to *realise* your fact, it takes on colour. It is all the difference between hearing of a man being stabbed to the heart, and seeing it done. In the stillness and the darkness, the knowledge that I was in deadly danger took to itself deeper and deeper meaning all the time; a something which was realisation crept inch by inch through my veins and turned me cold.

But it is a blessed provision of nature that at times like these, as soon as a man's mercury has got down to a certain point there comes a revulsion, and he rallies. Hope springs up, and cheerfulness along with it, and then he is in good shape to do something for himself, if anything can be done. When my rally came, it came with a bound; I said to myself that my eclipse would be sure to save me, and make me the greatest man in the kingdom besides; and straightway my mercury went up to the top of the tube, and my solicitudes all vanished. I was as happy a man as there was in the world. I was even impatient for to-morrow to come, I so wanted to gather-in that great triumph and be the centre of all the nation's wonder and reverence. Besides, in a business way it would be the making of me; I knew that.

Meantime there was one thing which had got pushed into the background of my mind. That was the half-conviction that when the nature of my proposed calamity should be reported to those superstitious people, it would have such an effect that they would want to compromise. So, by and by when I heard footsteps coming, that thought was recalled to me, and I said to myself, 'As sure as anything, it's the compromise. Well, if it is good, all right, I will accept; but if it isn't, I mean to stand my ground and play my hand for all it is worth.'

The door opened, and some men-at-arms appeared. The leader said:

'The stake is ready. Come!'

The stake! The strength went out of me, and I almost fell down. It is hard to get one's breath at such a time, such lumps come into one's throat, and such gaspings; but as soon as I could speak, I said:

'But this is a mistake—the execution is tomorrow.'

'Order changed; been set forward a day. Haste thee!'

I was lost. There was no help for me. I was dazed, stupefied; I had no command over myself; I only wandered purposelessly about, like one out of his mind; so the soldiers took hold of me, and pulled me along with them, out of the cell and along the maze of underground corridors, and finally into the fierce glare of daylight and the upper world. As we stepped into the vast enclosed court of the castle I got a shock; for the first thing I saw was the stake, standing in the centre, and near it the piled faggots and a monk. On all four sides of the court the seated multitudes rose rank above rank, forming sloping terraces that were rich with colour. The King and the Queen sat in their thrones, the most conspicuous figures there, of course.

To note all this occupied but a second. The next second Clarence had slipped from some place of concealment and was pouring news into my ear, his eyes beaming with triumph and gladness. He said:

"'Tis through *me* the change was wrought! And main hard have I worked to do it, too. But when I revealed to them the calamity in store, and saw how mighty was the terror it did engender, then saw I also that this was the time to strike! Wherefore I diligently pretended, unto this and that and the other one, that your power against the sun could not reach its full until the morrow; and so if any would save the sun and the world, you must be slain to-day, while your enchantments are but in the weaving and lack potency. Odsbodikins, it was but a dull lie, a most indifferent invention, but you should have seen them seize it and swallow it, in the frenzy of their fright, as it were salvation sent from heaven; and all the while was I laughing in my sleeve the one moment, to see them so cheaply deceived, and glorifying God the next, that He was content to let the meanest of His creatures be His instrument to the saving of thy life. Ah, how happily has the matter sped! You will not need to do the sun a *real hurt*—ah, forget not that, on your soul forget it not! Only make a little darkness—only the littlest little darkness, mind, and cease with that. It will be sufficient. They will see that I spoke falsely,—being ignorant, as they will fancy—and with the falling of the first shadow of that darkness you shall see them go mad with fear; and they will set you free and make you great! Go to thy triumph, now! But remember—ah, good friend, I implore thee remember my supplication, and do the blessed sun no hurt. For *my* sake, thy true friend.'

I choked out some words through my grief and misery—as much as to say I would spare the sun; for which the lad's eyes paid me back with such deep and loving gratitude that I had not the heart to tell him his good-hearted foolishness had ruined me and sent me to my death.

As the soldiers assisted me across the court the stillness was so profound that if I had been blindfold I should have supposed I was in a solitude instead of walled in by four thousand people. There was not a movement perceptible in those masses of humanity; they were as rigid as stone images, and as pale; and dread sat upon every countenance. This hush continued while I was being chained to the stake; it still continued while the faggots were carefully and tediously piled about my ankles, my knees, my thighs, my body. Then there was a pause, and a deeper hush, if possible, and a man knelt down at my feet with a blazing torch; the multitude strained forward, gazing, and parting slightly from their seats without knowing it; the monk raised his hands above my head, and his eyes toward the blue sky, and began some words in Latin; in this attitude he droned on and on, a little while, and then stopped. I waited two or three moments: then looked up; he was standing there petrified. With a common impulse the multitude rose slowly up and stared into the sky. I followed their eyes; as sure as guns, there was my eclipse beginning! The life went boiling through my veins; I was a new man! The rim of black spread slowly into the sun's disk, my heart beat higher and higher, and still the assemblage and the priest stared into the sky, motionless. I knew that this gaze would be turned upon me, next. When it was, l was ready. I was in one of the most grand attitudes I ever struck, with my arm stretched up, pointing to the sun. It was a noble effect. You could *see* the shudder sweep the mass like a wave. Two shouts rang out, one close upon the heels of the other:

'Apply the torch!'

'I forbid it!'

The one was from Merlin, the other from the King. Merlin started from his place—to apply the torch himself, I judged. I said:

'Stay where you are. If any man moves—even the King—before I give him leave, I will blast him with thunder, I will consume him with lightnings!'

The multitude sank meekly into their seats, and I was just expecting they would. Merlin hesitated a moment or two, and I was on pins and needles during that little while. Then he sat down, and I took a good breath; for I knew I was master of the situation now. The King said:

'Be merciful, fair sir, and essay no further in this perilous matter, lest disaster follow. It was reported to us that your powers could not attain unto their full strength until the morrow; but—'

'Your majesty thinks the report may have been a lie? It *was* a lie.'

That made an immense effect; up went appealing hands everywhere, and the King was assailed with a storm of supplications that I might be bought off at any price, and the calamity stayed. The King was eager to comply. He said:

'Name any terms, reverend sir, even to the halving of my kingdom; but banish this calamity, spare the sun!'

My fortune was made. I would have taken him up in a minute, but I couldn't stop an eclipse; the thing was out of the question. So I asked time to consider. The King said:

'How long—ah, how long, good sir? Be merciful; look, it groweth darker, moment by moment. Prithee how long?'

'Not long. Half an hour—maybe an hour.'

There were a thousand pathetic protests, but I couldn't shorten up any, for I couldn't remember how long a total eclipse lasts. I was in a puzzled condition, anyway, and wanted to think. Something was wrong about that eclipse, and the fact was very unsettling. If this wasn't the one I was after, how was I to tell whether this was the sixth century, or nothing but a dream? Dear me, if I could only prove it was the latter! Here was a glad new hope. If the boy was right about the date, and this was surely the 20th, it *wasn't* the sixth century. I reached for the monk's sleeve, in considerable excitement, and asked him what day of the month it was.

Hang him, he said it was the *twenty-first*! It made me turn cold to hear him. I begged him not to make any mistake about it; but he was sure; he knew it was the 21st. So, that feather-headed boy had botched things again! The time of the day was right for the eclipse; I had seen that for myself, in the beginning, by the dial that was near by. Yes, I *was* in King Arthur's court, and I might as well make the most out of it I could.

The darkness was steadily growing, the people becoming more and more distressed. I now said:

'I have reflected, Sir King. For a lesson, I will let this darkness proceed, and spread night in the world; but whether I blot out the sun for good, or restore it, shall rest with you. These are the terms, to wit: You shall remain King over all your dominions, and receive all the glories and honours that belong to the Kingship; but you shall appoint me your perpetual minister and executive, and give me for my services one per cent. of such actual increase of revenue over and above its present amount as I may succeed in creating for the State. If I can't live on that, I shan't ask anybody to give me a lift. Is it satisfactory?'

There was a prodigious roar of applause, and out of the midst of it the King's voice rose, saying:

'Away with his bonds, and set him free! and do him homage, high and low, rich and poor, for he is become the King's right hand, is clothed with power and authority, and his seat is upon the highest step of the throne! Now sweep away this creeping night, and bring the light and cheer again, that all the world may bless thee.'

But I said:

'That a common man should be shamed before the world, is nothing; but it were dishonor to the *King* if any that saw his minister naked should not also see him delivered from his shame. If I might ask that my clothes be brought again—'

'They are not meet,' the King broke in. 'Fetch raiment of another sort; clothe him like a prince!'

My idea worked. I wanted to keep things as they were till the eclipse was total, otherwise they would be trying again to get me to dismiss the darkness, and, of course, I couldn't do it. Sending for the clothes gained some delay, but not enough. So I had to make another excuse. I said it would be but natural if the King should change his mind and repent to some extent of what he had done under excitement; therefore I would let the darkness grow a while, and if at the end of a reasonable time the King had kept his mind the same, the darkness should be dismissed. Neither the King nor anybody else was satisfied with that arrangement, but I had to stick to my point.

It grew darker and darker and blacker and blacker, while I struggled with those awkward sixth-century clothes. It got to be pitch dark, at last, and the multitude groaned with horror to feel the cold uncanny night breezes fan through the place and see the stars come out and twinkle in the sky. At last the eclipse was total, and I was very glad of it, but everybody else was in misery; which was quite natural. I said:

'The King, by his silence, still stands to the terms.' Then I lifted up my hands—stood just so a moment—then I said, with the most awful solemnity: 'Let the enchantment dissolve, and pass harmless away!'

There was no response, for a moment, in that deep darkness and that graveyard hush. But when the silver rim of the sun pushed itself out, a moment or two later, the assemblage broke loose with a vast shout and came pouring down like a deluge to smother me with blessings and gratitude; and Clarence was not the last of the wash, to be sure.

from

The Three Musketeers

by Alexandre Dumas

Alexandre Dumas's (1802–1870) classic adventure novel tells the story of the young adventurer D'Artagnan. He arrives in Paris with a letter of introduction to M. De Treville, Captain of the King's elite guard—the Musketeers—but the letter is stolen. D'Artagnan, who has just informed De Treville of the loss, catches sight of the thief and runs to chase him.

D'Artagnan, in a state of fury, crossed the antechamber at three bounds, and was darting toward the stairs, which he reckoned upon descending four at a time, when, in his heedless course, he ran head foremost against a Musketeer who was coming out of one of M. de Treville's private rooms, and striking his shoulder violently, made him utter a cry, or rather a howl.

"Excuse me," said d'Artagnan, endeavoring to resume his course, "excuse me, but I am in a hurry."

Scarcely had he descended the first stair, when a hand of iron seized him by the belt and stopped him.

"You are in a hurry?" said the Musketeer, as pale as a sheet. "Under that pretense you run against me! You say. 'Excuse me,' and you believe that is sufficient? Not at all my young man. Do you fancy because you have heard Monsieur de Treville speak to us a little cavalierly today that other people are to treat us as he speaks to us? Undeceive yourself, comrade, you are not Monsieur de Treville."

"My faith!" replied d'Artagnan, recognizing Athos, who, after the dressing performed by the doctor, was returning to his own apartment. "I did not do it intentionally, and not doing it intentionally, I said 'Excuse me.' It appears to me that this is quite enough. I repeat to you, however, and this time on my word of honor—I think perhaps too often—that I am in haste, great haste. Leave your hold, then, I beg of you, and let me go where my business calls me."

"Monsieur," said Athos, letting him go, "you are not polite; it is easy to perceive that you come from a distance."

D'Artagnan had already strode down three or four stairs, but at Athos's last remark he stopped short.

"*Morbleu*, monsieur!" said he, "however far I may come, it is not you who can give me a lesson in good manners, I warn you."

"Perhaps," said Athos.

"Ah! If I were not in such haste, and if I were not running after someone," said d'Artagnan.

"Monsieur Man-in-a-hurry, you can find me without running—*me*, you understand?"

"And where, I pray you?"

"Near the Carmes-Deschaux."

"At what hour?"

"About noon."

"About noon? That will do; I will be there."

"Endeavor not to make me wait; for at quarter past twelve I will cut off your ears as you run."

"Good!" cried d'Artagnan, "I will be there ten minutes before twelve." And he set off running as if the devil possessed him, hoping that he might yet find the stranger, whose slow pace could not have carried him far.

But at the street gate, Porthos was talking with the soldier on guard. Between the two talkers there was just enough room for a man to pass. D'Artagnan thought it would suffice for him, and he sprang forward like a dart between them. But d'Artagnan had reckoned without the wind. As he was about to pass, the wind blew out Porthos's long cloak, and d'Artagnan rushed straight into the middle of it. Without doubt,

Porthos had reasons for not abandoning this part of his vestments, for instead of quitting his hold on the flap in his hand, he pulled it toward him, so that d'Artagnan rolled himself up in the velvet by a movement of rotation explained by the persistency of Porthos.

D'Artagnan, hearing the Musketeer swear, wished to escape from the cloak, which blinded him, and sought to find his way from under the folds of it. He was particularly anxious to avoid marring the freshness of the magnificent baldric we are acquainted with; but on timidly opening his eyes, he found himself with his nose fixed between the two shoulders of Porthos—that is to say, exactly upon the baldric.

Alas, like most things in this world which have nothing in their favor but appearances, the baldric was glittering with gold in the front, but was nothing but simple buff behind. Vainglorious as he was, Porthos could not afford to have a baldric wholly of gold, but had at least half. One could comprehend the necessity of the cold and the urgency of the cloak.

"Bless me!" cried Porthos, making strong efforts to disembarrass himself of d'Artagnan, who was wriggling about his back; "you must be mad to run against people in this manner."

"Excuse me," said d'Artagnan, reappearing under the shoulder of the giant, "but I am in such haste—I was running after someone and—"

"And do you always forget your eyes when you run?" asked Porthos.

"No," replied d'Artagnan, piqued, "and thanks to my eyes, I can see what other people cannot see."

Whether Porthos understood him or did not understand him, giving way to his anger, "Monsieur," said he, "you stand a chance of getting chastised if you rub Musketeers in this fashion."

"Chastised, Monsieur!" said d'Artagnan, "the expression is strong."

"It is one that becomes a man accustomed to look his enemies in the face."

"Ah, *pardieu!* I know full well that you don't turn your back to yours."

And the young man, delighted with his joke, went away laughing loudly.

Porthos foamed with rage, and made a movement to rush after d'Artagnan.

"Presently, presently," cried the latter, "when you haven't your cloak on."

"At one o'clock, then, behind the Luxembourg."

"Very well, at one o'clock, then," replied d'Artagnan, turning the angle of the street.

But neither in the street he had passed through, nor in the one which his eager glance pervaded, could he see anyone; however slowly the stranger had walked, he was gone on his way, or perhaps had entered some house. D'Artagnan inquired of everyone he met with, went down to the ferry, came up again by the Rue de Seine, and the Red Cross; but nothing, absolutely nothing! This chase was, however, advantageous to him in one sense, for in proportion as the perspiration broke from his forehead, his heart began to cool.

He began to reflect upon the events that had passed; they were numerous and inauspicious. It was scarcely eleven o'clock in the morning, and yet this morning had already brought him into disgrace with M. de Treville, who could not fail to think the manner in which d'Artagnan had left him a little cavalier.

Besides this, he had drawn upon himself two good duels with two men, each capable of killing three d'Artagnans—with two Musketeers, in short, with two of those beings whom he esteemed so greatly that he placed them in his mind and heart above all other men.

The outlook was sad. Sure of being killed by Athos, it may easily be understood that the young man was not very uneasy about Porthos. As hope, however, is the last thing extinguished in the heart of man, he finished by hoping that he might survive, even though with terrible wounds, in both these duels; and in case of surviving, he made the following reprehensions upon his own conduct:

"What a madcap I was, and what a stupid fellow I am! That brave and unfortunate Athos was wounded on that very shoulder against which I must run head foremost, like a ram. The only thing that astonishes me is that he did not strike me dead at once. He had good cause to do so; the pain I gave him must have been atrocious. As to Porthos—oh, as to Porthos, faith, that's a droll affair!"

And in spite of himself, the young man began to laugh aloud, looking round carefully, however, to see that his solitary laugh, without a cause in the eyes of passers-by, offended no one.

"As to Porthos, that is certainly droll; but I am not the less a giddy fool. Are people to be run against without warning? No! And have I any right to go and peep under their cloaks to see what is not there? He would have pardoned me, he would certainly have pardoned me, if I had not said anything to him about that cursed baldric—in ambiguous words, it is true, but rather drolly ambiguous. Ah, cursed Gascon that I am, I get from one hobble into another. Friend d'Artagnan," continued he, speaking to himself with all the amenity that he thought due himself, "if you escape, of which there is not much chance, I would advise you to practice perfect politeness for the future. You must henceforth be admired and quoted as a model of it. To be obliging and polite does not necessarily make a man a coward. Look at Aramis, now; Aramis is mildness and grace personified. Well, did anybody ever dream of calling Aramis a coward? No, certainly not, and from this moment I will endeavor to model myself after him. Ah! That's strange! Here he is!"

D'Artagnan, walking and soliloquizing, had arrived within a few steps of the hotel d'Arguillon and in front of that hotel perceived Aramis, chatting gaily with three gentlemen; but as he had not forgotten that it was in presence of this young man that M. de Treville had been so angry in the morning, and as a witness of the rebuke the Musketeers had received was not likely to be at all agreeable, he pretended not to see him. D'Artagnan, on the contrary, quite full of his plans of conciliation and courtesy, approached the young men with a profound bow, accompanied by a most gracious smile. All four, besides, immediately broke off their conversation.

D'Artagnan was not so dull as not to perceive that he was one too many; but he was not sufficiently broken into the fashions of the gay world to know how to extricate himself gallantly from a false position, like that of a man who begins to mingle with people he is scarcely acquainted with and in a conversation that does not concern him. He was seeking in his mind, then, for the least awkward means of retreat, when he remarked that Aramis had let his handkerchief fall, and by mistake, no doubt, had placed his foot upon it. This appeared to be a favorable opportunity to repair his intrusion. He stooped, and with the most gracious air he could assume, drew the handkerchief from under the foot of the Musketeer in spite of the efforts the latter made to detain it, and holding it out to him, said, "I believe, monsieur, that this is a handkerchief you would be sorry to lose?"

The handkerchief was indeed richly embroidered, and had a coronet and arms at one of its corners. Aramis blushed excessively, and snatched rather than took the handkerchief from the hand of the Gascon.

"Ah, ah!" cried one of the Guards, "will you persist in saying, most discreet Aramis, that you are not on good terms with Madame de Bois-Tracy, when that gracious lady has the kindness to lend you one of her handkerchiefs?"

Aramis darted at d'Artagnan one of those looks which inform a man that he has acquired a mortal enemy. Then, resuming his mild air, "You are deceived, gentlemen," said he, "this handkerchief is not mine, and I cannot fancy why Monsieur has taken it into his head to offer it to me rather than to one of you; and as a proof of what I say, here is mine in my pocket."

So saying, he pulled out his own handkerchief, likewise a very elegant handkerchief, and of fine cambric—though cambric was dear at the period—but a handkerchief without embroidery and without arms, only ornamented with a single cipher, that of its proprietor.

This time d'Artagnan was not hasty. He perceived his mistake; but the friends of Aramis were not at all convinced by his denial, and one of them addressed the young Musketeer with affected seriousness. "If it were as you pretend it is," said he, "I should be forced, my dear Aramis, to reclaim it myself; for, as you very well know, Bois-Tracy is an intimate friend of mine, and I cannot allow the property of his wife to be sported as a trophy."

"You make the demand badly," replied Aramis; "and while acknowledging the justice of your reclamation, I refuse it on account of the form."

"The fact is," hazarded d'Artagnan, timidly, "I did not see the handkerchief fall from the pocket of Monsieur Aramis. He had his foot upon it, that is all; and I thought from having his foot upon it the handkerchief was his."

"And you were deceived, my dear sir," replied Aramis, coldly, very little sensible to the reparation. Then turning toward that one of the guards who had declared himself the friend of Bois-Tracy, "Besides," continued he, "I have reflected, my dear intimate of Bois-Tracy, that I am not less tenderly his friend than you can possibly be; so that decidedly this handkerchief is as likely to have fallen from your pocket as mine."

"No, upon my honor!" cried his Majesty's Guardsman.

"You are about to swear upon your honor and I upon my word, and then it will be pretty evident that one of us will have lied. Now, here, Montaran, we will do better than that—let each take a half."

"Of the handkerchief?"

"Yes."

"Perfectly just," cried the other two Guardsmen, "the judgment of King Solomon! Aramis, you certainly are full of wisdom!"

The young men burst into a laugh, and as may be supposed, the affair had no other sequel. In a moment or two the conversation ceased, and the three Guardsmen and the Musketeer, after having cordially shaken hands, separated, the Guardsmen going one way and Aramis another.

"Now is my time to make peace with this gallant man," said d'Artagnan to himself, having stood on one side during the whole of the latter part of the conversation; and with this good feeling drawing near to Aramis, who was departing without paying any attention to him, "Monsieur," said he, "you will excuse me, I hope."

"Ah, monsieur," interrupted Aramis, "permit me to observe to you that you have not acted in this affair as a gallant man ought."

"What, monsieur!" cried d'Artagnan, "and do you suppose—"

"I suppose, monsieur, that you are not a fool, and that you knew very well, although coming from Gascony, that people do not tread upon handkerchiefs without a reason. What the devil! Paris is not paved with cambric!"

"Monsieur, you act wrongly in endeavoring to mortify me," said d'Artagnan, in whom the natural quarrelsome spirit began to speak more loudly than his pacific resolutions. "I am from Gascony, it is true; and since you know it, there is no occasion to tell you that Gascons are not very patient, so that when they have begged to be excused once, were it even for a folly, they are convinced that they have done already at least as much again as they ought to have done."

"Monsieur, what I say to you about the matter," said Aramis, "is not for the sake of seeking a quarrel. Thank God, I am not a bravo! And being a Musketeer but for a time, I only fight when I am forced to do so, and always with great repugnance; but this time the affair is serious, for here is a lady compromised by you."

"By *us*, you mean!" cried d'Artagnan.

"Why did you so maladroitly restore me the handkerchief?"

"Why did you so awkwardly let it fall?"

"I have said, monsieur, and I repeat, that the handkerchief did not fall from my pocket."

"And thereby you have lied twice, monsieur, for I saw it fall."

"Ah, you take it with that tone, do you, Master Gascon? Well, I will teach you how to behave yourself."

"And I will send you back to your Mass book, Master Abbe. Draw, if you please, and instantly—"

"Not so, if you please, my good friend—not here, at least. Do you not perceive that we are opposite the Hotel d'Arguillon, which is full of the cardinal's creatures? How do I know that this is not his Eminence who has honored you with the commission to procure my head? Now, I entertain a ridiculous partiality for my head, it seems to suit my shoulders so correctly. I wish to kill you, be at rest as to that, but to kill you quietly in a snug, remote place, where you will not be able to boast of your death to anybody."

"I agree, monsieur; but do not be too confident. Take your handkerchief; whether it belongs to you or another, you may perhaps stand in need of it."

"Monsieur is a Gascon?" asked Aramis.

"Yes. Monsieur does not postpone an interview through prudence?"

"Prudence, monsieur, is a virtue sufficiently useless to Musketeers, I know, but indispensable to churchmen; and as I am only a Musketeer provisionally, I hold it good to be prudent. At two o'clock I shall have the honor of expecting you at the hotel of Monsieur de Treville. There I will indicate to you the best place and time."

The two young men bowed and separated, Aramis ascending the street which led to the Luxembourg, while d'Artagnan, perceiving the appointed hour was approaching, took the road to the Carmes-Deschaux, saying to himself, "Decidedly I can't draw back; but at least, if I am killed, I shall be killed by a Musketeer."

D'Artagnan was acquainted with nobody in Paris. He went therefore to his appointment with Athos without a second, determined to be satisfied with those his adversary should choose. Besides, his intention was formed to make the brave Musketeer all suitable apologies, but without meanness or weakness, fearing that might result from this duel which generally results from an affair of this kind, when a young and vigorous man fights with an adversary who is wounded and weakened—if conquered, he doubles the triumph of his antagonist; if a conqueror, he is accused of foul play and want of courage.

Now, we must have badly painted the character of our adventure seeker, or our readers must have already perceived that d'Artagnan was not an ordinary man; therefore, while repeating to himself that his death was inevitable, he did not make up his mind to die quietly, as one less courageous and less restrained might have done in his place. He reflected upon the different characters of men he had to fight with, and began to view his situation more clearly. He hoped, by means of loyal excuses, to make a friend of Athos, whose lordly air and austere bearing pleased him much. He flattered himself he should be able to frighten Porthos with the adventure of the baldric, which he might, if not killed upon the spot, relate to everybody a recital which, well managed, would cover Porthos with ridicule. As to the astute Aramis, he did not entertain much dread of him; and supposing he should be able to get so far, he determined to dispatch him in good style or at least, by hitting him in the face, as Caesar recommended his soldiers do to those of Pompey, to damage forever the beauty of which he was so proud.

In addition to this, d'Artagnan possessed that invincible stock of resolution which the counsels of his father had implanted in his heart: "Endure nothing from anyone but the king, the cardinal, and Monsieur de Treville." He flew, then, rather than walked, toward the convent of the Carmes Dechausses, or rather Deschaux, as it was called at that period, a sort of building without a window, surrounded by barren fields—an accessory to the Preaux-Clercs, and which was generally employed as the place for the duels of men who had no time to lose.

When d'Artagnan arrived in sight of the bare spot of ground which extended along the foot of the monastery, Athos had been waiting about five minutes, and twelve o'clock was striking. He was, then, as punctual as the Samaritan woman, and the most rigorous casuist with regard to duels could have nothing to say.

Athos, who still suffered grievously from his wound, though it had been dressed anew by M. de Treville's surgeon, was seated on a post and waiting for his adversary with hat in hand, his feather even touching the ground.

"Monsieur," said Athos, "I have engaged two of my friends as seconds; but these two friends are not yet come, at which I am astonished, as it is not at all their custom."

"I have no seconds on my part, monsieur," said d'Artagnan; "for having only arrived yesterday in Paris, I as yet know no one but Monsieur de Treville, to whom I was recommended by my father, who has the honor to be, in some degree, one of his friends."

Athos reflected for an instant. "You know no one but Monsieur de Treville?" he asked.

"Yes, monsieur, I know only him."

"Well, but then," continued Athos, speaking half to himself, "if I kill you, I shall have the air of a boy-slayer."

"Not too much so," replied d'Artagnan, with a bow that was not deficient in dignity, "since you do me the honor to draw a sword with me while suffering from a wound which is very inconvenient."

"Very inconvenient, upon my word; and you hurt me devilishly, I can tell you. But I will take the left hand—it is my custom in such circumstances. Do not fancy that I do you a favor; I use either hand easily. And it will be even a disadvantage to you; a left-handed man is very troublesome to people who are not prepared for it. I regret I did not inform you sooner of this circumstance."

"You have truly, monsieur," said d'Artagnan, bowing again, "a courtesy, for which, I assure you, I am very grateful."

"You confuse me," replied Athos, with his gentlemanly air; "let us talk of something else, if you please. Ah, s'blood, how you have hurt me! My shoulder quite burns."

"If you would permit me—" said d'Artagnan, with timidity.

"What, monsieur?"

"I have a miraculous balsam for wounds—a balsam given to me by my mother and of which I have made a trial upon myself."

"Well?"

"Well, I am sure that in less than three days this balsam would cure you; and at the end of three days, when you would be cured— well, sir, it would still do me a great honor to be your man."

D'Artagnan spoke these words with a simplicity that did honor to his courtesy, without throwing the least doubt upon his courage.

"*Pardieu*, monsieur!" said Athos, "that's a proposition that pleases me; not that I can accept it, but a league off it savors of the gentleman. Thus spoke and acted the gallant knights of the time of Charlemagne, in whom every cavalier ought to seek his model. Unfortunately, we do not live in the times of the great emperor, we live in the times of the cardinal; and three days hence, however well the secret might be guarded, it would be known, I say, that we were to fight, and our combat would be prevented. I think these fellows will never come."

"If you are in haste, monsieur," said d'Artagnan, with the same simplicity with which a moment before he had proposed to him to put off the duel for three days, "and if it be your will to dispatch me at once, do not inconvenience yourself, I pray you."

"There is another word which pleases me," cried Athos, with a gracious nod to d'Artagnan. "That did not come from a man without a heart. Monsieur, I love men of your kidney; and I foresee plainly that if we don't kill each other, I shall hereafter have much pleasure in your conversation. We will wait for these gentlemen, so please you; I have plenty of time, and it will be more correct. Ah, here is one of them, I believe."

In fact, at the end of the Rue Vaugirard the gigantic Porthos appeared.

"What!" cried d'Artagnan, "is your first witness Monsieur Porthos?"

"Yes, that disturbs you?"

"By no means."

"And here is the second."

D'Artagnan turned in the direction pointed to by Athos, and perceived Aramis.

"What!" cried he, in an accent of greater astonishment than before, "your second witness is Monsieur Aramis?"

"Doubtless! Are you not aware that we are never seen one without the others, and that we are called among the Musketeers and the Guards, at court and in the city, Athos, Porthos, and Aramis, or the Three Inseparables? And yet, as you come from Dax or Pau—"

"From Tarbes," said d'Artagnan.

"It is probable you are ignorant of this little fact," said Athos.

"My faith!" replied d'Artagnan, "you are well named, gentlemen; and my adventure, if it should make any noise, will prove at least that your union is not founded upon contrasts."

In the meantime, Porthos had come up, waved his hand to Athos, and then turning toward d'Artagnan, stood quite astonished.

Let us say in passing that he had changed his baldric and relinquished his cloak.

"Ah, ah!" said he, "what does this mean?"

"This is the gentleman I am going to fight with," said Athos, pointing to d'Artagnan with his hand and saluting him with the same gesture.

"Why, it is with him I am also going to fight," said Porthos.

"But not before one o'clock," replied d'Artagnan.

"And I also am to fight with this gentleman," said Aramis, coming in his turn onto the place.

"But not until two o'clock," said d'Artagnan, with the same calmness.

"But what are you going to fight about, Athos?" asked Aramis.

"Faith! I don't very well know. He hurt my shoulder. And you, Porthos?"

"Faith! I am going to fight—because I am going to fight," answered Porthos, reddening.

Athos, whose keen eye lost nothing, perceived a faintly sly smile pass over the lips of the young Gascon as he replied, "We had a short discussion upon dress."

"And you, Aramis?" asked Athos.

"Oh, ours is a theological quarrel," replied Aramis, making a sign to d'Artagnan to keep secret the cause of their duel.

Athos indeed saw a second smile on the lips of d'Artagnan.

"Indeed?" said Athos.

"Yes; a passage of St. Augustine, upon which we could not agree," said the Gascon.

"Decidedly, this is a clever fellow," murmured Athos.

"And now you are assembled, gentlemen," said d'Artagnan, "permit me to offer you my apologies."

At this word *apologies*, a cloud passed over the brow of Athos, a haughty smile curled the lip of Porthos, and a negative sign was the reply of Aramis.

"You do not understand me, gentlemen," said d'Artagnan, throwing up his head, the sharp and bold lines of which were at the moment gilded by a bright ray of the sun. "I asked to be excused in case I should not be able to discharge my debt to all three; for Monsieur Athos has the right to kill me first, which must much diminish the face-value of your bill, Monsieur Porthos, and render yours almost null, Monsieur Aramis. And now, gentlemen, I repeat, excuse me, but on that account only, and—on guard!"

At these words, with the most gallant air possible, d'Artagnan drew his sword.

The blood had mounted to the head of d'Artagnan, and at that moment he would have drawn his sword against all the Musketeers in the kingdom as willingly as he now did against Athos, Porthos, and Aramis.

It was a quarter past midday. The sun was in its zenith, and the spot chosen for the scene of the duel was exposed to its full ardor.

"It is very hot," said Athos, drawing his sword in its turn, "and yet I cannot take off my doublet; for I just now felt my wound begin to bleed again, and I should not like to annoy Monsieur with the sight of blood which he has not drawn from me himself."

"That is true, Monsieur," replied d'Artagnan, "and whether drawn by myself or another, I assure you I shall always view with regret the blood of so brave a gentleman. I will therefore fight in my doublet, like yourself."

"Come, come, enough of such compliments!" cried Porthos. "Remember, we are waiting for our turns."

"Speak for yourself when you are inclined to utter such incongruities," interrupted Aramis. "For my part, I think what they say is very well said, and quite worthy of two gentlemen."

"When you please, monsieur," said Athos, putting himself on guard.

"I waited your orders," said d'Artagnan, crossing swords.

But scarcely had the two rapiers clashed, when a company of the Guards of his Eminence, commanded by M. de Jussac, turned the corner of the convent.

"The cardinal's Guards!" cried Aramis and Porthos at the same time. "Sheathe your swords, gentlemen, sheathe your swords!"

But it was too late. The two combatants had been seen in a position which left no doubt of their intentions.

"Halloo!" cried Jussac, advancing toward them and making a sign to his men to do so likewise, "halloo, Musketeers? Fighting here, are you? And the edicts? What is become of them?"

"You are very generous, gentlemen of the Guards," said Athos, full of rancor, for Jussac was one of the aggressors of the preceding day. "If we were to see you fighting, I can assure you that we would make no effort to prevent you. Leave us alone, then, and you will enjoy a little amusement without cost to yourselves."

"Gentlemen," said Jussac, "it is with great regret that I pronounce the thing impossible. Duty before everything. Sheathe, then, if you please, and follow us."

"Monsieur," said Aramis, parodying Jussac, "it would afford us great pleasure to obey your polite invitation if it depended upon ourselves; but unfortunately the thing is impossible—Monsieur de Treville has forbidden it. Pass on your way, then; it is the best thing to do."

This raillery exasperated Jussac. "We will charge upon you, then," said he, "if you disobey."

"There are five of them," said Athos, half aloud, "and we are but three; we shall be beaten again, and must die on the spot, for, on my part, I declare I will never appear again before the captain as a conquered man."

Athos, Porthos, and Aramis instantly drew near one another, while Jussac drew up his soldiers.

This short interval was sufficient to determine d'Artagnan on the part he was to take. It was one of those events which decide the life of a man; it was a choice between the king and the cardinal—the choice made, it must be persisted in. To fight, that was to disobey the law, that was to risk his head, that was to make at one blow an enemy of a minister more powerful than the king himself. All this the young man perceived, and yet, to his praise we speak it, he did not hesitate a second. Turning towards Athos and his friends, "Gentlemen," said he, "allow me to correct your words, if you please. You said you were but three, but it appears to me we are four."

"But you are not one of us," said Porthos.

"That's true," replied d'Artagnan; "I have not the uniform, but I have the spirit. My heart is that of a Musketeer; I feel it, monsieur, and that impels me on."

"Withdraw, young man," cried Jussac, who doubtless, by his gestures and the expression of his countenance, had guessed d'Artagnan's design. "You may retire; we consent to that. Save your skin; begone quickly."

D'Artagnan did not budge.

"Decidedly, you are a brave fellow," said Athos, pressing the young man's hand.

"Come, come, choose your part," replied Jussac.

"Well," said Porthos to Aramis, "we must do something."

"Monsieur is full of generosity," said Athos.

But all three reflected upon the youth of d'Artagnan, and dreaded his inexperience.

"We should only be three, one of whom is wounded, with the addition of a boy," resumed Athos; "and yet it will not be the less said we were four men."

"Yes, but to yield!" said Porthos.

"That *is* difficult," replied Athos.

D'Artagnan comprehended their irresolution.

"Try me, gentlemen," said he, "and I swear to you by my honor that I will not go hence if we are conquered."

"What is your name, my brave fellow?" said Athos.

"D'Artagnan, monsieur."

"Well, then, Athos, Porthos, Aramis, and d'Artagnan, forward!" cried Athos.

"Come, gentlemen, have you decided?" cried Jussac for the third time.

"It is done, gentlemen," said Athos.

"And what is your choice?" asked Jussac.

"We are about to have the honor of charging you," replied Aramis, lifting his hat with one hand and drawing his sword with the other.

"Ah! You resist, do you?" cried Jussac.

"S'blood; does that astonish you?"

And the nine combatants rushed upon each other with a fury which however did not exclude a certain degree of method.

Athos fixed upon a certain Cahusac, a favorite of the cardinal's. Porthos had Bicarat, and Aramis found himself opposed to two adversaries. As to d'Artagnan, he sprang toward Jussac himself.

The heart of the young Gascon beat as if it would burst through his side—not from fear, God he thanked, he had not the shade of it, but with emulation; he fought like a furious tiger, turning ten times round his adversary, and changing his ground and his guard twenty times. Jussac was, as was then said, a fine blade, and had had much practice; nevertheless it required all his skill to defend himself against an adversary who, active and energetic, departed every instant from received rules, attacking him on all sides at once, and yet parrying like a man who had the greatest respect for his own epidermis.

This contest at length exhausted Jussac's patience. Furious at being held in check by one whom he had considered a boy, he became warm and began to make mistakes. D'Artagnan, who though wanting in practice had a sound theory, redoubled his agility. Jussac, anxious to put an end to this, springing forward, aimed a terrible thrust at his adversary, but the latter parried it; and while Jussac was recovering himself, glided like a serpent beneath his blade, and passed his sword through his body. Jussac fell like a dead mass.

D'Artagnan then cast an anxious and rapid glance over the field of battle.

Aramis had killed one of his adversaries, but the other pressed him warmly. Nevertheless, Aramis was in a good situation, and able to defend himself.

Bicarat and Porthos had just made counterhits. Porthos had received a thrust through his arm, and Bicarat one through his thigh. But neither of these two wounds was serious, and they only fought more earnestly.

Athos, wounded anew by Cahusac, became evidently paler, but did not give way a foot. He only changed his sword hand, and fought with his left hand.

According to the laws of dueling at that period, d'Artagnan was at liberty to assist whom he pleased. While he was endeavoring to find out which of his companions stood in greatest need, he caught a glance from Athos. The glance was of sublime eloquence. Athos would have died rather than appeal for help; but he could look, and with that look ask assistance. D'Artagnan interpreted it; with a terrible bound he sprang to the side of Cahusac, crying, "To me, Monsieur Guardsman; I will slay you!"

Cahusac turned. It was time; for Athos, whose great courage alone supported him, sank upon his knee.

"S'blood!" cried he to d'Artagnan, "do not kill him, young man, I beg of you. I have an old affair to settle with him when I am cured and sound again. Disarm him only—make sure of his sword. That's it! Very well done!"

The exclamation was drawn from Athos by seeing the sword of Cahusac fly twenty paces from him. D'Artagnan and Cahusac sprang forward at the same instant, the one to recover, the other to obtain, the sword; but d'Artagnan, being the more active, reached it first and placed his foot upon it.

Cahusac immediately ran to the Guardsman whom Aramis had killed, seized his rapier, and returned toward d'Artagnan; but on his way he met Athos, who during his relief which d'Artagnan had procured him had recovered his breath, and who, for fear that d'Artagnan would kill his enemy, wished to resume the fight.

D'Artagnan perceived that it would be disobliging Athos not to leave him alone; and in a few minutes Cahusac fell, with a sword thrust through his throat.

At the same instant Aramis placed his sword point on the breast of his fallen enemy, and forced him to ask for mercy.

There only then remained Porthos and Bicarat. Porthos made a thousand flourishes, asking Bicarat what o'clock it could be, and offering him his compliments upon his brother's having just obtained a company in the regiment of Navarre; but, jest as he might, he gained nothing. Bicarat was one of those iron men who never fell dead.

Nevertheless, it was necessary to finish. The watch might come up and take all the combatants, wounded or not, royalists or cardinalists. Athos, Aramis, and d'Artagnan surrounded Bicarat, and required him to surrender. Though alone against all and with a wound in his thigh, Bicarat wished to hold out; but Jussac, who had risen upon his elbow, cried out to him to yield. Bicarat was a Gascon, as d'Artagnan was; he turned a deaf ear, and contented himself with laughing, and between two parries finding time to point to a spot of earth with his sword, "Here," cried he, parodying a verse of the Bible, "here will Bicarat die; for I only am left, and they seek my life."

"But there are four against you; leave off, I command you."

"Ah, if you command me, that's another thing," said Bicarat. "As you are my commander, it is my duty to obey." And springing backward, he broke his sword across his knee to avoid the necessity of surrendering it, threw the pieces over the convent wall, and crossed his arms, whistling a cardinalist air.

Bravery is always respected, even in an enemy. The Musketeers saluted Bicarat with their swords, and returned them to their sheaths. D'Artagnan did the same. Then, assisted by Bicarat, the only one left standing, he bore Jussac, Cahusac, and one of Aramis's adversaries who was only wounded, under the porch of the convent. The fourth, as we have said, was dead. They then rang the bell, and carrying away four swords out of five, they took their road, intoxicated with joy, toward the hotel of M. de Treville.

They walked arm in arm, occupying the whole width of the street and taking in every Musketeer they met, so that in the end it became a triumphal march. The heart of d'Artagnan swam in delirium; he marched between Athos and Porthos, pressing them tenderly.

"If I am not yet a Musketeer," said he to his new friends, as he passed through the gateway of M. de Treville's hotel, "at least I have entered upon my apprenticeship, haven't I?"

This affair made a great noise. M. de Treville scolded his Musketeers in public, and congratulated them in private; but as no time was to be lost in gaining the king, M. de Treville hastened to report himself at the Louvre. It was already too late. The king was closeted with the cardinal, and M. de Treville was informed that the king was busy and could not receive him at that moment. In the evening M. de Treville attended the king's gaming table. The king was winning; and as he was very avaricious, he was in an excellent humor. Perceiving M. de Treville at a distance—

"Come here, Monsieur Captain," said he, "come here, that I may growl at you. Do you know that his Eminence has been making fresh complaints against your Musketeers, and that with so much emotion, that this evening his Eminence is indisposed? Ah, these Musketeers of yours are very devils—fellows to be hanged."

"No, sire," replied Treville, who saw at the first glance how things would go, "on the contrary, they are good creatures, as meek as lambs, and have but one desire, I'll be their warranty. And that is that their swords may never leave their scabbards but in your Majesty's service. But what are they to do? The Guards of Monsieur the Cardinal are forever seeking quarrels with them, and for the honor of the corps even, the poor young men are obliged to defend themselves."

"Listen to Monsieur de Treville," said the king; "listen to him! Would not one say he was speaking of a religious community? In truth, my dear Captain, I have a great mind to take away your commission and give it to Mademoiselle de Chemerault, to whom I promised an abbey. But don't fancy that I am going to take you on your bare word. I am called Louis the Just, Monsieur de Treville, and by and by, by and by we will see."

"Ah, sire; it is because I confide in that justice that I shall wait patiently and quietly the good pleasure of your Majesty."

"Wait, then, monsieur, wait," said the king; "I will not detain you long."

In fact, fortune changed; and as the king began to lose what he had won, he was not sorry to find an excuse for playing Charlemagne—if we may use a gaming phrase of whose origin we confess our ignorance. The king therefore arose a minute after, and putting the money which lay before him into his pocket, the major part of which arose from his winnings, "La Vieuville," said he, "take my place; I must speak to Monsieur de Treville on an affair of importance. Ah, I had eighty louis before me; put down the same sum, so that they who have lost may have nothing to complain of. Justice before everything."

Then turning toward M. de Treville and walking with him toward the embrasure of a window, "Well, monsieur," continued he, "you say it is his Eminence's Guards who have sought a quarrel with your Musketeers?"

"Yes, sire, as they always do."

"And how did the thing happen? Let us see, for you know, my dear Captain, a judge must hear both sides."

"Good Lord! In the most simple and natural manner possible. Three of my best soldiers, whom your Majesty knows by name, and whose devotedness you have more than once appreciated, and who have, I dare affirm to the king, his service much at heart—three of my best soldiers, I say, Athos, Porthos, and Aramis, had made a party of pleasure with a young fellow from Gascony, whom I had introduced to them the same morning. The party was to take place at St. Germain, I believe, and they had appointed to meet at the Carmes-Deschaux, when they were disturbed by de Jussac, Cahusac, Bicarat, and two other Guardsmen, who certainly did not go there in such a numerous company without some ill intention against the edicts."

"Ah, ah! You incline me to think so," said the king. "There is no doubt they went thither to fight themselves."

"I do not accuse them, sire; but I leave your Majesty to judge what five armed men could possibly be going to do in such a deserted place as the neighborhood of the Convent des Carmes."

"Yes, you are right, Treville, you are right!"

"Then, upon seeing my Musketeers they changed their minds, and forgot their private hatred for partisan hatred; for your Majesty cannot be ignorant that the Musketeers, who belong to the king and nobody but the king, are the natural enemies of the Guardsmen, who belong to the cardinal."

"Yes, Treville, yes," said the king, in a melancholy tone; "and it is very sad, believe me, to see thus two parties in France, two heads to royalty.

But all this will come to an end, Treville, will come to an end. You say, then, that the Guardsmen sought a quarrel with the Musketeers?"

"I say that it is probable that things have fallen out so, but I will not swear to it, sire. You know how difficult it is to discover the truth; and unless a man be endowed with that admirable instinct which causes Louis XIII to be named the Just—"

"You are right, Treville; but they were not alone, your Musketeers. They had a youth with them?"

"Yes, sire, and one wounded man; so that three of the king's Musketeers—one of whom was wounded—and a youth not only maintained their ground against five of the most terrible of the cardinal's Guardsmen, but absolutely brought four of them to earth."

"Why, this is a victory!" cried the king, all radiant, "a complete victory!"

"Yes, sire; as complete as that of the Bridge of Ce."

"Four men, one of them wounded, and a youth, say you?"

"One hardly a young man; but who, however, behaved himself so admirably on this occasion that I will take the liberty of recommending him to your Majesty."

"How does he call himself?"

"D'Artagnan, sire; he is the son of one of my oldest friends—the son of a man who served under the king your father, of glorious memory, in the civil war."

"And you say this young man behaved himself well? Tell me how, Treville—you know how I delight in accounts of war and fighting."

And Louis XIII twisted his mustache proudly, placing his hand upon his hip.

"Sire," resumed Treville, "as I told you, Monsieur d'Artagnan is little more than a boy; and as he has not the honor of being a Musketeer, he was dressed as a citizen. The Guards of the cardinal, perceiving his youth and that he did not belong to the corps, invited him to retire before they attacked."

"So you may plainly see, Treville," interrupted the king, "it was they who attacked?"

"That is true, sire; there can be no more doubt on that head. They called upon him then to retire; but he answered that he was a Musketeer at heart, entirely devoted to your Majesty, and that therefore he would remain with Messieurs the Musketeers."

"Brave young man!" murmured the king.

"Well, he did remain with them; and your Majesty has in him so firm a champion that it was he who gave Jussac the terrible sword thrust which has made the cardinal so angry."

"He who wounded Jussac!" cried the king, "he, a boy! Treville, that's impossible!"

"It is as I have the honor to relate it to your Majesty."

"Jussac, one of the first swordsmen in the kingdom?"

"Well, sire, for once he found his master."

"I will see this young man, Treville—I will see him; and if anything can be done—well, we will make it our business."

"When will your Majesty deign to receive him?"

"Tomorrow, at midday, Treville."

"Shall I bring him alone?"

"No, bring me all four together. I wish to thank them all at once. Devoted men are so rare, Treville, by the back staircase. It is useless to let the cardinal know."

"Yes, sire."

"You understand, Treville—an edict is still an edict, it is forbidden to fight, after all."

"But this encounter, sire, is quite out of the ordinary conditions of a duel. It is a brawl; and the proof is that there were five of the cardinal's Guardsmen against my three Musketeers and Monsieur d'Artagnan."

"That is true," said the king; "but never mind, Treville, come still by the back staircase."

Treville smiled; but as it was indeed something to have prevailed upon this child to rebel against his master, he saluted the king respectfully, and with this agreement, took leave of him.

That evening the three Musketeers were informed of the honor accorded them. As they had long been acquainted with the king, they were not much excited; but d'Artagnan, with his Gascon imagination, saw in it his future fortune, and passed the night in golden dreams. By eight o'clock in the morning he was at the apartment of Athos.

D'Artagnan found the Musketeer dressed and ready to go out. As the hour to wait upon the king was not till twelve, he had made a party with Porthos and Aramis to play a game at tennis in a tennis court situated near the stables of the Luxembourg. Athos invited d'Artagnan to follow them; and although ignorant of the game, which he had never played, he accepted, not knowing what to do with his time from nine o'clock in the morning, as it then scarcely was, till twelve.

The two Musketeers were already there, and were playing together. Athos, who was very expert in all bodily exercises, passed with d'Artagnan to the opposite side and challenged them; but at the first effort he made, although he played with his left hand, he found that his wound was yet too recent to allow of such exertion. D'Artagnan remained, therefore, alone; and as he declared he was too ignorant of the game to play it regularly they only continued giving balls to one another without counting. But one of these balls, launched by Porthos' herculean hand, passed so close to d'Artagnan's face that he thought that if, instead of passing near, it had hit him, his audience would have been probably lost, as it would have been impossible for him to present himself before the king. Now, as upon this audience, in his Gascon imagination, depended his future life, he saluted Aramis and Porthos politely, declaring that he would not resume the game until he should be prepared to play with them on more equal terms, and went and took his place near the cord and in the gallery.

Unfortunately for d'Artagnan, among the spectators was one of his Eminence's Guardsmen, who, still irritated by the defeat of his companions, which had happened only the day before, had promised himself to seize the first opportunity of avenging it. He believed this opportunity was now come and addressed his neighbor: "It is not astonishing that that young man should be afraid of a ball, for he is doubtless a Musketeer apprentice."

D'Artagnan turned round as if a serpent had stung him, and fixed his eyes intensely upon the Guardsman who had just made this insolent speech.

"*Pardieu,* " resumed the latter, twisting his mustache, "look at me as long as you like, my little gentleman! I have said what I have said."

"And as since that which you have said is too clear to require any explanation," replied d'Artagnan, in a low voice, "I beg you to follow me."

"And when?" asked the Guardsman, with the same jeering air.

"At once, if you please."

"And you know who I am, without doubt?"

"I? I am completely ignorant; nor does it much disquiet me."

"You're in the wrong there; for if you knew my name, perhaps you would not be so pressing."

"What is your name?"

"Bernajoux, at your service."

"Well, then, Monsieur Bernajoux," said d'Artagnan, tranquilly, "I will wait for you at the door."

"Go, monsieur, I will follow you."

"Do not hurry yourself, monsieur, lest it be observed that we go out together. You must be aware that for our undertaking, company would be in the way."

"That's true," said the Guardsman, astonished that his name had not produced more effect upon the young man.

Indeed, the name of Bernajoux was known to all the world, d'Artagnan alone excepted, perhaps; for it was one of those which figured most frequently in the daily brawls which all the edicts of the cardinal could not repress.

Porthos and Aramis were so engaged with their game, and Athos was watching them with so much attention, that they did not even perceive their young companion go out, who, as he had told the Guardsman of his Eminence, stopped outside the door. An instant after, the Guardsman descended in his turn. As d'Artagnan had no time to lose, on account of the audience of the king, which was fixed for midday, he cast his eyes around, and seeing that the street was empty, said to his adversary, "My faith! It is fortunate for you, although your name is Bernajoux, to have only to deal with an apprentice Musketeer. Never mind; be content, I will do my best. On guard!"

"But," said he whom d'Artagnan thus provoked, "it appears to me that this place is badly chosen, and that we should be better behind the Abbey St. Germain or in the Pre-aux-Clercs."

"What you say is full of sense," replied d'Artagnan; "but unfortunately I have very little time to spare, having an appointment at twelve precisely. On guard, then, monsieur, on guard!"

Bernajoux was not a man to have such a compliment paid to him twice. In an instant his sword glittered in his hand, and he sprang upon his adversary, whom, thanks to his great youthfulness, he hoped to intimidate.

But d'Artagnan had on the preceding day served his apprenticeship. Fresh sharpened by his victory, full of hopes of future favor, he was resolved not to recoil a step. So the two swords were crossed close to the hilts, and as d'Artagnan stood firm, it was his adversary who made the retreating step; but d'Artagnan seized the moment at which, in this movement, the sword of Bernajoux deviated from the line. He freed his weapon, made a lunge, and touched his adversary on the shoulder. D'Artagnan immediately made a step backward and raised his sword; but Bernajoux cried out that it was nothing, and rushing blindly upon him, absolutely spitted himself upon d'Artagnan's sword. As, however, he did not fall, as he did not declare himself conquered, but only broke away toward the hotel of M. de la Tremouille, in whose service he had a relative, d'Artagnan was ignorant of the seriousness of the last wound his adversary had received, and pressing him warmly, without doubt would soon have completed his work with a third blow, when the noise which arose from the street being heard in the tennis court, two of the friends of the Guardsman, who had seen him go out after exchanging some words with d'Artagnan, rushed, sword in hand, from the court, and fell upon the conqueror. But Athos, Porthos, and Aramis quickly appeared in their turn, and the moment the two Guardsmen attacked their young companion, drove them back. Bernajoux now fell, and as the Guardsmen were only two against four, they began to cry, "To the rescue! The Hotel de la Tremouille!" At these cries, all who were in the hotel rushed out and fell upon the four companions, who on their side cried aloud, "To the rescue, Musketeers!"

This cry was generally heeded; for the Musketeers were known to be enemies of the cardinal, and were beloved on account of the hatred they bore to his Eminence. Thus the soldiers of other companies than those which belonged to the Red Duke, as Aramis had called him, often took part with the king's Musketeers in these quarrels. Of three Guardsmen of the company of M. Dessessart who were passing, two came to the assistance of the four companions, while the other ran toward the hotel of M. de Treville, crying, "To the rescue, Musketeers! To the rescue!" As usual, this hotel was full of soldiers of this company, who hastened to the succor of their comrades. The *melee* became general, but strength was on the side of the Musketeers. The cardinal's Guards and M. de la Tremouille's people retreated into the hotel, the doors of which they closed just in time to prevent their enemies from entering with them. As to the wounded man, he had been taken in at once, and, as we have said, in a very bad state.

Excitement was at its height among the Musketeers and their allies, and they even began to deliberate whether they should not set fire to the hotel to punish the insolence of M. de la Tremouille's domestics in daring to make a *sortie* upon the king's Musketeers. The proposition had been made, and received with enthusiasm, when fortunately eleven o'clock struck. D'Artagnan and his companions remembered their audience, and as they would very much have regretted that such an opportunity should be lost, they succeeded in calming their friends, who contented themselves with hurling some paving stones against the gates; but the gates were too strong. They soon tired of the sport. Besides, those who must be considered the leaders of the enterprise had quit the group and were making their way toward the hotel of M. de Treville, who was waiting for them, already informed of this fresh disturbance.

"Quick to the Louvre," said he, "to the Louvre without losing an instant, and let us endeavor to see the king before he is prejudiced by the cardinal. We will describe the thing to him as a consequence of the affair of yesterday, and the two will pass off together."

M. de Treville, accompanied by the four young fellows, directed his course toward the Louvre; but to the great astonishment of the captain of the Musketeers, he was informed that the king had gone stag hunting in the forest of St. Germain. M. de Treville required this intelligence to be repeated to him twice, and each time his companions saw his brow become darker.

"Had his Majesty," asked he, "any intention of holding this hunting party yesterday?"

"No, your Excellency," replied the valet de chambre, "the Master of the Hounds came this morning to inform him that he had marked down a stag. At first the king answered that he would not go; but he could not resist his love of sport, and set out after dinner."

"And the king has seen the cardinal?" asked M. de Treville.

"In all probability he has," replied the valet, "for I saw the horses harnessed to his Eminence's carriage this morning, and when I asked where he was going, they told me, 'To St. Germain.'"

"He is beforehand with us," said M. de Treville. "Gentlemen, I will see the king this evening; but as to you, I do not advise you to risk doing so."

This advice was too reasonable, and moreover came from a man who knew the king too well, to allow the four young men to dispute it. M. de Treville recommended everyone to return home and wait for news.

On entering his hotel, M. de Treville thought it best to be first in making the complaint. He sent one of his servants to M. de la Tremouille with a letter in which he begged of him to eject the cardinal's Guardsmen from his house, and to reprimand his people for their audacity in making *sortie* against the king's Musketeers. But M. de la Tremouille—already prejudiced by his esquire, whose relative, as we already know, Bernajoux was— replied that it was neither for M. de Treville nor the Musketeers to complain, but, on the contrary, for him, whose people the Musketeers had assaulted and whose hotel they had endeavored to burn. Now, as the debate between these two nobles might last a long time, each becoming, naturally, more firm in his own opinion, M. de Treville thought of an expedient which might terminate it quietly. This was to go himself to M. de la Tremouille.

He repaired, therefore, immediately to his hotel, and caused himself to be announced.

The two nobles saluted each other politely, for if no friendship existed between them, there was at least esteem. Both were men of courage and honor; and as M. de la Tremouille—a Protestant, and seeing the king seldom—was of no party, he did not, in general, carry any bias into his social relations. This time, however, his address, although polite, was cooler than usual.

"Monsieur," said M. de Treville, "we fancy that we have each cause to complain of the other, and I am come to endeavor to clear up this affair."

"I have no objection," replied M. de la Tremouille, "but I warn you that I am well informed, and all the fault is with your Musketeers."

"You are too just and reasonable a man, monsieur!" said Treville, "not to accept the proposal I am about to make to you."

"Make it, monsieur, I listen."

"How is Monsieur Bernajoux, your esquire's relative?"

"Why, monsieur, very ill indeed! In addition to the sword thrust in his arm, which is not dangerous, he has received another right through his lungs, of which the doctor says bad things."

"But has the wounded man retained his senses?"

"Perfectly."

"Does he talk?"

"With difficulty, but he can speak."

"Well, monsieur, let us go to him. Let us adjure him, in the name of the God before whom he must perhaps appear, to speak the truth. I will take him for judge in his own cause, monsieur, and will believe what he will say."

M. de la Tremouille reflected for an instant; then as it was difficult to suggest a more reasonable proposal, he agreed to it.

Both descended to the chamber in which the wounded man lay.

The latter, on seeing these two noble lords who came to visit him, endeavored to raise himself up in his bed; but he was too weak, and exhausted by the effort, he fell back again almost senseless.

M. de la Tremouille approached him, and made him inhale some salts, which recalled him to life. Then M. de Treville, unwilling that it should be thought that he had influenced the wounded man, requested M. de la Tremouille to interrogate him himself.

That happened which M. de Treville had foreseen. Placed between life and death, as Bernajoux was, he had no idea for a moment of concealing the truth; and he described to the two nobles the affair exactly as it had passed.

This was all that M. de Treville wanted. He wished Bernajoux a speedy convalescence, took leave of M. de la Tremouille, returned to his hotel, and immediately sent word to the four friends that he awaited their company at dinner.

M. de Treville entertained good company, wholly anticardinalst, though. It may easily be understood, therefore, that the conversation during the whole of dinner turned upon the two checks that his Eminence's Guardsmen had received. Now, as d'Artagnan had been the hero of these two fights, it was upon him that all the felicitations fell, which Athos, Porthos, and Aramis abandoned to him, not only as good comrades, but as men who had so often had their turn that could very well afford him his.

Toward six o'clock M. de Treville announced that it was time to go to the Louvre; but as the hour of audience granted by his Majesty was past, instead of claiming the *entree* by the back stairs, he placed himself with the four young men in the antechamber. The king had not yet returned from hunting. Our young men had been waiting about half an hour, amid a crowd of courtiers, when all the doors were thrown open, and his Majesty was announced.

At his announcement d'Artagnan felt himself tremble to the very marrow of his bones. The coming instant would in all probability decide the rest of his life. His eyes therefore were fixed in a sort of agony upon the door through which the king must enter.

Louis XIII appeared, walking fast. He was in hunting costume covered with dust, wearing large boots, and holding a whip in his hand. At the first glance, d'Artagnan judged that the mind of the king was stormy.

This disposition, visible as it was in his Majesty, did not prevent the courtiers from ranging themselves along his pathway. In royal antechambers it is worth more to be viewed with an angry eye than not to be seen at all. The three Musketeers therefore did not hesitate to make a step forward. D'Artagnan on the contrary remained concealed behind them; but although the king knew Athos, Porthos, and Aramis personally, he passed before them without speaking or looking— indeed, as if he had never seen them before. As for M. de Treville, when the eyes of the king fell upon him, he sustained the look with so much firmness that it was the king who dropped his eyes; after which his Majesty, grumbling, entered his apartment.

"Matters go but badly," said Athos, smiling; "and we shall not be made Chevaliers of the Order this time."

"Wait here ten minutes," said M. de Treville; "and if at the expiration of ten minutes you do not see me come out, return to my hotel, for it will be useless for you to wait for me longer."

The four young men waited ten minutes, a quarter of an hour, twenty minutes; and seeing that M. de Treville did not return, went away very uneasy as to what was going to happen.

M. de Treville entered the king's cabinet boldly, and found his Majesty in a very ill humor, seated on an armchair, beating his boot with the handle of his whip. This, however, did not prevent his asking, with the greatest coolness, after his Majesty's health.

"Bad, monsieur, bad!" replied the king; "I am bored."

This was, in fact, the worst complaint of Louis XIII, who would sometimes take one of his courtiers to a window and say, "Monsieur So-and-so, let us weary ourselves together."

"How! Your Majesty is bored? Have you not enjoyed the pleasures of the chase today?"

"A fine pleasure, indeed, monsieur! Upon my soul, everything degenerates; and I don't know whether it is the game which leaves no scent, or the dogs that have no noses. We started a stag of ten branches. We chased him for six hours, and when he was near being taken—when St. Simon was already putting his horn to his mouth to sound the mort—crack, all the pack takes the wrong scent and sets off after a two-year-older. I shall be obliged to give up hunting, as I have given up hawking. Ah, I am an unfortunate king, Monsieur de Treville! I had but one gerfalcon, and he died day before yesterday."

"Indeed, sire, I wholly comprehend your disappointment. The misfortune is great; but I think you have still a good number of falcons, sparrow hawks, and tiercets."

"And not a man to instruct them. Falconers are declining. I know no one but myself who is acquainted with the noble art of venery. After me it will all be over, and people will hunt with gins, snares, and traps. If I had but the time to train pupils! But there is the cardinal always at hand, who does not leave me a moment's repose; who talks to me about Spain, who talks to me about Austria, who talks to me about England! Ah! A *propos* of the cardinal, Monsieur de Treville, I am vexed with you!"

This was the chance at which M. de Treville waited for the king. He knew the king of old, and he knew that all these complaints were but a preface—a sort of excitation to encourage himself—and that he had now come to his point at last.

"And in what have I been so unfortunate as to displease your Majesty?" asked M. de Treville, feigning the most profound astonishment.

"Is it thus you perform your charge, monsieur?" continued the king, without directly replying to de Treville's question. "Is it for this I name you captain of my Musketeers, that they should assassinate a man, disturb a whole quarter, and endeavor to set fire to Paris, without your saying a word? But yet," continued the king, "undoubtedly my haste accuses you wrongfully; without doubt the rioters are in prison, and you come to tell me justice is done."

"Sire," replied M. de Treville, calmly, "on the contrary, I come to demand it of you."

"And against whom?" cried the king.

"Against calumniators," said M. de Treville.

"Ah! This is something new," replied the king. "Will you tell me that your three damned Musketeers, Athos, Porthos, and Aramis, and your youngster from Bearn, have not fallen, like so many furies, upon poor Bernajoux, and have not maltreated him in such a fashion that probably by this time he is dead? Will you tell me that they did not lay siege to the hotel of the Duc de la Tremouille, and that they did not endeavor to burn it?—which would not, perhaps, have been a great misfortune in time of war, seeing that it is nothing but a nest of Huguenots, but which is, in time of peace, a frightful example. Tell me, now, can you deny all this?"

"And who told you this fine story, sire?" asked Treville, quietly.

"Who has told me this fine story, monsieur? Who should it be but he who watches while I sleep, who labors while I amuse myself, who conducts everything at home and abroad—in France as in Europe?"

"Your Majesty probably refers to God," said M. de Treville; "for I know no one except God who can be so far above your Majesty."

"No, monsieur; I speak of the prop of the state, of my only servant, of my only friend—of the cardinal."

"His Eminence is not his holiness, sire."

"What do you mean by that, monsieur?"

"That it is only the Pope who is infallible, and that this infallibility does not extend to cardinals."

"You mean to say that he deceives me; you mean to say that he betrays me? You accuse him, then? Come, speak; avow freely that you accuse him!"

"No, sire, but I say that he deceives himself. I say that he is ill-informed. I say that he has hastily accused your Majesty's Musketeers, toward whom he is unjust, and that he has not obtained his information from good sources."

"The accusation comes from Monsieur de la Tremouille, from the duke himself. What do you say to that?"

"I might answer, sire, that he is too deeply interested in the question to be a very impartial witness; but so far from that, sire, I know the duke to be a royal gentleman, and I refer the matter to him—but upon one condition, sire."

"What?"

"It is that your Majesty will make him come here, will interrogate him yourself, *tête-à-tête*, without witnesses, and that I shall see your Majesty as soon as you have seen the duke."

"What, then! You will bind yourself," cried the king, "by what Monsieur de la Tremouille shall say?"

"Yes, sire."

"You will accept his judgment?"

"Undoubtedly."

"Any you will submit to the reparation he may require?"

"Certainly."

"La Chesnaye," said the king. "La Chesnaye!"

Louis XIII's confidential valet, who never left the door, entered in reply to the call.

"La Chesnaye," said the king, "let someone go instantly and find Monsieur de la Tremouille; I wish to speak with him this evening."

"Your Majesty gives me your word that you will not see anyone between Monsieur de la Tremouille and myself?"

"Nobody, by the faith of a gentleman."

"Tomorrow, then, sire?"

"Tomorrow, monsieur."

"At what o'clock, please your Majesty?"

"At any hour you will."

"But in coming too early I should be afraid of awakening your Majesty."

"Awaken me! Do you think I ever sleep, then? I sleep no longer, monsieur. I sometimes dream, that's all. Come, then, as early as you like—at seven o'clock; but beware, if you and your Musketeers are guilty."

"If my Musketeers are guilty, sire, the guilty shall be placed in your Majesty's hands, who will dispose of them at your good pleasure. Does your Majesty require anything further? Speak, I am ready to obey."

"No, monsieur, no; I am not called Louis the Just without reason. Tomorrow, then, monsieur—tomorrow."

"Till then, God preserve your Majesty!"

However ill the king might sleep, M. de Treville slept still worse. He had ordered his three Musketeers and their companion to be with him at half past six in the morning. He took them with him, without encouraging them or promising them anything, and without concealing from them that their luck, and even his own, depended upon the cast of the dice.

Arrived at the foot of the back stairs, he desired them to wait. If the king was still irritated against them, they would depart without being seen; if the king consented to see them, they would only have to be called.

On arriving at the king's private antechamber, M. de Treville found La Chesnaye, who informed him that they had not been able to find M. de la Tremouille on the preceding evening at his hotel, that he returned too late to present himself at the Louvre, that he had only that moment arrived and that he was at that very hour with the king.

This circumstance pleased M. de Treville much, as he thus became certain that no foreign suggestion could insinuate itself between M. de la Tremouille's testimony and himself.

In fact, ten minutes had scarcely passed away when the door of the king's closet opened, and M. de Treville saw M. de la Tremouille come out. The duke came straight up to him, and said: "Monsieur de Treville, his Majesty has just sent for me in order to inquire respecting the circumstances which took place yesterday at my hotel. I have told him the truth; that is to say, that the fault lay with my people, and that I was ready to offer you my excuses. Since I have the good fortune to meet you, I beg you to receive them, and to hold me always as one of your friends."

"Monsieur the Duke," said M. de Treville, "I was so confident of your loyalty that I required no other defender before his Majesty than yourself. I find that I have not been mistaken, and I thank you that there is still one man in France of whom may be said, without disappointment, what I have said of you."

"That's well said," cried the king, who had heard all these compliments through the open door; "only tell him, Treville, since he wishes to be considered your friend, that I also wish to be one of his, but he neglects me; that it is nearly three years since I have seen him, and that

I never do see him unless I send for him. Tell him all this for me, for these are things which a king cannot say for himself."

"Thanks, sire, thanks," said the duke; "but your Majesty may be assured that it is not those—I do not speak of Monsieur de Treville—whom your Majesty sees at all hours of the day that are most devoted to you."

"Ah! You have heard what I said? So much the better, Duke, so much the better," said the king, advancing toward the door. "Ah! It is you, Treville. Where are your Musketeers? I told you the day before yesterday to bring them with you; why have you not done so?"

"They are below, sire, and with your permission La Chesnaye will bid them come up."

"Yes, yes, let them come up immediately. It is nearly eight o'clock, and at nine I expect a visit. Go, Monsieur Duke, and return often. Come in, Treville."

The Duke saluted and retired. At the moment he opened the door, the three Musketeers and d'Artagnan, conducted by La Chesnaye, appeared at the top of the staircase.

"Come in, my braves," said the king, "come in; I am going to scold you."

The Musketeers advanced, bowing, d'Artagnan following closely behind them.

"What the devil!" continued the king. "Seven of his Eminence's Guards placed *hors de combat* by you four in two days! That's too many, gentlemen, too many! If you go on so, his Eminence will be forced to renew his company in three weeks, and I to put the edicts in force in all their rigor. One now and then I don't say much about; but seven in two days, I repeat, it is too many, it is far too many!"

"Therefore, sire, your Majesty sees that they are come, quite contrite and repentant, to offer you their excuses."

"Quite contrite and repentant! Hem!" said the king. "I place no confidence in their hypocritical faces. In particular, there is one yonder of a Gascon look. Come hither, monsieur."

D'Artagnan, who understood that it was to him this compliment was addressed, approached, assuming a most deprecating air.

"Why you told me he was a young man? This is a boy, Treville, a mere boy! Do you mean to say that it was he who bestowed that severe thrust at Jussac?"

"And those two equally fine thrusts at Bernajoux."

"Truly!"

"Without reckoning," said Athos, "that if he had not rescued me from the hands of Cahusac, I should not now have the honor of making my very humble reverence to your Majesty."

"Why he is a very devil, this Bearnais! *Ventre-Saint-Gris,* Monsieur de Treville, as the king my father would have said. But at this sort of work, many doublets must be slashed and many swords broken. Now, Gascons are always poor, are they not?"

"Sire, I can assert that they have hitherto discovered no gold mines in their mountains; though the Lord owes them this miracle in recompense for the manner in which they supported the pretensions of the king your father."

"Which is to say that the Gascons made a king of me, myself, seeing that I am my father's son, is it not, Treville? Well, happily, I don't say nay to it. La Chesnaye, go and see if by rummaging all my pockets you can find forty pistoles; and if you can find them, bring them to me. And now let us see, young man, with your hand upon your conscience, how did all this come to pass?"

D'Artagnan related the adventure of the preceding day in all its details; how, not having been able to sleep for the joy he felt in the expectation of seeing his Majesty, he had gone to his three friends three hours before the hour of audience; how they had gone together to the tennis court, and how, upon the fear he had manifested lest he receive a ball in the face, he had been jeered at by Bernajoux who had nearly paid for his jeer with his life and M. de la Tremouille, who had nothing to do with the matter, with the loss of his hotel.

"This is all very well," murmured the king, "yes, this is just the account the duke gave me of the affair. Poor cardinal! Seven men in two days, and those of his very best! But that's quite enough, gentlemen; please to understand, that's enough. You have taken your revenge for the Rue Ferou, and even exceeded it; you ought to be satisfied."

"If your Majesty is so," said Treville, "we are."

"Oh, yes; I am," added the king, taking a handful of gold from La Chesnaye, and putting it into the hand of d'Artagnan. "Here," said he, "is a proof of my satisfaction."

At this epoch, the ideas of pride which are in fashion in our days did not prevail. A gentleman received, from hand to hand, money from the king, and was not the least in the world humiliated. D'Artagnan put his forty pistoles into his pocket without any scruple—on the contrary, thanking his Majesty greatly.

"There," said the king, looking at a clock, "there, now, as it is half past eight, you may retire; for as I told you, I expect someone at nine. Thanks for your devotedness, gentlemen. I may continue to rely upon it, may I not?"

"Oh, sire!" cried the four companions, with one voice, "we would allow ourselves to be cut to pieces in your Majesty's service."

"Well, well, but keep whole; that will be better, and you will be more useful to me. Treville," added the king, in a low voice, as the others were retiring, "as you have no room in the Musketeers, and as we have besides decided that a novitiate is necessary before entering that corps, place this young man in the company of the Guards of Monsieur Dessessart, your brother-in-law. Ah, *pardieu*, Treville! I enjoy beforehand the face the cardinal will make. He will be furious; but I don't care. I am doing what is right."

The king waved his hand to Treville, who left him and rejoined the Musketeers, whom he found sharing the forty pistoles with d'Artagnan.

The cardinal, as his Majesty had said, was really furious, so furious that during eight days he absented himself from the king's gaming table. This did not prevent the king from being as complacent to him as possible whenever he met him, or from asking in the kindest tone, "Well, Monsieur Cardinal, how fares it with that poor Jussac and that poor Bernajoux of yours?"

The Hoard of the Gibbelins

by Lord Dunsany

Edward Plunkett (1875–1957), 18th Baron Dunsany, wrote plays, poetry and influential fantasy stories. This story appeared in his collection *The Book of Wonder*.

The Gibbelins eat, as is well known, nothing less good than man. Their evil tower is joined to Terra Cognita, to the lands we know, by a bridge. Their hoard is beyond reason; avarice has no use for it; they have a separate cellar for emeralds and a separate cellar for sapphires; they have filled a hole with gold and dig it up when they need it. And the only use that is known for their ridiculous wealth is to attract to their larder a continual supply of food. In times of famine they have even been known to scatter rubies abroad, a little trail of them to some city of man, and sure enough their larders would soon be full again.

Their tower stands on the other side of that river known to Homer— ό ρόος ω' χεανοίο, as he called it—which surrounds the world. And where the river is narrow and fordable the tower was built by the Gibbelins' gluttonous sires, for they liked to see burglars rowing easily to their steps. Some nourishment that common soil has not the huge trees drained there with their colossal roots from both banks of the river.

There the Gibbelins lived and discreditably fed.

Alderic, Knight of the Order of the City and the Assault, hereditary Guardian of the King's Peace of Mind, a man not unremembered among the makers of myth, pondered so long upon the Gibbelins' hoard that by now he deemed it his. Alas that I should say of so perilous a venture, undertaken at dead of night by a valorous man, that its motive was sheer avarice! Yet upon avarice only the Gibbelins relied to keep their larders full, and once in every hundred years sent spies into the cities of men to see how avarice did, and always the spies returned again to the tower saying that all was well.

It may be thought that, as the years went on and men came by fearful ends on that tower's wall, fewer and fewer would come to the Gibbelins' table: but the Gibbelins found otherwise.

Not in the folly and frivolity of his youth did Alderic come to the tower, but he studied carefully for several years the manner in which burglars met their doom when they went in search of the treasure that he considered his. *In every case they had entered by the door.*

He consulted those who gave advice on this quest; he noted every detail and cheerfully paid their fees, and determined to do nothing that they advised, for what were their clients now? No more than examples of the savoury art, mere half-forgotten memories of a meal; and many, perhaps, no longer even that.

These were the requisites for the quest that these men used to advise: a horse, a boat, mail armour, and at least three men-at-arms. Some said, "Blow the horn at the tower door"; others said, "Do not touch it."

Alderic thus decided: he would take no horse down to the river's edge, he would not row along it in a boat, and he would go alone and by way of the Forest Unpassable.

How pass, you may say, by the unpassable? This was his plan: there was a dragon he knew of who if peasants' prayers are heeded deserved to die, not alone because of the number of maidens he cruelly slew, but because he was bad for the crops; he ravaged the very land and was the bane of a dukedom.

Now Alderic determined to go up against him. So he took horse and spear and pricked till he met the dragon, and the dragon came out against him breathing bitter smoke. And to him Alderic shouted, "Hath foul dragon ever slain true knight?" And well the dragon knew that this had never been, and he hung his head and was silent, for he was glutted with blood. "Then," said the knight, "if thou would'st ever taste maiden's blood again thou shalt be my trusty steed, and if not, by this spear there shall befall thee all that the troubadours tell of the dooms of thy breed."

And the dragon did not open his ravening mouth, nor rush upon the knight, breathing out fire; for well he knew the fate of those that did these things, but he consented to the terms imposed, and swore to the knight to become his trusty steed.

It was on a saddle upon this dragon's back that Alderic afterwards sailed above the unpassable forest, even above the tops of those measureless trees, children of wonder. But first he pondered that subtle plan of his which was more profound than merely to avoid all that had been done before; and he commanded a blacksmith, and the blacksmith made him a pickaxe.

Now there was great rejoicing at the rumour of Alderic's quest, for all folk knew that he was a cautious man, and they deemed that he would succeed and enrich the world, and they rubbed their hands in the cities at the thought of largesse; and there was joy among all men in Alderic's country, except perchance among the lenders of money, who feared they would soon be paid. And there was rejoicing also because men hoped that when the Gibbelins were robbed of their hoard, they would shatter their high-built bridge and break the golden chains that bound them to the world, and drift back, they and their tower, to the moon, from which they had come and to which they rightly belonged. There was little love for the Gibbelins, though all men envied their hoard.

So they all cheered, that day when he mounted his dragon, as though he was already a conqueror, and what pleased them more than the good that they hoped he would do to the world was that he scattered gold as he rode away; for he would not need it, he said, if he found the Gibbelins' hoard, and he would not need it more if he smoked on the Gibbelins' table.

When they heard that he had rejected the advice of those that gave it, some said that the knight was mad, and others said he was greater than those that gave the advice, but none appreciated the worth of his plan.

He reasoned thus: for centuries men had been well advised and had gone by the cleverest way, while the Gibbelins came to expect them to come by boat and to look for them at the door whenever their larder was empty, even as a man looketh for a snipe in the marsh; but how, said Alderic, if a snipe should sit in the top of a tree, and would men find him there? Assuredly never! So Alderic decided to swim the river and not to go by the door, but to pick his way into the tower through the stone. Moreover, it was in his mind to work below the level of the ocean, the river (as Homer knew) that girdles the world, so that as soon as he made a hole in the wall the water should pour in, confounding the Gibbelins, and flooding the cellars rumoured to be 20 feet in depth, and therein he would dive for emeralds as a diver dives for pearls.

And on the day that I tell of he galloped away from his home scattering largesse of gold, as I have said, and passed through many kingdoms, the dragon snapping at maidens as he went, but being unable to eat them because of the bit in his mouth, and earning no gentler reward than a spur-thrust where he was softest. And so they came to the swart arboreal precipice of the unpassable forest. The dragon rose at it with a rattle of wings. Many a farmer near the edge of the world saw him up there where yet the twilight lingered, a faint, black, wavering line; and mistaking him for a row of geese going inland from the ocean, went into their houses cheerily rubbing their hands and saying that winter was coming, and that we should soon have snow. Soon even there the twilight faded away, and when they descended at the edge of the world it was night and the moon was shining. Ocean, the ancient river, narrow and shallow there, flowed by and made no murmur. Whether the Gibbelins banqueted or whether they watched by the door, they also made no murmur. And Alderic dismounted and took his armour off, and saying one prayer to his lady, swam with his pickaxe. He did not part from his sword, for fear that he met with a Gibbelin. Landed the other side, he began to work at once, and all went well with him. Nothing put out its head from any window, and all were lighted so that nothing within could see him in the dark. The blows of his pickaxe were dulled in the deep walls. All night he worked, no sound came to molest him, and at dawn the last rock swerved and tumbled inwards, and the river poured in after. Then Alderic took a stone, and went to the bottom step, and hurled the stone at the door; he heard the echoes roll into the tower, then he ran back and dived through the hole in the wall.

He was in the emerald cellar. There was no light in the lofty vault above him, but, diving through 20 feet of water, he felt the floor all rough with emeralds, and open coffers full of them. By a faint ray of the moon he saw that the water was green with them, and, easily filling a satchel, he rose again to the surface; and there were the Gibbelins waist-deep in the water, with torches in their hands! And, without saying a word, *or even smiling*, they neatly hanged him on the outer wall—and the tale is one of those that have not a happy ending.

The Legend of
Beowulf
by Wilhelm Wägner

The poem "Beowulf," probably composed in the early eighth century, is the oldest known epic in English literature. It tells the story of a great hero who does battle with terrible monsters. Here is Wilhelm Wägner's (1843–1880) prose translation of the Old English verse.

One evening while the warriors were feasting in King Hrodgar's hall, a minstrel was called upon to sing. He tuned his harp, and sang of the coming of Skiöld, the son whom Odin sent to live a human life among mortal men. He told how the babe had been seen lying on a shield floating on the waves of the sea, how he had been drawn ashore and carefully tended, and how he had become a mighty king and warrior in Jutland. He sang of Skiöld's glorious life, of the kingdom he had left to his children and grandchildren; and last of all he sang of Hrodgar, Skiöld's most famous grandson, who, like him, was the patron of all peaceful arts, the protector of all peaceful folk, and the punisher of evil-doers.

Many heroes were collected round the king that night at Hirschhalle,—so called from the gigantic antlers of a royal stag which, carved in stone, adorned the battlements. At length the time came for the warriors to separate for the night, and as there were too many of them to be accommodated elsewhere, beds were made up for them in the great hall. Two and thirty brave men lay down to sleep on the couches spread for them; but next morning, when the servants came to waken them, they were gone. The room was in confusion, here and there might be seen stains of blood, and other signs of struggle.

King Hrodgar came himself as soon as he heard what had chanced, and examined the place carefully to try and discover the cause of the disaster. He followed the bloodstains through the hall, and out of doors, and there, in the soft earth, he saw the deep footprints of a giant. The whole affair was clear to him now. He knew that the monster Grendel, who had been banished from the land by the aid of a great magician, had at length returned. When it became known that Grendel had come back, ten warriors offered to keep watch in the hall, and fight the giant if he tried to come in. Next morning they were gone. They had either been surprised in their sleep, or had not been strong enough to withstand the monster. The Skiöldungs' people were brave and fearless, so twelve other heroes immediately offered their services. Eleven of them laid themselves down to sleep in their armour, while the twelfth, a minstrel, kept watch.

At midnight the giant came, smacking his great lips, and slowly dragging his heavy body along. The minstrel saw and heard all that took place; but he could neither speak nor move; he was, as it were, paralyzed with fear, and at last sank back senseless. Next morning, when with infinite trouble they restored him to consciousness, he either could not, or would not, tell what he had seen. He picked up his arms and his harp, pointed to the stains on the floor, and strode down to the strand without a word or sign of farewell to any one. A vessel was on the point of sailing for Gothland, so he went on board, and had soon left the ill-fated shores of Jutland behind.

Hygelak, a brave and heroic man, ruled over Gothland at this time. He was surrounded by a band of famous warriors, chief among whom was his nephew Beowulf (bee-hunter, *i.e.*, woodpecker), son of Ektheov. When the harper arrived in Gothland, he found that the Swedes had invaded the country, and a great battle was about to take place. A few days later the battle was fought, and would have gone badly with the Goths had it not been for the almost superhuman prowess displayed by Beowulf, who, in spite of repeated disaster, always returned to the charge. His coolness and courage kept up the spirits of his men, and at last the Swedes had to return to their own land, mourning the loss of their king, and of many a valiant hero.

During the feast that was given in honour of this great victory, the stranger minstrel sang to the assembled warriors of the great deeds of past and present times. He sang of Siegmund (Siegfried) the brave Wölsung, and of all his adventures with giants and dragons. Then, striking yet louder chords upon his harp, he sang of Beowulf's victory, and called upon him to do yet greater things, to seek out and slay the horrible fiend of the fen, Grendel, who nightly crept into the Skiöldung's hall, and fed on the blood of heroes.

Beowulf promised to go and try to slay the monster that had done such incredible mischief. Now one of the great lords, Breka by name, was envious of Beowulf's fame, and proposed that they two should on the morrow go down to the sea, and fight the monsters of the deep. They would then see which of them was the better man; and the one that reached the shore first after the battle was over should receive the prize of victory. It was agreed that this trial of strength should take place on the morrow, and King Hygelak promised to give the gold chain he wore round his neck to whichever was the victor.

Next morning the sun rose red in the east, the stormy sea moaned, groaned, and dashed upon the shore, as though demanding a human sacrifice. The two bold swimmers stood on the strand, arrayed in their shirts of mail, their swords in their hands. When the signal was given, they flung themselves into the raging sea, and were soon lost to sight. They kept close together, that they might come to each other's help if hard pressed by the monsters of the deep, but were at length parted by waves which bore them in different directions. Breka soon found himself in calm water, where he swam about until it was time to return. Beowulf, on the contrary, was carried to a place where the waves beat fiercely against great cliffs that towered above the water, a place that swarmed with polypi, sea-dragons, and horrible nixies, all lying in wait for their prey. Gigantic arms were stretched out to grasp him, but he cut them down with his sword. Monsters of every sort tried to clutch and stifle him, but he stabbed them through their scales. A nixie clasped him in his arms, and would have dragged him down to his cave, but he stabbed the monster to the heart, and drew him to the surface of the water. After a long struggle he again reached the open sea, and then strove with all his might to reach home before the sun should quite have set. The storm was over, so that there was the less danger. Breka was the first of the bold swimmers to reach the shore. He turned with a triumphant smile to greet Beowulf, but what was his astonishment, and that of all present, when the hero dragged the monstrous form of the nixie on the sands, and stretched it out before them. The princes crowded round the hideous creature, and gazed at his enormous limbs in speechless amazement.

"Here is the gold chain," said the king to Breka. "You have won it by hard labour; but my bold nephew has done even more than you, in that he has conquered and slain one of the monsters of the deep. I shall therefore give him my good sword Nägling with the golden hilt, and the Runic letters engraved in gold, that are sure to bring good fortune to the possessor."

Beowulf was held in high honour by the Goths; but he was not satisfied with the deeds he had already done. He longed to free the royal palace of the Skiöldungs from the monster Grendel, so he presently took ship for King Hrodgar's castle, accompanied by the minstrel, and fifteen noble and courageous Goths.

On their ship touching the strand below the fortress the watchman asked them who they were, and what brought them to King Hrodgar's land. When he learnt their names and business, he was pleased, and sent them on to the king. Hrodgar also received them with joy and gratitude. The minstrel tuned his harp and sang of Beowulf's heroic deeds, and prophesied that he would conquer and slay the monster of the morass. This praise made Hunford, one of the courtiers, angry and jealous. He said it was Breka, not Beowulf, that had won the golden chain; that the Gothic hero was undertaking an enterprise that would very likely lead him to his death; and he advised him to think twice

before attacking Grendel. Upon this, Beowulf exclaimed indignantly
that he had won a good sword instead of the golden chain, and that it
was sharp enough both to pierce the hide of the monster and to cut out
a slanderous tongue. Hrodgar bade the courtier be silent, and promised the Goth that if he were victorious, he would give him rich presents, and would enter into a firm alliance with his people.

At night-fall Hrodgar and his warriors withdrew, and serving-men
came into the hall to make up beds for the strangers. Beowulf felt so
confident of victory that he laid aside his helmet and shirt of mail, and
then gave his sword to the groom in attendance.

"I intend to master Grendel with my fists," he said; "he is unarmed,
and I will meet him in like fashion."

Midnight came, and the fiend of the fen rose out of his hiding-
place. He expected a feast that night, and, wrapping himself in a veil of
mist, made his way to the palace. He entered the banqueting-hall, and
at sight of the Goths a grin of satisfaction spread over his countenance,
displaying his great teeth, which resembled boar's tusks in size and
shape. At the same time he stretched out his hairy hands, which were
furnished with claws like those of an eagle.

The warriors were all sunk in a sleep so profound as to seem like
enchantment. Beowulf alone remained awake, and that only by a
mighty effort. He watched the monster through his half-closed eyes,
and saw him stand gloating over his intended victims, uncertain with
whom to commence. At last he seemed to have made up his mind, for
he hurled himself upon one of the sleepers, whom he rapidly slew,
drinking his blood with evident eagerness and enjoyment. He turned
next to Beowulf. But the hero seized his outstretched arm in such a
firm grip that he bellowed with pain. And now began a terrible
struggle between the man and the demon. The hall trembled to its
foundation, and threatened every instant to fall in ruins. The sleepers
awoke. They drew their swords and fell upon the monster; but their
weapons glanced harmlessly off his scaly hide, and they were fain to
take refuge in out-of-the-way corners, that they might not be trampled
under foot by the wrestlers. At length Grendel had to acknowledge
Beowulf's mastery, and now only strove to escape. With a mighty effort

he succeeded in freeing himself from the hero's grasp, but at the price of one of his arms, which, torn out at the socket, remained in his antagonist's hands. Then, with a howl of rage and pain, the demon fled back to his morass, leaving a trail of blood to mark the path by which he had gone.

The Gothic hero stood in the middle of the vast hall, holding his trophy in his right hand. The rays of the rising sun streamed in at the window and lighted up his head as with a halo. His companions crowded round him and greeted him with awe and reverence. Then he fastened the trophy of his victory over the door of the hall, and, having done this, he returned thanks to All-father for having given him strength to withstand the monster. The warriors knelt round him and joined him in his praise and thanksgiving.

When the Goths rose from their knees, they saw the king and his courtiers assembled in the hall, gazing in astonishment, now at them, and now at the monster's arm over the doorway. They told Hrodgar all that had happened during the night.

The king was at first too much amazed to speak, but recovering himself he desired his nephew, Hrodulf, to bring the gifts he had prepared to reward the victor. The warrior soon returned with some servants bearing the presents, which Hrodgar gave to Beowulf with many words of gratitude for the service he had done him and the country. He then prayed the Goth to remain his friend and his son's friend as long as they all should live.

After these things the king ordered a great feast to be prepared in honour of Beowulf. While this was being done, Hunford came forward and said:

"Noble Beowulf, I wronged you yesterday evening by my scornful speech, which I never would have made had I known what you were. Will you accept my sword Hrunting? it was made by dwarfs and the blade was hardened in dragon's blood, and, in taking it, will you grant me your forgiveness and friendship?"

The two heroes shook hands in token of their reconciliation, and went together to the feast.

When the feast was over, and the warriors sat over their wine-cups, the minstrel sang of Beowulf's victory over Grendel, and of the alliance which had that day been concluded between the Goths and the Skiöldungs. When the song was finished, Queen Walchtheov filled the goblets of all present. To Beowulf she presented a golden cup, telling him to keep it in remembrance of her, together with a ring and a necklace that she put in his hand, saying they were the same that Hama (Heime) in the olden time stole from the Brosing (Harlung?) treasure.

"Wear them," she added, "for our sakes, but also for your own, that you may come whole and victorious out of all the battles you will have to fight during a long life."

Beowulf thanked the queen in seemly fashion, and then the Lady Walchtheov retired.

The king and his men, and Beowulf and his friends, retired to the royal apartments, and beds were spread in the hall for many warriors, who, no longer fearing a one-armed Grendel, had now flocked to the palace and filled it to overflowing.

The night, however, was not to pass as quietly as was hoped.

At midnight a great column of water rose in the midst of the sea, and out of it came a gigantic woman, whose face was as grey as her garments. Her eyes shone like coals of fire, her bristly hair stood up on end, and her long bony arms were stretched out as though in search for prey. It was Grendel's mother, who had come to avenge her son. She came up out of the sea, crossed the morass, and entered the great hall; there she slew one warrior after another, in spite of their resistance, and slaked her thirst with their warm blood.

Deep was the sorrow of both king and people next day when they heard of the new misery that had come upon the land. Then Beowulf said that the cause of all this wretchedness was Grendel's mother, and that she would never cease to persecute the Skiöldungs as long as she lived. The only thing to be done was to seek her out in her own place, and there to slay her. This he was prepared to do. He begged Hrodgar to send the treasures that he and the queen had given him to his uncle Hygelak, king of Gothland, should he fall in his struggle with the giantess.

The whole party then went down to the shore, and Beowulf, wading into the sea, sought to find the road leading to the monster's dwelling. Finding that it was a longer way than he had imagined he came back to the shore and took leave of his friends, who one and all entreated him to give up the enterprise; but in vain.

"Wait for me two days and nights," he said, "and if I do not then return, you may know that I have been conquered by the mer-woman; but that is a matter that is in the hands of the gods alone in whom I trust."

Having thus spoken, the hero tore himself away from his weeping friends, and plunged into the raging sea with all his armour on, and with Hunford's good sword at his side.

He swam a long way. At last he saw a light deep down in the water. "Her dwelling must be here," he thought; "may the gods have me in their keeping!" He dived down, down, down to the bottom of the sea. Many a monster of hideous shape snapped at him as he shot past, but his coat of mail was proof against their teeth. Suddenly he felt himself caught as with hooks, and dragged along so swiftly that he could scarcely breathe. In another moment he found himself in the crystal hall of a submarine palace, and face to face with the antagonist he had sought.

Then began a terrible struggle. Beowulf and the giantess wrestled together for life and death. The walls of the palace shook so that they threatened to fall. The two wrestlers fell to the ground, Beowulf the undermost. The mer-woman pulled out a sharp knife to cut his throat, but Wieland's armour was too well made to give way, and Beowulf struggled to his feet again. The giantess then drew a monstrous sword, so heavy that few mortal men could have wielded it; but, before she could use it, Beowulf made an unexpected spring upon her, and wrenched the sword out of her hand. He clutched it firmly in both hands, and, swinging it with all his strength, cut off the woman's head. He felt so exhausted with his labours that he rested awhile, leaning on his sword. After a few minutes he looked about him, and saw Grendel lying dead on a couch of sea-weed. He cut off his head, meaning to take it with him as a sign of victory; but no sooner had he done so than the blood began to flow from the monster's body in a great gurgling stream, then it mixed with that of his mother's, and flowed out of the entrance door into the sea. The blade of the giantess' sword melted in it, and vanished as completely as ice in the rays of the sun. The golden hilt of the sword and Grendel's head were the only booty that Beowulf brought with him out of the depths of the sea.

His friends were collected on the shore, their hearts filled with a deadly anxiety, for they had seen the sea reddened with blood, and knew not whose it was. So when the hero appeared, they received him with acclamation.

Hrodgar and his people could find no words that would fitly express their gratitude to the hero who had saved the land from two such foes as Grendel and his mother; and when Beowulf and his warriors set out on their journey home, they were laden with blessings and gifts of all kinds.

Hygelak received his nephew with great delight, and listened to the tale of his adventures in speechless amazement and ecstasy.

Many years passed away in peace and quiet. At last the Frisians made a viking raid on Gothland, burning defenseless granges and cottages. Before King Hygelak could reach the place of their depredation, and offer them battle, they had taken to their ships again and were far away. The king determined to make a descent upon Friesland and punish the marauders; he would not listen to Beowulf when he advised him to delay till better preparations could be made for the onslaught.

The Goths landed in Friesland without opposition, and, marching into the country, revenged themselves by burning many a farmstead, and taking many a castle and town. Now the Frisians were a free and warlike people, whose heroes had played an honourable part in the great Bravalla-fight; the time had come for them to preserve their homes and liberty, and they did not shun to make ready for battle. A murderous engagement took place between them and their Gothic invaders, in which the latter were defeated, and obliged to fly to their ships, terror-stricken by the loss of their king. Beowulf and the noblest of the warriors alone stood their ground, and, although severely wounded, did not join in the retreat until they had rescued and carried off Hygelak's body. Then the conquered army set sail for Gothland.

Queen Hygd was at first so overwhelmed with sorrow for the loss of her husband that she could give no thought to matters of state; but after a time she roused herself from her grief, and began to consider what was best for the nation. It was well that she did so, for while she was still wrapped up in her sorrow, the barons had been quarreling among themselves, and creating much disturbance. The royal widow therefore called a meeting of the notables, and standing up before the assembly, spoke of the anarchy into which the country was falling, and said that as her son Hardred was too young to govern the kingdom, and preserve it from civil or foreign war, she strongly advised that Beowulf should be made king. The notables all cheered, and shouted that Beowulf should be their king; but the hero came forward and said:

"And do you really think, ye men of Gothland, that I would rob the child of my uncle and friend of his rights and honours. May the gods, the avengers of all evil, preserve me from such a crime! Here," he cried, lifting young Hardred on his shield, and holding him aloft, "here is our king. I will be his faithful guardian, and will act in his name till he is old enough and wise enough to take the reins of government into his own hands."

Nobody ventured to remonstrate with Beowulf; indeed, they all knew that remonstrance would be in vain. And so the matter was settled.

Years passed on, and Beowulf kept his word. He ruled the kingdom with a strong hand, and with absolute justice; and with the help of Queen Hygd educated the young king with so much wisdom, that when the sovereign power was placed in his hands, there was every hope that he would use it for his people's good. But Hardred was not long to rule over the Goths. Like his former guardian and teacher Beowulf, the king was of a frank and honest nature, and trustful of all who had not shown themselves his enemies. So when Eanmund and Eadgils, the sons of Ohtere, king of Swithiod, came to him as fugitives, he received them with all kindness. He often tried to make them see that they had been wrong in rebelling against their father, and offered to arrange matters with him on their behalf. One day, when he was speaking to them very earnestly on this subject, Eanmund, a passionate, hot-tempered man, told him that he was too young to advise a tried warrior like him. Hardred sharply told him to remember to whom he was speaking; and Eanmund, completely losing the little self-control he ever had, drew his sword and stabbed his royal host to the heart. Young Wichstan (Weohstan) at once avenged the king's murder by slaying Eanmund; but Eadgils fled back to Swithiod, and soon after succeeded his father on the throne.

The Gothic Allthing, the assembly of all the free men of the nation, was called together as soon as Hardred's murder was made known, and by a unanimous vote Beowulf was elected king in his cousin's stead. He accepted the office, and swore to rule his people justly.

When Hardred's death was noised abroad, several of the neighbouring peoples made raids upon Gothland, but Beowulf kept so strict a watch on the borders that the enemy was beaten back at all points. Scarcely was the country freed from the attacks of these sea-wolves, when Eadgils, king of Swithiod, came at the head of a large army to avenge his brother's death. The Goths and Swedes met and fought a murderous battle, in which many men were slain, and among them King Eadgils. After the death of their king the Swedes retired to their ships, and sailed back to their own land. The consequence of this victory was a lasting peace. No vikings dared attack the well-defended shores of Gothland, and but few quarrels arose among the nobles to disturb the internal peace of the realm. Beowulf ruled the land with great justice and wisdom. No one entreating his help was ever sent empty away, and no act of tyranny remained unpunished.

Forty years or more passed after this fashion. The hero had grown an old man, and hoped that the national peace and happiness would last as long as he lived. But he was to be rudely awakened from this dream. An enemy attacked Gothland, against whom all weapons and armies were useless. This was how it happened. A dishonest slave, who feared discovery and punishment at his master's hands, fled from home, and took refuge in a wild, rocky place. When he got there, he looked about for some cave in which he might take up his abode. Coming to one, he entered, but found it already tenanted by an immense dragon, which lay stretched on the ground asleep. Behind it, at the back of the cave, were treasures of all sorts. The man looked greedily at the shining mass of jewels and gold, and thought in his heart, "If I had but a few of these treasures, I could buy my freedom, and need no longer fear my master." This idea made him bold. He slipped softly past the monster, and stole a golden pot, the knob on whose lid was formed of a shining carbuncle. He escaped safely, and going back to his master, bought his freedom. Neither of the men had the slightest notion of the harm this deed would bring down upon the land.

The dragon, which had watched over its hoard for hundreds of years, and knew each costly thing by heart, saw at once that it had been robbed. At nightfall it crept out of its hole to look for traces of the thief. Finding none, it lifted up its voice and howled so loud, that the earth shook, at the same time flames issued from its mouth and burnt up granges and homesteads far and wide. The men, who sought to put out the fire, fell victims to its fury, or else were dragged into the monster's cave, where they perished miserably. This happened night after night; the devastation had no end. Many brave warriors went out against the dragon, and tried to kill it, but none of them could withstand the fiery blasts with which the creature defended itself.

The old king heard the story of these events with infinite sorrow. He determined himself to attack the monster, and when his friends remonstrated with him on his rashness, he replied that it was his duty to defend his people from all their enemies, and that the gods would help him. He further announced that he would have fought the dragon unarmed, as he had done the monster Grendel, the son of the sea-witch, but that he feared he could not make his way through the flames without such protection. He therefore had a shield made three times as thick as usual, and so large that it covered him completely. This done, he chose eleven of his bravest warriors to be his comrades in this adventure, among them Wichstan, the man who avenged King Hardred's death.

Beowulf and his companions set out on their journey, and in due course arrived at the dragon's cave, out of which there flowed a brook whose waters were made boiling hot by the monster's breath.

The king bade his friends wait a little way off, until they saw whether he needed their help, and then advancing to the mouth of the cave, he called the dragon to come forth. The great beast came out at his call, and a terrible struggle ensued. Both combatants were hidden from view in a dense cloud of smoke and fire. The rocks trembled and shook at the bellowing of the monster, which at the same time slashed out with its tail, whose blows fell like a sledge-hammer both in sound and regularity. For a moment the smoke and flames were blown aside by a puff of wind, and Beowulf's comrades saw that the dragon had just seized their king in its great jaws. They could not bear the sight, and ten of them slipped aside and strove to hide behind rocks and trees; but the eleventh brave Wichstan hastened to help his master. His shield was burnt up in a twinkling, and he was obliged to seek shelter behind the king. Both heroes seemed lost. The dragon tore down Beowulf's iron shield, and caught him a second time in its great jaws, crushing him between its teeth with such force that the iron rings of his coat of mail cracked like so much crockery, though they had been forged by Wieland himself. Then Wichstan seized his opportunity, when the beast's head was raised, the better to champ his prey, and plunged his sword into the fleshy part of its throat under the lower jaw. Upon this the dragon dropped the king, and encircled both its adversaries with its tail, but Beowulf at the same moment made a lunge at its open mouth, driving his weapon so deep that the point came out at the dragon's throat. After that they soon dispatched the monster, and then threw themselves on a ledge of rock, panting and exhausted.

When they had recovered a little, the heroes loosened their armour, and Wichstan saw that blood was oozing slowly from under the king's gorget. He wanted to bind up the slight wound; but Beowulf forbade him, saying that it would be useless, as the hurt had been given by the dragon's tooth, and the poison was already in his veins.

"I must die," he added, "but I go to my forefathers without sadness, though I am the last of my race, for my wife has given me no son and heir. I can look back on my past life with pleasure, for I have wronged no man, but have shown justice to all."

He then asked Wichstan to fetch him a drink of water, and afterwards to bring him the treasure out of the dragon's cave, that he might see, with his own eyes, the last gift he should ever make to his people.

His commands were obeyed, and a few minutes later he had passed away quietly and peacefully. Wichstan gazed at him in silent grief. Beowulf had been his dearest friend, and he felt that, with his death, his last tie to life was loosed. Meanwhile the ten warriors had come out of their hiding-places, when they found that all danger was over. On seeing what had chanced, they raised their voices in mourning; but Wichstan bade them hold their peace, or if they must weep, at least weep for their own cowardice, and not for the hero who had died at his post. He then advised them to make the best of their way to other lands, as he could not answer for their lives when the Goths became aware of the way in which they had deserted their king in his hour of need.

With bowed heads and shame-stricken faces the men turned away. They departed out of Gothland, and sought to hide their heads in countries where their names were unknown.

The body of Beowulf was borne to its funeral pile on the height called Hronesnäs, and there burnt amid the tears and sorrow of a nation. When the funeral rites had all been performed, the great treasure was taken back to the dragon's cave. For the Goths would have none of the gold their beloved king had won for them in his death. So it still lies hidden in the heart of the earth as in the olden time when the dragon guarded it from mortal ken. If it is useless to men, it is at all events not hurtful.

from

The Hegeling Legend

by Wilhelm Wägner

Wilhelm Wägner's (1843–1880) translation of the Hegeling Legend is adapted from a 13th-century German epic poem called "Gudrun" (sometimes "Kudrun"). The poem tells the story of a family of kings and their many adventures.

Zealously strove the knights in tilt and tournament to uphold their country's honour before Sigeband their king, when he held the Midsummer feast at his high castle Balian in Ireland. Sweetly the minstrels sang the praise of warlike deeds; and eagerly did boys of noble birth contend in games of hurling the spear and shooting with the bow. But evermore did little Hagen, the king's son, bear him best in the gentle strife; and the heart of his mother, the Lady Ute, was pleased.

One day the boys were amusing themselves by throwing their spears at a target. Having thrown them all, they ran forward to get their weapons again, the prince among the rest. As he could run faster than his companions, he reached the target first, and was busy pulling out his spear, when an old man called to the children to run back and hide themselves, for danger was approaching. He pointed up at the sky, crying, "A griffin!"

The Lady Ute looked, and saw a dark spot in the sky. It seemed too small to be dangerous. But it approached with the swiftness of an arrow, and the nearer it came the bigger it grew. All could now hear the noise made by its wings, and the sound resembled the rushing of the storm. The other boys fled in terror, but Hagen stood his ground nobly, and flung his spear with all his childish strength at the great bird. The weapon grazed its feathers harmlessly, and, at the same moment, it swooped down upon the child and bore him off in its talons.

So the feasting and mirth that had reigned at Castle Balian were turned into mourning, for the heir to the kingdom was gone. There was no hope of rescue; for though many a hero would willingly have fought with the griffin, its flight was so swift that no one could see where it was gone. Years passed on, and the king and queen had no news of their boy.

The griffin carried Hagen over land and sea to its nest, which it had built on a rock rising out of the water. It gave the boy to its young ones to eat, and then flew away in search of new booty. The little griffins fell upon the child, and prepared to devour him, but he made ready for his defense, thrust back their bills with all his strength, and caught the birds by the throat, striving to throttle them. At length one of the griffins, which was old enough to fly, caught him up, and carried him to the branch of a tree, that it might enjoy the sweet morsel alone. The bough was too weak to bear their united weight; it bent, broke, and the monster fell with the boy into a thicket of thorns beneath. The griffin fluttered away, and Hagen crept deeper into the thicket, unheeding the thorns. At length he reached a dark cave, where he sank down utterly exhausted. When he came to his senses, he saw a little girl about his own age standing a little way off and looking at him in astonishment. He raised himself on his elbow to see her better, upon which she fled to a greater distance, and no wonder, his appearance was so frightful. He was dirty, wounded, and bleeding, and his clothes hung about him in rags. He limped and crept as well as he could after the girl, and found that she had taken refuge in a large cave with two companions. They all shrieked when they saw him, for they thought he was either a wicked dwarf or a merman, who had followed them to devour them;

but when he told them that he was a prince who had been carried off by the griffin, and had only escaped from the monster as by a miracle, they were comforted, and shared their scanty fare with him.

After that they told him their story, which was much the same as his own. He found that the girl he had first seen was called Hilde, and that she was an Indian princess; the second was Hildburg of Portugal; and the third came from Isenland. The maidens nursed their young companion with such care that his wounds were soon healed. When he was well again, he went out to provide the needful food, and ventured deeper into the land than the maidens had ever done. He made himself a bow and arrows, the latter of which he tipped with fish-bones, and brought home small game of all kinds. As the children had no fire, they were obliged to eat their food raw, but they became all the stronger and hardier for that, and when Hagen was twelve years old he was almost a man in size.

Meanwhile the young griffins were grown up, and were able to go out in search of food for themselves, so that the boy could no longer wander about as freely and fearlessly as before. Nevertheless, one evening he ventured down to the shore, and crept under an overhanging rock which hid him from view. He looked out at the foaming waves and the wild sea, which now looked dark as night, and again was lighted up by the vivid flashes of lightning that burst from the storm-clouds. He listened fearlessly to the loud peals of thunder, the howling of the wind, and the sound of the frantic waves dashing against the rocks. But suddenly he caught sight of a boat, struggling in unequal conflict with the elements, and his heart was filled with hope and fear; of hope because thoughts of home and his parents were awakened in his breast; of fear, because the boat seemed too weak to live on such a sea. Then he saw it drive upon a point of rock. There was one shriek of agony, and ship and crew were swallowed in the waves. The storm raged on, until morning came, and seemed with its soft light to calm the fury of the winds. On the strand were scattered pieces of the wreck, and the corpses of the luckless mariners. Hagen was going to sally out in hopes of picking up something useful, when he was stopped by hearing the whirr of griffins' wings, and knew that the great birds had come down to the shore, having scented the prey. While the monsters were busied with their meal, the boy crept out of his hiding-place in search of something to eat. But he only found drift-wood, and a drowned man in full armour, with sword and bow, and a quiverful of sharp-pointed arrows. He could have shouted for joy, for now he had arms, such as he used to see at his father's court. Quickly he donned the coat of mail, covered his head with the helmet, girded the sword to his side, picked up the steel bow and the arrows. It was high time, for at this moment one of the griffins swooped down upon him. He drew his bow with all his strength and the arrow struck his enemy in the breast, bringing it down with fluttering wings. It fell at his feet, dead. A second monster shared its fate, and now the three other birds attacked him all at once; but he slew them all with his sword. He took the heads of the dead monsters to his friends in the cave, who had passed a wakeful night in anxiety for him. Great was their joy when they found that the griffins were dead. They accompanied their hero to the place of his victory, they helped him to throw the great birds into the sea, and then, true to pious custom, they assisted him to heap up a mound over the dead warrior whose weapons had helped Hagen to victory. Vainly did they seek for provisions among the wreckage; but they found a well-preserved box with flint and steel, which enabled them to make a fire. So they were now able to enjoy a well-dressed meal, which after their former privations seemed a perfect banquet.

Hagen went out hunting much more frequently than before, and slew bears, wolves, panthers and other wild beasts. Once, however, he met with a curious creature. It was covered with shining scales, its eyes glowed like red-hot coals, and horrible grinders gleamed in its blood-red jaws.

He aimed a sharp arrow at its back; but the point glanced off the glittering scales, and the monster turned upon the lad. A second arrow was likewise without effect. Hagen now drew his sword; but all his efforts were useless, and he only escaped the terrible claws by his marvellous agility. When he was almost exhausted by the long struggle, he at length saw his opportunity, and plunged his weapon into the great jaws. Overcome with fatigue, he seated himself on the still heaving body of the creature. He longed for a few drops of water to quench his thirst, and as none was near, he eagerly drank of the blood that streamed from the monster's wounds. Scarcely had he done this than his weakness vanished, and an unaccustomed sense of power took possession of him. He sprang to his feet, longing to put his new strength to the test. He would not have hesitated to fight all the griffins and giants in the world. He drew his sword, and slew a bear with one stroke. In like manner he killed two panthers, and a huge wolf. He was covered with blood from head to foot, and looked so ferocious carrying the bear on his shoulders, that he frightened the maidens in the cave; but he regained his accustomed manner when he had seen the gentle Hilde.

Many years came and went. Hagen and his three friends had enough to eat and drink and were clothed in the skins of wild beasts. Although they were very happy together, they longed to return to the haunts of men, and often cast anxious looks over the sea in hopes of seeing some ship approach. At length one morning, when the three maidens were standing on the shore, a white sail appeared on the horizon, and came gradually nearer and nearer. They lighted a fire, and called Hagen, who joined them fully armed. Their signals were seen from the ship, and a boat was sent out, which soon approached the shore. The helmsman uttered a cry of astonishment when he saw their strange dress, and asked if they were human beings or water-sprites.

"We are poor unfortunate people," said Hagen; "take us with you, for God's sake."

So the sailors took them to the ship, and they were soon on board. The captain looked at them in amazement, and Hagen, in answer to his questions, told their whole story. When he spoke of his father Sigeband, the powerful king of Balian, the captain exclaimed:

"What! you can kill griffins like flies! Still you are a lucky catch for me, for I am that Count of Garadie to whom your father has done so much injury. You shall now be hostage till a proper sum of money is paid to me. Here, men, put this young fellow in chains, and steer for Garadin."

Scarcely had the Count said these words when Hagen fell into a Berserker rage. He flung the sailors, who would have laid hold of him, into the sea; then, drawing his sword, he rushed upon the master of the vessel, when a soft hand was laid upon his arm. He turned round furiously, but at the sight of Hilde's gentle, lovely face, his terrible anger vanished. Hilde spoke gentle words of conciliation, and Hagen listened. Then, turning to the Count, he promised to make all matters right between him and the king, if he would at once steer for Balian. The captain agreed to do so, and steered for Ireland. Favourable winds swelled the sails, and ten days later the walls and towers of Balian hove in sight. Naturally his parents did not at first recognize Hagen; but great was their rejoicing when they found who he was. A firm peace was concluded with the Count of Garadie, and the three maidens were received with all honour and courtesy.

Hagen did not long remain quietly at home in his father's house. He wished to see something of the world, and to gain both name and fame.

Time passed on, and Hagen, who was known far and wide for his great deeds, was appointed to rule the land in his old father's place. When urged by his mother to choose a wife, now that he had settled down after his wanderings, he wooed fair Hilde, the sweet companion of his childhood, and soon afterwards married her.

Queen Ute lived to hold a grandchild in her arms, who was called Hilde after her mother; but soon after that she and Sigeband died, leaving their son to rule alone.

The Princess Hilde grew up beautiful, and many wooers came to Balian to ask for her hand in marriage. But Hagen would receive no man as a son-in-law without first fighting with him, declaring that he would never give his daughter to one that was not stronger than himself. Whoever ventured to try conclusions with him had the worst of it. Wild Hagen, the terror of kings, became also the terror of wooers, and before long, he really had his house to himself.

from

The Iliad for Boys and Girls

by Alfred Church

The Iliad tells the story of the Trojan War, which pitted Greek heroes such as Achilles, Patroclus and Ajax against the Trojans, led by Hector. Achilles, sulking over a dispute with his friends, gives his armor to his beloved friend Patroclus, who leads the Greek Myrmidon troops into battle. Alfred Church (born 1933) in his prose translation of Homer's epic poem describes the results.

Patroclus stood by Achilles, weeping bitterly. And Achilles said to him: "What is the matter, Patroclus, that you weep? You are like a girl-child that runs along by her mother's side, and holds her gown and cries till she takes her up in her arms. Have you heard bad news from Phthia? Yet your father still lives, I know, and so does the old man Peleus. Or are you weeping for the Greeks because they perish for their folly, or, maybe, for the folly of their King?"

Then Patroclus answered: "Be not angry with me, great Achilles. The Greeks are in great trouble, for all the bravest of their chiefs are wounded, and yet you still keep your anger, and will not help them. They say that Peleus was your father and Thetis your mother. Yet I should say, so hard are you, that a rock was your father and your mother the sea. If you will not go forth to the battle because you have had some warning from the gods, then let me go, and let your people, the Myrmidons, go with me. And let me put on your armour; the Trojans will think that you have come back to the battle, and the Greeks will have a breathing space."

So Patroclus spoke, entreating Achilles, but he did not know that it was for his own death that he asked. And Achilles answered: "It is no warning that I heed, and that keeps me back from the battle. Such things trouble me not. But these men were not ashamed to stand by when their King took away from me the prize which I had won with my own hands. But let the past be past. I said that I would not fight again till the Trojans should bring the fire near to my own ships. But now, for I see that the people are in great need, you may put on my armour, and lead my people to the fight. And, indeed, it is time to give help, for I see that the Trojans are gathered about the ships, and that the Greeks have scarce standing ground between their enemies and the sea. And I do not see anywhere either Diomed with his spear, nor King Agamemnon; only I hear the voice of Hector, as he calls his people to the battle. Go, therefore, Patroclus, and keep the fire from the ships. But when you have done this, come back and fight no more with the Trojans, for it is my business to conquer them, and you must not take my glory from me. And mind this also: when you feel the joy of battle in your heart, be not over-bold; go not near to the wall of Troy, lest one of the gods meet you and harm you. For these gods love the Trojans, and especially the great archer Apollo with his deadly bow."

So these two talked together in the tent. But at the ships Ajax could hold out no longer. For the javelins came thick upon him and clattered on his helmet and his breastplate, and his shoulder was weary with the weight of his great shield. Heavily and hard did he breathe, and the great drops of sweat fell upon the ground. Then, at the last, Hector came near and struck at him with his sword. Him he did not hit, but he cut off the head of his spear. Great fear came on Ajax and he gave way, and the Trojans put torches to the ship's stern, and a great flame rose up into the air. When Achilles saw the flames, he struck his thigh with his hand and said: "Make haste, Patroclus, for I see the fire rising up from the ships."

Then Patroclus put on the armour—breastplate and shield and helmet—and bound the sword on his shoulder, and took a great spear in his hand. But the great Pelian spear he did not take, for that no man could wield but Achilles only. Then the charioteer yoked the horses to the chariot. Two of the horses, Bayard and Piebald, were immortal, but the third was of a mortal breed. And while he did this, Achilles called the Myrmidons to battle. Fifty ships he had brought to Troy, and fifty men in each. And when they were assembled he said: "Forget not, ye Myrmidons, what you said when first I kept you back from the battle, how angry you were, and how you blamed me, complaining that I kept you back against your will. Now you have the thing that you desired."

So the Myrmidons went forth to battle in close array, helmet to helmet and shield to shield, close together as are the stones which a builder builds into a wall. Patroclus went before them in the chariot of Achilles, with the charioteer by his side. And as they went, Achilles went to the chest which stood in his tent, and opened it, and took from it a great cup which Thetis his mother had given him. No man drank out of that cup but Achilles only. Nor did he pour libations out of it to any of the gods but to Zeus only. First he cleansed the cup with sulphur and then with water from the spring. After this he filled it with wine, and standing in the space before the tent he poured out from it to Zeus, saying: "O Zeus, this day I send my dear comrade to the battle. Be thou with him; make him strong and bold, and give him glory, and bring him home safe to the ships, and my people with him."

So he prayed; and Father Zeus heard his prayer: part he granted, but part he denied.

Meanwhile Patroclus with the Myrmidons had come to the place where the battle was so hot, namely, the ship to which Hector had put the torch and set it on fire. And when the Trojans saw him and the armour which he wore, they thought that it had been Achilles, who had put away his anger, and had come forth again to the battle. Nor was it long before they turned to flee. So the battle rolled back again to the trench, and many chariots of the Trojans were broken, for when they crossed it for the second time they took their chariots with them; but the horses of Achilles sprang across it in their stride, so nimble were they and so strong. And great was the fear of the Trojans; even the great Hector fled. The heart of Patroclus was set upon slaying him, for he had forgotten the command which Achilles had laid upon him, that when he had saved the ships from the fire he should not fight any more. But though he followed hard after him, he could not overtake him, so swift were the Trojan horses. Then he left following him and turned back, and caused the chariot to be driven backwards and forwards, so that he might slay the Trojans as they sought to fly to the city.

But there were some among the Trojans and their allies who would not flee. Among these was Sarpedon the Lycian; and he, when he saw his people flying before Patroclus, cried aloud to them: "Stand now and be of good courage: I myself will try this great warrior and see what he can do." So he leapt down from his chariot, and Patroclus also leapt down from his, and the two rushed at each other, fierce and swift as two eagles. Sarpedon carried a spear in either hand, and he threw both of them together. With the one he wounded to the death one of the horses of Achilles, that which was of a mortal strain, but the other missed its aim, flying over the left shoulder of Patroclus. But the spear of Patroclus missed not its aim. Full on the heart of Sarpedon it fell, and broke through his armour, and bore him to the earth. He fell, as a pine or a poplar falls on the hills before the woodman's axe. And as he fell, he called to Glaucus his kinsman "Now show yourself a man, O Glaucus; suffer not the Greeks to spoil me of my arms." And when he had said so much, he died. Now Glaucus was still troubled by the wound which Teucer the archer had given him. But when he heard the voice of Sarpedon he prayed to Apollo, saying: "Give me now strength that I may save the body of my kinsman from the hands of the Greeks." And Apollo heard him and made him whole of his wound. Then he called first to the Lycians, saying, "Fight for the body of your king," and next to the Trojans, that they should honour the man who had come from his own land to help them, and lastly to Hector himself, who had now returned to the battle. "Little care you, O Hector," he said, "for your allies. Lo! Sarpedon is dead, slain by Patroclus. Will you suffer the Myrmidons to carry off his body and do dishonour to it?"

Hector was much troubled by these words, and so were all the men of Troy, for among the allies there was none braver than Sarpedon. So they charged and drove back the Greeks from the body; and the Greeks charged again in their turn. No one would have known the great Sarpedon as he lay in the middle of the tumult, so covered was he with dust and blood. But at the last the Greeks drove back the Trojans from the body, and stripped it of its arms; but the body itself they harmed not. For at the bidding of Zeus, Apollo came down and carried it out of the tumult, and gave it to Sleep and Death that they should carry it to the land of Lycia. Then again Patroclus forgot the commands of Achilles, for he thought in his heart, "Now shall I take the city of Troy," for, when he had driven the Trojans up to the very gates, he himself climbed on to an angle of the wall. Three times did he climb upon it, and three times did Apollo push him back, laying his hand upon the boss of his shield. And when Patroclus climbed for the fourth time, then Apollo cried to him in a dreadful voice: "Go back, Patroclus; it is not for you to take the great city of Troy, no, nor even for Achilles, who is a far better man than you." Then Patroclus went back, for he feared the anger of the god. But though he thought no more of taking the city, he raged no less against the Trojans. Then did Apollo put it into the heart of Hector to go against the man. So Hector said to his charioteer: "We will see whether we cannot drive back this Patroclus, for it must be he; Achilles he is not, though he wears his armour." When Patroclus saw them coming he took a great stone from the ground, and cast it at the pair. The stone struck the charioteer full on the helmet. And as the man fell head foremost from the chariot, Patroclus laughed aloud, and said: "See now, how nimble is this man! See how well he dives! He might get many oysters from the bottom of the sea, diving from the deck of a ship, even though it should be a stormy day. Who would have thought that there would be such skillful divers in Troy?"

Three times did Patroclus charge into the ranks of the Trojans, and each time he slew nine warriors. But when he charged the fourth time, then, for the hour of his doom was come, Apollo stood behind him, and gave him a great blow on his neck, so that he could not see out of his eyes. And the helmet fell from his head, so that the plumes were soiled with the dust. Never before had it touched the ground, from the first day when Achilles wore it. The spear also which he carried in his hand was broken, and the shield fell from his arm, and the breastplate on his body was loosened. Then, as he stood without defence and confused, one of the Trojans wounded him in the back with his spear. And when he tried to hide himself behind his comrades, for the wound was not mortal, Hector thrust at him with his spear, and hit him above the hip, and he fell to the ground. And when the Greeks saw him fall they sent up a dreadful cry. Then Hector stood over him, and said: "Did you think, Patroclus, that you would take our city, and slay us with the sword, and carry away our wives and daughters in your ships? This you will not do, for, lo! I have overcome you with my spear, and the fowls of the air shall eat your flesh. And the great Achilles cannot help you at all. Did he not say to you, 'Strip the fellow's shirt from his back and bring it to me'? and you, in your folly, thought that you would do it."

Patroclus answered: "You boast too much, O Hector. It is not by your hand that I am overcome; it has been Apollo who has brought me to my death. Had twenty such as you are come against me, truly I had slain them all. And mark you this: death is very near to you, for the great Achilles will slay you."

Then said Hector: "Why do you prophesy my death? Who has shown you the things to come? Maybe, as I have slain you, so shall I also slay the great Achilles." So Hector spoke, but Patroclus was dead already. Then he drew the spear from the wound, and went after the charioteer of Achilles, hoping to slay him and to take the chariot for spoil, but the horses were so swift that he could not come up with them.

Very fierce was the fight for the body of Patroclus, and many warriors fell both on this side and on that; and the first to be killed was the man who had wounded him in the back; for when he came near to strip the dead man of his arms, King Menelaüs thrust at him with his spear and slew him. He slew him, but he could not strip off his arms, because Hector came and stood over the body, and Menelaüs did not dare to stand up against him, knowing that he was not a match for him in fighting. Then Hector spoiled the body of Patroclus of the arms which the great Achilles had given him to wear. But when he laid hold of the body, and began to drag it away to the ranks of the Trojans, the Greater Ajax came forward, and put his big shield before it. As a lioness stands before its cubs and will not suffer the hunter to take them, so did Ajax stand before the body of Patroclus and defend it from the Trojans. And Hector drew back when he saw him. Then Glaucus the Lycian spoke to him in great anger: "Are you not ashamed, O Hector, that you dare not stand before Ajax? How will you and the other Trojans save your city? Truly your allies will not fight any more for you, for though they help you much, yet you help them but little. Did not Sarpedon fall fighting for you, and yet you left him to be a prey to the dogs? And now, had you only stood up against this Ajax, and dragged away the body of Patroclus, we might have made an exchange, giving him and his arms, and receiving Sarpedon from the Greeks. But this may not be, because you are afraid of Ajax, and flee before him when he comes to meet you."

Hector answered: "I am not afraid of Ajax, nor of any man. But this I know, that Zeus gives victory now to one and now to another; this only do I fear, and this only, to go against the will of Zeus. But wait here, and see whether or no I am a coward."

Now he had sent the armour of Patroclus to the city; but when he heard Glaucus speak in this manner, he ran after the men who were carrying it and overtook them, and stripped off his own armour, and put on the armour of Achilles. And when Zeus saw him do this thing he was angry, and said to himself, "These arms will cost Hector dear." Nevertheless, when he came back to the battle, all men were astonished, for he seemed like to the great Achilles himself. Then the Trojans took heart again, and charged all together, and the battle grew fiercer and fiercer. For the Greeks said to themselves: "It were better that the earth should open her mouth and swallow us up alive than that we should let the Trojans carry off the body of Patroclus." And the Trojans said to themselves: "Now if we must all be slain fighting for the body of this man, be it so; but we will not yield." Now while they fought the horses of Achilles stood apart from the battle, and the tears rushed down from their eyes, for they loved Patroclus, and they knew that he was dead. Still they stood in the same place; they would not enter into the battle, neither would they turn back to the ships. And the charioteer could not move them with the lash, or with threats, or with gentle words. As a pillar stands by the grave of some dead man, so they stood; their heads drooped to the ground, and the tears trickled down from their eyes, and their long manes were trailed in the dust.

When Zeus saw them he pitied them in his heart. And he said: "It was not well that I gave you, immortal as you are, to a mortal man, for of all things that live and move upon the earth, surely man is the most miserable. But Hector shall not have you. It is enough for him, yea, it is too much that he should have the arms of Achilles."

Then the horses moved from their place, and obeyed their driver as before; and Hector could not take them, though he greatly desired so to do.

All this time the battle raged yet more and more fiercely about the body of Patroclus. At the last, when the Greeks were growing weary, and the Trojans pressed them more and more, Ajax said to Menelaüs, for these two had borne themselves more bravely in the battle than all the others: "See now if you can find Antilochus, Nestor's son, and bid him run and carry the news to Achilles that Patroclus is dead, and that the Greeks and Trojans are fighting for his body." So Menelaüs went, and found Antilochus on the left side of the battle. And he said to him: "I have bad news for you. You see that the Trojans prevail in the battle to-day. And now Patroclus lies dead. Run, therefore, to Achilles and tell him; maybe he can yet save the body; as for the arms, Hector has them."

Antilochus was greatly troubled to hear the news; his eyes filled with tears, and he could not speak for grief. But he gave heed to the words of Menelaüs, and ran to tell Achilles what had happened.

And Menelaüs went back to Ajax, where he had left him standing close by the body of Patroclus. And he said to him: "I have found Antilochus, and he is carrying the news to Achilles. Yet I doubt whether he will come to the battle, however great his anger may be and his grief, for he has no armour to cover him. Let us think, therefore, how we may best save the body of Patroclus from the Trojans."

Ajax said: "Do you and Meriones run forward and lift up the body and carry it away." So Menelaüs and Meriones ran forward and lifted up the body. But when they would have carried it away, then the Trojans ran fiercely at them. So the battle raged; neither could the Greeks save the body, nor could the Trojans carry it away. Meanwhile Antilochus came to Achilles where he sat by the door of his tent. With a great fear in his heart he sat, for he saw that the Greeks fled and the Trojans pursued after them. Then said Nestor's son: "I bring bad news. Patroclus is dead, and Hector has his arms, but the Greeks and Trojans are fighting for his body."

Then Achilles threw himself upon the ground, and took the dust in his hands, and poured it on his head, and tore his hair. And all the women wailed aloud. And Antilochus sat weeping; but while he wept he held the hands of Achilles, for he was afraid that in his anger he would do himself a mischief. But his mother heard his cry, where she sat in the depths of the sea, and came to him and laid her hand upon his head, and said "Why do you weep, my son? Tell me; hide not the matter from me." Achilles answered: "All that you asked from Zeus, and that he promised to do, he has done: but what is the good? The man whom I loved above all others is dead, and Hector has my arms, for Patroclus was wearing them. As for me, I do not wish to live except to avenge myself upon him."

Then said Thetis: "My son, do not speak so: do you not know that when Hector dies, the hour is near when you also must die?"

Then Achilles cried in great anger: "I would that I could die this hour, for I sent my friend to his death; and I, who am better in battle than all the Greeks, could not help him. Cursed be the anger that sets men to strive with one another, as it made me strive with King Agamemnon. And as for my fate—what matters it? Let it come when it may, so that I may first have vengeance on Hector. Seek not, therefore, my mother, to keep me back from the battle."

Thetis answered: "Be it so, my son: only you cannot go without arms, and these Hector has. But to-morrow I will go to Hephaestus, that he may make new arms for you."

But while they talked, the Trojans pressed the Greeks still more and more, so that Ajax himself could no longer stand against them. Then truly they would have taken the body of Patroclus, had not Zeus sent Iris to Achilles with this message: "Rouse yourself, son of Peleus, or, surely, Patroclus will be a prey to the dogs of Troy." But Achilles said: "How shall I go? For I have no arms, nor do I know of any one whose arms I could wear. I might shift with the shield of great Ajax; but this he is carrying, as is his custom, in the front of the battle."

Then said Iris: "Go only to the trench and show yourself, for the Trojans will be swift and draw back, and the Greeks will have a breathing-space."

So Achilles ran to the trench. And Athené put her great shield about his shoulders, and set as it were a circle of gold about his head, so that it shone like to a flame of fire. To the trench he went, but he obeyed the word of his mother, and did not mix in the battle. Only he shouted aloud, and his voice was as the voice of a trumpet. It was a terrible sound to hear, and the hearts of the men of Troy were filled with fear. The very horses were frightened, and started aside, so that the chariots clashed together. Three times did Achilles shout across the trench, and three times did the Trojans fall back. Twelve chiefs perished that hour; some were wounded by their own spears, and some were trodden down by their own horses; for the whole army was overcome with fear, from the front ranks to the hindermost. Then the Greeks took up the body of Patroclus from the place where it lay, and put it on the bier, and carried it to the tent of Achilles, and Achilles himself walked by its side weeping. This had been a sad day, and to bring it sooner to an end Hera commanded the sun to set before his time. So did the Greeks rest from their labours.

from

Grimbold's Other World

by Nicholas Stuart Gray

The boy in Nicholas Stuart Gray's (1922-1981) novel is named Muffler; he was found in a hen's nest when he was a baby. Two farmers adopted him, and he takes care of their animals. He also composes songs and poems.

One evening it was later than usual when Muffler came back from the mountain pastures. Meg grew anxious and begged Simon to go out in search. Then there was a thudding of hoofs in the lane outside, the click and creak of a gate, a voice calling good night. Muffler came into the kitchen, wet with dew, and apologetic. He said he had forgotten the time in making a poem.

"Silly boy," said Meg, rumpling his hair. "You're soaked to the skin! Oh my, you will get such a cold!"

And he did.

In the morning he sneezed thirty times. And Meg made him stay in bed, saying she had told him so. She brought an extra blanket and a hot brick to warm the truckle bed, and she lit a fire in the attic, for the boy seemed slightly feverish.

"Now you keep quiet," said she, "and sleep all day, my dear."

"My goats . . ." said Muffler, hoarsely.

"They'll do well enough," she laid her hand against his hot forehead. "Young Robin from up the lane can see to them till you're better."

And she went away. And Muffler fell asleep, and the day passed. Meg came several times with hot milk, and, in the evening, a potion of herbs. It was not nice, but she gave its recipient a spoonful of honey to sweeten the taste.

"The goats have been so naughty," she told him. "They ran from Robin, and came back here. Did you hear 'em bleating under your window? They ate nearly all my daffodils, too! We've put 'em in the big meadow, and there they can stay till you're well enough to deal with them. Wicked things!" and she laughed.

Muffler watched her then, while she banked charcoal round the smoldering logs in the fireplace. His eyes felt heavy, his head ached, and his feet seemed to be pinned to the bed. Meg came and looked down at him kindly. Then a very disapproving expression crossed her face.

"Ah," said she, "we'll have that out of here, for a start! When did he sneak in?"

She scooped up a large black cat who had been sprawling over Muffler's feet, dropped him on the floor with a thud, and shooed him toward the door. He glanced at her remotely and strolled without haste from the room.

"I didn't know he was there," wheezed Muffler.

"Nor I, my dear! He's a saucy brute, that one—not like my dear Dulcie." The farmer's wife was turning Muffler's pillows as she spoke. "He's been hanging about the farm all day. He must be a stray, though I've never seen him in the village before. And he's a big, handsome beast. But nervy! I don't know why I fed him!"

"I do," said Muffler. "He'd starve, otherwise."

"That one would never go hungry," smiled Meg. "He's a creature of darkness if ever I saw one! He can settle here, and work for his living, and welcome—but I think he'll go, as stealthy as he came."

She smoothed the hair from the boy's forehead and stooped to kiss him.

"There's water by you, if you wake. But I hope you sleep quiet all night. Good dreams to you, my dear."

She blew out the candle and went away. The door closed softly behind her, leaving the room to twilight and the gentle flicker of the fire.

A heavy weight landed with a thump on the bed, and a husky voice spoke in the stillness.

"Might I have your attention?" it said.

Muffler stared at the big cat. The light from the fire showed gleaming black fur and the glint of bright green eyes.

"I thought Mother Meg put you outside."

"I came back. No one puts me where I do not choose to go."

The cat began to work his paws, busily pulling long threads from the coverlet.

"I never heard a cat talk before," said Muffler sleepily. "Are you really a stray?"

The cat's eyes slitted. He arched his neck and licked his chest. It seemed he did not mean to answer. Then he favored Muffler with an impassive stare.

"You are thinking of some other animal," said he, coldly. "In order to stray, one must first belong. I do not belong."

"I beg your pardon."

"Cats are not like other creatures," said the ebony beast. "They live in two worlds. One is the world of daylight. The other, the world of night."

His tone was slightly sinister and Muffler was fascinated.

"Mother Meg was right, then," he said. "She called you a creature of darkness."

"I heard her," said the cat loftily. "And she doesn't know the half! For I am Grimbold."

Muffler pulled himself up higher against his pillow. His head throbbed. And the cat paced on the bed and sat bolt upright on the boy's middle. He was extremely heavy, but Muffler was too enthralled by him to protest. He held out his hand and Grimbold touched it delicately with the tip of his cool nose.

"I've heard that you are kind, as humans go," said he. "And that you make songs and tell tales of magic. I thought you might give me a hand."

"Me?" said Muffler doubtfully, and sneezed three times. "I've got a cold, you know."

The cat eyed him from the very end of the bed, where he had retired in a flash.

"I know," he said. "Please give me some warning before you do that again!"

"I had no idea I was going to," Muffler apologized. "I'll be glad to help you if I can. It'll be no trouble, I'm sure."

"Won't it, just!" said Grimbold darkly. "But your troubles don't concern me. Only those of my master."

"I thought cats didn't have masters?"

"A loose term," came the airy reply. "Put it like this—I have a *friend* in the night world. And he's in a frightful mess!"

The cat's eyes opened until they were like lamps against his dark fur. He looked most formidable. Muffler was enchanted.

"Who is your friend?" breathed the boy. "And what has he done?"

"He's the son of a great sorcerer and he has offended his father."

"Oh! And—and where is he?"

Grimbold closed his eyes. He said, in a slightly affected voice,

"Actually—he's tied hand and foot in the middle of a block of ice!"

He scratched his left ear. But Muffler thought he was more anxious than he seemed.

"Well, what can *I* do about it?"

"You know your farmer's wife's cat?" said Grimbold. "A small fat gray female. . . ."

"Dulcie?" said Muffler. "Oh, yes. She's sweet."

"That's as may be," purred Grimbold, deep in his throat. "Anyway, she told me that you once got up in the middle of the night and climbed the king oak in the meadow, because you heard her crying there. . . ."

"As I reached her," said Muffler indignantly, "she went down the other side."

"A misunderstanding," said Grimbold, in a dry voice. "She was not calling for help—but for me. And it isn't the point. You don't fear the dark, and you're good at climbing. And you're kind. Come with me."

The big cat stared at him compellingly and the boy got out of bed.

For a moment his head whirled like a top and his knees buckled. He shivered with cold. But he managed somehow to get to a stool where his clothes were folded. He began to dress, putting on his old woolen tunic and belting it.

"How can I leave the house without being seen?" said Muffler. "Mother Meg would never let me out."

"Easy," said the cat.

He stretched his gleaming body, limb by limb. He sprang from the bed and strolled over to the fireplace.

"You're shivering," said he. "Are you cold?"

"I *have* a cold."

"Ah, then you mustn't risk further chills. Have a word with the fire."

"A word with *what?*"

"How dull can humans be?" wondered Grimbold. "All living things speak, don't they? The fire is alive. Stoop close, boy, and listen to it."

Muffler blinked and obeyed. He knelt on the rag rug and leaned down toward the bars of the grate. He heard the crack and rustle of the little flames as they licked in and out of the charcoal. The warmth brought a flush to his cheek, though his hands and feet were cold as snow. Then he heard small voices whispering together.

"What's it like outside?" they hissed softly.

"Who knows?"

"We'll know soon. When we turn to smoke and fly away."

"Will it be frightening?"

"Will it be fun?"

"If we've been good, shall we be happy?"

"Who knows?"

"We'll know soon."

This conversation went on and on. For the flames were turning into smoke, even while they questioned, and went singing up the chimney. And new flames formed, wondered, and became smoke in their own turn. And, behind all the smaller voices, a vast, soft, faraway song was sighing:

"Out and away—away I go . . .
Now I am smoke, and now I know . . .

• • •

The boy listened with a catch in his breath to hear so sad and so happy a thing. The cat stirred by his side.

"Speak to them," he murmured. "Ask them for warmth. Preferably in rhyme. It always goes down well when there's magic in the air."

Muffler looked dubious, but he thought for a moment and then said timidly:

> "Smoke and flame, gray and gold,
> Help me, for I've got a cold."

He glanced at the cat.

"Go on," prompted that dark creature. "Ask for heat to take away with you. It's very important."

The boy hesitated and then spoke again to the fire:

> "Here I kneel and make a plea;
> Give me warmth to take with me."

"Oh, jolly good!" said the cat. "For the spur of the moment."

The flames went on rustling and whispering together.

"What's it like outside?"

"Who knows?"

"Did you hear what I heard?"

"Yes, if you heard what I did."

"Someone spoke to us."

"What's it like outside?"

"He fears it will be cold, from what he said."

"And he spoke so gently. Give him what he asks."

The voices in the fire seemed suddenly to fuse together and spoke in one soft murmur:

> "Flame and smoke, gold and gray,
> In your hands their magic lay;
> Take the gift that you desire,
> With the friendship of the fire:

Warmth of heart you had before;
Warmth go with you evermore."

And Muffler stopped shivering. A gentle glow started at his finger-
tips and crept all through him from head to foot. He felt like purring.
For a moment he thought he was. But it was the cat.

"Now follow me!" cried Grimbold.

And he sprang up the chimney. After a moment he came down again.

"Aren't you coming?" he said crossly.

"Up there?" faltered Muffler. "But—the fire. . . ."

"Don't tread on it!" snapped the cat. "Use your brain! The chimney
is wider than you think, and it's as easy to climb as a tree."

He vanished again in one huge bound. Muffler followed with some
misgiving.

Being banked low, the fire was not much of an obstacle. By taking
a deep breath before starting up, the boy escaped suffocation in the
smoke. But the brick chimney was not as easy to climb as the cat
seemed to think. Soot was everywhere, falling about in soft fluffy
lumps. But finally Muffler emerged into the moonlight and gasped and
coughed. Luckily for him, the chimney pot and part of the old stack
had been blown away in a gale long ago. He scrambled out on to the
roof and took a long breath of cool night air.

He was in a realm of sloping thatch, angled roofs, gables and curly
chimneys, for the farm was an old and rambling building. A bat sidestepped past his head, and owls were crying round the barns below.
Grimbold was sitting like a black statue on the roofridge nearby, his
ears alert, and his whiskers quivering with excitement. His mouth
opened in a silent laugh when he saw Muffler's soot-smeared face
emerge into the open, and he started to pick his way delicately down a
long slope of thatch.

"It's an easy jump at the bottom," said he, and leaped into darkness.

This also was not quite such an easy business for the boy. He tried
to clamber down slowly, but the pitch of the roof was too steep. He lost
his footing, rolled over on his back, and slid down—faster and faster—

until he shot over the eaves, with a startled squeak, and landed neck-deep in a full raintub.

Grimbold minced away from the splash.

"That's one way of doing it," he commented.

Muffler dragged himself out of the big barrel. He stood in a growing pool of water, but still felt as warm as toast. He said so, and the cat gave him a wondering glance.

"Surely you understood the spell of the fire?" he said. "You'll never be cold again. Which is just as well," he added, "considering how you come off roofs."

"I'm not in practice. . . ."

But the cat was out of earshot and the boy limped quickly after him.

"Where are we going?" he called.

"To the nearest gap," came back the voice of the cat.

He led the way, by winding brick paths, through the moonlit garden to the stone wall at the end; here were fruit trees, black-currant bushes, gooseberries, and rhubarb, and herbs; and here the cat paused. He twitched his tail and vanished. Muffler waited patiently until he reappeared.

"Why must I always come back for you?" snarled Grimbold.

"You never explain where you're going."

"This time, into the night world." The cat's teeth glinted as he drew back his lips. He said loftily, "All cats know the gaps. You must have noticed how they can disappear before your eyes when they choose. But I suppose it will take magic to get *you* through!"

He sniffed disparagingly and said something that sounded regrettably like:

> "Barriers of earth and sky,
> Let this hulking human by!"

And the ground shivered under Muffler's feet. A mist blew round him and cleared. He blinked and saw that he was standing in the same place—but it was not the same.

The stone wall looked transparent, as though made of glass. The trees had pale golden leaves and their trunks were dappled with shifting colors. Blossoms were like tiny lamps, alight. Even the rhubarb was ebony black and powdered with bright specks. A white bat went flicking through the strangely scented air. And the thatch on the farmhouse roof was as green as emerald.

Something touched Muffler's hand and he glanced down. He sprang back with a cry. A black panther looked at him with eyes of fire.

"It's me, silly," said Grimbold.

Muffler recovered slightly.

"You're—bigger!" he said.

"In the night world cats grow to their full stature," said Grimbold impressively. "This is not the world you know."

"It's beautiful."

"But very dangerous. Like everything else that is truly beautiful," the cat told him. "Those who see the night world can never again content themselves with the ordinary one. It changes them."

"Am I changed?"

An enigmatic expression flickered over the broad and whiskered face.

"I would not have brought you here," said the cat carefully, "but for what Dulcie told me. Poets and singers can wander in and out of the night kingdom, for they aren't quite like other humans anyway."

"Do many people come here?" said Muffler, puzzled by all this.

"We try to stop them. But sometimes they slip through. Ordinary people are never the same again. They become strangers to their own kind, and they are accused of witchcraft—madness . . . ! We discourage casual visitors," said Grimbold firmly.

"Except for poets."

"We can't stop those. They find the way for themselves. Once they reach *that* point," said the cat, "they hardly count as human anymore! Now, do stop gossiping and come along."

He sped toward the stone wall and shot through as though it had been made of mist. Muffler took a deep breath to encourage himself, and did the same. The wall *was* made of mist. On the far side was the duckpond. But not the duckpond as the boy knew it.

The trees at its margins had slender silver trunks and branches. Glass leaves tinkled in the night breeze. Underfoot the grass was white, as though there was a heavy frost. And the pond water was like milky, gleaming ice. Grimbold skidded as he loped across it, and, seeing the scratches left on the surface by his claws, Muffler realized that it *was* ice. He limped gingerly after the cat, and found him in the very center, crouching until his nose almost touched the crystal coldness.

"There he is," said Grimbold.

It gave Muffler quite a shock to look down and see a young man lying still and rigid some way beneath them, frozen into the solid ice. His hands and feet were tied with cords and his eyes were shut.

"Oh . . ." breathed Muffler, "is he dead?"

"No," said the cat. "But he's pretty cold! Mind you," he went on disapprovingly, "it's entirely his own fault. He will argue with his father, and the old man has some unbeatable back-answers!"

"He must be very cruel," said Muffler, "to treat his son like this."

"Actually," said the cat, "it's six of one and half a dozen of the other. Sometimes, I could wash my paws of the pair of them!"

"I don't consider this a fatherly way to behave, whatever the cause!"

"You," said Grimbold, "are not a sorcerer! He lost his temper. He said Gareth must find his own way out, and he set a spell on the ice so that *I* could not open it. Gareth's been there for a whole week now."

"And what am I supposed to do? Chip him out?"

In answer to his question, Grimbold asked another.

"Is it cold?"

"Not very," said Muffler, surprised. "In fact, considering all this ice—oh, it's the fire spell! I wish I could share it with your Gareth."

"Try," suggested Grimbold.

Muffler looked as doubtful as he felt. But he knelt on the ice and laid both hands on its surface. A pleasant glow tingled through his palms.

"I thought so! I thought so!" cried the cat.

Below them the sorcerer's son stirred. His pale hair floated round his face. Bubbles drifted from his lips. And the ice cracked across in thousands of fine hairlike lines. A deep pool of water spread in the middle of the pond, and Muffler found himself elbow-deep in the warmth of it.

"Get to the side!" hissed Grimbold. "You're melting the lot!"

There was crackling all round and more bubbles underneath. The young man floated to the surface, and Grimbold stretched a huge paw to drag him up onto the crumbling ice. Then, with Muffler's assistance, he slid him across it and safely onto the soft white grass. They all tumbled there in a damp heap, and the duckpond turned blue as the last of the ice vanished.

The son of the sorcerer sat up stiffly and shook back his wet hair.

"You were long in coming," he said to Grimbold.

"Serves you right," said the cat.

"Who's the boy?"

"Muffler. He got you out of that coil."

"Speaking of which," said Gareth, "it would be kind if someone untied me."

Muffler always carried a small knife in his belt and now he used it to saw through the cords. The sorcerer's son rubbed his wrists and shivered.

"Chilly for the time of year!" said he.

Then he gave his hand to Muffler. It was slender and wet, and without the fire spell, Muffler would have found it very cold. In the moonlight the eyes of Gareth were golden, and he was extremely handsome. But it was an unreliable sort of beauty, and his smile was indifferent.

"I'm most grateful," he said, and laughed. "The old man will be livid!"

"With me?" said Muffler, in some alarm.

Gareth gave him a flashing grin.

"With everyone!" said he, lightly.

"Oh, surely he will forgive you, if you apologize . . ."

Grimbold gave a small snicker, and the young man widened his strange and slanting eyes.

"Apologize?" said he, and turned to the cat. "You know that spell he's working at—to turn tadpoles into sponge cakes?"

The cat nodded.

"I," said Gareth, "have thought how to turn the whole thing to froth and frogs! It took some working out, but it kept me happy this last week."

He got to his feet, ran his hands down his wet tunic and gave Muffler another of his careless smiles.

"You are welcome to this world," he said. "Do come again."

He turned on his heel and went lightly away under the trees. Muffler shook his head admiringly.

"You can't help liking him," he said. "But surely he's asking for more trouble with all that tadpole stuff?"

"Oh, he's a madman," said Grimbold.

A faint golden light began to creep up the sky. The breeze freshened and the glass leaves rang like little bells. The cat yawned.

"You'd better get back," he said. "Time flies fast in your world and the dawn is breaking."

He scratched his jaw so that a few shining hairs drifted to the ground. He turned a thoughful stare on the boy.

"If the opportunity occurs for you to return to this world," he said, very seriously, "think twice before doing it. So far, no harm is done. But the knowledge of magic and mystery may change your life, if you let it. You're only a boy—and you might grow out of your singing and your rhymes. Be careful, Muffler—be very careful, and very sure, before you settle for poetry."

"Well," said the boy, "I love the daylight world, but magic draws me. If I never saw this place again, I would always dream of it."

The cat's eyes slitted to slanting lines of fire.

"I've warned you," said he.

He gave another yawn that curled his tongue like a pink petal in his mouth.

"You'll never get back up that roof," he stated. "But there's another gap somewhere hereabout."

He waved his tail, and said:

"Barriers of earth and sky,
Let the boy go safely by."

Muffler blinked. The mist cleared. The ground steadied. He was looking at the duckpond that he knew—green with water weeds and gently rippling, and apple trees leaning over to look at their morning reflections in it. A large white duck came stumping from the stable, plopped into the water, shouting raucously with pleasure, and stood on his head.

Something moved by Muffler's ankle. The boy stooped to stroke Grimbold, who was his daytime size again. The cat moved away, then relented and rubbed his head on the friendly hand.

"Doubtless we shall meet again," said he.

He minced away a few paces and turned.

"Must go, now," he said. "Gareth will have the old man hopping mad by breakfast time. Good-bye, and thank you. And remember what I told you."

He twitched his tail and vanished.

Muffler limped to the gate of the meadow behind the farm. The goats stopped everything that they were doing and crowded around, bleating affectionately.

"Hello, you woolly wickeds!" said Muffler.

The farmer's wife came from the house, carrying a trug of chicken food. She saw the boy and let it fall. And a fluster of hens came rushing from barns and stables to fall on the scattered grain.

"Muffler!" cried Meg. "What are you doing out of bed!"

"I'm quite all right, Mother Meg. I went up the chimney and into a world of . . ."

"You've certainly been messing with the fire," she scolded. "Look at you—all over soot! But your cold . . . !"

"It's gone. And I'll never have another," said Muffler hopefully. "The fire gave me a spell to keep me warm."

Meg was holding his hand very closely in her own.

"You're certainly warm enough," said she, wonderingly. "And not in fever. You've made a quick recovery, and no mistake! It must have been that potion I gave you. Never mind your tales of magic and your dreaming! You come along and have your breakfast!"

from

Peter and Wendy

by J. M. Barrie

Scottish writer J. M. Barrie (1860–1937) adapted the novel *Peter and Wendy* from his popular 1904 play *Peter Pan*. Peter Pan lives with his friends the Lost Boys in Never-Never Land. The boys and their friend Wendy are taken captive by the evil Captain Hook, who has a bo'sun named Smee and a metal hook in place of the hand he lost to a hungry crocodile.

One green light squinting over Kidd's Creek, which is near the mouth of the pirate river, marked where the brig, the *Jolly Roger*, lay, low in the water; a rakish-looking craft foul to the hull, every beam in her detestable like ground strewn with mangled feathers. She was the cannibal of the seas, and scarce needed that watchful eye, for she floated immune in the horror of her name.

She was wrapped in the blanket of night, through which no sound from her could have reached the shore. There was little sound, and none agreeable save the whir of the ship's sewing machine at which Smee sat, ever industrious and obliging, the essence of the commonplace, pathetic Smee. I know not why he was so infinitely pathetic, unless it were because he was so pathetically unaware of it; but even strong men had to turn hastily from looking at him, and more than once on summer evenings he had touched the fount of Hook's tears and made it flow. Of this, as of almost everything else, Smee was quite unconscious.

A few of the pirates leant over the bulwarks, drinking in the miasma of the night; others sprawled by barrels over games of dice and cards; and the exhausted four who had carried the little house lay prone on the deck, where even in their sleep they rolled skillfully to this side or that out of Hook's reach, lest he should claw them mechanically in passing.

Hook trod the deck in thought. O man unfathomable. It was his hour of triumph. Peter had been removed for ever from his path, and all the other boys were on the brig, about to walk the plank. It was his grimmest deed since the days when he had brought Barbecue to heel; and knowing as we do how vain a tabernacle is man, could we be surprised had he now paced the deck unsteadily, bellied out by the winds of his success?

But there was no elation in his gait, which kept pace with the action of his sombre mind. Hook was profoundly dejected.

He was often thus when communing with himself on board ship in the quietude of the night. It was because he was so terribly alone. This inscrutable man never felt more alone than when surrounded by his dogs. They were socially inferior to him.

Hook was not his true name. To reveal who he really was would even at this date set the country in a blaze; but as those who read between the lines must already have guessed, he had been at a famous public school; and its traditions still clung to him like garments, with which indeed they are largely concerned. Thus it was offensive to him even now to board a ship in the same dress in which he grappled her, and he still adhered in his walk to the school's distinguished slouch. But above all he retained the passion for good form.

Good form! However much he may have degenerated, he still knew that this is all that really matters.

From far within him he heard a creaking as of rusty portals, and through them came a stern tap-tap-tap, like hammering in the night when one cannot sleep. "Have you been good form to-day?" was their eternal question.

"Fame, fame, that glittering bauble, it is mine!" he cried.

"Is it quite good form to be distinguished at anything?" the tap-tap from his school replied.

"I am the only man whom Barbecue feared," he urged, "and Flint feared Barbecue."

"Barbecue, Flint—what house?" came the cutting retort.

Most disquieting reflection of all, was it not bad form to think about good form?

His vitals were tortured by this problem. It was a claw within him sharper than the iron one; and as it tore him, the perspiration dripped down his tallow countenance and streaked his doublet. Ofttimes he drew his sleeve across his face, but there was no damming that trickle.

Ah, envy not Hook.

There came to him a presentiment of his early dissolution. It was as if Peter's terrible oath had boarded the ship. Hook felt a gloomy desire to make his dying speech, lest presently there should be no time for it.

"Better for Hook," he cried, "if he had had less ambition!" It was in his darkest hours only that he referred to himself in the third person.

"No little children to love me!"

Strange that he should think of this, which had never troubled him before; perhaps the sewing machine brought it to his mind. For long he muttered to himself, staring at Smee, who was hemming placidly, under the conviction that all children feared him.

Feared him! Feared Smee! There was not a child on board the brig that night who did not already love him. He had said horrid things to them and hit them with the palm of his hand, because he could not hit with his fist, but they had only clung to him the more. Michael had tried on his spectacles.

To tell poor Smee that they thought him lovable! Hook itched to do it, but it seemed too brutal. Instead, he revolved this mystery in his mind: why do they find Smee lovable? He pursued the problem like the sleuth-hound that he was. If Smee was lovable, what was it that made him so? A terrible answer suddenly presented itself—"Good form?"

Had the bo'sun good form without knowing it, which is the best form of all?

He remembered that you have to prove you don't know you have it before you are eligible for Pop.

With a cry of rage he raised his iron hand over Smee's head; but he did not tear. What arrested him was this reflection:

"To claw a man because he is good form, what would that be?"

"Bad form!"

The unhappy Hook was as impotent as he was damp, and he fell forward like a cut flower.

His dogs thinking him out of the way for a time, discipline instantly relaxed; and they broke into a bacchanalian dance, which brought him to his feet at once, all traces of human weakness gone, as if a bucket of water had passed over him.

"Quiet, you scugs," he cried, "or I'll cast anchor in you"; and at once the din was hushed. "Are all the children chained, so that they cannot fly away?"

"Ay, ay."

"Then hoist them up."

The wretched prisoners were dragged from the hold, all except Wendy, and ranged in line in front of him. For a time he seemed unconscious of their presence. He lolled at his ease, humming, not unmelodiously, snatches of a rude song, and fingering a pack of cards. Ever and anon the light from his cigar gave a touch of colour to his face.

"Now then, bullies," he said briskly, "six of you walk the plank to-night, but I have room for two cabin boys. Which of you is it to be?"

"Don't irritate him unnecessarily," had been Wendy's instructions in the hold; so Tootles stepped forward politely. Tootles hated the idea of signing under such a man, but an instinct told him that it would be prudent to lay the responsibility on an absent person; and though a somewhat silly boy, he knew that mothers alone are always willing to be the buffer. All children know this about mothers, and despise them for it, but make constant use of it.

So Tootles explained prudently, "You see, sir, I don't think my mother would like me to be a pirate. Would your mother like you to be a pirate, Slightly?"

He winked at Slightly, who said mournfully, "I don't think so," as if he wished things had been otherwise. "Would your mother like you to be a pirate, Twin?"

"I don't think so," said the first twin, as clever as the others. "Nibs, would—"

"Stow this gab," roared Hook, and the spokesmen were dragged back. "You, boy," he said, addressing John, "you look as if you had a little pluck in you. Didst never want to be a pirate, my hearty?"

Now John had sometimes experienced this hankering at maths. prep.; and he was struck by Hook's picking him out.

"I once thought of calling myself Red-handed Jack," he said diffidently.

"And a good name too. We'll call you that here, bully, if you join."

"What do you think, Michael?" asked John.

"What would you call me if I join?" Michael demanded.

"Blackbeard Joe."

Michael was naturally impressed. "What do you think, John?" He wanted John to decide, and John wanted him to decide.

"Shall we still be respectful subjects of the King?" John inquired.

Through Hook's teeth came the answer: "You would have to swear, 'Down with the King.'"

Perhaps John had not behaved very well so far, but he shone out now.

"Then I refuse!" he cried, banging the barrel in front of Hook.

"And I refuse!" cried Michael.

"Rule Britannia!" squeaked Curly.

The infuriated pirates buffeted them in the mouth; and Hook roared out, "That seals your doom. Bring up their mother. Get the plank ready."

They were only boys, and they went white as they saw Jukes and Cecco preparing the fatal plank. But they tried to look brave when Wendy was brought up.

No words of mine can tell you how Wendy despised those pirates. To the boys there was at least some glamour in the pirate calling; but all that she saw was that the ship had not been tidied for years. There was not a porthole on the grimy glass of which you might not have written with your finger "Dirty pig"; and she had already written it on several. But as the boys gathered round her she had no thought, of course, save for them.

"So, my beauty," said Hook, as if he spoke in syrup, "you are to see your children walk the plank."

Fine gentleman though he was, the intensity of his communings had soiled his ruff, and suddenly he knew that she was gazing at it. With a hasty gesture he tried to hide it, but he was too late.

"Are they to die?" asked Wendy, with a look of such frightful contempt that he nearly fainted.

"They are," he snarled. "Silence all," he called gloatingly, "for a mother's last words to her children."

At this moment Wendy was grand. "These are my last words, dear boys," she said firmly. "I feel that I have a message to you from your real mothers, and it is this: 'We hope our sons will die like English gentlemen.'"

Even the pirates were awed, and Tootles cried out hysterically, "I am going to do what my mother hopes. What are you to do, Nibs?"

"What my mother hopes. What are you to do, Twin?"

"What my mother hopes. John, what are—"

But Hook had found his voice again.

"Tie her up!" he shouted.

It was Smee who tied her to the mast. "See here, honey," he whispered, "I'll save you if you promise to be my mother."

But not even for Smee would she make such a promise. "I would almost rather have no children at all," she said disdainfully.

It is sad to know that not a boy was looking at her as Smee tied her to the mast; the eyes of all were on the plank: that last little walk they were about to take. They were no longer able to hope that they would walk it manfully, for the capacity to think had gone from them; they could stare and shiver only.

Hook smiled on them with his teeth closed, and took a step toward Wendy. His intention was to turn her face so that she should see the boys walking the plank one by one. But he never reached her, he never heard the cry of anguish he hoped to wring from her. He heard something else instead.

It was the terrible tick-tick of the crocodile.

They all heard it—pirates, boys, Wendy—and immediately every head was blown in one direction; not to the water whence the sound proceeded, but toward Hook. All knew that what was about to happen concerned him alone, and that from being actors they were suddenly become spectators.

Very frightful was it to see the change that came over him. It was as if he had been clipped at every joint. He fell in a little heap.

The sound came steadily nearer; and in advance of it came this ghastly thought, "The crocodile is about to board the ship!"

Even the iron claw hung inactive; as if knowing that it was no intrinsic part of what the attacking force wanted. Left so fearfully alone, any other man would have lain with his eyes shut where he fell: but the gigantic brain of Hook was still working, and under its guidance he crawled on his knees along the deck as far from the sound as he could go. The pirates respectfully cleared a passage for him, and it was only when he brought up against the bulwarks that he spoke.

"Hide me!" he cried hoarsely.

They gathered round him, all eyes averted from the thing that was coming aboard. They had no thought of fighting it. It was Fate.

Only when Hook was hidden from them did curiosity loosen the limbs of the boys so that they could rush to the ship's side to see the crocodile climbing it. Then they got the strangest surprise of the Night of Nights; for it was no crocodile that was coming to their aid. It was Peter.

He signed to them not to give vent to any cry of admiration that might arouse suspicion. Then he went on ticking.

Odd things happen to all of us on our way through life without our noticing for a time that they have happened. Thus, to take an instance, we suddenly discover that we have been deaf in one ear for we don't know how long, but, say, half an hour. Now such an experience had come that night to Peter. When last we saw him he was stealing across the island with one finger to his lips and his dagger at the ready. He had seen the crocodile pass by without noticing anything peculiar about it, but by and by he remembered that it had not been ticking. At first he thought this eerie, but soon concluded rightly that the clock had run down.

Without giving a thought to what might be the feelings of a fellow-creature this abruptly deprived of its closest companion, Peter began to consider how he could turn the catastrophe to his own use; and he decided to tick, so that wild beasts should believe he was the crocodile and let him pass unmolested. He ticked superbly, but with one unforeseen result. The crocodile was among those who heard the sound, and it followed him, though whether with the purpose of regaining what it had lost, or merely as a friend under the belief that it was again ticking itself, will never be certainly known, for, like slaves to a fixed idea, it was a stupid beast.

Peter reached the shore without mishap, and went straight on, his legs encountering the water as if quite unaware that they had entered a new element. Thus many animals pass from land to water, but no other human of whom I know. As he swam he had but one thought: "Hook or me this time." He had ticked so long that he now went on ticking without knowing that he was doing it. Had he known he would have stopped, for to board the brig by help of the tick, though an ingenious idea, had not occurred to him.

On the contrary, he thought he had scaled her side as noiseless as a mouse; and he was amazed to see the pirates cowering from him, with Hook in their midst as abject as if he had heard the crocodile.

The crocodile! No sooner did Peter remember it than he heard the ticking. At first he thought the sound did come from the crocodile, and he looked behind him swiftly. They he realised that he was doing it himself, and in a flash he understood the situation. "How clever of me!" he thought at once, and signed to the boys not to burst into applause.

It was at this moment that Ed Teynte the quartermaster emerged from the forecastle and came along the deck. Now, reader, time what happened by your watch. Peter struck true and deep. John clapped his hands on the ill-fated pirate's mouth to stifle the dying groan. He fell forward. Four boys caught him to prevent the thud. Peter gave the signal, and the carrion was cast overboard. There was a splash, and then silence. How long has it taken?

"One!" (Slightly had begun to count.)

None too soon, Peter, every inch of him on tiptoe, vanished into the cabin; for more than one pirate was screwing up his courage to look round. They could hear each other's distressed breathing now, which showed them that the more terrible sound had passed.

"It's gone, captain," Smee said, wiping off his spectacles. "All's still again."

Slowly Hook let his head emerge from his ruff, and listened so intently that he could have caught the echo of the tick. There was not a sound, and he drew himself up firmly to his full height.

"Then here's to Johnny Plank!" he cried brazenly, hating the boys more than ever because they had seen him unbend. He broke into the villainous ditty:

> "Yo ho, yo ho, the frisky plank,
>   You walks along it so,
> Till it goes down and you goes down
>   To Davy Jones below!"

To terrorize the prisoners the more, though with a certain loss of dignity, he danced along an imaginary plank, grimacing at them as he sang; and when he finished he cried, "Do you want a touch of the cat before you walk the plank?"

At that they fell on their knees. "No, no!" they cried so piteously that every pirate smiled.

"Fetch the cat, Jukes," said Hook; "it's in the cabin."

The cabin! Peter was in the cabin! The children gazed at each other.

"Ay, ay," said Jukes blithely, and he strode into the cabin. They followed him with their eyes; they scarce knew that Hook had resumed his song, his dogs joining in with him:

> *"Yo ho, yo ho, the scratching cat,*
> *Its tails are nine, you know,*
> *And when they're writ upon your back—"*

What was the last line will never be known, for of a sudden the song was stayed by a dreadful screech from the cabin. It wailed through the ship, and died away. Then was heard a crowing sound which was well understood by the boys, but to the pirates was almost more eerie than the screech.

"What was that?" cried Hook.

"Two," said Slightly solemnly.

The Italian Cecco hesitated for a moment and then swung into the cabin. He tottered out, haggard.

"What's the matter with Bill Jukes, you dog?" hissed Hook, towering over him.

"The matter wi' him is he's dead, stabbed," replied Cecco in a hollow voice.

"Bill Jukes dead!" cried the startled pirates.

"The cabin's as black as a pit," Cecco said, almost gibbering, "but there is something terrible in there: the thing you heard crowing."

The exultation of the boys, the lowering looks of the pirates, both were seen by Hook.

"Cecco," he said in his most steely voice, "go back and fetch me out that doodle-doo."

Cecco, bravest of the brave, cowered before his captain, crying "No, no"; but Hook was purring to his claw.

"Did you say you would go, Cecco?" he said musingly.

Cecco went, first flinging his arms despairingly. There was no more singing, all listened now; and again came a death-screech and again a crow.

No one spoke except Slightly. "Three," he said.

Hook rallied his dogs with a gesture. "'S'death and odds fish," he thundered, "who is to bring me that doodle-doo?"

"Wait till Cecco comes out," growled Starkey, and the others took up the cry.

"I think I heard you volunteer, Starkey," said Hook, purring again.

"No, by thunder!" Starkey cried.

"My hook thinks you did," said Hook, crossing to him. "I wonder if it would not be advisable, Starkey, to humour the hook?"

"I'll swing before I go in there," replied Starkey doggedly, and again he had the support of the crew.

"Is this mutiny?" asked Hook more pleasantly than ever. "Starkey's ringleader!"

"Captain, mercy!" Starkey whimpered, all of a tremble now.

"Shake hands, Starkey," said Hook, proffering his claw.

Starkey looked round for help, but all deserted him. As he backed Hook advanced, and now the red spark was in his eye. With a despairing scream the pirate leapt upon Long Tom and precipitated himself into the sea.

"Four," said Slightly.

"And now," Hook said courteously, "did any other gentlemen say mutiny?" Seizing a lantern and raising his claw with a menacing gesture, "I'll bring out that doodle-doo myself," he said, and sped into the cabin.

"Five." How Slightly longed to say it. He wetted his lips to be ready, but Hook came staggering out, without his lantern.

"Something blew out the light," he said a little unsteadily.

"Something!" echoed Mullins.

"What of Cecco?" demanded Noodler.

"He's as dead as Jukes," said Hook shortly.

His reluctance to return to the cabin impressed them all unfavourably, and the mutinous sounds again broke forth. All pirates are superstitious, and Cookson cried, "They do say the surest sign a ship's accurst in when there's one on board more than can be accounted for."

"I've heard," muttered Mullins, "he always boards the pirate craft last. Had he a tail, captain?"

"They say," said another, looking viciously at Hook, "that when he comes it's in the likeness of the wickedest man aboard."

"Had he a hook, captain?" asked Cookson insolently; and one after another took up the cry, "The ship's doomed!" At this the children could not resist raising a cheer. Hook had well-nigh forgotten his prisoners, but as he swung round on them now his face lit up again.

"Lads," he cried to his crew, "here's a notion. Open the cabin door and drive them in. Let them fight the doodle-doo for their lives. If they kill him, we're so much the better; if he kills them, we're none the worse."

For the last time his dogs admired Hook, and devotedly they did his bidding. The boys, pretending to struggle, were pushed into the cabin and the door was closed on them.

"Now, listen!" cried Hook, and all listened. But not one dared to face the door. Yes, one, Wendy, who all this time had been bound to the mast. It was for neither a scream nor a crow that she was watching, it was for the reappearance of Peter.

She had not long to wait. In the cabin he had found the thing for which he had gone in search: the key that would free the children of their manacles, and now they all stole forth, armed with such weapons as they could find. First signing them to hide, Peter cut Wendy's bonds, and then nothing could have been easier than for them all to fly off together; but one thing barred the way, an oath, "Hook or me this time." So when he had freed Wendy, he whispered for to her to conceal herself with the others, and himself took her place by the mast, her cloak around him so that he should pass for her. Then he took a great breath and crowed.

To the pirates it was a voice crying that all the boys lay slain in the cabin; and they were panic-stricken. Hook tried to hearten them, but like the dogs he had made them they showed him their fangs, and he knew that if he took his eyes off them now they would leap at him.

"Lads," he said, ready to cajole or strike as need be, but never quailing for an instant, "I've thought it out. There's a Jonah aboard."

"Ay," they snarled, "a man wi' a hook."

"No, lads, no, it's the girl. Never was luck on a pirate ship wi' a woman on board. We'll right the ship when she's gone."

Some of them remembered that this had been a saying of Flint's. "It's worth trying," they said doubtfully.

"Fling the girl overboard," cried Hook; and they made a rush at the figure in the cloak.

"There's none can save you now, missy," Mullins hissed jeeringly.

"There's one," replied the figure.

"Who's that?"

"Peter Pan the avenger!" came the terrible answer; and as he spoke Peter flung off his cloak. Then they all knew who 'twas that had been undoing them in the cabin, and twice Hook essayed to speak and twice he failed. In that frightful moment I think his fierce heart broke.

At last he cried, "Cleave him to the brisket!" but without conviction.

"Down, boys, and at them!" Peter's voice rang out; and in another moment the clash of arms was resounding through the ship. Had the pirates kept together it is certain that they would have won; but the onset came when they were all unstrung, and they ran hither and thither, striking wildly, each thinking himself the last survivor of the crew. Man to man they were the stronger; but they fought on the defensive only, which enabled the boys to hunt in pairs and choose their quarry. Some of the miscreants leapt into the sea, others hid in dark recesses, where they were found by Slightly, who did not fight, but ran about with a lantern which he flashed in their faces, so that they were half blinded and fell an easy prey to the reeking swords of the other boys. There was little sound to be heard but the clang of weapons, an occasional screech or splash, and Slightly monotonously counting— five—six—seven—eight—nine—ten—eleven.

I think all were gone when a group of savage boys surrounded

Hook, who seemed to have a charmed life, as he kept them at bay in that circle of fire. They had done for his dogs, but this man alone seemed to be a match for them all. Again and again they closed upon him, and again and again he hewed a clear space. He had lifted up one boy with his hook, and was using him as a buckler, when another, who had just passed his sword through Mullins, sprang into the fray.

"Put up your swords, boys," cried the newcomer, "this man is mine."

Thus suddenly Hook found himself face to face with Peter. The others drew back and formed a ring around them.

For long the two enemies looked at one another, Hook shuddering slightly, and Peter with the strange smile upon his face.

"So, Pan," said Hook at last, "this is all your doing."

"Ay, James Hook," came the stern answer, "it is all my doing."

"Proud and insolent youth," said Hook, "prepare to meet thy doom."

"Dark and sinister man," Peter answered, "have at thee."

Without more words they fell to, and for a space there was no advantage to either blade. Peter was a superb swordsman, and parried with dazzling rapidity; ever and anon he followed up a feint with a lunge that got past his foe's defence, but his shorter reach stood him in ill stead, and he could not drive the steel home. Hook, scarcely his inferior in brilliancy, but not quite so nimble in wrist play, forced him back by the weight of his onset, hoping suddenly to end all with a favourite thrust, taught him long ago by Barbecue at Rio; but to his astonishment he found this thrust turned aside again and again. Then he sought to close and give the quietus with his iron hook, which all this time had been pawing the air; but Peter doubled under it and, lunging fiercely, pierced him in the ribs. At the sight of his own blood, whose peculiar colour, you remember, was offensive to him, the sword fell from Hook's hand, and he was at Peter's mercy.

"Now!" cried all the boys, but with a magnificent gesture Peter invited his opponent to pick up his sword. Hook did so instantly, but with a tragic feeling that Peter was showing good form.

Hitherto he had thought it was some fiend fighting him, but darker suspicions assailed him now.

"Pan, who and what art thou?" he cried huskily.

"I'm youth, I'm joy," Peter answered at a venture, "I'm a little bird that has broken out of the egg."

This, of course, was nonsense; but it was proof to the unhappy Hook that Peter did not know in the least who or what he was, which is the very pinnacle of good form.

"To't again," he cried despairingly.

He fought now like a human flail, and every sweep of that terrible sword would have severed in twain any man or boy who obstructed it; but Peter fluttered round him as if the very wind it made blew him out of the danger zone. And again and again he darted in and pricked.

Hook was fighting now without hope. That passionate breast no longer asked for life; but for one boon it craved: to see Peter show bad form before it was cold forever.

Abandoning the fight he rushed into the powder magazine and fired it.

"In two minutes," he cried, "the ship will be blown to pieces."

Now, now, he thought, true form will show.

But Peter issued from the powder magazine with the shell in his hands, and calmly flung it overboard.

What sort of form was Hook himself showing? Misguided man though he was, we may be glad, without sympathising with him, that in the end he was true to the traditions of his race. The other boys were flying around him now, flouting, scornful; and as he staggered about the deck striking up at them impotently, his mind was no longer with them; it was slouching in the playing fields of long ago, or being sent up for good, or watching the wall-game from a famous wall. And his shoes were right, and his waistcoat was right, and his tie was right, and his socks were right.

James Hook, thou not wholly unheroic figure, farewell.

For we have come to his last moment.

Seeing Peter slowly advancing upon him through the air with dagger poised, he sprang upon the bulwarks to cast himself into the sea. He did not know that the crocodile was waiting for him; for we purposely stopped the clock that this knowledge might be spared him: a little mark of respect from us at the end.

He had one last triumph, which I think we need not grudge him. As he stood on the bulwark looking over his shoulder at Peter gliding through the air, he invited him with a gesture to use his foot. It made Peter kick instead of stab.

At last Hook had got the boon for which he craved.

"Bad form," he cried jeeringly, and went content to the crocodile.

Thus perished James Hook.

"Seventeen," Slightly sang out; but he was not quite correct in his figures. Fifteen paid the penalty for their crimes that night; but two reached the shore: Starkey to be captured by the redskins, who made him nurse for all their papooses, a melancholy come-down for a pirate; and Smee, who henceforth wandered about the world in his spectacles, making a precarious living by saying he was the only man that Jas. Hook had feared.

Wendy, of course, had stood by taking no part in the fight, though watching Peter with glistening eyes; but now that all was over she became prominent again. She praised them equally, and shuddered delightfully when Michael showed her the place where he had killed one; and then she took them into Hook's cabin and pointed to his watch which was hanging on a nail. It said "half-past one!"

The lateness of the hour was almost the biggest thing of all. She got them to bed in the pirates' bunks pretty quickly, you may be sure; all but Peter, who strutted up and down on the deck, until at last he fell asleep by the side of Long Tom. He had one of his dreams that night, and cried in his sleep for a long time, and Wendy held him tight.

from

Musashi

by Eiji Yoshikawa,
translated by Charles S. Terry

Eiji Yoshikawa's (1892–1962) book *Musashi* is a fictional account of a real Samurai warrior named Miyamoto Musashi (1584–1645). Musashi traveled around Japan to find dueling opponents who could help him become a more skillful fighter. He travels with a boy named Jotaro.

S tudents of the martial arts invariably knew of the Hozoin. For a man who claimed to be a serious student to refer to it as just another temple was sufficient reason for him to be regarded as an impostor. It was well known among the local populace too, though, oddly enough, few were familiar with the much more important Shosoin Repository and its priceless collection of ancient art objects.

The temple was located on Abura Hill in a large, dense forest of cryptomeria trees. It was just the kind of place goblins might inhabit. Here, too, were reminders of the glories of the Nara period—the ruins of a temple, the Ganrin'in, and of the huge public bathhouse built by the Empress Komyo for the poor—but today all that was left was a scattering of foundation stones peeking out through the moss and weeds.

Musashi had no difficulty getting directions to Abura Hill, but once there he stood looking all around in bewilderment, for there were quite a few other temples nestled in the forest. The cryptomerias had weathered the winter and been bathed in the early spring rains, and their leaves were now at their darkest. Above them one could make out in the approaching twilight the soft feminine curves of Mount Kasuga. The distant mountains still lay in bright sunlight.

Although none of the temples looked like the right one, Musashi went from gate to gate inspecting the plaques on which their names were inscribed. His mind was so preoccupied with the Hozoin that when he saw the plaque of the Ozoin, he at first misread it, since only the first character, that for *O*, was different. Although he immediately realized his mistake, he took a look inside anyway. The Ozoin appeared to belong to the Nichiren sect; as far as he knew, the Hozoin was a Zen temple having no connection with Nichiren.

As he stood there, a young monk returning to the Ozoin passed by him, staring suspiciously.

Musashi removed his hat and said, "Could I trouble you for some information?"

"What would you like to know?"

"This temple is called the Ozoin?"

"Yes. That's what it says on the plaque."

"I was told that the Hozoin is on Abura Hill. Isn't it?"

"It's just in back of this temple. Are you going there for a fencing bout?"

"Yes."

"Then let me give you some advice. Forget it."

"Why?"

"It's dangerous. I can understand someone born crippled going there to get his legs straightened out, but I see no reason why anyone with good straight limbs should go there and be maimed."

The monk was well built and somehow different from the ordinary Nichiren monk. According to him, the number of would-be warriors had reached the point where even the Hozoin had come to regard them as a nuisance. The temple was, after all, a holy sanctuary for the light of the Buddha's Law, as its name indicated. Its real concern was religion. The martial arts were only a sideline, so to speak.

Kakuzenbo In'ei, the former abbot, had often called on Yagyu Muneyoshi. Through his association with Muneyoshi and with Lord Koizumi of Ise, Muneyoshi's friend, he had developed an interest in the martial arts and eventually taken up swordsmanship as a pastime.

From that he had gone on to devise new ways of using the lance, and this, as Musashi already knew, was the origin of the highly regarded Hozoin Style.

In'ei was now eighty-four years old and completely senile. He saw almost no one. Even when he did receive a caller, he was unable to carry on a conversation; he could only sit and make unintelligible movements with his toothless mouth. He didn't seem to comprehend anything said to him. As for the lance, he had forgotten about it completely.

"And so you see," concluded the monk after explaining all this, "it wouldn't do you much good to go there. You probably couldn't meet the master, and even if you did, you wouldn't learn anything." His brusque manner made it clear that he was eager to be rid of Musashi.

Though aware he was being made light of, Musashi persisted. "I've heard about In'ei, and I know what you've said about him is true. But I've also heard that a priest named Inshun has taken over as his successor. They say he's still studying but already knows all the secrets of the Hozoin Style. According to what I've heard, although he already has many students, he never refuses to give guidance to anyone who calls on him."

"Oh, Inshun," said the monk disdainfully. "There's nothing in those rumors. Inshun is actually a student of the abbot of the Ozoin. After In'ei began to show his age, our abbot felt it would be a shame for the reputation of the Hozoin to go to waste, so he taught Inshun the secrets of lance fighting—what he himself had learned from In'ei— and then saw to it that Inshun became abbot."

"I see," said Musashi.

"But you still want to go over there?"

"Well, I've come all this distance . . ."

"Yes, of course."

"You said it's behind here. Is it better to go around to the left or to the right?"

"You don't have to go around. It's much quicker just to walk straight through our temple. You can't miss it."

Thanking him, Musashi walked past the temple kitchen to the back of the compound, which with its woodshed, a storehouse for bean paste and a vegetable garden of an acre or so, very much resembled the area around the house of a well-to-do farmer. Beyond the garden he saw the Hozoin.

Walking on the soft ground between rows of rape, radishes and scallions, he noticed, off to one side, an old man hoeing vegetables. Hunched over his hoe, he was looking intently at the blade. All Musashi could see of his face was a pair of snow-white eyebrows, and save for the clank of the hoe against the rocks, it was perfectly quiet.

Musashi assumed that the old man must be a monk from the Ozoin. He started to speak, but the man was so absorbed in his work that it seemed rude to disturb him.

As he walked silently by, however, he suddenly became aware that the old man was staring out of the corner of his eye at Musashi's feet. Although the other man neither moved nor spoke, Musashi felt a terrifying force attack him—a force like lightning splitting the clouds. This was no daydream. He actually felt the mysterious power pierce his body and, terrified, he leaped into the air. He felt hot all over, as if he'd just narrowly avoided a death blow from a sword or lance.

Looking over his shoulder, he saw that the hunched back was stlll turned toward him, the hoe continuing its unbroken rhythm. "What on earth was that all about?" he wondered, dumbfounded by the power he'd been hit with.

He found himself in front of the Hozoin, his curiosity unabated. While waiting for a servant to appear, he thought: "Inshun should still be a young man. The young monk said In'ei was senile and had forgotten all about the lance, but I wonder. . . ." The incident in the garden lingered in the back of his mind.

He called out loudly two more times, but the only reply was an echo from the surrounding trees. Noticing a large gong beside the entrance, he struck it. Almost immediately an answering call came from deep inside the temple.

A priest came to the door. He was big and brawny; had he been one

of the warrior-priests of Mount Hiei, he might well have been the commander of a battalion. Accustomed as he was to receiving visits from
people like Musashi day in and day out, he gave him a brief glance and
said, "You're a *shugyosha?*"

"Yes."

"What are you here for?"

"I'd like to meet the master."

The priest said, "Come in," and gestured to the right of the entrance,
suggesting obliquely that Musashi should wash his feet first. There was
a barrel overflowing with water supplied by a bamboo pipe and,
pointing this way and that, about ten pairs of worn and dirty sandals.

Musashi followed the priest down a wide dark corridor and was
shown into an anteroom. There he was told to wait. The smell of
incense was in the air, and through the window he could see the broad
leaves of a plantain tree. Aside from the offhand manner of the giant
who'd let him in, nothing he saw indicated there was anything unusual
about this particular temple.

When he reappeared, the priest handed him a registry and ink box,
saying, "Write down your name, where you studied, and what style you
use." He spoke as though instructing a child.

The title on the registry was: "List of Persons Visiting This Temple to
Study. Steward of the Hozoin." Musashi opened the book and glanced
over the names, each listed under the date on which the samurai or student had called. Following the style of the last entry, he wrote down the
required information, omitting the name of his teacher.

The priest, of course, was especially interested in that.

Musashi's answer was essentially the one he'd given at the Yoshioka
School. He had practiced the use of the truncheon under his father,
"without working very hard at it." Since making up his mind to study
in earnest, he had taken as his teacher everything in the universe, as
well as the examples set by his predecessors throughout the country.
He ended up by saying, "I'm still in the process of learning."

"Mm. You probably know this already, but since the time of our
first master, the Hozoin has been celebrated everywhere for its lance

techniques. The fighting that goes on here is rough, and there are no exceptions. Before you go on, perhaps you'd better read what's written at the beginning of the registry."

Musashi picked up the book, opened it and read the stipulation, which he had skipped over before. It said: "Having come here for the purpose of study, I absolve the temple of all responsibility in the event that I suffer bodily injury or am killed."

"I agree to that," said Musashi with a slight grin—it amounted to no more than common sense for anyone committed to becoming a warrior.

"All right. This way."

The dojo was immense. The monks must have sacrificed a lecture hall or some other large temple building in favor of having it. Musashi had never before seen a hall with columns of such girth, and he also observed traces of paint, gold foil and Chinese-white primer on the frame of the transom—things not to be found in ordinary practice halls.

He was by no means the only visitor. More than ten student-warriors were seated in the waiting area, with a similar number of student-priests. In addition, there were quite a few samurai who seemed to be merely observers. All were tensely watching two lancers fighting a practice bout. No one even glanced Musashi's way as he sat down in a corner.

According to a sign on the wall, if anyone wanted to fight with real lances, the challenge would be accepted, but the combatants now on the floor were using long oak practice poles. A strike could, nevertheless, be extremely painful, even fatal.

One of the fighters was eventually thrown in the air, and as he limped back to his seat in defeat, Musashi could see that his thigh had already swollen to the size of a tree trunk. Unable to sit down, he dropped awkwardly to one knee and extended the wounded leg out before him.

"Next!" came the summons from the man on the floor, a priest of singularly arrogant manner. The sleeves of his robe were tied up behind him, and his whole body—legs, arms, shoulders, even his forehead—

seemed to consist of bulging muscles. The oak pole he held vertically was at least ten feet in length.

A man who seemed to be one of those who'd arrived that day spoke up. He fastened up his sleeves with a leather thong and strode into the practice area. The priest stood motionless as the challenger went to the wall, chose a halberd, and came to face him. They bowed, as was customary, but no sooner had they done this than the priest let out a howl like that of a wild hound, simultaneously bringing his pole down forcefully on the challenger's skull.

"Next," he called, reverting to his original position.

That was all: the challenger was finished. While he did not appear to be dead yet, the simple act of lifting his head from the floor was more than he could manage. A couple of the student-priests went out and dragged him back by the sleeves and waist of his kimono. On the floor behind him stretched a thread of saliva mixed with blood.

"Next!" shouted the priest again, as surly as ever.

At first Musashi thought he was the second-generation master Inshun, but the men sitting around him said no, he was Agon, one of the senior disciples who were known as the "Seven Pillars of the Hozoin." Inshun himself, they said, never had to engage in a bout, because challengers were always put down by one of these.

"Is there no one else?" bellowed Agon, now holding his practice lance horizontally.

The brawny steward was comparing his registry with the faces of the waiting men. He pointed at one.

"No, not today. . . . I'll come again some other time."

"How about you?"

"No. I don't feel quite up to it today."

One by one they backed out, until Musashi saw the finger pointing at him.

"How about you?"

"If you please."

" 'If you please'? What's that supposed to mean?"

"It means I'd like to fight."

All eyes focused on Musashi as he rose. The haughty Agon had retired from the floor and was talking and laughing animatedly with a group of priests, but when it appeared that another challenger had been found, a bored look came over his face, and he said lazily, "Somebody take over for me."

"Go ahead," they urged. "There's only one more."

Giving in, Agon walked nonchalantly back to the center of the floor. He took a fresh grip on the shiny black wooden pole, with which he seemed totally familiar. In quick order, he assumed an attacking stance, turned his back on Musashi, and charged off in the other direction.

"Yah-h-h-h!" Screaming like an enraged roc, he hurtled toward the back wall and thrust his lance viciously into a section used for practice purposes. The boards had been recently replaced, but despite the resilience of the new wood, Agon's bladeless lance plowed straight through.

"Yow-w-w!" His grotesque scream of triumph reverberated through the hall as he disengaged the lance and started to dance, rather than walk, back toward Musashi, steam rising from his muscle-bound body. Taking a stance some distance away, he glared at his latest challenger ferociously. Musashi had come forward with only his wooden sword and now stood quite still, looking a little surprised.

"Ready!" cried Agon.

A dry laugh was heard outside the window, and a voice said, "Agon, don't be a fool! Look, you stupid oaf, look! That's not a board you're about to take on."

Without relaxing his stance, Agon looked toward the window. "Who's there?" he bellowed.

The laughter continued, and then there came into view above the windowsill, as though it had been hung there by an antique dealer, a shiny pate and a pair of snow-white eyebrows.

"It won't do you any good, Agon. Not this time. Let the man wait until the day after tomorrow, when Inshun returns."

Musashi, who had also turned his head toward the window, saw that the face belonged to the old man he had seen on his way to the Hozoin, but no sooner had he realized this than the head disappeared.

Agon heeded the old man's warning to the extent of relaxing his hold on his weapon, but the minute his eyes met Musashi's again, he swore in the direction of the now empty window—and ignored the advice he had received.

As Agon tightened his grip on his lance, Musashi asked, for the sake of form, "Are you ready now?"

This solicitude drove Agon wild. His muscles were like steel, and when he jumped, he did so with awesome lightness. His feet seemed to be on the floor and in the air at the same time, quivering like moonlight on ocean waves.

Musashi stood perfectly still, or so it seemed. There was nothing unusual about his stance; he held his sword straight out with both hands, but being slightly smaller than his opponent and not so conspicuously muscular, he looked almost casual. The greatest difference was in the eyes. Musashi's were as sharp as a bird's, their pupils a clear coral tinted with blood.

Agon shook his head, perhaps to shake off the streams of sweat pouring down from his forehead, perhaps to shake off the old man's warning words. Had they lingered on? Was he attempting to cast them out of his mind? Whatever the reason, he was extremely agitated. He repeatedly shifted his position, trying to draw out Musashi, but Musashi remained motionless.

Agon's lunge was accompanied by a piercing scream. In the split second that decided the encounter, Musashi parried and counterattacked.

"What happened?"

Agon's fellow priests hastily ran forward and crowded around him in a black circle. In the general confusion, some tripped over his practice lance and went sprawling.

A priest stood up, his hands and chest smeared with blood, shouting, "Medicine! Bring the medicine. Quick!"

"You won't need any medicine." It was the old man, who had come in the front entrance and quickly assessed the situation. His face turned sour. "If I'd thought medicine would save him, I wouldn't have tried to stop him in the first place. The idiot!"

No one paid any attention to Musashi. For lack of anything better to do, he walked to the front door and began putting his sandals on.

The old man followed him. "You!" he said.

Over his shoulder, Musashi replied, "Yes?"

"I'd like to have a few words with you. Come back inside."

He led Musashi to a room behind the practice hall—a simple, square cell, the only opening in the four walls being the door.

After they were seated, the old man said, "It would be more proper for the abbot to come and greet you, but he's on a trip and won't be back for two or three days. So I'll act on his behalf."

"This is very kind of you," said Musashi, bowing his head. "I'm grateful for the good training I received today, but I feel I should apologize for the unfortunate way it turned out—"

"Why? Things like that happen. You have to be ready to accept it before you start fighting. Don't let it worry you."

"How are Agon's injuries?"

"He was killed instantly," said the old man. The breath with which he spoke felt like a cold wind on Musashi's face.

"He's dead?" To himself, he said: "So, it's happened again." Another life cut short by his wooden sword. He closed his eyes and in his heart called on the name of the Buddha, as he had on similar occasions in the past.

"Young man!"

"Yes, sir."

"Is your name Miyamoto Musashi?"

"That's correct."

"Under whom did you study the martial arts?"

"I've had no teacher in the ordinary sense. My father taught me how to use the truncheon when I was young. Since then, I've picked up a number of points from older samurai in various provinces. I've also spent some time traveling about the countryside, learning from the mountains and the rivers. I regard them, too, as teachers."

"You seem to have the right attitude. But you're so strong! Much too strong!"

Believing he was being praised, Musashi blushed and said, "Oh, no! I'm still immature. I'm always making blunders."

"That's not what I mean. Your strength is your problem. You must learn to control it, become weaker."

"What?" Musashi asked perplexedly.

"You will recall that a short while ago you passed through the vegetable garden where I was at work."

"Yes."

"When you saw me, you jumped away, didn't you?"

"Yes."

"Why did you do that?"

"Well, somehow I imagined that you might use your hoe as a weapon and strike my legs with it. Then, too, though your attention seemed to be focused on the ground, my whole body felt transfixed by your eyes. I felt something murderous in that look, as though you were searching for my weak spot—so as to attack it."

The old man laughed. "It was the other way around. When you were still fifty feet from me, I perceived what you call 'something murderous' in the air. I sensed it in the tip of my hoe—that's how strongly your fighting spirit and ambition manifest themselves in every step you take. I knew I had to be prepared to defend myself.

"If it had been one of the local farmers passing by, I myself would have been no more than an old man tending vegetables. True, you sensed belligerence in me, but it was only a reflection of your own."

So Musashi had been right in thinking, even before they first exchanged words, that here was no ordinary man. Now he keenly felt that the priest was the master, and he the pupil. His attitude toward the old man with the bent back became appropriately deferential.

"I thank you for the lesson you have given me. May I ask your name and your position in this temple?"

"Oh, I don't belong to the Hozoin. I'm the abbot of the Ozoin. My name is Nikkan."

"I see."

"I'm an old friend of In'ei, and since he was studying the use of the lance, I decided to study along with him. Later, I had an afterthought or two. Now I never touch the weapon."

"I guess that means that Inshun, the present abbot here, is your disciple."

"Yes, it could be put that way. But priests shouldn't have any use for weapons, and I consider it unfortunate that the Hozoin has become famous for a martial art, rather than for its religious fervor. Still, there were people who felt that it would be a pity to let the Hozoin Style die out, so I taught it to Inshun. And to no one else."

"I wonder if you'd let me stay in your temple until Inshun returns."

"Do you propose to challenge him?"

"Well, as long as I'm here, I'd like to see how the foremost master uses his lance."

Nikkan shook his head reproachfully. "It's a waste of time. There's nothing to be learned here."

"Is that so?"

"You've already seen the Hozoin lancemanship, just now, when you fought Agon. What more do you need to see? If you want to learn more, watch me. Look into my eyes."

Nikkan drew up his shoulders, put his head slightly forward, and stared at Musashi. His eyes seemed about to jump from their sockets. As Musashi stared back, Nikkan's pupils shone first with a coral flame, then gradually took on an azure profundity. The glow burned and numbed Musashi's mind. He looked away. Nikkan's crackling laugh was like the clatter of bone-dry boards.

He relaxed his stare only when a younger priest came in and whispered to him. "Bring it in," he commanded.

Presently the young priest returned with a tray and a round wooden rice container, from which Nikkan scooped rice into a bowl. He gave it to Musashi.

"I recommend the tea gruel and pickles. It's the practice of the Hozoin to serve them to all those who come here to study, so don't feel they're going to any special trouble for you. They make their own pickles—called Hozoin pickles, in fact—cucumbers stuffed with basil and red pepper. I think you'll find they taste rather good."

As Musashi picked up his chopsticks, he felt Nikkan's keen eyes on him again. He could not tell at this point whether their piercing quality originated within the priest or was a response to something he himself emitted. As he bit into a pickle, the feeling swept over him that Takuan's fist was about to smite him again, or perhaps the lance near the threshold was about to fly at him.

After he had finished a bowl of rice mixed with tea and two pickles, Nikkan asked, "Would you care for another helping?"

"No, thank you. I've had plenty."

"What do you think of the pickles?"

"Very good, thank you."

Even after he'd left, the sting of the red pepper on Musashi's tongue was all he could recall of the pickles' flavor. Nor was that the only sting he felt, for he came away convinced that somehow he'd suffered a defeat. "I lost," he grumbled to himself, walking slowly through a grove of cryptomerias. "I've been outclassed!" In the dim light, fleeting shadows ran across his path, a small herd of deer, frightened by his footsteps.

"When it was only a matter of physical strength, I won, but I left there feeling defeated. Why? Did I win outwardly only to lose inwardly?"

Suddenly remembering Jotaro, he retraced his steps to the Hozoin, where the lights were still burning. When he announced himself, the priest standing watch at the door poked his head out and said casually, "What is it? Did you forget something?"

"Yes. Tomorrow, or the next day, I expect someone to come here looking for me. When he does, will you tell him I'll be staying in the neighborhood of Sarusawa Pond? He should ask for me at the inns there."

"All right."

Since the reply was so casual, Musashi felt constrained to add, "It'll be a boy. His name is Jotaro. He's very young, so please be sure you make the message clear to him."

Once again striding down the path he had taken earlier, Musashi muttered to himself, "That proves I lost. I even forgot to leave a message for Jotaro. I was beaten by the old abbot!" Musashi's dejection persisted. Although he had won against Agon, the only thing that stuck in his mind was the immaturity he had felt in Nikkan's presence. How could he ever become a great swordsman, the greatest of them all? This was the question that obsessed him night and day, and today's encounter had left him utterly depressed.

During the past twenty years or so, the area between Sarusawa Pond and the lower reaches of the Sai River had been built up steadily, and there was a jumble of new houses, inns and shops. Only recently, Okubo Nagayasu had come to govern the city for the Tokugawas and had set up his administrative offices nearby. In the middle of the town was the establishment of a Chinese who was said to be a descendant of Lin Ho-ching; he had done so well with his stuffed dumplings that an expansion of his shop in the direction of the pond was under way.

Musashi stopped amid the lights of the busiest district and wondered where he should stay. There were plenty of inns, but he had to be careful about his expenses; at the same time, he wanted to choose a place not too far off the beaten track, so Jotaro could find him easily.

He had just eaten at the temple, but when he caught a whiff of the stuffed dumplings, he felt hungry again. Entering the shop, he sat down and ordered a whole plateful. When they arrived, Musashi noted that the name Lin was burned into the bottom of the dumplings. Unlike the hot pickles at the Hozoin, the dumplings had a flavor he could savor with pleasure.

The young girl who poured his tea asked politely, "Where are you planning to stay tonight?"

Musashi, unfamiliar with the district, welcomed the opportunity to explain his situation and ask her advice. She told him one of the proprietor's relatives had a private boardinghouse where he would be welcome, and without waiting for his answer, trotted off. She returned with a youngish woman, whose shaved eyebrows indicated she was married—presumably the proprietor's wife.

The boardinghouse was on a quiet alley not far from the restaurant, apparently an ordinary residence that sometimes took in guests. The eyebrowless mistress of the shop, who had shown him the way, tapped lightly on the door, then turned to Musashi and said quietly, "It's my elder sister's house, so don't worry about tipping or anything."

The maid came out of the house and the two of them exchanged whispers for a moment or two. Apparently satisfied, she led Musashi to the second floor.

The room and its furnishings were too good for an ordinary inn, making Musashi feel a bit ill at ease. He wondered why a house as well-off as this one would take in boarders and asked the maid about it, but she just smiled and said nothing. Having already eaten, he had his bath and went to bed, but the question was still on his mind when he went off to sleep.

Next morning, he said to the maid, "Someone is supposed to come looking for me. Will it be all right if I stay over for a day or two until he arrives?"

"By all means," she replied, without even asking the lady of the house, who soon came herself to pay her respects.

She was a good-looking woman of about thirty, with fine smooth skin. When Musashi tried to satisfy his curiosity about why she was accepting roomers, she laughingly replied, "To tell the truth, I'm a widow—my husband was a Nō actor by the name of Kanze—and I'm afraid to be without a man in the house, what with all these ill-bred ronin in the vicinity." She went on to explain that while the streets were full of drinking shops and prostitutes, many of the indigent samurai were not satisfied with these diversions. They would pump information from the local youths and attack houses where there were no men about. They spoke of this as "calling on the widows."

"In other words," said Musashi, "you take in people like me to act as your bodyguard, right?"

"Well," she said, smiling, "as I said, there are no men in the household. Please feel free to stay as long as you like."

"I understand perfectly. I hope you'll feel safe as long as I'm here. There's only one request I'd like to make. I'm expecting a visitor, so I wonder if you'd mind putting a marker with my name on it outside the gate."

The widow, not at all unhappy to let it be known that she had a man in the house, obligingly wrote "Miyamoto Musashi" on a strip of paper and pasted it on the gatepost.

Jotaro did not show up that day, but on the next, Musashi received a visit from a group of three samurai. Pushing their way past the protesting maid, they came straight upstairs to his room. Musashi saw immediately that they were among those who had been present at the Hozoin when he had killed Agon. Sitting down around him as though they'd known him all their lives, they started pouring on the flattery.

"I never saw anything like it in my life," said one. "I'm sure nothing of the kind ever happened at the Hozoin before. Just think! An unknown visitor arrives and, just like that, downs one of the Seven Pillars. And not just anyone—the terrifying Agon himself. One grunt and he was spitting blood. You don't often see sights like that!"

Another went on in the same vein. "Everyone we know is talking about it. All the ronin are asking each other just who this Miyamoto Musashi is. That was a bad day for the Hozoin's reputation."

"Why, you must be the greatest swordsman in the country!"

"And so young, too!"

"No doubt about it. And you'll get even better with time."

"If you don't mind my asking, how does it happen that with your ability you're only a ronin? It's a waste of your talents not to be in the service of a daimyo!"

They paused only long enough to slurp some tea and devour the tea cakes with gusto, spilling crumbs all over their laps and on the floor.

Musashi, embarrassed by the extravagance of their praise, shifted his eyes from right to left and back again. For a time, he listened with an impassive face, thinking that sooner or later their momentum would run down. When they showed no signs of changing the subject, he took the initiative by asking their names.

"Oh, I'm sorry. I'm Yamazoe Dampachi. I used to be in the service of Lord Gamo," said the first.

The man next to him said, "I'm Otomo Banryu. I've mastered the Bokuden Style, and I have a lot of plans for the future."

"I'm Yasukawa Yasubei," said the third with a chuckle, "and I've never been anything but a ronin, like my father before me."

Musashi wondered why they were taking up their time and his with their small talk. It became apparent that he would not find out unless he asked, so the next time there was a break in the conversation, he said, "Presumably you came because you had some business with me."

They feigned surprise at the very idea but soon admitted they had come on what they regarded as a very important mission. Moving quickly forward, Yasubei said, "As a matter of fact, we do have some business with you. You see, we're planning to put on a public 'entertainment' at the foot of Mount Kasuga, and we wanted to talk to you about it. Not a play or anything like that. What we have in mind is a series of matches that would teach the people about the martial arts, and at the same time give them something to lay bets on."

He went on to say that the stands were already being put up, and that the prospects looked excellent. They felt, however, that they needed another man, because with just the three of them, some really strong samurai might show up and beat them all, which would mean that their hard-earned money would go down the drain. They had decided that Musashi was just the right person for them. If he would join in with them, they would not only split the profits but pay for his food and lodging while the matches were in progress. That way he could easily earn some fast money for his future travels.

Musashi listened with some amusement to their blandishments, but by and by he grew tired and broke in. "If that's all you want, there's no point in discussing it. I'm not interested."

"But why?" asked Dampachi. "Why aren't you interested?"

Musashi's youthful temper erupted. "I'm not a gambler!" he stated indignantly. "And I eat with chopsticks, not with my sword!"

"What's that?" protested the three, insulted by his implication. "What do you mean by that?"

"Don't you understand, you fools? I am a samurai, and I intend to remain a samurai. Even if I starve in the process. Now clear out of here!"

One man's mouth twisted into a nasty snarl, and another, red with anger, shouted, "You'll regret this!"

They well knew that the three of them together were no match for Musashi, but to save face, they stamped out noisily, scowling and doing their best to give the impression they weren't through with him yet.

That night, as on other recent nights, there was a milky, slightly overcast moon. The young mistress of the house, free from worry as long as Musashi was in residence, was careful to provide him with delicious food and sake of good quality. He ate downstairs with the family and in the process drank himself into a mellow mood.

Returning to his room, he sprawled on the floor. His thoughts soon came to rest on Nikkan.

"It's humiliating," he said to himself.

The adversaries he had defeated, even the ones he had killed or half killed, always disappeared from his mind like so much froth, but he couldn't forget anyone who got the better of him in any way or, for that matter, anyone in whom he sensed an overpowering presence. Men like that dwelt in his mind like living spirits, and he thought constantly of how one day he might be able to overshadow them.

"Humiliating!" he repeated.

He clutched at his hair and pondered how he could get the better of Nikkan, how he could face that unearthly stare without flinching. For two days this question had gnawed at him. It wasn't that he wished Nikkan any harm, but he was sorely disappointed with himself.

"Is it that I'm no good?" he asked himself ruefully. Having learned swordsmanship on his own, and thus lacking an objective appraisal of his own strength, he couldn't help but doubt his own ability to ever achieve power such as the old priest exuded.

Nikkan had told him he was too strong, that he had to learn to become weaker. This was the point that sent his mind off on tangent after tangent, for he couldn't fathom the meaning. Wasn't strength a warrior's most important quality? Was that not what made one warrior superior to others? How could Nikkan speak of it as a flaw?

"Maybe," thought Musashi, "the old rascal was toying with me. Maybe he considered my youth and decided to talk in riddles just to confuse me and amuse himself. Then after I left, he had a good laugh. It's possible."

At times like this, Musashi wondered whether it had been wise to read all those books at Himeji Castle. Until then, he had never bothered much about figuring things out, but now, whenever something happened, he couldn't rest until he'd found an explanation satisfying to his intellect. Previously he'd acted on instinct; now he had to understand each small thing before he could accept it. And this applied not only to swordsmanship but to the way he viewed humanity and society.

It was true that the daredevil in him had been tamed. Yet Nikkan said he was "too strong." Musashi assumed that Nikkan was referring not to physical strength but to the savage fighting spirit with which he had been born. Could the priest really have perceived it, or was he guessing?

"The knowledge that comes from books is of no use to the warrior," he reassured himself. "If a man worries too much about what others think or do, he's apt to be slow to act. Why, if Nikkan himself closed his eyes for a moment and made one misstep, he'd crumble and fall to pieces!"

The sound of footsteps on the stairs intruded upon his musings. The maid appeared, and after her Jotaro, his dark skin further blackened by the grime acquired on his journey, but his spritelike hair white with dust. Musashi, truly happy to have the diversion of his little friend, welcomed him with open arms.

The boy plopped down on the floor and stretched his dirty legs out straight. "Am I tired!" he sighed.

"Did you have trouble finding me?"

"Trouble! I almost gave up. I've been searching all over!"

"Didn't you ask at the Hozoin?"

"Yes, but they said they didn't know anything about you."

"Oh, they did, did they?" Musashi's eyes narrowed. "And after I said specifically that you'd find me near Sarusawa Pond. Oh, well, I'm glad you made it."

"Here's the answer from the Yoshioka School." He handed Musashi the bamboo tube. "I couldn't find Hon'iden Matahachi, so I asked the people at his house to give him the message."

"Fine. Now run along and have a bath. They'll give you some dinner downstairs."

Musashi took the letter from its container and read it. It said that Seijuro looked forward to a "second bout"; if Musashi didn't show up as promised the following year, it would be assumed that he'd lost his nerve. Should that happen, Seijuro would make sure that Musashi became the laughingstock of Kyoto. This braggadocio was set down in clumsy handwriting, presumably by someone other than Seijuro.

As Musashi tore the letter to bits and burned it, the charred pieces fluttered up into the air like so many black butterflies.

Seijuro had spoken of a "bout," but it was clear that it was going to be more than that. It would be a battle to the death. Next year, as a result of this insulting note, which one of the combatants would end up in ashes?

Musashi took it for granted that a warrior must be content to live from day to day, never knowing each morning if he'd live to see nightfall. Nevertheless, the thought that he might really die in the coming year worried him somewhat. There were so many things he still wanted to do. For one thing, there was his burning desire to become a great swordsman. But that wasn't all. So far, he reflected, he hadn't done any of the things people ordinarily do in the course of a lifetime.

At this stage of his life, he was still vain enough to think he'd like to have retainers—a lot of them—leading his horses and carrying his falcons, just like Bokuden and Lord Koizumi of Ise. He would like, too, to have a proper house, with a good wife and loyal servants. He wanted to be a good master and to enjoy the warmth and comfort of home life. And of course, before he settled down, he had a secret longing to have a passionate love affair. During all these years of thinking solely about the Way of the Samurai he had, not unnaturally, remained chaste. Still, he was struck by some of the women he saw on the streets of Kyoto and Nara, and it was not their aesthetic qualities alone that pleased him; they aroused him physically.

His thoughts turned to Otsu. Though she was now a creature of the distant past, he felt closely bound to her. How many times, when he was lonely or melancholy, had the vague recollection of her alone cheered him up.

Presently he came out of his reverie. Jotaro had rejoined him, bathed, satiated and proud to have carried out his mission successfully. Sitting with his short legs crossed and his hands between his knees, he didn't take long to succumb to fatigue. He was soon snoozing blissfully, his mouth open. Musashi put him to bed.

When morning came, the boy was up with the sparrows. Musashi also arose early, since he intended to resume his travels.

As he was dressing, the widow appeared and said in a regretful tone, "You seem in a hurry to leave." In her arms she was carrying some clothing, which she offered him. "I've sewn these things together for you as a parting gift—a kimono with a short cloak. I'm not sure you'll like them, but I hope you'll wear them."

Musashi looked at her in astonishment. The garments were much too expensive for him to accept after having stayed there only two days. He tried to refuse, but the widow insisted. "No, you must take them. They aren't anything very special anyway. I have a lot of old kimono and No costumes left by my husband. I have no use for them. I thought it would be nice for you to have some. I do hope you won't refuse. Now that I've altered them to fit you, if you don't take them, they'll just go to waste."

She went behind Musashi and held up the kimono for him to slip his arms into. As he put it on, he realized that the silk was of very good quality and felt more embarrassed than ever. The sleeveless cloak was particularly fine; it must have been imported from China. The hem was gold brocade, the lining silk crepe, and the leather fastening straps had been dyed purple.

"It looks perfect on you!" exclaimed the widow.

Jotaro, looking on enviously, suddenly said to her, "What're you going to give me?"

The widow laughed. "You should be happy for the chance to accompany your fine master."

"Aw," grumbled Jotaro, "who wants an old kimono anyway?"

"Is there anything you do want?"

Running to the wall in the anteroom and taking a No mask down from its hook, the boy said, "Yes, this!" He'd coveted it since first spying it the night before, and now he rubbed it tenderly against his cheek.

Musashi was surprised at the boy's good taste. He himself had found it admirably executed. There was no way of knowing who had made it, but it was certainly two or three centuries old and had evidently been used in actual No performances. The face, carved with exquisite care, was that of a female demon, but whereas the usual mask of this type was grotesquely painted with blue spots, this was the face of a beautiful and elegant young girl. It was peculiar only in that one side of her mouth curved sharply upward in the eeriest fashion imaginable. Obviously not a fictitious face conjured up by the artist, it was the portrait of a real, living madwoman, beautiful yet bewitched.

"That you cannot have," said the widow firmly, trying to take the mask away from the boy.

Evading her reach, Jotaro put the mask on the top of his head and danced about the room, shouting defiantly, "What do you need it for? It's mine now; I'm going to keep it!"

Musashi, surprised and embarrassed by his ward's conduct, made an attempt to catch him, but Jotaro stuffed the mask into his kimono and fled down the stairs, the widow giving chase. Although she was laughing, not angry at all, she clearly didn't intend to part with the mask.

Presently Jotaro climbed slowly back up the stairs. Musashi, ready to scold him severely, was seated with his face toward the door. But as the boy entered, he cried, "Boo!" and held the mask out before him. Musashi was startled; his muscles tensed and his knees shifted inadvertently.

He wondered why Jotaro's prank had such an effect on him, but as he stared at the mask in the dim light, he began to understand. The carver had put something diabolical into his creation. That crescent smile, curving up on the left side of the white face, was haunted, possessed of a devil.

"If we're going, let's go," said Jotaro.

Musashi, without rising, said, "Why haven't you given the mask back yet? What do you want with a thing like that?"

"But she said I could keep it! She gave it to me."

"She did not! Go downstairs and give it back to her."

"But she gave it to me! When I offered to return it, she said that if I wanted it so badly, I could keep it. She just wanted to make sure I'd take good care of it, so I promised her I would."

"What am I going to do with you!" Musashi felt ashamed about accepting, first, the beautiful kimono and then this mask that the widow seemed to treasure. He would have liked to do something in return, but she was obviously not in need of money—certainly not the small amount he could have spared—and none of his meager possessions would make a suitable gift. He descended the stairs, apologizing for Jotaro's rudeness and attempting to return the mask.

The widow, however, said, "No, the more I think of it, the more I think I'd be happier without it. And he does want it so badly. . . . Don't be too hard on him."

Suspecting the mask had some special significance for her, Musashi tried once more to return it, but by this time Jotaro had his straw sandals on and was outside waiting by the gate, a smug look on his face. Musashi, eager to be off, gave in to her kindness and accepted the gift. The young widow said she was sorrier to see Musashi go than she was to lose the mask, and begged him several times to come back and stay there whenever he was in Nara.

Musashi was tying the thongs of his sandals when the dumpling-maker's wife came running up. "Oh," she said breathlessly, "I'm so glad you haven't left yet. You can't go now! Please, go back upstairs. Something terrible is going on!" The woman's voice trembled as though she thought some fearful ogre was about to attack her.

Musashi finished tying his sandals and calmly raised his head. "What is it? What's so terrible?"

"The priests at the Hozoin have heard you're leaving today, and more than ten of them have taken their lances and are lying in wait for you in Hannya Plain."

"Oh?"

"Yes, and the abbot, Inshun, is with them. My husband knows one of the priests, and he asked him what was going on. The priest said the man who's been staying here for the last couple of days, the man named Miyamoto, was leaving Nara today, and the priests were going to waylay him on the road."

Her face twitching with fright, she assured Musashi that it would be suicide to leave Nara this morning and fervently urged him to lie low for another night. It would be safer, in her opinion, to try and sneak away the next day.

"I see," said Musashi without emotion. "You say they plan to meet me on Hannya Plain?"

"I'm not sure exactly where, but they went off in that direction. Some of the townspeople told me it wasn't only the priests. They said a whole lot of the ronin, too, had got together, saying they'd catch you and turn you over to the Hozoin. Did you say something bad about the temple, or insult them in some way?"

"No."

"Well, they say the priests are furious because you hired somebody to put up posters with verses on them making fun of the Hozoin. They took this to mean you were gloating over having killed one of their men."

"I didn't do anything of the sort. There's been a mistake."

"Well, if it's a mistake, you shouldn't go out and get yourself killed over it!"

His brow beaded with sweat, Musashi looked thoughtfully up at the sky, recalling how angry the three ronin had been when he turned down their business deal. Maybe he was indebted to them for all this. It would be just like them to put up offensive posters and then spread the word that he'd done it.

Abruptly he stood up. "I'm leaving," he said.

He strapped his traveling bag to his back, took his basket hat in hand, and turning to the two women, thanked them for their kindness. As he started toward the gate, the widow, now in tears, followed along, begging him not to go.

"If I stay over another night," he pointed out, "there's bound to be trouble at your house. I certainly wouldn't want that to happen, after you've been so good to us."

"I don't care," she insisted. "You'd be safer here."

"No, I'll go now. Jo! Say thank you to the lady."

Dutifully, the boy bowed and did as he was told. He, too, appeared to be in low spirits, but not because he was sorry to leave. When it came right down to it, Jotaro did not really know Musashi. In Kyoto, he had heard that his master was a weakling and a coward, and the thought that the notorious lancers of the Hozoin were set to attack him was very depressing. His youthful heart was filled with gloom and foreboding.

Jotaro trudged along sadly behind his master, fearing each step was taking them closer to certain death. A little earlier, on the damp, shady road near the Todaiji, a dewdrop falling on his collar had almost made him cry out. The black crows he saw along the way gave him an eerie feeling.

Nara was far behind them. Through the rows of cryptomeria trees along the road, they could make out the gently sloping plain leading up to Hannya Hill; to their right were the rolling peaks of Mount Mikasa, above them the peaceful sky.

That he and Musashi were heading straight for the place where the Hozoin lancers were waiting in ambush made absolutely no sense to him. There were plenty of places to hide, if one put one's mind to it. Why couldn't they go into one of the many temples along the way and bide their time? That would surely be more sensible.

He wondered if perhaps Musashi meant to apologize to the priests, even though he hadn't wronged them in any way. Jotaro resolved that if Musashi begged their forgiveness, he would too. This was no time to be arguing about the right and wrong of things.

"Jotaro!"

The boy started at the sound of his name being called. His eyebrows shot up and his body became tense. Realizing his face was probably pale from fright and not wanting to appear childish, he turned his eyes bravely toward the sky. Musashi looked up at the sky too, and the boy felt more dispirited than ever.

When Musashi continued, it was in his usual cheerful tone. "Feels good, doesn't it, Jo? It's as though we were walking along on the songs of the nightingales."

"What?" asked the boy, astonished.

"Nightingales, I said."

"Oh, yeah, nightingales. There are some around here, aren't there?"

Musashi could see from the paleness of the boy's lips that he was dejected. He felt sorry for him. After all, in a matter of minutes he might be suddenly alone in a strange place.

"We're getting near Hannya Hill, aren't we?" said Musashi.

"That's right."

"Well, now what?"

Jotaro didn't reply. The singing of the nightingales fell coldly on his ears. He couldn't shake off the foreboding that they might soon be parted forever. The eyes that had bristled with mirth when surprising Musashi with the mask were now worried and mournful.

"I think I'd better leave you here," said Musashi. "If you come along, you may get hurt accidentally. There's no reason to put yourself in harm's way."

Jotaro broke down, tears streaming down his cheeks as if a dam had broken. The backs of his hands went up to his eyes and his shoulders quivered. His crying was punctuated by tiny spasms, as if he had the hiccups.

"What's this? Aren't you supposed to be learning the Way of the Samurai? If I break and run, you run in the same direction. If I get killed, go back to the sake shop in Kyoto. But for now, go to that little hill and watch from there. You'll be able to keep an eye on everything that happens."

Having wiped his tears away, Jotaro grabbed Musashi's sleeves and blurted out, "Let's run away!"

"That's no way for a samurai to talk! That's what you want to be, isn't it?"

"I'm afraid! I don't want to die!" With trembling hands, he kept trying to pull Musashi back by the sleeve. "Think about me," he pleaded. "Please, let's get away while we can!"

"When you talk like that, you make me want to run too. You've got no parents who'll look after you, just like me when I was your age. But—"

"Then come on. What are we waiting for?"

"No!" Musashi turned, and planting his feet wide apart, faced the child squarely. "I'm a samurai. You're a samurai's son. We're not going to run away."

Hearing the finality in Musashi's tone, Jotaro gave up and sat down, dirty tears rolling off his face as he rubbed his red and swollen eyes with his hands.

"Don't worry!" said Musashi. "I have no intention of losing. I'm going to win! Everything will be all right then, don't you think?"

Jotaro took little comfort from this speech. He couldn't believe a word of it. Knowing that the Hozoin lancers numbered more than ten, he doubted whether Musashi, considering his reputation for weakness, could beat them one at a time, let alone all together.

Musashi, for his part, was beginning to lose patience. He liked Jotaro, felt sorry for him, but this was no time to be thinking about children. The lancers were there for one purpose: to kill him. He had to be prepared to face them. Jotaro was becoming a nuisance.

His voice took on a sharp edge. "Stop your blubbering! You'll never be a samurai, carrying on this way. Why don't you just go on back to the sake shop?" Firmly and not too gently, he pushed the boy from him.

Jotaro, stung to the core, suddenly stopped crying and stood straight, a surprised look on his face. He watched his master stride off toward Hannya Hill. He wanted to call out after him, but resisted the urge. Instead he forced himself to remain silent for several minutes. Then he squatted under a nearby tree, buried his face in his hands, and gritted his teeth.

Musashi did not look back, but Jotaro's sobs echoed in his ears. He felt he could see the hapless, frightened little boy through the back of his head and regretted having brought him along. It was more than enough just to take care of himself; still immature, with only his sword to rely on and no idea of what the morrow might bring—what need had he of a companion?

The trees thinned out. He found himself on an open plain, actually the slightly rising skirt of the mountains in the distance. On the road branching off toward Mount Mikasa, a man raised his hand in greeting.

"Hey, Musashi! Where are you going?"

Musashi recognized the man coming toward him; it was Yamazoe Dampachi. Though Musashi sensed immediately that Dampachi's objective was to lead him into a trap, he nevertheless greeted him heartily.

Dampachi said, "Glad I ran into you. I want you to know how sorry I am about that business the other day." His tone was too polite, and as he spoke, he was obviously examining Musashi's face with great care. "I hope you'll forget about it. It was all a mistake."

Dampachi himself was none too sure what to make of Musashi. He had been very impressed by what he had seen at the Hozoin. Indeed, just thinking about it sent chills up his spine. Be that as it may, Musashi was still only a provincial ronin, who couldn't be more than twenty-one or twenty-two years old, and Dampachi was far from ready to admit to himself that anyone of that age and status could be his better.

"Where are you going?" he asked again.

"I'm planning to go through Iga over to the Ise highroad. And you?"

"Oh, I have some things to do in Tsukigase."

"That's not far from Yagyu Valley, is it?"

"No, not far."

"That's where Lord Yagyu's castle is, isn't it?"

"Yes, it's near the temple called Kasagidera. You must go there sometime. The old lord, Muneyoshi, lives in retirement, like a tea master, and his son, Munenori, is in Edo, but you should still stop in and see what it's like."

"I don't really think Lord Yagyu would give a lesson to a wanderer like me."

"He might. Of course, it'd help if you had an introduction. As it happens, I know an armorer in Tsukigase who does work for the Yagyus. If you'd like, I could ask if he'd be willing to introduce you."

The plain stretched out broadly for several miles, the skyline broken occasionally by a lone cryptomeria or Chinese black pine. There were gentle rises here and there, however, and the road rose and fell too. Near the bottom of Hannya Hill, Musashi spotted the brown smoke of a fire rising beyond a low hillock.

"What's that?" he asked.

"What's what?"

"That smoke over there."

"What's so strange about smoke?" Dampachi had been sticking close to Musashi's left side, and as he stared into the latter's face, his own hardened perceptibly.

Musashi pointed. "That smoke over there: there's something suspicious about it," he said. "Doesn't it look that way to you?"

"Suspicious? In what way?"

"Suspicious—you know, like the look on your face right now," Musashi said sharply, abruptly sweeping his finger toward Dampachi.

A sharp whistling sound broke the stillness on the plain. Dampachi gasped as Musashi struck. His attention diverted by Musashi's finger, Dampachi never realized that Musashi had drawn his sword. His body rose, flew forward, and landed face down. Dampachi would not rise again.

From the distance there was a cry of alarm, and two men appeared at the top of the hillock. One of the men screamed, and both spun round and took to their heels, their arms flailing the air wildly.

The sword that Musashi was pointing toward the earth glittered in the sunlight; fresh blood dripped from its tip. He marched directly on toward the hillock, and although the spring breeze blew softly against his skin, Musashi felt his muscles tauten as he ascended. From the top, he looked down at the fire burning below.

"He's come!" shouted one of the men who had fled to join the others. There were about thirty men. Musashi picked out Dampachi's cohorts, Yasukawa Yasubei and Otomo Banryu.

"He's come!" parroted another.

They'd been lolling in the sun. Now they all jumped to their feet. Half were priests, the other half nondescript ronin. When Musashi came into view, a wordless but nonetheless savage stir went through the group. They saw the bloodstained sword and suddenly realized that the battle had already begun. Instead of challenging Musashi, they had been sitting around the fire and had let him challenge them!

Yasukawa and Otomo were talking as fast as they could, explaining with broad rapid gestures how Yamazoe had been cut down. The ronin scowled with fury, the Hozoin priests eyed Musashi menacingly while grouping themselves for battle.

All of the priests carried lances. Black sleeves tucked up, they were ready for action, apparently set upon avenging the death of Agon and restoring the temple's honor. They looked grotesque, like so many demons from hell.

The ronin formed a semicircle, so they could watch the show and at the same time keep Musashi from escaping.

This precaution, however, proved unnecessary, for Musashi showed no sign of either running or backing down. In fact, he was walking steadily and directly toward them. Slowly, pace by pace, he advanced, looking as if he might pounce at any moment.

For a moment, there was an ominous silence, as both sides contemplated approaching death. Musashi's face went deadly white and through his eyes stared the eyes of the god of vengeance, glittering with venom. He was selecting his prey.

Neither the ronin nor the priests were as tense as Musashi. Their numbers gave them confidence, and their optimism was unshakable. Still, no one wanted to be the first attacked.

A priest at the end of the column of lancers gave a signal, and without breaking formation, they rushed around to Musashi's right.

"Musashi! I am Inshun," shouted the same priest. "I'm told that you came while I was away and killed Agon. That you later publicly insulted the honor of the Hozoin. That you mocked us by having posters put up all over town. Is this true?"

"No!" shouted Musashi. "If you're a priest, you should know better than to trust only what you see and hear. You should consider things with your mind and spirit."

It was like pouring oil on the flames. Ignoring their leader, the priests began to shout, saying talk was cheap, it was time to fight.

They were enthusiastically seconded by the ronin, who had grouped themselves in close formation at Musashi's left. Screaming, cursing and waving their swords in the air, they egged the priests on to action.

Musashi, convinced that the ronin were all mouth and no fight, suddenly turned to them and shouted, "All right! Which one of you wants to come forward?"

All but two or three fell back a pace, each sure that Musashi's evil eye was upon him. The two or three brave ones stood ready, swords outstretched, issuing a challenge.

In the wink of an eye, Musashi was on one of them like a fighting cock. There was a sound like the popping of a cork, and the ground turned red. Then came a chilling noise—not a battle cry, not a curse, but a truly blood-curdling howl.

Musashi's sword screeched back and forth through the air, a reverberation in his own body telling him when he connected with human bone. Blood and brains spattered from his blade; fingers and arms flew through the air.

The ronin had come to watch the carnage, not to participate in it, but their weakness had led Musashi to attack them first. At the very beginning, they held together fairly well, because they thought the priests would soon come to their rescue. But the priests stood silent and motionless as Musashi quickly slaughtered five or six ronin, throwing the others into confusion. Before long they were slashing wildly in all directions, as often as not injuring one other.

For most of the time, Musashi wasn't really conscious of what he was doing. He was in a sort of trance, a murderous dream in which body and soul were concentrated in his three-foot sword. Unconsciously, his whole life experience—the knowledge his father had beaten into him, what he had learned at Sekigahara, the theories he had heard at the various schools of swordsmanship, the lessons taught him by the mountains and the trees—everything came into play in the rapid movements of his body. He became a disembodied whirlwind mowing down the herd of ronin, who by their stunned bewilderment left themselves wide open to his sword.

For the short duration of the battle, one of the priests counted the number of times he inhaled and exhaled. It was all over before he had taken his twentieth breath.

Musashi was drenched with the blood of his victims. The few remaining ronin were also covered with gore. The earth, the grass, even the air was bloody. One of their number let out a scream, and the surviving ronin scattered in all directions.

While all this was going on, Jotaro was absorbed in prayer. His hands folded before him and his eyes lifted skyward, he implored, "Oh, God in heaven, come to his aid! My master, down there on the plain, is hopelessly outnumbered. He's weak, but he isn't a bad man. Please help him!"

Despite Musashi's instructions to go away, he couldn't leave. The place where he had finally chosen to sit, his hat and his mask beside him, was a knoll from which he could see the scene around the bonfire in the distance.

"Hachiman! Kompira! God of Kasuga Shrine! Look! My master is walking directly into the enemy. Oh, gods of heaven, protect him. He isn't himself. He's usually mild and gentle, but he's been a little bit strange ever since this morning. He must be crazy, or else he wouldn't take on that many at once! Oh, please, please, help him!"

After calling on the deities a hundred times or more, he noticed no visible results of his efforts and started getting angry. Finally, he was shouting: "Aren't there any gods in this land? Are you going to let the wicked people win, and the good man be killed? If you do that, then everything they've always told me about right and wrong is a lie! You can't let him be killed! If you do, I'll spit on you!"

When he saw that Musashi was surrounded, his invocations turned to curses, directed not only at the enemy but at the gods themselves. Then, realizing that the blood being spilled on the plain was not his teacher's, he abruptly changed his tune. "Look! My master's not a weakling after all! He's beating them!"

This was the first time Jotaro had ever witnessed men fighting like beasts to the death, the first time he had ever seen so much blood. He began to feel that he was down there in the middle of it, himself smeared with gore. His heart turned somersaults, he felt giddy and light-headed.

"Look at him! I told you he could do it! What an attack! And look at those silly priests, lined up like a bunch of cawing crows, afraid to take a step!"

But this last was premature, for as he spoke the priests of the Hozoin began moving in on Musashi.

"Oh, oh! This looks bad. They're all attacking him at once. Musashi's in trouble!" Forgetting everything, out of his senses with anxiety, Jotaro darted like a fireball toward the scene of impending disaster.

Abbot Inshun gave the command to charge, and in an instant, with a tremendous roar of voices, the lancers flew into action. Their glittering weapons whistled in the air as the priests scattered like bees sprung from a hive, shaved heads making them appear all the more barbaric.

The lances they carried were all different, with a wide variety of blades—the usual pointed, cone-shaped ones, others flat, cross-shaped or hooked—each priest using the type he favored most. Today they had a chance to see how the techniques they honed in practice worked in real battle.

As they fanned out, Musashi, expecting a trick attack, jumped back and stood on guard. Weary and a little dazed from the earlier bout, he gripped his sword handle tightly. It was sticky with gore, and a mixture of blood and sweat clouded his vision, but he was determined to die magnificently, if die he must.

To his amazement, the attack never came. Instead of making the anticipated lunges in his direction, the priests fell like mad dogs on their erstwhile allies, chasing down the ronin who had fled and slashing at them mercilessly as they screamed in protest. The unsuspecting ronin, futilely trying to direct the lancers toward Musashi, were slit, skewered, stabbed in the mouth, sliced in two, and otherwise slaughtered until not one of them was left alive. The massacre was as thorough as it was bloodthirsty.

Musashi could not believe his eyes. Why had the priests attacked their supporters? And why so viciously? He himself had only moments earlier been fighting like a wild animal; now he could hardly bear to watch the ferocity with which these men of the cloth slew the ronin. Having been transformed for a time into a mindless beast, he was now restored to his normal state by the sight of others similarly transformed. The experience was sobering.

Then he became aware of a tugging at his arms and legs. Looking down, he found Jotaro weeping tears of relief. For the first time, he relaxed.

As the battle ended, the abbot approached him, and in a polite, dignified manner, said, "You are Miyamoto, I assume. It is an honor to meet you." He was tall and of light complexion. Musashi was somewhat overcome by his appearance, as well as by his poise. With a certain amount of confusion, he wiped his sword clean and sheathed it, but for the moment words failed him.

"Let me introduce myself," continued the priest. "I am Inshun, abbot of the Hozoin."

"So you are the master of the lance," said Musashi.

"I'm sorry I was away when you visited us recently. I'm also embarrassed that my disciple Agon put up such a poor fight."

Sorry about Agon's performance? Musashi felt that perhaps his ears needed cleaning. He remained silent for a moment, for before he could decide on a suitable way to respond to Inshun's courteous tone, he had to straighten out the confusion in his mind. He still couldn't figure out why the priests had turned on the ronin—could imagine no possible explanation. He was even somewhat puzzled to find himself still alive.

"Come," said the abbot, "and wash off some of that blood. You need a rest." Inshun led him toward the fire, Jotaro tagging along close behind.

The priests had torn a large cotton cloth into strips and were wiping their lances. Gradually they gathered by the fire, sitting down with Inshun and Musashi as though nothing unusual had occurred. They began chatting among themselves.

"Look, up there," said one, pointing upward.

"Ah, the crows have caught the whiff of blood. Cawing over the dead bodies, they are."

"Why don't they dig in?"

"They will, as soon as we leave. They'll be scrambling to get at the feast."

The grisly banter went on in this leisurely vein. Musashi got the impression that he wasn't going to find out anything unless he asked. He looked at Inshun and said, "You know, I thought you and your men had come here to attack me, and I'd made up my mind to take along as many of you as I could to the land of the dead. I can't understand why you're treating me this way."

Inshun laughed. "Well, we don't necessarily regard you as an ally, but our real purpose today was to do a little housecleaning."

"You call what's been going on housecleaning?"

"That's right," said Inshun, pointing toward the horizon. "But I think we might as well wait and let Nikkan explain it to you. I'm sure that speck on the edge of the plain is he."

At the same moment, on the other side of the plain, a horseman was saying to Nikkan, "You walk fast for your age, don't you?"

"I'm not fast. You're slow."

"You're nimbler than the horses."

"Why shouldn't I be? I'm a man."

The old priest, who alone was on foot, was pacing the horsemen as they advanced toward the smoke of the fire. The five riders with him were officials.

As the party approached, the priests whispered among themselves, "It's the Old Master." Having confirmed this, they fell back a good distance and lined themselves up ceremoniously, as for a sacred rite, to greet Nikkan and his entourage.

The first thing Nikkan said was, "Did you take care of everything?"

Inshun bowed and replied, "Just as you commanded." Then, turning to the officials, "Thank you for coming."

As the samurai jumped one by one off their horses, their leader replied, "It's no trouble. Thank *you* for doing the real work! . . . Let's get on with it, men."

The officials went about inspecting the corpses and making a few notes; then their leader returned to where Inshun was standing. "We'll send people from the town to clean up the mess. Please feel free to leave everything as it is." With that, the five of them remounted their horses and rode off.

Nikkan let the priests know that they were no longer needed. Having bowed to him, they started walking away silently. Inshun, too, said good-bye to Nikkan and Musashi and took his leave.

As soon as the men were gone, there was a great cacophony. The crows descended, flapping their wings joyfully.

Grumbling over the noise, Nikkan walked over to Musashi's side and said casually, "Forgive me if I offended you the other day."

"Not at all. You were very kind. It is I who should thank you." Musashi knelt and bowed deeply before the old priest.

"Get off the ground," commanded Nikkan. "This field is no place for bowing."

Musashi got to his feet.

"Has the experience here taught you anything?" the priest asked.

"I'm not even sure what happened. Can you tell me?"

"By all means," replied Nikkan. "Those officials who just left work under Okubo Nagayasu, who was recently sent to administer Nara. They're new to the district, and the ronin have been taking advantage of their unfamiliarity with the place—waylaying innocent passersby, blackmailing, gambling, making off with the women, breaking into widows' houses—causing all sorts of trouble. The administrator's office couldn't bring them under control, but they did know that there were about fifteen ringleaders, including Dampachi and Yasukawa.

"This Dampachi and his cohorts took a disliking to you, as you know. Since they were afraid to attack you themselves, they concocted what they thought was a clever plan, whereby the priests of the Hozoin would do it for them. The slanderous statements about the temple, attributed to you, were their work; so were the posters. They made sure everything was reported to me, presumably on the theory that I'm stupid."

Musashi's eyes laughed as he listened.

"I thought about it for a while," said the abbot, "and it occurred to me that this was an ideal opportunity to have a housecleaning in Nara. I spoke to Inshun about my plan, he agreed to undertake it, and now everybody's happy—the priests, the administrators; also the crows. Ha, ha!"

There was one other person who was supremely happy. Nikkan's story had wiped away all of Jotaro's doubts and fears, and the boy was ecstatic. He began singing an improvised ditty while dancing about like a bird flapping its wings:

> A housecleaning, oh,
> A housecleaning!

At the sound of his unaffected voice, Musashi and Nikkan turned to watch him. He was wearing his mask with the curious smile and pointing his wooden sword at the scattered bodies. Taking an occasional swipe at the birds, he continued:

> Yes, you crows,
> Once in a while

There's a need for housecleaning,
But not only in Nara.
It's nature's way
To make everything new again.
So spring can rise from the ground,
We burn leaves,
We burn fields.
Sometimes we want snow to fall,
Sometimes we want a housecleaning.
Oh, you crows!
Feast away! What a spread!
Soup straight from the eye sockets,
And thick red sake.
But don't have too much
Or you'll surely get drunk.

"Come here, boy!" shouted Nikkan sharply.

"Yes, sir." Jotaro stood still and turned to face the abbot.

"Stop acting the fool. Fetch me some rocks."

"This kind?" asked Jotaro, snatching a stone that lay near his feet and holding it up.

"Yes, like that. Bring lots of them!"

"Yes, sir!"

As the boy gathered the stones, Nikkan sat down and wrote on each one "Namu Myoho Renge-kyo," the sacred invocation of the Nichiren sect. Then he gave them back to the boy and ordered him to scatter them among the dead. While Jotaro did this, Nikkan put his palms together and chanted a section of the Lotus Sutra.

When he had finished, he announced, "That should take care of them. Now you two can be on your way. I shall return to Nara." As abruptly as he had come, he departed, walking at his customary break-neck speed, before Musashi had a chance to thank him or make arrangements to see him again.

For a moment, Musashi just stared at the retreating figure, then suddenly he darted off to catch up with it. "Reverend priest!" he called. "Haven't you forgotten something?" He patted his sword as he said this.

"What?" asked Nikkan.

"You have given me no word of guidance, and since there is no way of knowing when we'll meet again, I'd appreciate some small bit of advice."

The abbot's toothless mouth let out its familiar crackling laugh. "Don't you understand *yet?*" he asked. "That you're too strong is the only thing I have to teach you. If you continue to pride yourself on your strength, you won't live to see thirty. Why, you might easily have been killed today. Think about that, and decide how to conduct yourself in the future."

Musashi was silent.

"You accomplished something today, but it was not well done, not by a long shot. Since you're still young, I can't really blame you, but it's a grave error to think the Way of the Samurai consists of nothing but a show of strength.

"But then, I tend to have the same fault, so I'm not really qualified to speak to you on the subject. You should study the way that Yagyu Sekishusai and Lord Koizumi of Ise have lived. Sekishusai was my teacher, Lord Koizumi was his. If you take them as your models and try to follow the path they have followed, you may come to know the truth."

When Nikkan's voice ceased, Musashi, who had been staring at the ground, deep in thought, looked up. The old priest had already vanished.

The Gallant Tailor

by the Brothers Grimm,
translated by Lucy Crane

German brothers Jakob Grimm (1785–1863) and Wilhelm Grimm (1786–1858) wrote popular stories based upon traditional folk tales. This story is about a tailor who isn't afraid of anyone.

One summer morning a little tailor was sitting on his board near the window, and working cheerfully with all his might, when an old woman came down the street crying,

"Good jelly to sell! good jelly to sell!"

The cry sounded pleasant in the little tailor's ears, so he put his head out of the window, and called out,

"Here, my good woman—come here, if you want a customer."

So the poor woman climbed the steps with her heavy basket, and was obliged to unpack and display all her pots to the tailor. He looked at every one of them, and lifting all the lids, applied his nose to each, and said at last,

"The jelly seems pretty good; you may weigh me out four half ounces, or I don't mind having a quarter of a pound."

The woman, who had expected to find a good customer, gave him what he asked for, but went off angry and grumbling.

"This jelly is the very thing for me," cried the little tailor; "it will give me strength and cunning"; and he took down the bread from the cupboard, cut a whole round of the loaf, and spread the jelly on it, laid it near him, and went on stitching more gallantly than ever. All the while the scent of the sweet jelly was spreading throughout the room, where there were quantities of flies, who were attracted by it and flew to partake.

"Now then, who asked you to come?" said the tailor, and drove the unbidden guests away. But the flies, not understanding his language, were not to be got rid of like that, and returned in larger numbers than before. Then the tailor, not being able to stand it any longer, took from his chimney-corner a ragged cloth, and saying,

"Now, I'll let you have it!" beat it among them unmercifully. When he ceased, and counted the slain, he found seven lying dead before him.

"This is indeed somewhat," he said, wondering at his own gallantry; "the whole town shall know this."

So he hastened to cut out a belt, and he stitched it, and put on it in large capitals "Seven at one blow!"

"—The town, did I say!" said the little tailor; "the whole world shall know it!" And his heart quivered with joy, like a lamb's tail.

The tailor fastened the belt round him, and began to think of going out into the world, for his workshop seemed too small for his worship. So he looked about in all the house for something that it would be useful to take with him, but he found nothing but an old cheese, which he put in his pocket. Outside the door he noticed that a bird had got caught in the bushes, so he took that and put it in his pocket with the cheese. Then he set out gallantly on his way, and as he was light and active he felt no fatigue. The way led over a mountain, and when he reached the topmost peak he saw a terrible giant sitting there, and looking about him at his ease. The tailor went bravely up to him, called out to him, and said,

"Comrade, good day! there you sit looking over the wide world! I am on the way thither to seek my fortune: have you a fancy to go with me?"

The giant looked at the tailor contemptuously, and said,

"You little rascal! you miserable fellow!"

"That may be!" answered the little tailor, and undoing his coat he showed the giant his belt; "you can read there whether I am a man or not!"

The giant read: "Seven at one blow!" and thinking it meant men that the tailor had killed, felt at once more respect for the little fellow. But as he wanted to prove him, he took up a stone and squeezed it so hard that water came out of it.

"Now you can do that," said the giant,—"that is, if you have the strength for it."

"That's not much," said the little tailor, "I call that play," and he put his hand in his pocket and took out the cheese and squeezed it, so that the whey ran out of it.

"Well," said he, "what do you think of that?"

The giant did not know what to say to it, for he could not have believed it of the little man. Then the giant took up a stone and threw it so high that it was nearly out of sight.

"Now, little fellow, suppose you do that!"

"Well thrown," said the tailor; "but the stone fell back to earth again,—I will throw you one that will never come back." So he felt in his pocket, took out the bird, and threw it into the air. And the bird, when it found itself at liberty, took wing, flew off, and returned no more.

"What do you think of that, comrade?" asked the tailor.

"There is no doubt that you can throw," said the giant; "but we will see if you can carry."

He led the little tailor to a mighty oak-tree which had been felled, and was lying on the ground, and said,

"Now, if you are strong enough, help me to carry this tree out of the wood."

"Willingly," answered the little man; "you take the trunk on your shoulders, I will take the branches with all their foliage, that is much the most difficult."

So the giant took the trunk on his shoulders, and the tailor seated himself on a branch, and the giant, who could not see what he was doing, had the whole tree to carry, and the little man on it as well. And the little man was very cheerful and merry, and whistled the tune: *"There were three tailors riding by,"* as if carrying the tree was mere child's play. The giant, when he had struggled on under his heavy load a part of the way, was tired out, and cried,

"Look here, I must let go the tree!"

The tailor jumped off quickly, and taking hold of the tree with both arms, as if he were carrying it, said to the giant,

"You see you can't carry the tree though you are such a big fellow!"

They went on together a little farther, and presently they came to a cherry-tree, and the giant took hold of the topmost branches, where the ripest fruit hung, and pulling them downwards, gave them to the tailor to hold, bidding him eat. But the little tailor was much too weak to hold the tree, and as the giant let go, the tree sprang back, and the tailor was caught up into the air. And when he dropped down again without any damage, the giant said to him,

"How is this? haven't you strength enough to hold such a weak sprig as that?"

"It is not strength that is lacking," answered the little tailor; "how should it to one who has slain seven at one blow. I just jumped over the tree because the hunters are shooting down there in the bushes. You jump it too, if you can."

The giant made the attempt, and not being able to vault the tree, he remained hanging in the branches, so that once more the little tailor got the better of him. Then said the giant,

"As you are such a gallant fellow, suppose you come with me to our den, and stay the night."

The tailor was quite willing, and he followed him. When they reached the den there sat some other giants by the fire, and each had a roasted sheep in his hand, and was eating it. The little tailor looked round and thought,

"There is more elbow-room here than in my workshop."

And the giant showed him a bed, and told him he had better lie down upon it and go to sleep. The bed was, however, too big for the tailor, so he did not stay in it, but crept into a corner to sleep. As soon as it was midnight the giant got up, took a great staff of iron and beat the bed through with one stroke, and supposed he had made an end of that grasshopper of a tailor. Very early in the morning the giants went into the wood and forgot all about the little tailor, and when they saw him coming after them alive and merry, they were terribly frightened, and, thinking he was going to kill them, they ran away in all haste.

So the little tailor marched on, always following his nose. And after he had gone a great way he entered the courtyard belonging to a King's palace, and there he felt so overpowered with fatigue that he lay down and fell asleep. In the meanwhile came various people, who looked at him very curiously and read on his belt, "Seven at one blow!"

"Oh!" said they, "why should this great lord come here in time of peace? what a mighty champion he must be."

Then they went and told the King about him, and they thought that if war should break out what a worthy and useful man he would be, and that he ought not to be allowed to depart at any price. The King then summoned his council, and sent one of his courtiers to the little tailor to beg him, so soon as he should wake up, to consent to serve in the King's army. So the messenger stood and waited at the sleeper's side until his limbs began to stretch, and his eyes to open, and then he carried his answer back. And the answer was,

"That was the reason for which I came," said the little tailor, "I am ready to enter the King's service."

So he was received into it very honourably, and a separate dwelling set apart for him.

But the rest of the soldiers were very much set against the little tailor, and they wished him a thousand miles away.

"What shall be done about it?" they said among themselves; if we pick a quarrel and fight with him then seven of us will fall at each blow. That will be of no good to us."

So they came to a resolution, and went all together to the King to ask for their discharge.

"We never intended," said they, "to serve with a man who kills seven at a blow."

The King felt sorry to lose all his faithful servants because of one man, and he wished that he had never seen him, and would willingly get rid of him if he might. But he did not dare to dismiss the little tailor for fear he should kill all the King's people, and place himself upon the throne. He thought a long while about it, and at last made up his mind what to do. He sent for the little tailor, and told him that as he was so great a warrior he had a proposal to make to him. He told him that in a wood in his dominions dwelt two giants, who did great damage by robbery, murder, and fire, and that no man durst go near them for fear of his life. But that if the tailor should overcome and slay both these giants the King would give him his only daughter in marriage, and half his kingdom as dowry, and that a hundred horsemen should go with him to give him assistance.

"That would be something for a man like me!" thought the little tailor, "a beautiful princess and half a kingdom are not to be had every day," and he said to the King,

"Oh yes, I can soon overcome the giants, and yet have no need of the hundred horsemen; he who can kill seven at one blow has no need to be afraid of two."

So the little tailor set out, and the hundred horsemen followed him. When he came to the border of the wood he said to his escort,

"Stay here while I go to attack the giants."

Then he sprang into the wood, and looked about him right and left. After a while he caught sight of the two giants; they were lying down under a tree asleep, and snoring so that all the branches shook. The little tailor, all alive, filled both his pockets with stones and climbed up into the tree, and made his way to an overhanging bough, so that he could seat himself just above the sleepers; and from there he let one stone after another fall on the chest of one of the giants. For a long time the giant was quite unaware of this, but at last he waked up and pushed his comrade, and said,

"What are you hitting me for?"

"You are dreaming," said the other, "I am not touching you." And they composed themselves again to sleep, and the tailor let fall a stone on the other giant.

"What can that be?" cried he, "what are you casting at me?"

"I am casting nothing at you," answered the first grumbling.

They disputed about it for a while, but as they were tired, they gave it up at last, and their eyes closed once more. Then the little tailor began his game anew, picked out a heavier stone and threw it down with force upon the first giant's chest.

"This is too much!" cried he, and sprang up like a madman and struck his companion such a blow that the tree shook above them. The other paid him back with ready coin, and they fought with such fury that they tore up trees by their roots to use for weapons against each other, so that at last they both of them lay dead upon the ground. And now the little tailor got down.

"Another piece of luck!" said he, "that the tree I was sitting in did not get torn up too, or else I should have had to jump like a squirrel from one tree to another."

Then he drew his sword and gave each of the giants a few hacks in the breast, and went back to the horsemen and said,

"The deed is done, I have made an end of both of them: but it went hard with me, in the struggle they rooted up trees to defend themselves, but it was of no use, they had to do with a man who can kill seven at one blow."

"Then are you not wounded?" asked the horsemen.

"Nothing of the sort!" answered the tailor, "I have not turned a hair."

The horsemen still would not believe it, and rode into the wood to see, and there they found the giants wallowing in their blood, and all about them lying the uprooted trees.

The little tailor then claimed the promised boon, but the King repented him of his offer, and he sought again how to rid himself of the hero.

"Before you can possess my daughter and the half of my kingdom," said he to the tailor, "you must perform another heroic act. In the wood lives a unicorn who does great damage; you must secure him."

"A unicorn does not strike more terror into me than two giants. Seven at one blow!—that is my way," was the tailor's answer.

So, taking a rope and an axe with him, he went out into the wood, and told those who were ordered to attend him to wait outside. He had not far to seek, the unicorn soon came out and sprang at him, as if he would make an end of him without delay. "Softly, softly," said he, "most haste, worst speed," and remained standing until the animal came quite near, then he slipped quietly behind a tree. The unicorn ran with all his might against the tree and stuck his horn so deep into the trunk that he could not get it out again, and so was taken.

"Now I have you," said the tailor, coming out from behind the tree, and, putting the rope round the unicorn's neck, he took the axe, set free the horn, and when all his party were assembled he led forth the animal and brought it to the King.

The King did not yet wish to give him the promised reward, and set him a third task to do. Before the wedding could take place the tailor was to secure a wild boar which had done a great deal of damage in the wood.

The huntsmen were to accompany him.

"All right," said the tailor, "this is child's play."

But he did not take the huntsmen into the wood, and they were all the better pleased, for the wild boar had many a time before received them in such a way that they had no fancy to disturb him. When the boar caught sight of the tailor he ran at him with foaming mouth and gleaming tusks to bear him to the ground, but the nimble hero rushed into a chapel which chanced to be near, and jumped quickly out of a window on the other side. The boar ran after him, and when he got inside the door shut after him, and there he was imprisoned, for the creature was too big and unwieldy to jump out of the window too. Then the little tailor called the huntsmen that they might see the prisoner with their own eyes; and then he betook himself to the King, who now, whether he liked it or not, was obliged to fulfil his promise, and give him his daughter and the half of his kingdom. But if he had known that the great warrior was only a little tailor he would have taken it still more to heart. So the wedding was celebrated with great splendour and little joy, and the tailor was made into a king.

One night the young queen heard her husband talking in his sleep and saying,

"Now, boy, make me that waistcoat and patch me those breeches, or I will lay my yard measure about your shoulders!"

And so, as she perceived of what low birth her husband was, she went to her father the next morning and told him all, and begged him to set her free from a man who was nothing better than a tailor. The King bade her be comforted, saying,

"To-night leave your bedroom door open, my guard shall stand outside, and when he is asleep they shall come in and bind him and carry him off to a ship, and he shall be sent to the other side of the world."

So the wife felt consoled, but the King's water-bearer, who had been listening all the while, went to the little tailor and disclosed to him the whole plan.

"I shall put a stop to all this," said he.

At night he lay down as usual in bed, and when his wife thought that he was asleep, she got up, opened the door and lay down again. The little tailor, who only made believe to be asleep, began to murmur plainly,

"Now, boy, make me that waistcoat and patch me those breeches, or I will lay my yard measure about your shoulders! I have slain seven at one blow, killed two giants, caught a unicorn, and taken a wild boar, and shall I be afraid of those who are standing outside my room door?"

And when they heard the tailor say this, a great fear seized them; they fled away as if they had been wild hares, and none of them would venture to attack him.

And so the little tailor all his lifetime remained a king.

Morgan le Fay

by John Steinbeck

John Steinbeck (1902–1968) as a boy read Mallory's *Morte d'Arthur*, the poem that helped popu-
larize the legend of King Arthur. Steinbeck later
retold Mallory's tale in prose. This story describes
the treachery of Arthur's half-sister Morgan le Fay.

Morgan le Fay, King Arthur's half-sister,
was a dark, handsome, passionate woman, and cruel and ambitious. In
a nunnery she studied necromancy and became proficient in the dark
and destructive magic which is the weapon of the jealous. She joyed in
bending and warping men to her will through beauty and enchantment, and when these failed she used the blacker arts of treason and
murder. It was her pleasure to use men against men, fashioning from
their weaknesses weapons for their strength. Having Sir Uryens for her
husband, she made promises to Sir Accolon of Gaul and so enmeshed
him in dreams and enchantments that his will was slack and his honor
drugged, and he became the implement of her deepest wish. For
Morgan hated her brother, Arthur, hated his nobility and was jealous
of his crown. Morgan le Fay planned her brother's murder with intri-
cate care. She would give the crown to Uryens but keep its power for
herself, and the entangled Accolon would be the murder weapon.

By her arts Morgan the witch made a sword and sheath exactly like
Excalibur in appearance, and secretly she substituted it for Arthur's

sword. Then she beguiled Accolon with promises, canceled his conscience with his lust, and instructed him in the part he was to play, and when he agreed he thought her eyes lighted with love when they were fired with triumph, for Morgan le Fay loved no one. Hatred was her passion and destruction her pleasure.

Then Accolon by instruction took his place near Arthur and never left his side.

When there were no wars or tournaments it was the custom of knights and fighting men to hunt in the great forests which covered so much of England. In the breakneck chase of deer through forest and swamp and over rutted and rock-strewn hills, they tempered their horsemanship, and meeting the savage charge of wild boars, they kept their courage high and their dexterity keen. And also their mild enterprise loaded the turning spits in the kitchens with succulent meat for the long tables of the great hall.

On a day when King Arthur and many of his knights quartered the forest in search of quarry, the king and Sir Uryens and Sir Accolon of Gaul started a fine stag and gave chase. They were well horsed, so that before they knew it they were ten miles from the rest of the fellowship. The proud, high-antlered stag drew them on, and with whip and spur they pushed their foaming horses through tangled undergrowth and treacherous bogs, leaped streams and fallen trees until they overdrove their mounts and the foundered horses fell heaving to the ground, with bloody bits and rowel stripes on their sides.

The three knights, now footbound, watched the stag move wearily away. "This is a pretty thing," said Arthur. "We are miles from help."

Sir Uryens said, "We haven't any choice but to go on foot and look for some place to lodge and wait for help." They walked heavily through the oak forest until they came to the bank of a deep, wide river, and on the bank lay the exhausted stag, ringed with hounds, a brachet tearing at his throat. King Arthur scattered the hounds and killed the stag, and he raised his hunting horn and sounded the death call of a prize taken.

And only then did the knights look about them. On the smooth dark water they saw a little ship covered with silken cloth that hung over the sides and dipped into the water, and the boat moved silently toward the bank and grounded itself in the sandy shallows nearby. Arthur waded to the boat and looked under the silken hangings and saw no one there. He called to his friends to come, and the three boarded the little vessel and found it laden with luxury, with soft cushions and rich hangings, but they could see no occupants. The three men sat tiredly down on the soft cushions and rested while the evening came and the forest darkened around them. Night birds called in the forest and wild ducks came coasting in and the black wall of the forest reared over them.

As the companions nodded sleepily, a ring of torches flared up around them, and from the cabin of the ship twelve lovely damsels emerged, dressed in flowing silken gowns. The ladies curtsied to the king and saluted him by his name and welcomed him, and Arthur thanked them for their courtesy. Then they led the king and his fellows to a cabin hung with tapestry, and at a rich table they served wine and meats of many kinds, and such delicacies that all sat in wonder at the variety and profusion of the supper. And after they had supped long and pleasantly, and their eyes were heavy with good wine, the damsels led each to separate cabins richly hung with beds deep and soft. Then the three sank into the beds and instantly they fell into a deep, drugged sleep.

In the dawn Sir Uryens opened his wine-swollen eyes and saw that he lay in his own bed in his own lodgings in Camelot and Morgan le Fay seemingly asleep beside him. He had gone to sleep two days' journey away, and he could remember nothing else. He studied his wife through slitted lids, for there were many things he did not know about her and many other things he did not want to know. And so he held his peace and concealed his wonder.

King Arthur came to his senses on the cold stones of a dungeon floor. Dusky light from a high slit in the wall showed him the restless figures of many other prisoners. The king sat up, asking, "Where am I, and who are you?"

"We are captive knights," they told him. "There are twenty of us here and some of us have been kept in this dark cell for as much as eight years."

"For what reason?" asked the king. "Is it for ransom?"

"No," said one of the knights. "I will tell you the cause. The lord of this castle is Sir Damas, a mean and recreant man, and also a coward. His younger brother is Sir Outlake, a good, brave, honorable knight. Sir Damas has refused to share the inherited lands with his brother, except for a small manor house and lands Sir Outlake holds by force and guards against his brother. The people of the countryside love Sir Outlake for his kindness and justice, but they hate Sir Damas, because he is cruel and vengeful, as most cowards are. For many years there has been war and contention between the brothers, and Sir Outlake has issued a challenge to fight in single combat for his rights against his brother or any knight Sir Damas may appoint. But Sir Damas has not the courage to fight, and moreover he is so hated that no knight will enter the field for him. And so he with a gang of hired fighting men has laid traps for good knights venturing alone, and fallen on them and brought them captive to this place. He offers freedom if we will fight for him, but everyone has refused and some he has tortured and some starved to death. All of us are faint from hunger and the cramping prison so that we could not fight even if we wished to."

And Arthur said, "May God in his mercy deliver you."

Now a damsel looked through the iron grill of the dungeon door and beckoned to Arthur, and she said softly, "How do you like it here?"

"Am I supposed to like a prison?" said Arthur. "Why do you ask?"

"Because you have a choice," the damsel said. "If you will fight for my lord you will be released, but if you refuse, as these other fools have, you will spend your life here."

"It is a strange way to get a champion," said the king, "but for myself I would rather combat with a knight than live in a dungeon. If I agree to fight, will you release these other prisoners?"

"Yes," said the damsel.

"Then I am ready," the king said, "but I have neither horse nor armor."

"You shall have everything you need, sir."

The king looked closely at her and he said, "It seems to me that I have seen you at King Arthur's court."

"No," she said. "I have never been there. I am the daughter of the lord of this castle."

While the girl went to make arrangements, Arthur searched his memory, and he was quite sure he had seen her attending his sister Morgan le Fay.

Sir Damas accepted Arthur's offer and he took an oath to deliver the prisoners and the king swore to fight his utmost against Sir Damas's enemy. Then the twenty weak and starving knights were brought out of the dungeon and given food, and they all remained to see the combat.

Now we must go to Sir Accolon, the third knight, who had slept the enchanted sleep. He awakened close beside a deep well where a movement in his sleep would have cast him down. From the well there issued a silver pipe spouting water into a marble fountain. Morgan's magic had weakened with her absence, so that Accolon blessed himself, and he said aloud, "Jesus save my lord King Arthur and Sir Uryens. Those were not ladies in the ship but fiends from hell. If I can come clear of this misadventure I will destroy them and all others who practice evil magic."

And at that moment an ugly dwarf with thick lips and a flat nose came out of the forest and saluted Sir Accolon. "I come from Morgan le Fay," said the dwarf, and the spell settled back on the knight. "She greets you and bids you be strong-hearted, because tomorrow in the morning you are to fight with a knight. Because she loves you, she sends you this sword Excalibur and its scabbard. And she says if you love her you will fight without mercy, as you promised her in private. She will also expect the king's head as proof that you have fulfilled your oath."

Sir Accolon was deep enchanted now. He said, "I understand. I shall keep my promise and I can, now that I have Excalibur. When did you see my lady?"

"A little time ago," said the dwarf.

Then Accolon in his rapture embraced the ugly dwarf and kissed him and said, "Greet my lady for me and tell her I will keep my promise or die in the attempt. Now I understand the little ship and the sleep. My lady has arranged all of it, isn't that true?"

"You may well believe it, sir," said the dwarf and he slipped away into the forest and left Accolon dreaming beside the silver fountain.

And soon there came a knight accompanied by a lady and six squires, and he begged Accolon to come to a manor nearby to dine and rest, and Accolon accepted. All this was planned by Morgan le Fay, for the lord of the manor was Sir Outlake, who lay wounded by a spear thrust in the thigh. And as Sir Accolon sat with him, word was brought that Sir Damas had a champion to fight against his brother in the morning.

Then Sir Outlake was furious with his wound, for he had wanted this test of arms for a long time, but his legs were so hurt that he could not sit a horse.

Sir Accolon was confident because he had the protection of the sword Excalibur, and he offered to fight as Sir Outlake's champion.

Then Sir Outlake was glad and he thanked Sir Accolon with all his heart for his offer, and he sent Sir Damas a message saying that his champion would fight for him.

This combat had the blessing of custom and the authority of religion. It was an appeal to God to decide which of two men was right and to show His decision in the victor. The outcome had the force of law. And because of the hatred men felt for Sir Damas and the esteem in which Sir Outlake was held, the whole countryside assembled to see the trial by arms, knights and free men, and on the fringes of the gathering bondsmen and serfs. Twelve honorable men of the country were chosen to wait upon the champions where they sat with their horses, shields dressed, visors down, and spears booted, waiting for the signal to begin. The morning sun slanted through the leaves of great oaks which surrounded the jousting ground. Mass had been sung and each champion had prayed for the decision, and now they waited.

Then a damsel rode onto the field and from under her riding cloak she drew a sword and scabbard—the counterfeit Excalibur. The damsel said, "Because of her great love for you, your sister Morgan le Fay sends you Excalibur, my lord, the sheath to protect your life and the sword to give you victory."

"How kind my sister is," said Arthur. "Give her my thanks and love." And he took the false sword and belted it to his side.

Now the horn blew its savage signal, and both knights couched their spears and hurtled together, and both spears struck true and held, and both men were hurled to the ground, and they sprang up and drew their swords and faced each other. They circled and feinted, each testing the other and looking for a weakness or an opening.

And as they opened the fight, Nyneve of the Lake rode up, driving her horse fast, the same damsel who had beguiled Merlin and sealed him in the rock. The necromantic art she had wrung from the adoring old man had given her power, but also it aroused rivalry and suspicion in Morgan le Fay. Nyneve loved the king and hated his evil sister. She knew the plot against Arthur's life and she had come at speed to save him before the combat joined and the laws against interference were applied. But she arrived late and had to watch the unequal contest, for although each knight delivered strokes and cuts, Excalibur bit deep and ripped its wounding way through Arthur's armor, while the false sword of the king glanced harmlessly from the shield and helm of Accolon.

When Arthur felt his blood pouring from his wounds and felt the blunt uselessness of his sword, he was dismayed, and suspicion grew in him that he had been tricked. Then he was afraid, for every stroke of Accolon bit deep while Arthur's strongest blows were impotent. The counterfeit sword in his hand was forged of base metal, soft and useless.

Now Accolon felt his advantage and pressed on, and the king struck such a furious stroke that the very weight of it staggered Accolon, who stepped away to get his breath and clear his head, but in a moment he came on again, and without art or skill the two rained strokes until Arthur bled from a hundred wounds, while Accolon was unhurt, protected by the sheath of the true Excalibur.

Then a murmur of wonder went through the circle of watchers. They saw that Arthur fought well and yet could not wound his enemy, and they were amazed that he could continue with such loss of blood. Then

Arthur drew back to rest and gather his strength, but Accolon cried out in triumph, "Come! Fight. This is no time to let you rest," and he charged forward and forced the battle so that Arthur in despair leaped in and swung a great stroke to the helm, and his sword blade broke and left only the pommel in his hand. Helpless, he covered himself with his shield while Accolon showered cuts upon him, trying to finish him. And as he attacked Sir Accolon said, "You are finished, helpless and lost. I don't want to kill you. Surrender and give up the cause."

The king said weakly, "I can't. I promised to fight as long as I had life. I would rather die with honor than live in shame. If you kill an unarmed man you will never live down the shame."

"It is not your affair to worry about my shame," said Accolon. "You are a dead man." And he pressed home his attack, careless of defense.

Arthur took the only possible opening. He pressed close and thrust his shield against Accolon's sword arm and swung at his exposed helmet with the broken pommel of his sword with such force that Accolon reeled back three steps and stood swaying dizzily.

Nyneve had watched the combat hoping for the decision of God against the treason of Morgan le Fay, but when she saw Arthur's last despairing stroke with the broken sword and Accolon recover his strength and advance on the weak and disarmed king, she knew that he was lost without her help. Then she searched her memory for Merlin's teaching and she forged a spell and flung it with her eyes at the advancing traitor. Sir Accolon raised Excalibur, measured his distance, and aimed a deadly finishing stroke, but as the blade touched the shield, the hand that held it lost its grip and the fingers went lax. The sword fell to the ground and Accolon watched with helpless horror as Arthur picked it up. The pommel felt good in his hand and he knew it was the true Excalibur and he said, "My dear sword, you have been too long out of my hand and you have wounded me. Now, be my friend again, Excalibur." He looked at Accolon and saw the scabbard, and leaped forward and tore it free and flung it as far as he could over the heads of the circled people.

"Now, Sir Knight," he said to Accolon, "you have had your turn and

I my wounds. Now we change places and you shall have what you have given me." He rushed on Accolon, shield forward to raise his guard, but Accolon fell to the ground rigid with paralyzing fear. Arthur dashed off his helm and struck him on the head with the flat of Excalibur so that blood started from his nose and ears. "Now I will kill you," said Arthur.

"That is your right," said Sir Accolon. "I see now that God is on your side and your cause is right. But as you promised to fight to the end, so did I, and I cannot beg for mercy. Do what you will."

Arthur looked at the unvisored face, distorted and dirtied with dust and blood, and he said, "I know your face. Who are you?"

"Sir Knight, I am of the royal court of King Arthur. My name is Accolon of Gaul."

Then Arthur thought of the enchantment of the ship and the treachery whereby Excalibur came into his enemy's hand, and he asked softly, "Tell me, Sir Knight, who gave you this sword?"

"The sword is my misfortune. It has brought death to me," said Accolon.

"Whatever it has brought, where did you get it?"

Sir Accolon sighed, for the power of his promised mistress had failed and disappeared. "I see no reason now to conceal anything," he said hopelessly. "The king's sister hates him with a death hate because he has the crown and because he is loved and honored above her. She loves me and I love her to the point of treason. She has betrayed Sir Uryens, her husband, and been my paramour. She promised me that if I would kill Arthur with her help, she would rid herself of her husband and make me king, and she would be my queen, and we would reign in England and live in happiness." He fell silent, remembering, and then he said, "It is all over now. My plans have invited my death."

Arthur spoke through his closed visor. "If you had won this fight, do you know you would have been king? But how could you have contained the sin of treason against your anointed king?"

"I don't know, Sir Knight," said Accolon. "My mind and soul have been under a spell so that even treason seemed a nothing. But that is gone now like a dream. Tell me who you are, before I die."

"I am your king," said Arthur.

Then Accolon cried out in sorrow and in pain. "My lord, I did not know. I thought I fought a champion. I have been tricked as you have. Can you grant mercy to a man who has been cheated and beguiled even to plotting your death?"

The king thought long and then he said, "I can grant mercy because I believe you did not know me. I have honored Morgan le Fay, my sister, given in to her, and loved her better than my other kin. And I have trusted her more even than my wife, even though I knew her jealousy and lust of flesh and hunger for power, and even though I knew she practiced the black arts. If she could do this to me, I can believe and forgive what she has done to you. But I will not have mercy on her. My vengeance on my evil sister will be the talk of Christendom. Now rise, Sir Accolon. I have granted mercy." Then Arthur helped him to his feet and he called to the people clustered about the field, "Come closer." And when they had gathered around him he said, "We have fought and wounded each other sorely, but if we had known each other there would have been no combat."

Accolon cried out, "This is the best and bravest knight in the world, but he is more than that. He is our lord and sovereign, King Arthur. By mischance I have fought against my king. He can grant mercy, but I cannot forgive myself, for there is no sin or crime worse than treason against the king."

Then all the people kneeled down and begged for mercy.

"Mercy you shall have," said Arthur. "You did not know. Only remember from this what strange and fatal adventures and accidents may come to errant knights. Now I am weak and wounded and I must rest, but first here is my judgment of the test of right by combat.

"Sir Damas, as your champion I have fought and won. But because you are proud and cowardly and full of villainy, hear my decision. You will give this whole manor to your brother, Sir Outlake, with all its equipment of farms and houses. He in payment will send you a palfrey every year, for you are better fit to ride a lady's hackney than a war horse. I charge you on pain of death never to distress or injure knights errant who ride through your lands. As for the twenty knights in prison, you will return their armor and any other things you have taken from them. And if any of them comes to my court to complain of you, you shall die. That is my judgment."

Then Arthur, weak from loss of blood, turned to Sir Outlake. "Because you are a good knight, brave and true and courteous, I charge you to come to my court to be my knight, and I shall so favor you that you will live in comfort and in honor."

"Thank you, my lord," said Sir Outlake. "I am at your command. Only be sure, sir, that if I had not been wounded I would have fought my own combat."

"I wish it had been so," said Arthur, "for then I would not have been so hurt, and hurt by treachery and enchantment by one near to me."

Sir Outlake said, "I can't imagine anyone plotting against you, my lord."

"I will deal with that person," said the king. "Now, how far am I from Camelot?"

"Two days' journey," said Outlake. "Too far to travel with your wounds. Three miles from here there is an abbey with nuns to care for you, and learned men to heal your wounds."

"I will go there to rest," said the king, and he called farewell to the people and helped Sir Accolon to his horse, and mounted and rode slowly away.

At the abbey their wounds were cleansed and cared for with the best-known salves and unguents, but within four days Sir Accolon died of the terrible last wound on his unshielded head.

Then Arthur ordered his body to be taken to Camelot by six knights and delivered to Morgan le Fay. He said, "Tell my dear sister I send him to her as a present in payment for her kindness to me."

Meanwhile, Morgan believed her plan had been carried out and the king killed with his own sword. The time had come, she thought, to rid herself of her husband, Sir Uryens. In the night she waited until he was asleep and then called a maiden who attended her. "Fetch me my lord's sword," she said. "There will never be a better time to kill him."

The maid cried out in terror, "If you kill your husband, you will never escape."

"That is not your worry," Morgan said. "Go quickly and bring the sword."

Then in fear the damsel crept to the bed of Sir Ewain, Morgan's son, and she awakened him. "Get up," she whispered. "Your mother is going to kill your father in his sleep. She has sent me for a sword."

Ewain started awake and rubbed his eyes, and then he said quietly, "Obey her orders. Get the sword. I will take care of it," and he slipped from his bed and armed himself and crept along dark corridors and hid himself in his father's room.

The damsel brought the sword with shaking hands, and Morgan le Fay took it from her and boldly she stood over her sleeping husband, coldly judging the proper place to drive in the blade. When she raised the sword to strike, Sir Ewain leaped from his hiding place and caught her wrist and held her, struggling. "What are you doing?" he demanded. "It is said that Merlin was sired by a fiend. You must be an earthly fiend. If you were not my mother, I would kill you."

But Morgan trapped was doubly dangerous. She stared wildly about as though awakened suddenly. "What is this?" she cried. "Where am I? What is this sword?—Oh, my son, protect me! Some evil spirit has entered while I slept. Have mercy on me, my son. Do not tell of this. Protect my honor. It is your honor, too."

Sir Ewain said reluctantly, "I will forgive you if you promise to give up your magic crafts."

"I promise," said Morgan. "I will swear it. You are my good son, my dear son." Then Ewain, half-believing, released her and took the sword away.

In the morning one of her secret people brought news to Morgan le Fay that her plan had failed. Sir Accolon was dead and Arthur, alive, had Excalibur again. Inwardly she raged against her brother and mourned the death of Accolon, but her face was cold and composed and she showed no anger nor fear or shed any open tears for her lover. She well knew that if she stayed for the king's return her life was forfeit, for there could be no clemency for her unmentionable crime against her brother and her king.

Morgan went sweetly to Queen Guinevere and asked permission to leave the court.

"Can you not wait until your brother, the king, comes home?" asked Guinevere.

"I wish I might, but I cannot," said Morgan. "Bad news has come of revolt on my estates and I must go."

"In that case you may go," said the queen.

Then in the dark, before morning, Morgan le Fay assembled forty trusted followers and she rode out and gave no rest to horse or man for a day and a night. And early on the second morning she came to the abbey where she knew King Arthur lay.

She entered boldly and demanded to see her brother, and a nun replied, "He is sleeping now at last. For three nights his wounds have given him little rest."

"Do not awaken him," said Morgan. "I will go quietly to see my brother's dear face." And she dismounted and went inside with such authority that no one dared stop the sister of the king.

She found his room and saw by a small rush light that the king lay on his bed asleep, but his hand gripped the handle of Excalibur and its naked blade lay beside him on the bed. Morgan did not dare to take the sword for fear he might awaken, for he slept restlessly. But on a chest nearby she saw the scabbard and slipped it under her cloak and went out thanking the nuns, and she mounted and rode away with speed.

When the king awakened, he missed his scabbard. "Who has taken it?" he demanded angrily. "Who has been here?"

"Only your sister Morgan le Fay, and she has gone."

"You have not guarded me," he cried. "She has taken my scabbard."

"Sir," said the nuns, "we could not disobey your sister."

Then Arthur struggled from his bed and ordered the best horse to be found, and he asked Sir Outlake to arm and come with him, and the two galloped after Morgan.

At a wayside cross they asked a cowherd if he had seen a lady pass.

"Aye, that I did," he said. "A little time ago she went riding by and forty horsemen with her. They rode toward yonder forest."

Then Arthur and Sir Outlake gave chase, and in a short time they sighted her and whipped up their horses.

Morgan saw them coming and she drove her horse through the forest and out on an open plain beyond it, and when she saw the pursuers gaining on her, she spurred her horse into a little lake. "Whatever happens to me, he shall not have this sheath to protect him," she said, and she threw the scabbard as far out as she could in the water. It was heavy with gold and cut jewels and sank quickly out of sight.

Then she rejoined her men and galloped on into a valley where there were rings of great standing stones. And Morgan cast enchantment so that her men and she became tall stones like the others. When Arthur entered the valley and saw the stones, he said, "She has drawn the vengeance of God on her. My vengeance is not needed." He looked about on the ground for his scabbard and could not find it, for it was in the lake. And after a time he rode slowly back toward the abbey.

As soon as he had gone, Morgan le Fay resumed her form and freed her men from the skins of stone. "Now you are free," she said, "but did you see the king's face?"

"We did, and it was icy rage. If we had not been turned to stone we would have run away."

"I believe you would," said she.

They took up their march again, and on their way they met a knight leading a prisoner bound and blindfolded.

"What are you doing with that knight?" Morgan asked.

"I am going to drown him. I found him with my wife. And I will drown her too."

Morgan asked the prisoner, "Is this true what he says?"

"No, madame, it is not true."

"Where do you come from? What is your name?" she asked.

"I am of King Arthur's court," he said. "My name is Manessen. I am Sir Accolon's cousin."

Morgan le Fay said, "I loved Sir Accolon. In his memory I shall deliver you to do to this man what he would have done to you."

Her men unbound him and tied the other with the same cords. Sir Manessen put on the armor and weapons of his captor and took him to a deep spring and threw him in. Then he returned to Morgan. "I will return to Arthur's court. Have you any message for him?"

She smiled bitterly. "I have," she said. "Tell my dear brother that I rescued you not for love of him but for love of Accolon. And tell him I have no fear of him, for I can turn myself and my followers into stones. Lastly, tell him I can do much more than that and I will prove it to him when the time comes."

She went to her lands in the country of Gore, and she strengthened her castles and towns, and armed and provisioned them, because in spite of her brave message she lived in fear of King Arthur.

from

King Arthur and His Knights

by Sir James Knowles

Sir James Knowles (1784–1862) wrote plays and novels. He retold Thomas Mallory's 15th-century epic *Morte d'Arthur* for his 1923 book *King Arthur and His Knights*. This selection tells of the quarrel between Arthur and his strongest knight, Sir Lancelot.

Within a while thereafter was a jousting at the court, wherein Sir Lancelot won the prize. And two of those he smote down were Sir Agravaine, the brother of Sir Gawain, and Sir Modred, his false brother—King Arthur's son by Belisent. And because of his victory they hated Sir Lancelot, and sought how they might injure him.

So on a night when King Arthur was hunting in the forest, and the queen sent for Sir Lancelot to her chamber, they two espied him; and thinking now to make a scandal and a quarrel between Lancelot and the king, they found twelve others, and said Sir Lancelot was even now in the queen's chamber and King Arthur was dishonoured.

Then, all armed, they came suddenly round the queen's door, and cried, "Traitor! now art thou taken."

"Madam, we be betrayed," said Sir Lancelot; "yet shall my life cost these men dear."

Then did the queen weep sore, and dismally she cried, "Alas! there is no armour here whereby ye might withstand so many; wherefore ye will be slain, and I be burnt for the dread crime they will charge on me."

But while she spake the shouting of the knights was heard without, "Traitor, come forth, for now thou art snared!"

"Better were twenty deaths at once than this vile outcry," said Sir Lancelot.

Then he kissed her and said, "Most noble lady, I beseech ye, as I have ever been your own true knight, take courage; pray for my soul if I be now slain, and trust my faithful friends, Sir Bors and Sir Lavaine, to save you from the fire."

But ever bitterly she wept and moaned, and cried, "Would God that they would take and slay me, and that thou couldst escape."

"That shall never be," said he. And wrapping his mantle round his arm he unbarred the door a little space, so that but one could enter.

Then first rushed in Sir Chalaunce, a full strong knight, and lifted up his sword to smite Sir Lancelot; but lightly he avoided him, and struck Sir Chalaunce, with his hand such a sore buffet on the head as felled him dead upon the floor.

Then Sir Lancelot pulled in his body and barred the door again, and dressed himself in his armour, and took his drawn sword in his hand.

But still the knights cried mightily without the door, "Traitor, come forth!"

"Be silent and depart," replied Sir Lancelot; "for be ye sure ye will not take me, and to-morrow will I meet ye face to face before the king."

"Ye shall have no such grace," they cried; "but we will slay thee, or take thee as we list."

"Then save yourselves who may," he thundered, and therewith suddenly unbarred the door and rushed forth at them. And at the first blow he slew Sir Agravaine, and after him twelve other knights, with twelve more mighty buffets. And none of all escaped him save Sir Modred, who, sorely wounded, fled away for life.

Then returned he to the queen, and said, "Now, madam, will I depart, and if ye be in any danger I pray ye come to me."

"Surely will I stay here, for I am queen," she answered; "yet if to-morrow any harm come to me I trust to thee for rescue."

"Have ye no doubt of me," said he, "forever while I live am I your own true knight."

Therewith he took his leave, and went and told Sir Bors and all his kindred of this adventure. "We will be with thee in this quarrel," said they all; "and if the queen be sentenced to the fire, we certainly will save her."

Meanwhile Sir Modred, in great fear and pain, fled from the court, and rode until he found King Arthur, and told him all that had befallen. But the king would scarce believe him till he came and saw the bodies of Sir Agravaine and all the other knights.

Then felt he in himself that all was true, and with his passing grief his heart nigh broke. "Alas!" cried he, "now is the fellowship of the Round Table forever broken: yea, woe is me! I may not with my honour spare my queen."

Anon it was ordained that Queen Guinevere should be burnt to death because she had dishonoured King Arthur.

But when Sir Gawain heard thereof, he came before the king, and said, "My lord, I counsel thee be not too hasty in this matter, but stay the judgment of the queen a season, for it may well be that Sir Lancelot was in her chamber for no evil, seeing she is greatly beholden to him for so many deeds done for her sake, and peradventure she had sent to him to thank him, and did it secretly that she might avoid slander."

But King Arthur answered, full of grief, "Alas! I may not help her; she is judged as any other woman."

Then he required Sir Gawain and his brethren, Sir Gaheris and Sir Gareth, to be ready to bear the queen to-morrow to the place of execution.

"Nay, noble lord," replied Sir Gawain, "that can I never do; for neither will my heart suffer me to see the queen die, nor shall men ever say I was of your counsel in this matter."

Then said his brothers, "Ye may command us to be there, but since it is against our will, we will be without arms, that we may do no battle against her."

So on the morrow was Queen Guinevere led forth to die by fire, and a mighty crowd was there, of knights and nobles, armed and unarmed. And all the lords and ladies wept sore at that piteous sight. Then was she shriven by a priest, and the men came nigh to bind her to the stake and light the fire.

At that Sir Lancelot's spies rode hastily and told him and his kindred, who lay hidden in a wood hard by; and suddenly, with twenty knights, he rushed into the midst of all the throng to rescue her.

But certain of King Arthur's knights rose up and fought with them, and there was a full great battle and confusion. And Sir Lancelot drave fiercely here and there among the press, and smote on every side, and at every blow struck down a knight, so that many were slain by him and his fellows.

Then was the queen set free, and caught up on Sir Lancelot's saddle and fled away with him and all his company to the Castle of La Joyous Garde.

Now so it chanced that, in the turmoil of the fighting, Sir Lancelot had unawares struck down and slain the two good knights Sir Gareth and Sir Gaheris, knowing it not, for he fought wildly, and saw not that they were unarmed.

When King Arthur heard thereof, and of all that battle, and the rescue of the queen, he sorrowed heavily for those good knights, and was passing wroth with Lancelot and the queen.

But when Sir Gawain heard of his brethren's death he swooned for sorrow and wrath, for he wist that Sir Lancelot had killed them in malice. And as soon as he recovered he ran in to the king, and said, "Lord, king and uncle, hear this oath which now I swear, that from this day I will not fail Sir Lancelot till one of us hath slain the other. And now, unless ye haste to war with him, that we may be avenged, will I myself alone go after him."

Then the king, full of wrath and grief, agreed thereto, and sent letters throughout the realm to summon all his knights, and went with a vast army to besiege the Castle of La Joyous Garde. And Sir Lancelot, with his knights, mightily defended it; but never would he suffer any to go forth and attack one of the king's army, for he was right loth to fight against him.

So when fifteen weeks were passed, and King Arthur's army wasted itself in vain against the castle, for it was passing strong, it chanced upon a day Sir Lancelot was looking from the walls and espied King Arthur and Sir Gawain close beside.

"Come forth, Sir Lancelot," said King Arthur right fiercely, "and let us two meet in the midst of the field."

"God forbid that I should encounter with thee, lord, for thou didst make me a knight," replied Sir Lancelot.

Then cried Sir Gawain, "Shame on thee, traitor and false knight, yet be ye well assured we will regain the queen and slay thee and thy company; yea, double shame on ye to slay my brother Gaheris unarmed, Sir Gareth also, who loved ye so well. For that treachery, be sure I am thine enemy till death."

"Alas!" cried Sir Lancelot, "that I hear such tidings, for I knew not I had slain those noble knights, and right sorely now do I repent it with a heavy heart. Yet abate thy wrath, Sir Gawain, for ye know full well I did it by mischance, for I loved them ever as my own brothers."

"Thou liest, false recreant," cried Sir Gawain fiercely.

At that Sir Lancelot was wroth, and said, "I well see thou art now mine enemy, and that there can be no more peace with thee, or with my lord the king, else would I gladly give back the queen."

Then the king would fain have listened to Sir Lancelot, for more than all his own wrong did he grieve at the sore waste and damage of the realm, but Sir Gawain persuaded him against it, and ever cried out foully on Sir Lancelot.

When Sir Bors and the other knights of Lancelot's party heard the fierce words of Sir Gawain, they were passing wroth, and prayed to ride forth and be avenged on him, for they were weary of so long waiting to no good. And in the end Sir Lancelot, with a heavy heart, consented.

So on the morrow the hosts on either side met in the field, and there was a great battle. And Sir Gawain prayed his knights chiefly to set upon Sir Lancelot; but Sir Lancelot commanded his company to forbear King Arthur and Sir Gawain.

So the two armies jousted together right fiercely, and Sir Gawain proffered to encounter with Sir Lionel, and overthrew him. But Sir

Bors, and Sir Blamor, and Sir Palomedes, who were on Sir Lancelot's side, did great feats of arms, and overthrew many of King Arthur's knights.

Then the king came forth against Sir Lancelot, but Sir Lancelot forbore him and would not strike again.

At that Sir Bors rode up against the king and smote him down. But Sir Lancelot cried, "Touch him not on pain of thy head," and going to King Arthur he alighted and gave him his own horse, saying, "My lord, I pray thee forbear this strife, for it can bring to neither of us any honour."

And when King Arthur looked on him the tears came to his eyes as he thought of his noble courtesy, and he said within himself, "Alas! that ever this war began."

But on the morrow Sir Gawain led forth the army again, and Sir Bors commanded on Sir Lancelot's side. And they two struck together so fiercely that both fell to the ground sorely wounded; and all the day they fought till night fell, and many were slain on both sides, yet in the end neither gained the victory.

But by now the fame of this fierce war spread through all Christendom, and when the Pope heard thereof he sent a Bull, and charged King Arthur to make peace with Lancelot, and receive back Queen Guinevere; and for the offence imputed to her, absolution should be given by the Pope.

Thereto would King Arthur straightway have obeyed, but Sir Gawain ever urged him to refuse.

When Sir Lancelot heard thereof, he wrote thus to the king: "It was never in my thought, lord, to withhold thy queen from thee; but since she was condemned for my sake to death, I deemed it but a just and knightly part to rescue her therefrom; wherefore I recommend me to your grace, and within eight days will I come to thee and bring the queen in safety."

Then, within eight days, as he had said, Sir Lancelot rode from out the castle with Queen Guinevere, and a hundred knights for company, each carrying an olive branch, in sign of peace. And so they came to the court, and found King Arthur sitting on his throne, with Sir Gawain and many other knights around him. And when Sir Lancelot entered with the queen, they both kneeled down before the king.

Anon Sir Lancelot rose and said, "My lord, I have brought hither my lady the queen again, as right requireth, and by commandment of the Pope and you. I pray ye take her to your heart again and forget the past. For myself I may ask nothing, and for my sin I shall have sorrow and sore punishment; yet I would to Heaven I might have your grace."

But ere the king could answer, for he was moved with pity at his words, Sir Gawain cried aloud, "Let the king do as he will, but be sure, Sir Lancelot, thou and I shall never be accorded while we live, for thou hast slain my brethren traitorously and unarmed."

"As Heaven is my help," replied Sir Lancelot, "I did it ignorantly, for I loved them well, and while I live I shall bewail their death; but to make war with me were no avail, for I must needs fight with thee if thou assailest, and peradventure I might kill thee also, which I were right loth to do."

"I will forgive thee never," cried Sir Gawain, "and if the king accordeth with thee he shall lose my service."

Then the knights who stood near tried to reconcile Sir Gawain to Sir Lancelot, but he would not hear them. So, at the last, Sir Lancelot said, "Since peace is vain, I will depart, lest I bring more evil on my fellowship."

And as he turned to go, the tears fell from him, and he said, "Alas, most noble Christian realm, which I have loved above all others, now shall I see thee never more!" Then said he to the queen, "Madam, now must I leave ye and this noble fellowship forever. And, I beseech ye, pray for me, and if ye ever be defamed of any, let me hear thereof, and as I have been ever thy true knight in right and wrong, so will I be again."

With that he kneeled and kissed King Arthur's hands, and departed on his way. And there was none in all that court, save Sir Gawain, alone, but wept to see him go.

So he returned with all his knights to the Castle of La Joyous Garde, and, for his sorrow's sake, he named it Dolorous Garde thenceforth.

Anon he left the realm, and went with many of his fellowship beyond the sea to France, and there divided all his lands among them equally, he sharing but as the rest.

And from that time forward peace had been between him and King Arthur, but for Sir Gawain, who left the king no rest, but constantly persuaded him that Lancelot was raising mighty hosts against him.

So in the end his malice overcame the king, who left the government in charge of Modred, and made him guardian of the queen, and went with a great army to invade Sir Lancelot's lands.

Yet Sir Lancelot would make no war upon the king, and sent a message to gain peace on any terms King Arthur chose. But Sir Gawain met the herald ere he reached the king, and sent him back with taunting and bitter words. Whereat Sir Lancelot sorrowfully called his knights together and fortified the Castle of Benwicke, and there was shortly besieged by the army of King Arthur.

Yet every day Sir Gawain rode up to the walls, and cried out foully on Sir Lancelot, till, upon a time, Sir Lancelot answered him that he would meet him in the field and put his boasting to the proof. So it was agreed on both sides that there should none come nigh them or separate them till one had fallen or yielded; and they two rode forth.

Then did they wheel their horses apart, and turning, came together as it had been thunder, so that both horses fell, and both their lances broke. At that they drew their swords and set upon each other fiercely, with passing grievous strokes.

Now Sir Gawain had through magic a marvellous great gift. For every day, from morning till noon, his strength waxed to the might of seven men, but after that waned to his natural force. Therefore till noon he gave Sir Lancelot many mighty buffets, which scarcely he endured. Yet greatly he forbore Sir Gawain, for he was aware of his enchantment, and smote him slightly till his own knights marvelled. But after noon Sir Gawain's strength sank fast, and then, with one full blow, Sir Lancelot laid him on the earth. Then Sir Gawain cried out, "Turn not away, thou traitor knight, but slay me if thou wilt, or else I will arise and fight with thee again some other time."

"Sir Knight," replied Sir Lancelot, "I never yet smote a fallen man."

At that they bore Sir Gawain sorely wounded to his tent, and King Arthur withdrew his men, for he was loth to shed the blood of so many knights of his own fellowship.

But now came tidings to King Arthur from across the sea, which caused him to return in haste. For thus the news ran, that no sooner was Sir Modred set up in his regency, than he had forged false tidings from abroad that the king had fallen in a battle with Sir Lancelot. Whereat he had proclaimed himself the king, and had been crowned at Canterbury, where he had held a coronation feast for fifteen days. Then he had gone to Winchester, where Queen Guinevere abode, and had commanded her to be his wife; whereto, for fear and sore perplexity, she had feigned consent, but under pretext of preparing for the marriage, had fled in haste to London and taken shelter in the Tower, fortifying it and providing it with all manner of victuals, and defending it against Sir Modred, and answering to all his threats that she would rather slay herself than be his queen.

Thus was it written to King Arthur. Then, in passing great wrath and haste, he came with all his army swiftly back from France and sailed to England. But when Sir Modred heard thereof, he left the Tower and marched with all his host to meet the king at Dover.

Then fled Queen Guinevere to Amesbury to a nunnery, and there she clothed herself in sackcloth, and spent her time in praying for the king and in good deeds and fasting. And in that nunnery evermore she lived, sorely repenting and mourning for her sin, and for the ruin she had brought on all the realm. And there anon she died.

And when Sir Lancelot heard thereof, he put his knightly armour off, and bade farewell to all his kin, and went a mighty pilgrimage for many years, and after lived a hermit till his death.

When Sir Modred came to Dover, he found King Arthur and his army but just landed; and there they fought a fierce and bloody battle, and many great and noble knights fell on both sides.

But the king's side had the victory, for he was beyond himself with might and passion, and all his knights so fiercely followed him, that, in spite of all their multitude, they drove Sir Modred's army back with fearful wounds and slaughter, and slept that night upon the battlefield.

But Sir Gawain was smitten by an arrow in the wound Sir Lancelot gave him, and wounded to the death. Then was he borne to the king's tent, and King Arthur sorrowed over him as it had been his own son. "Alas!" said he; "in Sir Lancelot and in you I had my greatest earthly joy, and now is all gone from me."

And Sir Gawain answered, with a feeble voice, "My lord and king, I know well my death is come, and through my own wilfulness, for I am smitten in the wound Sir Lancelot gave me. Alas! that I have been the cause of all this war, for but for me thou hadst been now at peace with Lancelot, and then had Modred never done this treason. I pray ye, therefore, my dear lord, be now agreed with Lancelot, and tell him, that although he gave me my deathwound, it was through my own seeking; wherefore I beseech him to come back to England, and here to visit my tomb, and pray for my soul."

When he had thus spoken, Sir Gawain gave up his ghost, and the king grievously mourned for him.

Then they told him that the enemy had camped on Barham Downs, whereat, with all his hosts, he straightway marched there, and fought again a bloody battle, and overthrew Sir Modred utterly. Howbeit, he raised yet another army, and retreating ever from before the king, increased his numbers as he went, till at the farthest west in Lyonesse, he once more made a stand.

Now, on the night of Trinity Sunday, being the eve of the battle, King Arthur had a vision, and saw Sir Gawain in a dream, who warned him not to fight with Modred on the morrow, else he would be surely slain; and prayed him to delay till Lancelot and his knights should come to aid him.

So when King Arthur woke he told his lords and knights that vision, and all agreed to wait the coming of Sir Lancelot. Then a herald was sent with a message of truce to Sir Modred, and a treaty was made that neither army should assail the other.

But when the treaty was agreed upon, and the heralds returned,

King Arthur said to his knights, "Beware, lest Sir Modred deceive us, for I in no wise trust him, and if swords be drawn be ready to encounter!" And Sir Modred likewise gave an order, that if any man of the king's army drew his sword, they should begin to fight.

And as it chanced, a knight of the king's side was bitten by an adder in the foot, and hastily drew forth his sword to slay it. That saw Sir Modred, and forthwith commanded all his army to assail the king's.

So both sides rushed to battle, and fought passing fiercely. And when the king saw there was no hope to stay them, he did right mightily and nobly as a king should do, and ever, like a lion, raged in the thickest of the press, and slew on the right hand and on the left, till his horse went fetlock deep in blood. So all day long they fought, and stinted not till many a noble knight was slain.

But the king was passing sorrowful to see his trusty knights lie dead on every side. And at the last but two remained beside him, Sir Lucan and his brother, Sir Bedivere, and both were sorely wounded.

"Now am I come to mine end," said King Arthur; "but, lo! that traitor Modred liveth yet, and I may not die till I have slain him. Now, give me my spear, Sir Lucan."

"Lord, let him be," replied Sir Lucan; "for if ye pass through this unhappy day, ye shall be right well revenged upon him. My good lord, remember well your dream, and what the spirit of Sir Gawain did forewarn ye."

"Betide me life, betide me death," said the king; "now I see him yonder alone, he shall never escape my hands, for at a better revenge shall I never have him."

"God speed you well," said Sir Bedivere.

Then King Arthur got his spear in both his hands, and ran towards Sir Modred, crying, "Traitor, now is thy death-day come!" And when Sir Modred heard his words, and saw him come, he drew his sword and stood to meet him. Then King Arthur smote Sir Modred through the body more than a fathom. And when Sir Modred felt he had his death-wound, he thrust himself with all his might up to the end of King Arthur's spear, and smote his father, Arthur, with his sword upon the head, so that it pierced both helm and brain-pan.

And therewith Sir Modred fell down stark dead to the earth, and King Arthur fell down also in a swoon, and swooned many times.

Then Sir Lucan and Sir Bedivere came and bare him away to a little chapel by the sea-shore. And there Sir Lucan sank down with the bleeding of his own wounds, and fell dead.

And King Arthur lay long in a swoon, and when he came to himself, he found Sir Lucan lying dead beside him, and Sir Bedivere weeping over the body of his brother.

Then said the king to Sir Bedivere, "Weeping will avail no longer, else would I grieve for evermore. Alas! now is the fellowship of the Round Table dissolved forever, and all my realm I have so loved is wasted with war. But my time hieth fast, wherefore take thou Excalibur, my good sword, and go therewith to yonder water-side and throw it in, and bring me word what thing thou seest."

So Sir Bedivere departed; but as he went he looked upon the sword, the hilt whereof was all inlaid with precious stones exceeding rich. And presently he said within himself, "If I now throw this sword into the water, what good should come of it?" So he hid the sword among the reeds, and came again to the king.

"What sawest thou?" said he to Sir Bedivere.

"Lord," said he, "I saw nothing else but wind and waves."

"Thou hast untruly spoken," said the king; "wherefore go lightly back and throw it in, and spare not."

Then Sir Bedivere returned again, and took the sword up in his hand; but when he looked on it, he thought it sin and shame to throw away a thing so noble. Wherefore he hid it yet again, and went back to the king.

"What saw ye?" said King Arthur.

"Lord," answered he, "I saw nothing but the water ebbing and flowing."

"Oh, traitor and untrue!" cried out the king; "twice hast thou now betrayed me. Art thou called of men a noble knight, and wouldst betray me for a jewelled sword? Now, therefore, go again for the last time, for thy tarrying hath put me in sore peril of my life, and I fear my wound hath taken cold; and if thou do it not this time, by my faith I will arise and slay thee with my hands."

Then Sir Bedivere ran quickly and took up the sword, and went down to the water's edge, and bound the girdle round the hilt and threw it far into the water. And lo! an arm and hand came forth above the water, and caught the sword, and brandished it three times, and vanished.

So Sir Bedivere came again to the king and told him what he had seen.

"Help me from hence," said King Arthur; "for I dread me I have tarried over long."

Then Sir Bedivere took the king up in his arms, and bore him to the water's edge. And by the shore they saw a barge with three fair queens therein, all dressed in black, and when they saw King Arthur they wept and wailed.

"Now put me in the barge," said he to Sir Bedivere, and tenderly he did so.

Then the three queens received him, and he laid his head upon the lap of one of them, who cried, "Alas! dear brother, why have ye tarried so long, for your wound hath taken cold?"

With that the barge put from the land, and when Sir Bedivere saw it departing, he cried with a bitter cry, "Alas! my lord King Arthur, what shall become of me now ye have gone from me?"

"Comfort ye," said King Arthur, "and be strong, for I may no more help ye. I go to the Vale of Avilion to heal me of my grievous wound, and if ye see me no more, pray for my soul."

Then the three queens kneeled down around the king and sorely wept and wailed, and the barge went forth to sea, and departed slowly out of Sir Bedivere's sight.

The Story of Ali Baba and the Forty Thieves

by Kate Douglas Wiggin
and Nora A. Smith

Sisters Kate Douglas Wiggin (1856–1923) and Nora A. Smith (c. 1859–1934) retold their favorite Arabian folktales for a 1909 collection.

In a town in Persia, there lived two brothers, one named Cassim, the other Ali Baba. Their father left them scarcely anything; but as he had divided his little property equally between them, it would seem that their fortune ought to have been equal; but chance determined otherwise.

Cassim married a wife, who soon after became heiress to a large sum, and to a warehouse full of rich goods; so that he all at once became one of the richest and most considerable merchants, and lived at his ease. Ali Baba, on the other hand, who had married a woman as poor as himself, lived in a very wretched habitation, and had no other means to maintain his wife and children but his daily labour of cutting wood, and bringing it to town to sell, upon three asses, which were his whole substance.

One day, when Ali Baba was in the forest, and had just cut wood enough to load his asses, he saw at a distance a great cloud of dust, which seemed to be driven toward him: he observed it very attentively, and distinguished soon after a body of horse. Though there had been no rumour of robbers in that country, Ali Baba began to think that they might prove such, and without considering what might become of his asses, was resolved to save himself. He climbed up a large, thick tree, whose branches, at a little distance from the ground, were so close to one another that there was but little space between them. He placed himself in the middle, from whence he could see all that passed without being discovered; and the tree stood at the base of a single rock, so steep and craggy that nobody could climb up it.

The troop, who were all well mounted and armed, came to the foot of this rock, and there dismounted. Ali Baba counted forty of them, and, from their looks and equipage, was assured that they were robbers. Nor was he mistaken in his opinion; for they were a troop of banditti, who, without doing any harm to the neighbourhood, robbed at a distance, and made that place their rendezvous; but what confirmed him in his opinion was, that every man unbridled his horse, tied him to some shrub, and hung about his neck a bag of corn which they brought behind them. Then each of them took his saddle wallet, which seemed to Ali Baba to be full of gold and silver from its weight. One, who was the most personable amongst them, and whom he took to be their captain, came with his wallet on his back under the tree in which Ali Baba was concealed, and making his way through some shrubs, pronounced these words so distinctly: *"Open, Sesame,"* that Ali Baba heard him. As soon as the captain of the robbers had uttered these words, a door opened in the rock; and after he had made all his troop enter before him, he followed them, when the door shut again of itself. The robbers stayed some time within the rock, and Ali Baba, who feared that some one, or all of them together, might come out and catch him, if he should endeavour to make his escape, was obliged to sit patiently in the tree. He was nevertheless tempted to get down, mount one of their horses, and lead another, driving his asses before him with all the haste he could to town; but the uncertainty of the event made him choose the safest course.

At last the door opened again, and the forty robbers came out. As the captain went in last, he came out first, and stood to see them all pass by him, when Ali Baba heard him make the door close by pronouncing these words: *"Shut, Sesame."* Every man went and bridled his horse, fastened his wallet, and mounted again; and when the captain saw them all ready, he put himself at their head, and they returned the way they had come. Ali Baba did not immediately quit his tree; for, said he to himself, they may have forgotten something and may come back again, and then I shall be taken. He followed them with his eyes as far as he could see them; and afterward stayed a considerable time before he descended. Remembering the words the captain of the robbers used to cause the door to open and shut, he had the curiosity to try if his pronouncing them would have the same effect. Accordingly, he went among the shrubs, and perceiving the door concealed behind them, stood before it, and said: *"Open, Sesame!"* The door instantly flew wide open. Ali Baba, who expected a dark dismal cavern, was surprised to see it well lighted and spacious, in the form of a vault, which received the light from an opening at the top of the rock. He saw all sorts of provisions, rich bales of silk stuff, brocade, and valuable carpeting, piled upon one another; gold and silver ingots in great heaps, and money in bags. The sight of all these riches made him suppose that this cave must have been occupied for ages by robbers, who had succeeded one another. Ali Baba did not stand long to consider what he should do, but went immediately into the cave, and as soon as he had entered, the door shut of itself, but this did not disturb him, because he knew the secret to open it again. He never regarded the silver, but made the best use of his time in carrying out as much of the gold coin as he thought his three asses could carry. He collected his asses, which were dispersed, and when he had loaded them with the bags, laid wood over in such a manner that they could not be seen. When he had done he stood before the door, and pronouncing the words: *"Shut, Sesame!"* the door closed after him, for it had shut of itself while he was within, but remained open while he was out. He then made the best of his way to town.

When Ali Baba got home, he drove his asses into a little yard, shut the gates very carefully, threw off the wood that covered the bags, carried them into his house, and ranged them in order before his wife, who sat on a sofa. His wife handled the bags, and finding them full of money, suspected that her husband had been robbing, insomuch that she could not help saying: "Ali Baba, have you been so unhappy as to—" "Be quiet, wife," interrupted Ali Baba, "do not frighten yourself; I am no robber, unless he may be one who steals from robbers. You will no longer entertain an ill opinion of me, when I shall tell you my good fortune." He then emptied the bags, which raised such a great heap of gold as dazzled his wife's eyes; and when he had done, told her the whole adventure from beginning to end; and, above all, recommended her to keep it secret. The wife, cured of her fears, rejoiced with her husband at their good fortune, and would count all the gold piece by piece. "Wife," replied Ali Baba, "you do not know what you undertake, when you pretend to count the money; you will never have done. I will dig a hole, and bury it; there is no time to be lost." "You are in the right, husband," replied she; "but let us know, as nigh as possible, how much we have. I will borrow a small measure in the neighbourhood, and measure it, while you dig the hole." "What you are going to do is to no purpose, wife," said Ali Baba; "if you would take my advice, you had better let it alone; but keep the secret, and do what you please." Away the wife ran to her brother-in-law Cassim, who lived just by, but was not then at home; and addressing herself to his wife, desired her to lend her measure for a little while. Her sister-in-law asked her, whether she would have a great or a small one. The wife asked for a small one. The sister-in-law agreed to lend one, but as she knew Ali Baba's poverty, she was curious to know what sort of grain his wife wanted to measure, and artfully putting some suet at the bottom of the measure, brought it to her with an excuse, that she was sorry that she had made her stay so long, but that she could not find it sooner. Ali Baba's wife went home, set the measure upon the heap of gold, filled it and emptied it often upon the sofa, till she had done: when she was very well satisfied to find the number of measures amounted to so many as they did, and went to tell her husband, who had almost finished digging the hole. While Ali Baba was burying the gold, his wife, to show her exactness and diligence to her sister-in-law, carried the measure back again, but without taking notice that a piece of gold had stuck to the bottom. "Sister," said she, giving it to her again, "you see that I have not kept your measure long; I am obliged to you for it, and return it with thanks."

As soon as her sister-in-law was gone, Cassim's wife looked at the bottom of the measure, and was inexpressibly surprised to find a piece of gold stuck to it. Envy immediately possessed her breast. "What!" said she, "has Ali Baba gold so plentiful as to measure it? Where has that poor wretch got all this wealth?" Cassim, her husband, was not at home, but at his counting-house, which he left always in the evening. His wife waited for him, and thought the time an age; so great was her impatience to tell him the circumstances, at which she guessed he would be as much surprised as herself.

When Cassim came home, his wife said to him: "Cassim, I know you think yourself rich, but you are much mistaken; Ali Baba is infinitely richer than you; he does not count his money, but measures it." Cassim desired her to explain the riddle, which she did, by telling him the stratagem she had used to make the discovery, and showed him the piece of money, which was so old that they could not tell in what prince's reign it was coined. Cassim, instead of being pleased, conceived a base envy at his brother's prosperity; he could not sleep all that night, and went to him in the morning before sunrise, although after he had married the rich widow, he had never treated him as a brother, but neglected him. "Ali Baba," said he, accosting him, "you are very reserved in your affairs; you pretend to be miserably poor, and yet you measure gold." "How, brother?" replied Ali Baba; "I do not know what you mean: explain yourself." "Do not pretend ignorance," replied Cassim, showing him the piece of gold his wife had given him. "How many of these pieces," added he, "have you? My wife found this at the bottom of the measure you borrowed yesterday."

By this discourse, Ali Baba perceived that Cassim and his wife, through his own wife's folly, knew what they had so much reason to conceal; but what was done could not be recalled; therefore, without showing the least surprise or trouble, he confessed all, told his brother by what chance he had discovered this retreat of the thieves, in what place it was; and offered him part of his treasure to keep the secret. "I expect as much," replied Cassim haughtily; "but I must know exactly where this treasure is, and how I may visit it myself when I choose; otherwise I will go and inform against you, and then you will not only get no more, but will lose all you have, and I shall have a share for my information."

Ali Baba, more out of his natural good temper, than frightened by the menaces of his unnatural brother, told him all he desired, and even the very words he was to use to gain admission into the cave.

Cassim, who wanted no more of Ali Baba, left him, resolving to be beforehand with him, and hoping to get all the treasure to himself. He rose the next morning long before the sun, and set out for the forest with ten mules bearing great chests, which he designed to fill; and followed the road which Ali Baba had pointed out to him. He was not long before he reached the rock, and found out the place by the tree, and other marks, which his brother had given him. When he reached the entrance of the cavern, he pronounced the words: *"Open, Sesame!"* and the door immediately opened, and when he was in, closed upon him. In examining the cave, he was in great admiration to find much more riches than he had apprehended from Ali Baba's account. He was so covetous, and greedy of wealth, that he could have spent the whole day in feasting his eyes with so much treasure, if the thought that he came to carry some away had not hindered him. He laid as many bags of gold as he could carry at the door of the cavern, but his thoughts were so full of the great riches he should possess, that he could not think of the necessary word to make it open, but instead of *"Sesame,"* said: *"Open, Barley!"* and was much amazed to find that the door remained fast shut. He named several sorts of grain, but still the door would not open. Cassim had never expected such an incident, and was so alarmed at the danger he was in that, the more he endeavoured to remember the word *"Sesame,"* the more his memory was confounded, and he had as much forgotten it as if he had never heard it mentioned. He threw down the bags he had loaded himself with and walked distractedly up and down the cave, without having the least regard to the riches that were round him. About noon the robbers chanced to visit their cave, and at some distance from it saw Cassim's mules straggling about the rock, with great chests on their backs. Alarmed at this novelty, they galloped full speed to the cave. They drove away the mules, which Cassim had neglected to fasten, and they strayed through the forest so far, that they were soon out of sight. The robbers never gave themselves the trouble to pursue them, being more concerned to know to whom they belonged, and while some of them searched about the rock, the captain and the rest went directly to the door with their naked sabres in their hands, and pronouncing proper words, it opened.

Cassim, who heard the noise of the horses' feet from the middle of the cave, never doubted of the arrival of the robbers and his approaching death; but was resolved to make one effort to escape from them. To this end he rushed to the door, and no sooner heard the word *Sesame*, which he had forgotten, and saw the door open, than he ran out and threw the leader down, but could not escape the other robbers, who with their sabres soon deprived him of life. The first care of the robbers after this was to examine the cave. They found all the bags which Cassim had brought to the door, to be ready to load his mules, and carried them again to their places, without missing what Ali Baba had taken away before. Then holding a council, and deliberating upon this occurrence, they guessed that Cassim, when he was in, could not get out again; but could not imagine how he had entered. It came into their heads that he might have got down by the top of the cave; but the aperture by which it received light was so high, and the rocks so inaccessible without, that they gave up this conjecture. That he came in at the door they could not believe, however, unless he had the secret of making it open. In short, none of them could imagine which way he had entered; for they were all persuaded nobody knew their secret, little imagining that Ali Baba had watched them. It was a matter of the greatest importance to them to secure their riches. They agreed therefore to cut Cassim's body into quarters, to hang two on one side and two on the other, within the door of the cave, to terrify any person who should attempt again to enter. They had no sooner taken this resolution than they put it in execution, and when they had nothing more to detain them, left the place of their hoards well closed. They then mounted their horses, went to beat the roads again, and to attack the caravans they might meet.

In the meantime, Cassim's wife was very uneasy when night came, and her husband was not returned. She ran to Ali Baba in alarm, and said: "I believe, brother-in-law, that you know Cassim, your brother, is gone to the forest, and upon what account; it is now night, and he is not returned; I am afraid some misfortune has happened to him." Ali Baba, who had expected that his brother, after what he had said, would go to the forest, had declined going himself that day, for fear of giving him any umbrage; therefore told her, without any reflection upon her husband's unhandsome behaviour, that she need not frighten herself, for that certainly Cassim would not think it proper to come into the town till the night should be pretty far advanced.

Cassim's wife, considering how much it concerned her husband to keep the business secret, was the more easily persuaded to believe her brother-in-law. She went home again, and waited patiently till midnight. She repented of her foolish curiosity, and cursed her desire of penetrating into the affairs of her brother- and sister-in-law. She spent all the night in weeping; and as soon as it was day, went to them, telling them, by her tears, the cause of her coming. Ali Baba did not wait for his sister-in-law to desire him to go and see what was become of Cassim, but departed immediately with his three asses, begging of her first to moderate her affliction. He went to the forest, and when he came near the rock, having seen neither his brother nor the mules in his way, was seriously alarmed at finding some blood spilt near the door which he took for an ill omen; but when he had pronounced the word, and the door had opened, he was struck with horror at the dismal sight of his brother's body. Without adverting to the little fraternal affection his brother had shewn for him, Ali Baba went into the cave to find something to enshroud his remains, and having loaded one of his asses with them covered them over with wood. The other two asses he loaded with bags of gold, covering them with wood also as before; and then bidding the door shut, came away; but was so cautious as to stop some time at the end of the forest, that he might not go into the town before night. When he came home, he drove the two asses loaded with gold into his little yard, and left the care of unloading them to his wife, while he led the other to his sister-in-law's house.

Ali Baba knocked at the door, which was opened by Morgiana, an intelligent slave, fruitful in inventions to insure success in the most difficult undertakings: and Ali Baba knew her to be such. When he came into the court, he unloaded the ass, and taking Morgiana aside, said to her: "The first thing I ask of you is an inviolable secrecy, both for your mistress's sake and mine. Your master's body is contained in these two bundles, and our business is, to bury him as if he had died a natural death. Go, tell your mistress I want to speak with her; and mind what I have said to you."

Morgiana went to her mistress, and Ali Baba followed her. "Well, brother," said she, with impatience, "what news do you bring me of my husband? I perceive no comfort in your countenance." "Sister," answered Ali Baba, "I cannot satisfy your inquiries unless you hear my story without speaking a word; for it is of as great importance to you as to me to keep what has happened secret." "Alas!" said she, "this preamble lets me know that my husband is not to be found; but at the same time I know the necessity of secrecy, and I must constrain myself: say on, I will hear you."

Ali Baba then detailed the incidents of his journey, till he came to the finding of Cassim's body. "Now," said he, "sister, I have something to relate which will afflict you the more, because it is what you so little expect; but it cannot now be remedied; if my endeavours can comfort you, I offer to put that which God hath sent me to what you have, and marry you: assuring you that my wife will not be jealous, and that we shall live happily together. If this proposal is agreeable to you, we must think of acting so that my brother should appear to have died a natural death. I think you may leave the management of the business to Morgiana, and I will contribute all that lies in my power to your consolation." What could Cassim's widow do better than accept of this proposal? for though her first husband had left behind him a plentiful substance, his brother was now much richer, and by the discovery of this treasure might be still more so. Instead, therefore, of rejecting the offer, she regarded it as the sure means of comfort; and drying up her tears, which had begun to flow abundantly, and suppressing the outcries usual with women who have lost their husbands, showed Ali Baba that she approved of his proposal. Ali Baba left the widow, recommended to Morgiana to act her part well, and then returned home with his ass.

Morgiana went out at the same time to an apothecary, and asked for a sort of lozenges which he prepared, and were very efficacious in the most dangerous disorders. The apothecary inquired who was ill at her master's? She replied with a sigh, her good master Cassim himself: that they knew not what his disorder was, but that he could neither eat nor speak. After these words, Morgiana carried the lozenges home with her, and the next morning went to the same apothecary's again, and with tears in her eyes, asked for an essence which they used to give to sick people only when at the last extremity. "Alas!" said she, taking it from the apothecary, "I am afraid that this remedy will have no better effect than the lozenges; and that I shall lose my good master." On the other hand, as Ali Baba and his wife were often seen to go between Cassim's and their own house all that day, and to seem melancholy, nobody was surprised in the evening to hear the lamentable shrieks and cries of Cassim's wife and Morgiana, who gave out everywhere that her master was dead. The next morning, soon after day appeared, Morgiana, who knew a certain old cobbler that opened his stall early, before other people, went to him, and bidding him good morrow, put a piece of gold into his hand. "Well," said Baba Mustapha, which was his name, and who was a merry old fellow, looking at the gold, "this is good hansel: what must I do for it? I am ready."

"Baba Mustapha," said Morgiana, "you must take with you your sewing tackle, and go with me; but I must tell you, I shall blindfold you when you come to such a place." Baba Mustapha seemed to hesitate a little at these words. "Oh! oh!" replied he, "you would have me do something against my conscience or against my honour?" "God forbid!" said Morgiana, putting another piece of gold into his hand, "that I should ask anything that is contrary to your honour; only come along with me, and fear nothing."

Baba Mustapha went with Morgiana, who, after she had bound his eyes with a handkerchief, conveyed him to her deceased master's house, and never unloosed his eyes till he had entered the room where she had put the corpse together. "Baba Mustapha," said she, "you must make haste and sew these quarters together; and when you have done, I will give you another piece of gold." After Baba Mustapha had finished his task, she blindfolded him again, gave him the third piece of gold as she had promised, and recommending secrecy to him, carried him back to the place where she first bound his eyes, pulled off the bandage, and let him go home, but watched him that he returned toward his stall, till he was quite out of sight, for fear he should have the curiosity to return and track her.

By the time Morgiana had warmed some water to wash the body, Ali Baba came with incense to embalm it, after which it was sewn up in a winding-sheet. Not long after, the joiner, according to Ali Baba's orders, brought the bier, which Morgiana received at the door, and helped Ali Baba to put the body into it; when she went to the mosque to inform the imaum that they were ready. The people of the mosque, whose business it was to wash the dead, offered to perform their duty, but she told them that it was done already. Morgiana had scarcely got home before the imaum and the other ministers of the mosque arrived. Four neighbours carried the corpse on their shoulders to the burying-ground, following the imam, who recited some prayers. Morgiana, as a slave to the deceased, followed the corpse, weeping, beating her breast, and tearing her hair; and Ali Baba came after with some neighbours, who often relieved the others in carrying the corpse to the burying-ground. Cassim's wife stayed at home mourning, uttering lamentable cries with the women of the neighbourhood, who came according to custom during the funeral, and joining their lamentations with hers, filled the quarter far and near with sorrow. In this manner Cassim's melancholy death was concealed and hushed up between Ali

Baba, his wife, Cassim's widow, and Morgiana, with so much contrivance, that nobody in the city had the least knowledge or suspicion of the cause of it.

Three or four days after the funeral, Ali Baba removed his few goods openly to the widow's house; but the money he had taken from the robbers he conveyed thither by night: soon after the marriage with his sister-in-law was published, and as these marriages are common in the Mussulman religion, nobody was surprised. As for Cassim's warehouse, Ali Baba gave it to his own eldest son, promising that if he managed it well, he would soon give him a fortune to marry very advantageously according to his situation.

Let us now leave Ali Baba to enjoy the beginning of his good fortune, and return to the forty robbers. They came again at the appointed time to visit their retreat in the forest; but great was their surprise to find Cassim's body taken away, with some of their bags of gold. "We are certainly discovered," said the captain, "and if we do not speedily apply some remedy, shall gradually lose all the riches which we have, with so much pains and danger, been so many years amassing together. All that we can think of the loss which we have sustained is, that the thief whom we surprised had the secret of opening the door, and we arrived luckily as he was coming out: but his body being removed, and with it some of our money, plainly shows that he had an accomplice; and as it is likely that there were but two who had discovered our secret, and one has been caught, we must look narrowly after the other. What say you, my lads?" All the robbers thought the captain's proposal so advisable, that they unanimously approved of it, and agreed that they must lay all other enterprises aside, to follow this closely, and not give it up till they had succeeded.

"I expected no less," said the captain, "from your fidelity: but, first of all, one of you who is artful, and enterprising, must go into the town disguised as a traveller, to try if he can hear any talk of the strange death of the man whom we have killed, as he deserved; and endeavour to find out who he was, and where he lived. This is a matter of the first importance for us to ascertain, that we may do nothing which we may have reason to repent of, by discovering ourselves in a country where we have lived so long unknown. But to warn him who shall take upon himself this commission, and to prevent our being deceived by his giving us a false report, I ask you all, if you do not think that in case of treachery, or even error of judgment, he should suffer death?" Without waiting for the suffrages of his companions, one of the robbers started up, and said: "I submit to this condition, and think it an honour to expose my life, by taking the commission upon me; but remember, at least, if I do not succeed, that I neither wanted courage nor good will to serve the troop." After this robber had received great commendations from the captain, he disguised himself, and taking his leave of the troop that night, went into the town just at daybreak; and walked up and down, till accidentally he came to Baba Mustapha's stall, which was always open before any of the shops.

Baba Mustapha was seated with an awl in his hand, just going to work. The robber saluted him, bidding him good morrow; and perceiving that he was old, said: "Honest man, you begin to work very early: is it possible that one of your age can see so well? I question, even if it were somewhat lighter, whether you could see to stitch."

"Certainly," replied Baba Mustapha, "you must be a stranger, and do not know me; for old as I am, I have extraordinarily good eyes; and you will not doubt it when I tell you that I sewed a dead body together in a place where I had not so much light as I have now." The robber was overjoyed to think that he had addressed himself, at his first coming into the town, to a man who in all probability could give him the intelligence he wanted. "A dead body!" replied he with affected amazement. "What could you sew up a dead body for? You mean you sewed up his winding-sheet." "No, no," answered Baba Mustapha, "I perceive your meaning; you want to have me speak out, but you shall know no more." The robber wanted no farther assurance to be persuaded that he had discovered what he sought. He pulled out a piece of gold, and putting it into Baba Mustapha's hand, said to him: "I do not want to learn your secret, though I can assure you I would not divulge it, if you trusted me with it; the only thing which I desire of you is, to do me the favour to shew me the house where you stitched up the dead body."

"If I were disposed to do you that favour," replied Baba Mustapha, holding the money in his hand, ready to return it, "I assure you I cannot. I was taken to a certain place, where I was blinded, I was then led to the house, and afterward brought back again in the same manner; you see, therefore, the impossibility of my doing what you desire."

"Well," replied the robber, "you may, however, remember a little of the way that you were led blindfolded. Come, let me blind your eyes at the same place. We will walk together; perhaps you may recognise some part; and as everybody ought to be paid for his trouble, there is another piece of gold for you; gratify me in what I ask you." So saying, he put another piece of gold into his hand.

The two pieces of gold were great temptations to Baba Mustapha. He looked at them a long time in his hand, without saying a word, thinking with himself what he should do; but at last he pulled out his purse, and put them in. "I cannot assure you," said he to the robber, "that I can remember the way exactly; but since you desire, I will try what I can do." At these words Baba Mustapha rose up, to the great joy of the robber, and without shutting his shop, where he had nothing valuable to lose, he led the robber to the place where Morgiana had bound his eyes. "It was here," said Baba Mustapha, "I was blindfolded; and I turned as you see me." The robber, who had his handkerchief ready, tied it over his eyes, walked by him till he stopped, partly leading, and partly guided by him. "I think," said Baba Mustapha, "I went no farther," and he had now stopped directly at Cassim's house, where Ali Baba then lived. The thief, before he pulled off the band, marked the door with a piece of chalk, which he had ready in his hand; and then asked him if he knew whose house that was; to which Baba Mustapha replied, that as he did not live in that neighbourhood he could not tell. The robber, finding he could discover no more from Baba Mustapha, thanked him for the trouble he had taken, and left him to go back to his stall, while he returned to the forest, persuaded that he should be very well received. A little after the robber and Baba

Mustapha had parted, Morgiana went out of Ali Baba's house upon some errand, and upon her return, seeing the mark the robber had made, stopped to observe it. "What can be the meaning of this mark?" said she to herself. "Somebody intends my master no good: however, with whatever intention it was done, it is advisable to guard against the worst." Accordingly, she fetched a piece of chalk, and marked two or three doors on each side in the same manner, without saying a word to her master or mistress.

In the meantime the thief rejoined his troop in the forest, and recounted to them his success. All the robbers listened to him with the utmost satisfaction; when the captain, after commending his diligence, addressing himself to them all, said: "Comrades, we have no time to lose: let us set off well armed; but that we may not excite any suspicion, let only one or two go into the town together, and join at our rendezvous, which shall be the great square. In the meantime, our comrade who brought us the good news, and I, will go and find out the house that we may consult what had best be done."

This plan was approved of by all, and they were soon ready. They filed off in parties of two each, and got into the town without being in the least suspected. The captain, and he who had visited the town in the morning as spy, came in the last. He led the captain into the street where he had marked Ali Baba's residence; and when they came to the first of the houses which Morgiana had marked, he pointed it out. But the captain observed that the next door was chalked in the same manner; and shewing it to his guide, asked him which house it was, that, or the first? The guide was so confounded, that he knew not what answer to make; but still more puzzled, when he saw five or six houses similarly marked. He assured the captain, with an oath, that he had marked but one, and could not tell who had chalked the rest so that he could not distinguish the house which the cobbler had stopped at.

The captain, finding that their design had proved abortive, went directly to the place of rendezvous, and told the first of his troop whom he met that they had lost their labour, and must return to their cave. When the troop was all got together, the captain told them the reason of their returning; and presently the conductor was declared by all worthy of death. He condemned himself, acknowledging that he ought to have taken better precaution, and prepared to receive the stroke from him who was appointed to cut off his head. Another of the gang, who promised himself that he should succeed better, immediately presented himself, and his offer being accepted, he went and corrupted Baba Mustapha, as the other had done; and being shewn the house, marked it in a place more remote from sight, with red chalk.

Not long after, Morgiana, whose eyes nothing could escape, went out, and seeing the red chalk, and arguing with herself as she had done before, marked the other neighbours' houses in the same place and manner. The robber, at his return to his company, valued himself much on the precaution he had taken, which he looked upon as an infallible way of distinguishing Ali Baba's house from the others; and the captain and all of them thought it must succeed. They conveyed themselves into the town with the same precaution as before; but when the robber and his captain came to the street, they found the same difficulty: at which the captain was enraged, and the robber in as great confusion as his predecessor. Thus the captain and his troop were forced to retire a second time, and much more dissatisfied; while the unfortunate robber, who had been the author of the mistake, underwent the same punishment; which he willingly submitted to.

The captain, having lost two brave fellows of his troop, was afraid of diminishing it too much by pursuing this plan to get information of the residence of their plunderer. He found by their example that their heads were not so good as their hands on such occasions; and therefore resolved to take upon himself the important commission. Accordingly, he went and addressed himself to Baba Mustapha, who did him the same service he had done to the other robbers. He did not set any particular mark on the house, but examined and observed it so carefully, by passing often by it, that it was impossible for him to mistake it.

The captain, well satisfied with his attempt, and informed what he wanted to know, returned to the forest; and when he came into the cave, where the troop waited for him, said: "Now, comrades, nothing can prevent our full revenge, as I am certain of the house, and in my way hither I have thought how to put it into execution, but if any one can form a better expedient, let him communicate it." He then told them his contrivance; and as they approved of it, ordered them to go into the villages about, and buy nineteen mules, with thirty-eight large leather jars, one full of oil, and the others empty. In two or three days' time the robbers had purchased the mules and jars, and as the mouths of the jars were rather too narrow for his purpose, the captain caused them to be widened; and after having put one of his men into each, with the weapons which he thought fit, leaving open the seam which had been undone to leave them room to breathe, he rubbed the jars on the outside with oil from the full vessel. Things being thus prepared, when the nineteen mules were loaded with thirty-seven robbers in jars, and the jar of oil, the captain, as their driver, set out with them, and reached the town by the dusk of the evening, as he had intended. He led them through the streets till he came to Ali Baba's, at whose door he designed to have knocked; but was prevented by his sitting there after supper to take a little fresh air. He stopped his mules, addressed himself to him, and said: "I have brought some oil a great way, to sell at to-morrow's market; and it is now so late that I do not know where to lodge. If I should not be troublesome to you, do me the favour to let me pass the night with you, and I shall be very much obliged by your hospitality."

Though Ali Baba had seen the captain of the robbers in the forest, and had heard him speak, it was hardly possible to know him in the disguise of an oil merchant. He told him he should be welcome, and immediately opened his gates for the mules to go into the yard. At the same time he called to a slave, and ordered him, when the mules were unloaded, to put them into the stable, and give them fodder; and then went to Morgiana, to bid her get a good supper. He did more. When he saw the captain had unloaded his mules, and that they were put into the stables as he had ordered, and he was looking for a place to pass the night in the air, he brought him into the hall where he received his company, telling him he would not suffer him to be in the

court. The captain excused himself on pretence of not being troublesome; but really to have room to execute his design, and it was not till
after the most pressing importunity that he yielded. Ali Baba, not content to keep company, till supper was ready, with the man who had a
design on his life, continued talking with him till it was ended, and
repeating his offer of service. The captain rose up at the same time with
his host; and while Ali Baba went to speak to Morgiana he withdrew
into the yard, under pretence of looking at his mules. Ali Baba, after
charging Morgiana afresh to take care of his guest, said to her: "To-
morrow morning I design to go to the bath before day; take care my
bathing linens be ready, give them to Abdoollah," which was the
slave's name, "and make me some good broth against I return." After
this he went to bed.

In the meantime, the captain went from the stable to give his people
orders what to do; and beginning at the first jar, and so on to the last,
said to each man: "As soon as I throw some stones out of the chamber
window where I lie, do not fail to cut the jar open with the knife you
have about you for the purpose, and come out, and I will immediately
join you." After this he returned into the house, when Morgiana, taking
up a light, conducted him to his chamber, where she left him; and he,
to avoid any suspicion, put the light out soon after, and laid himself
down in his clothes, that he might be the more ready to rise.

Morgiana, remembering Ali Baba's orders, got his bathing linens
ready, and ordered Abdoollah to set on the pot for the broth; but while
she was preparing it, the lamp went out, and there was no more oil in
the house, nor any candles. What to do she did not know, for the broth
must be made. Abdoollah seeing her very uneasy, said: "Do not fret and
tease yourself, but go into the yard, and take some oil out of one of the
jars." Morgiana thanked Abdoollah for his advice, took the oil-pot, and
went into the yard; when as she came nigh the first jar, the robber within
said softly: "Is it time?" Though the robber spoke low, Morgiana was
struck with the voice the more, because the captain, when he unloaded
the mules, had taken the lids off this and all the other jars to give air to
his men, who were ill enough at their ease, almost wanting room to

breathe. As much surprised as Morgiana naturally was at finding a man in a jar, instead of the oil she wanted, many would have made such an outcry as to have given an alarm; whereas Morgiana comprehending immediately the importance of keeping silence, and the necessity of applying a speedy remedy without noise, conceived at once the means, and collecting herself without showing the least emotion, answered: "Not yet, but presently." She went in this manner to all the jars, giving the same answer, till she came to the jar of oil.

By this means, Morgiana found that her master Ali Baba, who thought that he had entertained an oil merchant, had admitted thirty-eight robbers into his house, regarding this pretended merchant as their captain. She made what haste she could to fill her oil-pot, and returned into her kitchen; where, as soon as she had lighted her lamp, she took a great kettle, went again to the oil-jar, filled the kettle, set it on a large wood-fire, and as soon as it boiled went and poured enough into every jar to stifle and destroy the robber within.

When this action, worthy of the courage of Morgiana, was executed without any noise, she returned into the kitchen with the empty kettle; and having put out the great fire she had made to boil the oil, and leaving just enough to make the broth, put out the lamp also, and remained silent; resolving not to go to rest till she had observed what might follow through a window of the kitchen, which opened into the yard.

She had not waited long before the captain of the robbers got up, opened the window, and finding no light, and hearing no noise, or any one stirring in the house, gave the appointed signal, by throwing little stones, several of which hit the jars, as he doubted not by the sound they gave. He then listened, but not hearing or perceiving anything whereby he could judge that his companions stirred, he began to grow very uneasy, threw stones again a second and also a third time, and could not comprehend the reason that none of them should answer his signal. Much alarmed, he went softly down into the yard, and going to the first jar, whilst asking the robber, whom he thought alive, if he was in readiness, smelt the hot boiled oil, which sent forth a steam out of the jar. Hence he suspected that his plot to murder Ali Baba and plunder his house was discovered. Examining all the jars one after another, he found that all the members of his gang were dead; and by the oil he missed out of the last jar guessed the means and manner of their death. Enraged to despair at having failed in his design, he forced the lock of a door that led from the yard to the garden, and climbing over the walls, made his escape.

When Morgiana heard no noise, and found, after waiting some time, that the captain did not return, she concluded that he had chosen rather to make his escape by the garden than the street door, which was double-locked. Satisfied and pleased to have succeeded so well, in saving her master and family, she went to bed.

Ali Baba rose before day, and, followed by his slave, went to the baths, entirely ignorant of the important event which had happened at home; for Morgiana had not thought it safe to wake him before, for fear of losing her opportunity; and after her successful exploit she thought it needless to disturb him.

When he returned from the baths, the sun was risen; he was very much surprised to see the oil jars and that the merchant was not gone with the mules. He asked Morgiana, who opened the door, and had let all things stand as they were, that he might see them, the reason of it. "My good master," answered she, "God preserve you and all your family; you will be better informed of what you wish to know when you have seen what I have to show you, if you will but give yourself the trouble to follow me."

As soon as Morgiana had shut the door, Ali Baba followed her; when she requested him to look into the first jar and see if there was any oil. Ali Baba did so, and seeing a man, started back in alarm, and cried out. "Do not be afraid," said Morgiana; "the man you see there can neither do you nor anybody else any harm. He is dead." "Ah, Morgiana!" said Ali Baba, "what is it you show me? Explain yourself." "I will," replied Morgiana; "moderate your astonishment, and do not excite the curiosity of your neighbours. Look into all the other jars."

Ali Baba examined all the other jars, and when he came to that which had the oil in, found it prodigiously sunk, and stood for some time motionless, sometimes looking at the jars, and sometimes at Morgiana, without saying a word, so great was his surprise: at last, when he had recovered himself, he said: "And what is become of the merchant?"

"Merchant!" answered she, "he is as much one as I am; I will tell you who he is, and what is become of him: but you had better hear the story in your own chamber; for it is time for your health that you had your broth after your bathing."

While Ali Baba retired to his chamber, Morgiana went into the kitchen to fetch the broth, but before he would drink it, he first entreated her to satisfy his impatience, and tell him what had happened, with all the circumstances; and she obeyed him.

"This," she said, when she had completed her story, "is the account you asked of me; and I am convinced it is the consequence of what I observed some days ago, but did not think fit to acquaint you with; for when I came in one morning early I found our street door marked with white chalk, and the next morning with red; upon which, both times without knowing what was the intention of those chalks, I marked two or three neighbours' doors on each side in the same manner. If you reflect on this, and what has since happened, you will find it to be a plot of the robbers of the forest, of whose gang there are two wanting, and now they are reduced to three: all this shows that they had sworn your destruction, and it is proper you should be upon your guard, while there is one of them alive: for my part, I shall neglect nothing necessary to your preservation, as I am in duty bound."

When Morgiana had left off speaking, Ali Baba was so sensible of the great service she had done him, that he said to her: "I will not die without rewarding you as you deserve; I owe my life to you, and for the first token of my acknowledgment, give you your liberty from this moment, till I can complete your recompense as I intend. I am persuaded with you, that the forty robbers have laid snares for my destruction. God, by your means, has delivered me from them as yet, and I hope will continue to preserve me from their wicked designs, and deliver the world from their persecution. All that we have to do is to bury the bodies of these pests of mankind immediately, and with all the secrecy imaginable, that nobody may suspect what is become of them. But that labour Abdoollah and I will undertake."

Ali Baba's garden was very long, and shaded at the farther end by a great number of large trees. Under these he and the slave dug a trench, long and wide enough to hold all the robbers. Afterward they lifted the bodies out of the jars, took away their weapons, carried them to the end of the garden, laid them in the trench, and levelled the ground again. When this was done, Ali Baba hid the jars and weapons, and as he had no occasion for the mules, he sent them at different times to be sold in the market by his slave.

While Ali Baba took these measures to prevent the public from knowing how he came by his riches in so short a time, the captain of the forty robbers returned to the forest with inconceivable mortification; and in his confusion at his ill success, so contrary to what he had promised himself, entered the cave, not being able, all the way from the town, to come to any resolution how to revenge himself of Ali Baba.

The loneliness of the gloomy cavern became frightful to him. "Where are you, my brave lads," cried he, "old companions of my watchings, inroads, and labour? What can I do without you? Did I collect you only to lose you by so base a fate, and so unworthy of your courage! Had you died with your sabres in your hands, like brave men, my regret had been less! When shall I enlist so gallant a troop again? And if I could, can I undertake it without exposing so much gold and treasure to him who hath already enriched himself out of it? I cannot, I ought not to think of it, before I have taken away his life. I will undertake that alone, which I could not accomplish with your powerful assistance; and when I have taken measures to secure this treasure from being pillaged, I will provide for it new masters and successors after me, who shall preserve and augment it to all posterity." This resolution being taken, he was not at a loss how to execute his purpose; but full of hopes, slept all that night very quietly.

When he awoke early next morning, he dressed himself, agreeably to the project he had formed, went to the town, and took a lodging in a khan. As he expected what had happened at Ali Baba's might make a great noise, he asked his host what news there was in the city. Upon which the innkeeper told him a great many circumstances, which did not concern him in the least. He judged by this, that the reason why Ali Baba kept his affairs so secret, was for fear people should know where the treasure lay; and because he knew his life would be sought on account of it. This urged him the more to neglect nothing to rid himself of so cautious an enemy.

The captain now assumed the character of a merchant, and conveyed gradually a great many sorts of rich stuffs and fine linen to his lodging from the cavern, but with all the necessary precautions imaginable to conceal the place whence he brought them. In order to dispose of the merchandise, when he had amassed them together, he took a warehouse, which happened to be opposite to Cassim's, which Ali Baba's son had occupied since the death of his uncle.

He took the name of Khaujeh Houssain, and as a newcomer, was, according to custom, extremely civil and complaisant to all the merchants his neighbours. Ali Baba's son was from his vicinity one of the first to converse with Khaujeh Houssain, who strove to cultivate his friendship more particularly when, two or three days after he was settled, he recognised Ali Baba, who came to see his son, and stopped to talk with him as he was accustomed to do. When he was gone, the impostor learnt from his son who he was. He increased his assiduities, caressed him in the most engaging manner, made him some small presents, and often asked him to dine and sup with him.

Ali Baba's son did not choose to lie under such obligation to Khaujeh Houssain, without making the like return; but was so much straitened for want of room in his house, that he could not entertain him so well as he wished; he therefore acquainted his father Ali Baba with his intention, and told him that it did not look well for him to receive such favours from Khaujeh Houssain without inviting him in return.

Ali Baba, with great pleasure, took the treat upon himself. "Son," said he, "to-morrow being Friday, which is a day that the shops of such great merchants as Khaujeh Houssain and yourself are shut, get him to take a walk with you, and as you come back, pass by my door and call in. It will look better to have it happen accidentally, than if you gave him a formal invitation. I will go and order Morgiana to provide a supper."

The next day Ali Baba's son and Khaujeh Houssain met by appointment, took their walk, and as they returned, Ali Baba's son led Khaujeh Houssain through the street where his father lived; and when they came to the house, stopped and knocked at the door. "This, sir," said he, "is my father's house; who, from the account I have given him of your friendship, charged me to procure him the honour of your acquaintance."

Though it was the sole aim of Khaujeh Houssain to introduce himself into Ali Baba's house, that he might kill him without hazarding his own life or making any noise; yet he excused himself, and offered to take his leave. But a slave having opened the door, Ali Baba's son took him obligingly by the hand, and in a manner forced him in.

Ali Baba received Khaujeh Houssain with a smiling countenance, and in the most obliging manner. He thanked him for all the favours he had done his son; adding withal, the obligation was the greater, as he was a young man not much acquainted with the world.

Khaujeh Houssain returned the compliment, by assuring Ali Baba, that though his son might not have acquired the experience of older men, he had good sense equal to the knowledge of many others. After a little more conversation on different subjects, he offered again to take his leave; when Ali Baba, stopping him, said: "Where are you going, sir, in so much haste? I beg you would do me the honour to sup with me, though what I have to give you is not worth your acceptance; but such as it is, I hope you will accept it as heartily as I give it." "Sir," replied Khaujeh Houssain, "I am thoroughly persuaded of your good will; and if I ask the favour of you not to take it ill that I do not accept your obliging invitation, I beg of you to believe that it does not proceed from any slight or intention to affront, but from a reason which you would approve if you knew it."

"And what may that reason be, sir," replied Ali Baba, "if I may be so bold as to ask you?" "It is," answered Khaujeh Houssain, "that I can eat no victuals that have any salt in them; therefore judge how I should feel at your table." "If that is the only reason," said Ali Baba, "it ought not to deprive me of the honour of your company at supper; for, in the first place, there is no salt ever put into my bread, and as to the meat we shall have to-night, I promise you there shall be none in that. Therefore you must do me the favour to stay. I will return immediately."

Ali Baba went into the kitchen, and ordered Morgiana to put no salt to the meat that was to be dressed that night; and to make quickly two or three ragouts besides what he had ordered, but be sure to put no salt in them.

Morgiana, who was always ready to obey her master, could not help seeming somewhat dissatisfied at his strange order. "Who is this difficult man," said she, "who eats no salt with his meat? Your supper will be spoiled, if I keep it back so long." "Do not be angry, Morgiana," replied Ali Baba; "he is an honest man; therefore do as I bid you."

Morgiana obeyed, though with no little reluctance, and had a curiosity to see this man who ate no salt. To this end, when she had finished what she had to do in the kitchen, she helped Abdoollah to carry up the dishes; and looking at Khaujeh Houssain, knew him at first sight, notwithstanding his disguise, to be the captain of the robbers, and examining him very carefully, perceived that he had a dagger under his garment. "I am not in the least amazed," said she to herself, "that this wicked wretch, who is my master's greatest enemy, would eat no salt with him, since he intends to assassinate him; but I will prevent him."

Morgiana, while they were eating, made the necessary preparations for executing one of the boldest acts ever meditated, and had just determined, when Abdoollah came for the dessert of fruit, which she carried up, and as soon as he had taken the meat away, set upon the table; after that, she placed three glasses by Ali Baba, and going out, took Abdoollah with her to sup, and to give Ali Baba the more liberty of conversation with his guest.

Khaujeh Houssain, or rather the captain of the robbers, thought he had now a favourable opportunity of being revenged on Ali Baba. "I will," said he to himself, "make the father and son both drunk: the son, whose life I intend to spare, will not be able to prevent my stabbing his father to the heart; and while the slaves are at supper, or asleep in the kitchen, I can make my escape over the gardens as before."

Instead of going to supper, Morgiana, who had penetrated the intentions of the counterfeit Khaujeh Houssain, would not give him time to put his villainous design into execution, but dressed herself neatly with a suitable head-dress like a dancer, girded her waist with a silver-gilt girdle, to which there hung a poniard with a hilt and guard of the same metal, and put a handsome mask on her face. When she had thus disguised herself, she said to Abdoollah: "Take your tabor, and let us go and divert our master and his son's guest, as we do sometimes when he is alone."

Abdoollah took his tabor and played all the way into the hall before Morgiana, who when she came to the door made a low obeisance, with a deliberate air, in order to draw attention, and by way of asking leave to exhibit her skill. Abdoollah, seeing that his master had a mind to say something, left off playing. "Come in, Morgiana," said Ali Baba, "and let Khaujeh Houssain see what you can do, that he may tell us what he thinks of you. But, sir," said he, turning toward his guest, "do not think that I put myself to any expense to give you this diversion, since these are my slave and my cook and housekeeper; and I hope you will not find the entertainment they give us disagreeable."

Khaujeh Houssain, who did not expect this diversion after supper, began to fear he should not be able to improve the opportunity he thought he had found: but hoped, if he now missed his aim, to secure it another time, by keeping up a friendly correspondence with the father and son; therefore, though he could have wished Ali Baba would have declined the dance, he had the complaisance to express his satisfaction at what he saw pleased his host.

As soon as Abdoollah saw that Ali Baba and Khaujeh Houssain had done talking, he began to play on the tabor, and accompanied it with an air; to which Morgiana, who was an excellent performer, danced in such a manner as would have created admiration in any other company besides that before which she now exhibited, among whom, perhaps, none but the false Khaujeh Houssain was in the least attentive to her, the rest having seen her so frequently.

After she had danced several dances with equal propriety and grace, she drew the poniard, and holding it in her hand, began a dance, in which she outdid herself, by the many different figures, light movements, and the surprising leaps and wonderful exertions with which she accompanied it. Sometimes she presented the poniard to one person's breast, sometimes to another's, and oftentimes seemed to strike her own. At last, as if she was out of breath, she snatched the tabor from Abdoollah with her left hand, and holding the dagger in her right, presented the other side of the tabor, after the manner of those who get a livelihood by dancing, and solicit the liberality of the spectators.

Ali Baba put a piece of gold into the tabor, as did also his son: and Khaujeh Houssain, seeing that she was coming to him, had pulled his purse out of his bosom to make her a present; but while he was putting his hand into it, Morgiana, with a courage and resolution worthy of herself, plunged the poniard into his heart. Ali Baba and his son, shocked at this action, cried out aloud. "Unhappy wretch!" exclaimed Ali Baba, "what have you done to ruin me and my family?" "It was to preserve, not to ruin you," answered Morgiana; "for see here," continued she (opening the pretended Khaujeh Houssain's garment, and showing the dagger), "what an enemy you had entertained! Look well at him, and you will find him to be both the fictitious oil merchant, and the captain of the gang of forty robbers. Remember, too, that he would eat no salt with you; and what would you have more to persuade you of his wicked design? Before I saw him, I suspected him as soon as you told me you had such a guest. I knew him, and you now find that my suspicion was not groundless."

Ali Baba, who immediately felt the new obligation he had to Morgiana for saving his life a second time, embraced her: "Morgiana," said he, "I gave you your liberty, and then promised you that my gratitude should not stop there, but that I would soon give you higher proofs of its sincerity, which I now do by making you my daughter-in-law." Then, addressing himself to his son, he said: "I believe you, son, to be so dutiful a child, that you will not refuse Morgiana for your wife. You see that Khaujeh Houssain sought your friendship with a treacherous design to take away my life; and, if he had succeeded, there is no doubt but he would have sacrificed you also to his revenge. Consider, that by marrying Morgiana you marry the preserver of my family and your own."

The son, far from showing any dislike, readily consented to the marriage; not only because he would not disobey his father, but also because it was agreeable to his inclination.

After this, they thought of burying the captain of the robbers with his comrades, and did it so privately that nobody discovered their bones till many years after, when no one had any concern in the publication of this remarkable history.

A few days afterward, Ali Baba celebrated the nuptials of his son and Morgiana with great solemnity, a sumptuous feast, and the usual dancing and spectacles; and had the satisfaction to see that his friends and neighbours, whom he invited, had no knowledge of the true motives of the marriage; but that those who were not unacquainted with Morgiana's good qualities commended his generosity and goodness of heart.

Ali Baba forbore, after this marriage, from going again to the robbers' cave, as he had done, for fear of being surprised, from the time he had brought away his brother Cassim's mangled remains. He had kept away after the death of the thirty-seven robbers and their captain, supposing the other two, whom he could get not account of, might be alive.

At the year's end, when he found that they had not made any attempt to disturb him, he had the curiosity to make another journey, taking the necessary precautions for his safety. He mounted his horse, and when he came to the cave, and saw no footsteps of men or beasts, looked upon it as a good sign. He alighted, tied his horse to a tree, then approaching the entrance and pronouncing the words, *Open, Sesame!*

the door opened. He entered the cavern, and by the condition he found things in, judged that nobody had been there since the false Khaujeh Houssain, when he had fetched the goods for his shop; that the gang of forty robbers was completely destroyed, and no longer doubted that he was the only person in the world who had the secret of opening the cave, so that all the treasure was at his sole disposal. Having brought with him a wallet, he put into it as much gold as his horse would carry, and returned to town.

Afterward Ali Baba carried his son to the cave, and taught him the secret, which they handed down to their posterity, who, using their good fortune with moderation, lived in great honour and splendour.

from

Excalibur

by Bernard Cornwell

This tale by Bernard Cornwell (born 1944) describes King Arthur's dealings with neighboring rulers. Lord Derfel is son of the Saxon King Aelle, but supports Arthur—a Briton. Derfel carries to his father a peace offering from Arthur—but doesn't know whether Aelle and his allies (who include Arthur's enemies Cerdic and Lancelot) will welcome him or kill him.

I am a Saxon. My Saxon mother, Erce, while she was still pregnant, was taken captive by Uther and made a slave and I was born soon after. I was taken from my mother as a small child, but not before I had learned the Saxon tongue. Later, much later, on the very eve of Lancelot's rebellion, I found my mother and learned that my father was Aelle.

My blood then is pure Saxon, and half royal at that, though because I was raised among the Britons I feel no kinship with the Sais. To me, as to Arthur or to any other free-born Briton, the Sais are a plague carried to us across the Eastern Sea.

From whence they come, no one really knows. Sagramor, who has travelled more widely than any other of Arthur's commanders, tells me the Saxon land is a distant, fog-shrouded place of bogs and woodland, though he admits he has never been there. He just knows it is somewhere across the sea and they are leaving it, he claims, because the land of Britain is better, though I have also heard that the Saxons' homeland is under siege from other, even stranger, enemies who come from the world's farthest edge. But for whatever reason, for a hundred years now the Saxons have been crossing the sea to take our land and now they hold all eastern Britain. We call that stolen territory Lloegyr, the Lost Lands, and there is not a soul in free Britain who does not dream of taking back the Lost Lands. Merlin and Nimue believe that the lands will only be recovered by the Gods, while Arthur wishes to do it with the sword. And my task was to divide our enemies to make the task easier for either the Gods or for Arthur.

I travelled in the autumn when the oaks had turned to bronze, the beeches to red and the cold was misting the dawns white. I travelled alone, for if Aelle was to reward an emissary's coming with death then it was better that only one man should die. Ceinwyn had begged me to take a warband, but to what purpose? One band could not hope to take on the power of Aelle's whole army, and so, as the wind stripped the first yellow leaves from the elms, I rode eastwards. Ceinwyn had tried to persuade me to wait until after Samain, for if Merlin's invocations worked at Mai Dun then there would surely be no need for any emissaries to visit the Saxons, but Arthur would not countenance any delay. He had put his faith in Aelle's treachery and he wanted an answer from the Saxon King, and so I rode, hoping only that I would survive and that I would be back in Dumnonia by Samain Eve. I wore my sword and I had a shield hung on my back, but I carried no other weapons or armour.

I did not ride directly eastwards, for that route would have taken me dangerously close to Cerdic's land, so instead I went north into Gwent and then eastwards, aiming for the Saxon frontier where Aelle ruled. For a day and a half I journeyed through the rich farmlands of Gwent, passing villas and homesteads where smoke blew from roof holes. The fields were churned muddy by the hoofs of beasts being penned for the winter slaughter, and their lowing added a melancholy to my journey. The air had that first hint of winter and in the mornings the swollen sun hung low and pale in the mist. Starlings flocked on fallow fields.

The landscape changed as I rode eastwards. Gwent was a Christian country and at first I passed large, elaborate churches, but by the second day the churches were much smaller and the farms less prosperous until at last I reached the middle lands, the waste places where neither Saxon nor Briton ruled, but where both had their killing grounds. Here the meadows that had once fed whole families were thick with oak saplings, hawthorn, birch and ash, the villas were roofless ruins and the halls were stark burned skeletons. Yet some folk still lived here, and when I once heard footsteps running through a nearby wood I drew Hywelbane in fear of the masterless men who had their refuge in these wild valleys, but no one accosted me until that evening when a band of spearmen barred my path. They were men of Gwent and, like all King Meurig's soldiers, they wore the vestiges of old Rome's uniform; bronze breastplates, helmets crested with plumes of red-dyed horsehair, and rust-red cloaks. Their leader was a Christian named Carig and he invited me to their fortress that stood in a clearing on a high wooded ridge. Carig's job was to guard the frontier and he brusquely demanded to know my business, but enquired no further when I gave him my name and said I rode for Arthur.

Carig's fortress was a simple wooden palisade inside which was built a pair of huts that were thick with smoke from their open fires. I warmed myself as Carig's dozen men busied themselves with cooking a haunch of venison on a spit made from a captured Saxon spear. There were a dozen such fortresses within a day's march, all watching eastwards to guard against Aelle's raiders. Dumnonia had much the same precautions, though we kept an army permanently close to our border. The expense of such an army was exorbitant, and resented by those whose taxes of grain and leather and salt and fleeces paid for the troops. Arthur had always struggled to make the taxes fair and keep their burden light, though now, after the rebellion, he was ruthlessly levying a stiff penalty on all those wealthy men who had followed Lancelot. That levy fell disproportionately on Christians, and Meurig, the Christian King of Gwent, had sent a protest that Arthur had ignored. Carig, Meurig's loyal follower, treated me with a certain reserve, though he did do his best to warn me of what waited across the border. 'You do know, Lord,' he said, 'that the Sais are refusing to let men cross the frontier?'

'I had heard, yes.'

'Two merchants went by a week ago,' Carig said. 'They were carrying pottery and fleeces. I warned them, but,' he paused and shrugged, 'the Saxons kept the pots and the wool, but sent back two skulls.'

'If my skull comes back,' I told him, 'send it to Arthur.' I watched the venison fat drip and flare in the fire. 'Do any travellers come out of Lloegyr?'

'Not for weeks now,' Carig said, 'but next year, no doubt, you will see plenty of Saxon spearmen in Dumnonia.'

'Not in Gwent?' I challenged him.

'Aelle has no quarrel with us,' Carig said firmly. He was a nervous young man who did not much like his exposed position on Britain's frontier, though he did his duty conscientiously enough and his men, I noted, were well disciplined.

'You're Britons,' I told Carig, 'and Aelle's a Saxon, isn't that quarrel enough?'

Carig shrugged. 'Dumnonia is weak, Lord, the Saxons know that. Gwent is strong. They will attack you, not us.' He sounded horribly complacent.

'But once they have beaten Dumnonia,' I said, touching the iron in my sword hilt to avert the ill-luck implicit in my words, 'how long before they come north into Gwent?'

'Christ will protect us,' Carig said piously, and made the sign of the cross. A crucifix hung on the hut wall and one of his men licked his fingers then touched the feet of the tortured Christ. I surreptitiously spat into the fire.

I rode east next morning. Clouds had come in the night and the dawn greeted me with a thin cold rain that blew into my face. The Roman road, broken and weed-grown now, stretched into a dank wood and the further I rode the lower my spirits sank. Everything I had heard in Carig's frontier fort suggested that Gwent would not fight for Arthur. Meurig, the young King of Gwent, had ever been a reluctant warrior. His father, Tewdric, had known that the Britons must unite against their common enemy, but Tewdric had resigned his throne and gone to live as a monk beside the River Wye and his son was no warlord.

Without Gwent's well-trained troops Dumnonia was surely doomed unless a glowing naked nymph presaged some miraculous intervention by the Gods. Or unless Aelle believed Arthur's lie. And would Aelle even receive me? Would he even believe that I was his son? The Saxon King had been kind enough to me on the few occasions we had met, but that meant nothing for I was still his enemy, and the longer I rode through that bitter drizzle between the towering wet trees, the greater my despair. I was sure Arthur had sent me to my death, and worse, that he had done it with the callousness of a losing gambler risking everything on one final cast on the throwboard.

At mid morning the trees ended and I rode into a wide clearing through which a stream flowed. The road forded the small water, but beside the crossing and stuck into a mound that stood as high as a man's waist, there stood a dead fir tree that was hung with offerings. The magic was strange to me so I had no idea whether the bedecked tree guarded the road, placated the stream or was merely the work of children. I slid off my horse's back and saw that the objects hung from the brittle branches were the small bones of a man's spine. No child's play, I reckoned, but what? I spat beside the mound to avert its evil, touched the iron of Hywelbane's hilt, then led my horse through the ford.

The woods began again thirty paces beyond the stream and I had not covered half that distance when an axe hurtled out of the shadows beneath the branches. It turned as it came towards me, the day's grey light flickering from the spinning blade. The throw was bad, and the axe hissed past a good four paces away. No one challenged me, but nor did any other weapon come from the trees.

'I am a Saxon!' I shouted in that language. Still no one spoke, but I heard a mutter of low voices and the crackle of breaking twigs. 'I am a Saxon!' I called again, and wondered whether the hidden watchers were not Saxons but outlaw Britons, for I was still in the wasteland where the masterless men of every tribe and country hid from justice.

I was about to call in the British tongue that I meant no harm when a voice shouted from the shadows in Saxon. 'Throw your sword here!' a man commanded me.

'You may come and take the sword,' I answered.

There was a pause. 'Your name?' the voice demanded.

'Derfel,' I said, 'son of Aelle.'

I called my father's name as a challenge, and it must have unsettled them because once again I heard the low murmur of voices, and then, a moment later, six men pushed through the brambles to come into the clearing. All were in the thick furs that Saxons favoured as armour and all carried spears. One of them wore a horned helmet and he, evidently the leader, walked down the edge of the road towards me. 'Derfel,' he said, stopping a half dozen paces from me. 'Derfel,' he said again. 'I have heard that name, and it is no Saxon name.'

'It is my name,' I answered, 'and I am a Saxon.'

'A son of Aelle?' He was suspicious.

'Indeed.'

He considered me for a moment. He was a tall man with a mass of brown hair crammed into his horned helmet. His beard reached almost to his waist and his moustaches hung to the top edge of the leather breastplate he wore beneath his fur cloak. I supposed he was a local chieftain, or maybe a warrior deputed to guard this part of the frontier. He twisted one of his moustaches in his free hand, then let the strands unwind. 'Hrothgar, son of Aelle, I know,' he said musingly, 'and Cyrning, son of Aelle, I call a friend. Penda, Saebold and Yffe, sons of Aelle, I have seen in battle, but Derfel, son of Aelle?' He shook his head.

'You see him now,' I said.

He hefted his spear, noting that my shield was still hanging from my horse's saddle. 'Derfel, friend of Arthur, I have heard of,' he said accusingly.

'You see him also,' I said, 'and he has business with Aelle.'

'No Briton has business with Aelle,' he said, and his men growled their assent.

'I am a Saxon,' I retorted.

'Then what is your business?'

'That is for my father to hear and for me to speak. You are not part of it.'

He turned and gestured towards his men. 'We make it our business.'
'Your name?' I demanded.

He hesitated, then decided that imparting his name would do no
harm. 'Ceolwulf,' he said, 'son of Eadbehrt.'

'So, Ceolwulf,' I said, 'do you think my father will reward you when
he hears that you delayed my journey? What will you expect of him?
Gold? Or a grave?'

It was a fine bluff, but it worked. I had no idea whether Aelle would
embrace me or kill me, but Ceolwulf had sufficient fear of his King's
wrath to give me grudging passage and an escort of four spearmen who
led me deeper and deeper into the Lost Lands.

And so I travelled through places where few free Britons had
stepped in a generation. These were the enemy heartlands, and for two
days I rode through them. At first glance the country looked little different from British land, for the Saxons had taken over our fields and
they farmed them in much the same manner as we did, though I noted
their haystacks were piled higher and made squarer than ours, and their
houses were built more stoutly. The Roman villas were mostly deserted,
though here and there an estate still functioned. There were no Christian churches here, indeed no shrines at all that I could see, though we
did once pass a British idol which had some small offerings left at its
base. Britons still lived here and some even owned their own land, but
most were slaves or else were wives to Saxons. The names of the places
had all changed and my escort did not even know what they had been
called when the British ruled. We passed through Lycceword and Ste-
ortford, then Leodasham and Celmeresfort, all strange Saxon names
but all prosperous places. These were not the homes and farms of
invaders, but the settlements of a fixed people. From Celmeresfort we
turned south through Beadewan and Wicford, and as we rode my companions proudly told me that we now rode across farmland that Cerdic
had yielded back to Aelle during the summer. The land was the price,
they said, of Aelle's loyalty in the coming war that would take these
people clean across Britain to the Western Sea. My escort was confident
that they would win. They had all heard how Dumnonia had been

weakened by Lancelot's rebellion, and that revolt had encouraged the Saxon Kings to unite in an effort to take all southern Britain.

Aelle's winter quarters were at a place the Saxons called Thunreslea. It was a high hill in a flat landscape of clay fields and dark marshes, and from the hill's flat summit a man could stare southwards across the wide Thames towards the misty land where Cerdic ruled. A great hall stood on the hill. It was a massive building of dark oak timbers, and fixed high on its steep pointed gable was Aelle's symbol: a bull's skull painted with blood. In the dusk the lonely hall loomed black and huge, a baleful place. Off to the east there was a village beyond some trees and I could see the flicker of a myriad fires there. It seemed I had arrived in Thunreslea at the time of a gathering, and the fires showed where folk camped. 'It's a feast,' one of my escort told me.

'In honour of the Gods?' I enquired.

'In honour of Cerdic. He's come to talk with our King.'

My hopes, that were already low, plummeted. With Aelle I stood some chance of survival, but with Cerdic, I thought, there was none. Cerdic was a cold, hard man, while Aelle had an emotional, even a generous, soul.

I touched Hywelbane's hilt and thought of Ceinwyn. I prayed the Gods would let me see her again, and then it was time to slide off my weary horse's back, twitch my cloak straight, unhook the shield from my saddle's pommel and go to face my enemies.

Three hundred warriors must have been feasting on the rush-covered floor of that high, gaunt hall on its damp hilltop. Three hundred raucous, cheerful men, bearded and red-faced, who, unlike us Britons, saw nothing wrong in carrying weapons into a lord's feasting-hall. Three huge fires flared in the hall's centre and so thick was the smoke that at first I could not see the men sitting behind the long table at the hall's far end. No one noticed my entrance, for with my long fair hair and thick beard I looked like a Saxon spearman, but as I was led past the roaring fires a warrior saw the five-pointed white star on my shield and he remembered facing that symbol in battle. A growl erupted through the tumult of talk and laughter. The growl spread until every man in that hall was howling at me as I walked towards the dais on which the high table stood. The howling warriors put down their horns of ale and began to beat their hands against the floor or against their shields so that the high roof echoed with the death-beat.

The crash of a blade striking the table ended the noise. Aelle had stood, and it was his sword that had driven splinters from the long rough table where a dozen men sat behind heaped plates and full horns. Cerdic was beside him, and on Cerdic's other side was Lancelot. Nor was Lancelot the only Briton there. Bors, his cousin, slouched beside him while Amhar and Loholt, Arthur's sons, sat at the table's end. All of them were enemies of mine, and I touched Hywelbane's hilt and prayed for a good death.

Aelle stared at me. He knew me well enough, but did he know I was his son? Lancelot looked astonished to see me, he even blushed, then he beckoned to an interpreter, spoke to him briefly and the interpreter leant towards Cerdic and whispered in the monarch's ear. Cerdic also knew me, but neither Lancelot's words, nor his recognition of an enemy, changed the impenetrable expression on his face. It was a clerk's face, clean-shaven, narrow-chinned, and with a high broad forehead. His lips were thin and his sparse hair was combed severely back to a knot behind his skull, but the otherwise unremarkable face was made memorable by his eyes. They were pale eyes, merciless eyes, a killer's eyes.

Aelle seemed too astonished to speak. He was much older than Cerdic, indeed he was a year or two beyond fifty which made him an old man by any reckoning, but he still looked formidable. He was tall, broad-chested, and had a flat, hard face, a broken nose, scarred cheeks and a full black beard. He was dressed in a fine scarlet robe and had a thick gold torque at his neck and more gold about his wrists, but no finery could disguise the fact that Aelle was first and foremost a soldier, a great bear of a Saxon warrior. Two fingers were missing from his right hand, struck off in some long-ago battle where, I daresay, he had taken a bloody revenge. He finally spoke. 'You dare come here?'

'To see you, Lord King,' I answered and went down on one knee. I

bowed to Aelle, then to Cerdic, but ignored Lancelot. To me he was a
nothing, a client King of Cerdic's, an elegant British traitor whose dark
face was filled with loathing for me.

Cerdic speared a piece of meat on a long knife, brought it towards
his mouth, then hesitated. 'We are receiving no messengers from
Arthur,' he said casually, 'and any who are foolish enough to come are
killed.' He put the meat in his mouth, then turned away as though he
had disposed of me as a piece of trivial business. His men bayed for
my death.

Aelle again silenced the hall by banging his sword blade on the
table. 'Do you come from Arthur?' he challenged me.

I decided the Gods would forgive an untruth. 'I bring you greetings,
Lord King,' I said, 'from Erce, and the filial respect of Erce's son who is
also, to his joy, your own.'

The words meant nothing to Cerdic. Lancelot, who had listened to
a translation, again whispered urgently to his interpreter and that man
spoke once more to Cerdic. I did not doubt that he had encouraged
what Cerdic now uttered. 'He must die,' Cerdic insisted. He spoke very
calmly, as though my death were a small thing. 'We have an agreement,'
he reminded Aelle.

'Our agreement says we shall receive no embassies from our enemies,' Aelle said, still staring at me.

'And what else is he?' Cerdic demanded, at last showing some
temper.

'He is my son,' Aelle said simply, and a gasp sounded all around the
crowded hall. 'He is my son,' Aelle said again, 'are you not?'

'I am, Lord King.'

'You have more sons,' Cerdic told Aelle carelessly, and gestured
towards some bearded men who sat at Aelle's left hand. Those men—
I presumed they were my half-brothers—just stared at me in confusion.
'He brings a message from Arthur!' Cerdic insisted. 'That dog,' he
pointed his knife towards me, 'always serves Arthur.'

'Do you bring a message from Arthur?' Aelle asked.

'I have a son's words for a father,' I lied again, 'nothing more.'

'He must die!' Cerdic said curtly, and all his supporters in the hall growled their agreement.

'I will not kill my own son,' Aelle said, 'in my own hall.'

'Then I may?' Cerdic asked acidly. 'If a Briton comes to us then he must be put to the sword.' He spoke those words to the whole hall. 'That is agreed between us!' Cerdic insisted and his men roared their approval and beat spear shafts against their shields. 'That thing,' Cerdic said, flinging a hand towards me, 'is a Saxon who fights for Arthur! He is vermin, and you know what you do with vermin!' The warriors bellowed for my death and their hounds added to the clamour with howls and barks. Lancelot watched me, his face unreadable, while Amhar and Loholt looked eager to help put me to the sword. Loholt had an especial hatred for me, for I had held his arm while his father had struck off his right hand.

Aelle waited until the tumult had subsided. 'In my hall,' he said, stressing the possessive word to show that he ruled here, not Cerdic, 'a warrior dies with his sword in his hand. Does any man here wish to kill Derfel while he carries his sword?' He looked about the hall, inviting someone to challenge me. No one did, and Aelle looked down at his fellow King. 'I will break no agreement with you, Cerdic. Our spears will march together and nothing my son says can prevent that victory.'

Cerdic picked a scrap of meat from between his teeth. 'His skull,' he said, pointing to me, 'will make a fine standard for battle. I want him dead.'

'Then you kill him,' Aelle said scornfully. They might have been allies, but there was little affection between them. Aelle resented the younger Cerdic as an upstart, while Cerdic believed the older man lacked ruthlessness.

Cerdic half smiled at Aelle's challenge. 'Not me,' he said mildly, 'but my champion will do the work.' He looked down the hall, found the man he wanted and pointed a finger. 'Liofa! There is vermin here. Kill it!'

The warriors cheered again. They relished the thought of a fight, and doubtless before the night was over the ale they were drinking

would cause more than a few deadly battles, but a fight to the death
between a King's champion and a King's son was a far finer entertainment than any drunken brawl and a much better amusement than the
melody of the two harpists who watched from the hall's edges.

I turned to see my opponent, hoping he would prove to be already
half drunk and thus easy meat for Hywelbane, but the man who
stepped through the feasters was not at all what I had expected. I
thought he would be a huge man, not unlike Aelle, but this champion
was a lean, lithe warrior with a calm, shrewd face that carried not a
single scar. He gave me an unworried glance as he let his cloak fall,
then he pulled a long thin-bladed sword from its leather scabbard. He
wore little jewellery, nothing but a plain silver torque, and his clothes
had none of the finery that most champions affected. Everything about
him spoke of experience and confidence, while his unscarred face suggested either monstrous good luck or uncommon skill. He also looked
frighteningly sober as he came to the open space in front of the high
table and bowed to the Kings.

Aelle looked troubled. 'The price for speaking with me,' he told me,
'is to defend yourself against Liofa. Or you may leave now and go
home in safety.' The warriors jeered that suggestion.

'I would speak with you, Lord King,' I said.

Aelle nodded, then sat. He still looked unhappy and I guessed that
Liofa had a fearsome reputation as a swordsman. He had to be good,
or else he would not be Cerdic's champion, but something about
Aelle's face told me that Liofa was more than just good.

Yet I too had a reputation, and that seemed to worry Bors who was
whispering urgently in Lancelot's ear. Lancelot, once his cousin had
finished, beckoned to the interpreter who in turn spoke with Cerdic.
The King listened, then gave me a dark look. 'How do we know,' he
asked, 'that this son of yours, Aelle, is not wearing some charm of
Merlin's?'

The Saxons had always feared Merlin, and the suggestion made
them growl angrily.

Aelle frowned. 'Do you have one, Derfel?'

'No, Lord King.'

Cerdic was not convinced. 'These men would recognize Merlin's magic,' he insisted, waving at Lancelot and Bors; then he spoke to the interpreter, who passed on his orders to Bors. Bors shrugged, stood up and walked round the table and off the dais. He hesitated as he approached me, but I spread my arms as though to show that I meant him no harm. Bors examined my wrists, maybe looking for strands of knotted grass or some other amulet, then tugged open the laces of my leather jerkin. 'Be careful of him, Derfel,' he muttered in British, and I realized, with surprise, that Bors was no enemy after all. He had persuaded Lancelot and Cerdic that I needed to be searched just so that he could whisper his warning to me. 'He's quick as a weasel,' Bors went on, 'and he fights with both hands. Watch the bastard when he seems to slip.' He saw the small golden brooch that had been a present from Ceinwyn. 'Is it charmed?' he asked me.

'No.'

'I'll keep it for you anyway,' he said, unpinning the brooch and showing it to the hall, and the warriors roared their anger that I might have been concealing the talisman. 'And give me your shield,' Bors said, for Liofa had none.

I slipped the loops from my left arm and gave the shield to Bors. He took it and placed it against the dais, then balanced Ceinwyn's brooch on the shield's top edge. He looked at me as if to make sure I had seen where he put it and I nodded.

Cerdic's champion gave his sword a cut in the smoky air. 'I have killed forty-eight men in single combat,' he told me in a mild, almost bored voice, 'and lost count of the ones who have fallen to me in battle.' He paused and touched his face. 'In all those fights,' he said, 'I have not once taken a scar. You may yield to me now if you want your death to be swift.'

'You may give me your sword,' I told him, 'and spare yourself a beating.'

The exchange of insults was a formality. Liofa shrugged away my offer and turned to the kings. He bowed again and I did the same. We were standing ten paces apart in the middle of the open space between the dais and the nearest of the three big fires, and on either flank the hall was crammed with excited men. I could hear the chink of coins as wagers were placed.

Aelle nodded to us, giving his permission for the fight to begin. I drew Hywelbane and raised her hilt to my lips. I kissed one of the little slivers of pig bone that were set there. The two bone scraps were my real talismans and they were far more powerful than the brooch, for the pig bones had once been a part of Merlin's magic. The scraps of bone gave me no magical protection, but I kissed the hilt a second time, then faced Liofa.

Our swords are heavy and clumsy things that do not hold their edge in battle and so become little more than great iron clubs that take considerable strength to wield. There is nothing delicate about sword fighting, though there is skill. The skill lies in deception, in persuading an opponent that a blow will come from the left and, when he guards that side, striking from the right, though most sword fights are not won by such skill, but by brute strength. One man will weaken and so his guard will be beaten down and the winner's sword will hack and beat him to death.

But Liofa did not fight like that. Indeed, before or since, I have never fought another quite like Liofa. I sensed the difference as he approached me, for his sword blade, though as long as Hywelbane, was much slimmer and lighter. He had sacrificed weight for speed, and I realized that this man would be as fast as Bors had warned me, lightning fast, and just as I realized that, so he attacked, only instead of sweeping the blade in a great curve he lunged with it, trying to rake its point through the muscles of my right arm.

I walked away from the lunge. These things happen so fast that afterwards, trying to remember the passages of a fight, the mind cannot pin down each move and counter-stroke, but I had seen a flicker in his eye, saw that his sword could only stab forward and I had moved just as he whipped the stab towards me. I pretended that the speed of his lunge had given me no surprise and I made no parry, but just walked past him and then, when I reckoned he must be off balance I snarled and backswung Hywelbane in a blow that would have disembowelled an ox.

He leapt backwards, not off balance at all, and spread his arms wide so that my blow scythed a harmless six inches from his belly. He waited for me to swing again, but instead I was waiting for him. Men were shouting at us, calling for blood, but I had no ears for them. I kept my gaze fixed on Liofa's calm grey eyes. He hefted the sword in his right hand, flicked it forward to touch my blade, then swung at me.

I parried easily, then countered his backswing which followed as naturally as the day follows the night. The clangour of the swords was loud, but I could feel that there was no real effort in Liofa's blows. He was offering me the fight I might have expected, but he was also judging me as he edged forward and as he swung blow after blow. I parried the cuts, sensing when they became harder, and just when I expected him to make a real effort he checked a blow, let go of the sword in mid-air, snatched it with his left hand and slashed it straight down towards my head. He did it with the speed of a viper striking.

Hywelbane caught that downward cut. I do not know how she did it. I had been parrying a sideways blow and suddenly there was no sword there, but only death above my skull, yet somehow my blade was in the right place and his lighter sword slid down to Hywelbane's hilt and I tried to convert the parry into a counter-cut, but there was no force in my response and he leapt easily backwards. I kept going forward, cutting as he had cut, only doing it with all my strength so that any one of the blows would have gutted him, and the speed and force of my attacks gave him no choice but to retreat. He parried the blows as easily as I had parried his, but there was no resistance in the parries. He was letting me swing, and instead of defending with his sword he was protecting himself by constantly retreating. He was also letting me exhaust my strength on thin air instead of on bone and muscle and blood. I gave a last massive cut, checked the blade in mid swing and twisted my wrist to lunge Hywelbane at his belly.

His sword edged towards the lunge, then whipped back at me as he sidestepped. I made the same quick sidestep, so that each of us missed. Instead we clashed, breast to breast, and I smelt his breath. There was a faint smell of ale, though he was certainly not drunk. He froze for a heartbeat, then courteously moved his sword arm aside and looked quizzically at me as if to suggest that we agree to break apart. I nodded, and we both stepped backwards, swords held wide, while the crowd talked excitedly. They knew they were watching a rare fight. Liofa was famous among them, and I dare say my name was not obscure, but I knew I was probably outmatched. My skills, if I had any, were a soldier's skills. I knew how to break a shield wall, I knew how to fight with spear and shield, or with sword and shield, but Liofa, Cerdic's champion, had only one skill and that was to fight man on man with a sword. He was lethal.

We drew back six or seven paces, then Liofa skipped forward, as light on his feet as a dancer, and cut at me fast. Hywelbane met the cut hard and I saw him draw back from the solid parry with a flinch. I was faster than he expected, or maybe he was slower than usual for even a small amount of ale will slow a man. Some men only fight drunk, but those who live longest fight sober.

I wondered about that flinch. He had not been hurt, yet I had obviously worried him. I cut at him and he leapt back, and that leap gave me another pause to think. What had made him flinch? Then I remembered the weakness of his parries and I realized he dared not risk his blade against mine, for it was too light. If I could strike that blade with all my force then it would as like as not break and so I slashed again, only this time I kept slashing and I roared at him as I stamped towards him. I cursed him by air, by fire and by sea. I called him woman, I spat on his grave and on the dog's grave where his mother was buried, and all the while he said not a word, but just let his sword meet mine and slide away and always he backed away and those pale eyes watched me.

Then he slipped. His right foot seemed to slide on a patch of rushes and his leg went out from under him. He fell backwards and reached out with his left hand to check himself and I roared his death and raised Hywelbane high.

Then I stepped away from him, without even trying to finish the killing blow.

I had been warned of that slip by Bors and I had been waiting for it. To watch it was marvellous, and I had very nearly been fooled for I could have sworn the slip was an accident, but Liofa was an acrobat as well as a sword fighter and the apparently unbalanced slip turned into a sudden supple motion that swept his sword around to where my feet should have been. I can still hear that long slim blade hissing as it swept just inches above the floor rushes. The blow should have sliced into my ankles, crippling me, only I was not there.

I had stepped back and now watched him calmly. He looked up ruefully. 'Stand, Liofa,' I said, and my voice was steady, telling him that all my rage had been a pretence.

I think he knew then that I was truly dangerous. He blinked once or twice and I guessed he had used his best tricks on me, but none had worked, and his confidence was sapped. But not his skill, and he came forward hard and fast to drive me back with a dazzling succession of short cuts, quick lunges and sudden sweeps. I let the sweeps go unparried, while the other attacks I touched away as best I could, deflecting them and trying to break his rhythm, but at last one cut beat me squarely. I caught it on my left forearm and the leather sleeve broke the sword's force, though I bore a bruise for the best part of a month afterwards. The crowd sighed. They had watched the fight keenly and were eager to see the first blood drawn. Liofa ripped the blade back from my forearm, trying to saw its edge through the leather to the bone, but I flicked my arm out of the way, lunged with Hywelbane and so drove him back.

He waited for me to follow up the attack, but it was my turn to play the tricks now. I deliberately did not move towards him, but instead let my sword drop a few inches as I breathed heavily. I shook my head, trying to flick the sweat-soaked hanks of hair from my forehead. It was hot beside that great fire. Liofa watched me cautiously. He could see I was out of breath, he saw my sword falter, but he had not killed forty-eight men by taking risks. He gave me one of his quick cuts to test my reaction. It was a short swing that demanded a parry, but would not thump home like an axe biting into flesh. I parried it late, deliberately late, and let the tip of Liofa's sword strike my upper arm as Hywelbane clanged on the thicker part of his blade. I grunted, feigned a swing, then pulled my blade back as he stepped easily away.

Again I waited for him. He lunged, I struck his sword aside, but this time I did not try to counter his attack with one of my own. The crowd had fallen silent, sensing this fight was about to end. Liofa tried another lunge and again I parried. He preferred the lunge, for that would kill without endangering his precious blade, but I knew that if I parried those quick stabs often enough he would eventually kill me the old way instead. He tried two more lunges and I knocked the first clumsily aside, stepped back from the second, then cuffed at my eyes with my left sleeve as though the sweat was stinging them.

He swung then. He shouted aloud for the first time as he gave a mighty swing that came from high above his head and angled down towards my neck. I parried it easily, but staggered as I slid his scything blow safely over my skull with Hywelbane's blade, then I let her drop a little and he did what I expected him to do.

He backswung with all his force. He did it fast and well, but I knew his speed now and I was already bringing Hywelbane up in a counter-stroke that was just as fast. I had both hands on her hilt and I put all my strength into that slashing upward blow that was not aimed at Liofa, but at his sword.

The two swords met plumb.

Only this time there was no ringing sound, but a crack.

For Liofa's blade had broken. The outer two thirds of it sheared clean away to fall among the rushes, leaving only a stump in his hand. He looked horrified. Then, for a heartbeat, he seemed tempted to attack me with the remnants of his sword, but I gave Hywelbane two fast cuts that drove him back. He could see now that I was not tired at all. He could also see that he was a dead man, but still he tried to parry Hywelbane with his broken weapon, but she beat that feeble metal stump aside and then I stabbed.

And held the blade still at the silver torque about his throat. 'Lord King?' I called, but keeping my eyes on Liofa's eyes. There was a silence in the hall. The Saxons had seen their champion beaten and they had no voices left. 'Lord King!' I called again.

'Lord Derfel?' Aelle answered.

'You asked me to fight King Cerdic's champion, you did not ask me to kill him. I beg his life of you.'

Aelle paused. 'His life is yours, Derfel.'

'Do you yield?' I asked Liofa. He did not answer at once. His pride was still seeking a victory, but while he hesitated I moved Hywelbane's tip from his throat to his right cheek. 'Well?' I prompted him.

'I yield,' he said, and threw down the stump of his sword.

I thrust with Hywelbane just hard enough to gouge the skin and flesh away from his cheekbone. 'A scar, Liofa,' I said, 'to remind you that you fought the Lord Derfel Cadarn, son of Aelle, and that you lost.' I left him bleeding. The crowd was cheering. Men are strange things. One moment they had been baying for my blood, now they were shouting plaudits because I had spared their champion's life. I retrieved Ceinwyn's brooch, then picked up my shield and gazed up at my father. 'I bring you greetings from Erce, Lord King,' I said.

'And they are welcome, Lord Derfel,' Aelle said, 'they are welcome.'

He gestured to a chair on his left that one of his sons had vacated and thus I joined Arthur's enemies at their high table. And feasted.

Acknowledgments

Many people made this anthology.

At Thunder's Mouth Press and Avalon Publishing Group:
Thanks to Ghadah Alrawi, Tracy Armstead, Will Balliett, Sue Canavan, Kristen Couse, Maria Fernandez, Linda Kosarin, Shona McCarthy, Dan O'Connor, Neil Ortenberg, Paul Paddock, Susan Reich, David Riedy, Simon Sullivan and Mike Walters for their support, dedication and hard work.

At The Writing Company:
Kate Fletcher and Nathaniel May did most of the research. Nathaniel May also oversaw rights research and negotiations. Nate Hardcastle, Mark Klimek, Taylor Smith and March Truedsson took up slack on other projects.

At the Portland Public Library in Portland, Maine:
The librarians helped collect books from around the country.

Finally, I am grateful to the writers whose work appears in this book.

Permissions

Bibliography

The selections used in this anthology were taken from the editions listed below. In some cases, other editions may be easier to find. Hard-to-find or out-of-print titles often are available through inter-library loan services or through Internet booksellers.

Barrie, J. M. *Peter and Wendy*. New York: Charles Scribner's Sons, 1911.

Church, Alfred. *The Iliad for Boys and Girls: Told from Homer in Simple Language*. New York: MacMillan, 1932.

Clemens, Samuel (Mark Twain). *A Connecticut Yankee at King Arthur's Court*. New York: Penguin Books, 1980.

Cornwell, Bernard. *Excalibur: A Novel of Arthur*. New York: St. Martin's Press, 1997.

Dumas, Alexandre, *The Three Musketeers*. http://www.literature.org/authors/dumas-alexandre/the-three-musketeers/

Dunsany, Lord. *The Book of Wonder*. New York: Boni and Liveright, Inc., 1918. (For "The Hoard of the Gibbelins")

Goldman, William. *The Princess Bride: S. Morgenstern's Classic Tale of True Love and High Adventure, The 'good parts' version abridged by William Goldman*. New York: Harcourt Brace, 1973.

Gray, Nicholas Stuart. *Grimbold's Other World*. New York: Meredith Press, 1968.

Grimm, Jakob, and Wilhelm Grimm, translated by Lucy Crane. *Household Stories from the Collection of the Brothers Grimm*. New York: Dover Publications, 1963. (For "The Gallant Tailor")

Knowles, Sir James. *King Arthur and His Knights*. New York: Dilithium Press, 1986.

Pyle, Howard. *The Merry Adventures of Robin Hood of Great Renown in Nottinghamshire as Written and Illustrated by Howard Pyle*. New York: Charles Scribner's Sons, 1946.

Steinbeck, John. *The Acts of King Arthur and His Noble Knights*. New York: Farrar, Straus and Giroux, 1976. (For "Morgan le Fay")

Wägner, Wilhelm. *Romances and Epics of Our Northern Ancestors, Norse, Celt and Teuton; translated from the works of Dr. W. Wägner*. New York: The Norrœna Society, 1907. (For "The Legend of Beowulf" and "The Hegeling Legend")

Wiggin, Kate Douglas, and Nora A. Smith. *The Arabian Nights: Their Best Known Tales*. New York: Charles Scribner's Sons, 1937. (For "The Story of Ali Baba and the Forty Thieves")

Wu Chêng-ên, translated by Arthur Waley. *Monkey*. London: Penguin, 1977.

Yoshikawa, Eiji, translated by Charles S. Terry. *Musashi*. New York: Kodansha International, 1995.